A GIRL LIKE I

ALSO BY ANITA LOOS

Novels

Gentlemen Prefer Blondes
But They Marry Brunettes
A Mouse Is Born
No Mother to Guide Her

Screen Plays

The New York Hat
Nellie the Female Villain
American Aristocracy
The Redheaded Woman
  (*from the novel by Katharine Brush*)
San Francisco
  (*in collaboration with Robert Hopkins*)
Gentlemen Prefer Blondes
and 200 others

Plays

Happy Birthday
The King's Mare
  (*adapted from the French by Carolle*)
Gigi (*from the novel by Colette*)
Gentlemen Prefer Blondes

A Girl Like I

ANITA LOOS

New York ✒ THE VIKING PRESS

The lines on page 134 from "Mae Marsh, Motion Picture Actress" are Copyright 1917, The Macmillan Company, renewed 1945 by Elizabeth C. Lindsay; "What Her Best Young Man Should Say To That Golden Haired Girl Over There If He Has Any Nerve" on pages 142-43 is Copyright, under title "To A Golden Haired Girl In a Louisiana Town," 1923, The Macmillan Company, renewed 1951 by Elizabeth C. Lindsay. Both from *Collected Poems* by Vachel Lindsay and used by permission of The Macmillan Company.

The excerpts from letters of Vachel Lindsay are used with the permission of Nicholas C. Lindsay.

"Résumé" (page 150) is from *The Portable Dorothy Parker*. Copyright 1926, 1954 by Dorothy Parker. By permission of The Viking Press, Inc.

FOR GLADYS

ILLUSTRATIONS

A GIRL LIKE I

ᴥ§ CHAPTER I

ᴥ§Sometime in mid-1850, at a church in Hartford, Connecticut, a girl with the incredible name of Cleopatra Fairbrother was married to a certain prosperous and respectable George Smith. The newlyweds, who were my grandparents, had met when Cleopatra was sixteen and living on the Vermont farm where she was born. Why the child of a New England farmer came to be called after the Serpent of the Nile has never been explained. The family name of Fairbrother sounds proper enough, and no doubt the Fairbrothers were people of moral rectitude, for they were Shakers; moreover, they must have been industrious or they would never have taken root in so grim a territory as Vermont. Whoever named that baby must have had visions of exotic luxury or at any rate been fed up with the meager life of a frontier farm.

In addition to this, one of our forebears was reputed to have been the historic firebrand Ethan Allen, hero of Crown Point and Ticonderoga and the French and Indian War. Seeing that Allen never married and that he preferred native American girls to the white-skinned settlers, Cleopatra must have had Indian blood in her veins, along with bastardy and a hankering for excitement.

On the other hand, George Smith had been a worthy citizen from the days of his boyhood on a farm in Bedfordshire, England, where he was born in 1825. An early daguerreotype shows him rugged and humorless, with the stern expression of a young George Washington. When only seventeen he already had the ambition, initiative, and price of a ticket to get to America on a clipper ship. After a voyage that took forty-two days, George Smith landed in New York and immediately proceeded by horseback to Wisconsin, where he had heard there was a shortage of farm labor and hoped he might quickly earn enough money to buy a farm of his own. But before he achieved his stake, news of the discovery of gold in California electrified the world, and Grandpa determined to join the stream of argonauts heading for the Far West. In company with several other young men he fitted out an ox team and started across the plains. For seven months they hacked their way through virgin country, beset by Indians, buffaloes, personal bickering, food shortages, and scurvy until, at long last, they came upon the site of the Great Discovery itself at Sutter's Fort in the Sacramento Valley.

Even there Grandpa found the going tough. Other prospectors who arrived ahead of him had already grabbed the best locations in the valley. So Grandpa set forth into the far north. At that period fortune seekers were interested in gold only as bullion; they ignored the golden sunshine of Southern California and the golden citrus fruit to be grown there, and had no premonition of the golden curls of Mary Pickford, which were to give rise one day to a fabulous new prosperity, including my own.

During Grandpa's pilgrimage along Indian trails to the north he was one of the first white men ever to penetrate the awesome forest of Big Trees. The sight must have staggered him, unprepared as he was for the wonders he beheld. Nor could he visualize a time when the California Chamber of Commerce would install electronic devices in those redwoods so that the wayfarer could deposit a quarter in a coin box and listen to a voice declaiming "Only God can make a tree." In those days there was no interference to jam George Smith's earnest communion with the Infinite, or to disturb his dreams of finding untold wealth in some far corner of the wilderness.

But hard times still pursued George Smith. He met up with a shyster who offered, for cash in advance, to guide him to a spot where he could wash out a pint of gold dust every day. After pocketing his fee, that snake-in-the-grass led Grandpa farther into the wilderness and then disappeared, leaving him to shift for himself.

As a child I used to listen wide-eyed to Grandpa's account of that misadventure; but instead of sharing the outrage which never ceased to irk him, I only felt a lively admiration for the trickster who had put it over on Grandpa. It appears that I had inherited a love of larceny from someone in my ancestral line. As it obviously wasn't Grandpa, I have a suspicion that Grandma Cleopatra was to blame.

When George Smith reached the northern border of California, he finally attained his goal. In his own words, quoted from an interview in a local newspaper: "As I was making my way along a creek, I noticed some gravel on the opposite side that looked favorable for gold. I crossed the creek, scooped up a shovel full of gravel and in two minutes washed out five dollars' worth of gold dust. I immediately staked out a claim and began mining. My method was to carry the gravel quite a distance to the creek, where I could wash the gold out in rockers. I didn't seem to know enough to dam the creek from above and force it to run conveniently near the gravel bank." Poor Grandpa always did things the hard way, but even so he was able to take out forty or fifty dollars' worth of gold a day.

By the time his hoard of gold ran out, George Smith had amassed enough to be considered rich, and he determined to go to New England, find himself a worthy helpmeet, buy a farm, and settle down to a life of peaceful endeavor. In San Francisco he boarded one of the clipper ships which at that time negotiated a tortuous route around the Horn. Arriving in New England, George Smith started to look for both a farm and a farmer's wife, and the quest happened to take him past the Fairbrother place in Vermont. Later events proved that he might have done better to look for a helpmeet in some frontier saloon, for while he was wooing Cleopatra in her stuffy parlor, she was only dreaming of adventure and had no intention of spending the rest of her life on a farm.

Cleopatra must have listened wide-eyed to her suitor's tales about the Far West, the Indian savages, and pioneer life on a grander scale than the one she knew, and about the long ocean voyage that had brought George Smith her way. Even their wedding picture hints that Grandma would never be the "home" type. She was a sultry brunette with her hair draped low over the ears and parted down the middle in a very curious manner, for the parting had been widened by the use of tweezers. Girls of that period might have gotten the idea from old prints of red Indians which illustrate such a fad. It was of short duration and, as yet, has never been revived; so if the young men who hold sway in modern beauty parlors would like a new way to torture hair, I hereby hand on the tip.

At any rate, Cleopatra went in for the more advanced fashions to an extent that should have worried her serious young husband. Scarcely was the honeymooon over before his visions of a Yankee fireside began to be invaded by his bride's artful suggestions that they go West for more adventures in the gold fields. At length she talked him into returning to California. She may have argued that the trip had recently become less of an ordeal; clipper ships no longer took a course around the Horn; instead, they sailed to Panama, where passengers disembarked, after which they crossed the isthmus by mule train and boarded a clipper on the Pacific side that took them to San Francisco.

Before they started out, Cleo wheedled her bridegroom into buying her a baby grand piano. It was among the first ever to be shipped to California and had to be taken apart in New York, put into packing cases, and sent by freight around the Horn. But the young wife's greatest victory was when she made her husband agree to take along a piano tuner who could put the instrument back into proper condition on arrival.

Cleopatra must have felt that to sail for San Francisco on the high seas would be a breezy adventure, but she was soon to learn that a clipper ship could be more stuffy than any farmhouse parlor in Vermont. True, it was immaculately clean, but quarters were cramped and the air fetid. The entire ship stank of hemp, axle grease, coal oil used in the lamps, and smudge from the stove in the galley. Not even an Atlantic gale could blow away the stench; one felt as queasy as if the sea itself flowed coal oil. To get a breath of air Cleo, seasick and weighed down by her numberless petticoats, would have had to climb the mizzen mast. The sailors were of such feeble wit that they signed up to do superhuman labors to earn the price of a single binge in the first waterfront saloon. They weren't even worth a flirtation.

Before the clipper docked at Panama, Cleopatra was pregnant, which added a new dimension to seasickness. Their trip across the isthmus on mule-back along jungle trails was plagued by tropical heat, insects, nasty drinking water, and malaria. Awaiting them on the Pacific side was another clipper ship, and an interminable repetition of the same agonies, climaxed when the frail young piano tuner actually died during a violent spell of seasickness.

When at long last they docked in San Francisco, Cleopatra found it to be a shanty town half sunk in mud, its international glitter yet to be purchased with gold that was still being mined. In spite of her pregnancy, Cleopatra was more than willing to leave at once for the northern part of the state, which her husband assured her was a land of pristine grandeur; so they set forth by pack in the bitter cold of winter. There is a family legend that when they finally reached the straggling settlement of Yreka, Cleopatra's skirts were frozen to the saddle and had to be chopped loose with a hatchet before she could be carried into the tavern.

George Smith waited around Yreka until his son was born and then started prospecting again in the Salmon Mountains, where he discovered the rich Steamboat Mine, which he named after the miracle of transportation that had recently been invented in the East. But presently, when a second child was on its way, he started to clear an extensive tract of land for a ranch in Scott's Valley at the foot of the Klamath Mountains.

From the very first, Cleopatra must have resented the gray spruce-covered mountains which imprisoned her. In her longing for adventure she had married a man whom she scarcely knew, but when she finally got to know him she discovered his pioneer spirit was motivated by a desire for security and a fondness for hard work. Offspring arrived, not as a result of ardor but because of mute physical urge. And, when at length the Steamboat Mine ran dry, George Smith was more than satisfied with the life of a prosperous rancher.

Today the original ranch house still stands; it crowns a gently sloping hilltop, a Georgian structure of two stories and attic, painted white. A front door of hospitable width opens directly into the living room, which has wings on either side. The parlor in the right wing is still furnished in its original English mahogany, but the piano is as nonexistent as its fragile tuner. Cleopatra's bedroom in the left wing has a big wardrobe which once held her voluminous dresses and petticoats. At the rear of the house is a spacious dining room, built to accommodate a dozen or more extra hands when the thousands of acres of wheat were harvested. Behind it are a kitchen and pantry. There was no bath except for a portable tub, and other conveniences required a walk of some distance into the back yard. The front lawn, enclosed by a picket fence, has a mossy spring at its lower end that remains at the same frosty temperature in the hottest weather. Even today it is a landmark where passersby stop to refresh themselves.

As time went on, George Smith built barns, stables, a granary, a smokehouse, a laundry, and a dairy where the milk was kept in enormous shallow copper pans and produced a type of cream now found only in Devonshire. The best breeds of cattle and horses were imported from England; there was every facility for opulent living and good food, except that there were never any fresh vegetables. Ranch hands were too busy with the more important crops of wheat and oats to spend any time in a truck garden. Cleopatra might have taken charge in that area, but she wasn't interested and she had a good alibi in that she was always pregnant. Even so, she could have played Lady Bountiful to the Indians, but they too were a disappointment. She might have welcomed an Indian attack or even an abduction, but it was no thrill to see handsome Indian braves doing the work of handymen.

Although there was every type of vehicle in the stables, there wasn't any place to go. Roads were bad, and even to reach the town of Etna, in the center of Scott's Valley, required an hour's

drive. While Etna did boast a tavern with a gaming room patronized by the rowdier citizens of the area, no lady ever went there;
and finally, Cleopatra, like her illustrious namesake, found that she
had worked her way into a trap.

As long as the Steamboat Mine was producing, Grandpa divided
his labors between there and the ranch, making the trip every
month to be at the mine on payday. As an employer he was meticu-
lous and paid his miners according to the hours they put in, so that
copper pennies were required to make up the exact amounts in
their pay envelopes. During those days of largess, pennies didn't
exist in California and Grandpa had to import them in packages by
Wells Fargo Express. His miners didn't appreciate the trouble he
took and contemptuously tossed his pennies into the creek. Years
later, when I spent summer vacations at the ranch, we children
would fish them out of the creek when we went wading, but we
also were too snobbish to think of pennies as money. We collected
them as we did the flint arrowheads of the Indian huntsmen, which
were equally plentiful.

Grandpa's caretaker at the mine was a bearded old boy named
Floyd, who used to lead a lonely existence when the mine closed
down in winter. Yet Floyd had his diversions, one of which was to
hang some ladies' garments on his clothesline as an innuendo that he
was entertaining a female on the premises. Since the washing was
never removed, it danced there limp and faded in the frosty air and
didn't fool anybody; but the ruse provided Floyd with a certain
cachet.

One winter Floyd took in a fellow miner as house guest, but the
arrangement worked out badly, for a tiff developed over the equal
division of a jar of raspberry jam and ended in the hatchet-murder
of Floyd's guest. Floyd was never required to pay for his crime,
which was considered justifiable homicide. After the murder,
Floyd returned to his life of single blessedness, and the Mother
Hubbard wrappers continued to flap on his clothesline.

Aside from a few such pathological divertissements, life on the
Smith ranch was without untoward incident and, on the whole,
quite comfortable. Grandpa sent to San Francisco for a Chinese

cook, and to my mind nothing can be more exciting than a Chinese in the house. Our Sukey spent a major part of his wages importing exotic gifts for us from the native land he was never to see again: lichee nuts, embroidered slippers made for feet which had been bound, dolls with sophisticated hairdos, firecrackers, and tea in red and gold packages so flashy they almost made us blink.

Aside from Sukey, Cleopatra's staff was recruited from local Klamath Indians whom Grandpa lured from their woodland ease and inoculated with the curse of labor. I remember a sister-and-brother team which went by the nicknames of "Smoothy" and "Roughy." Smoothy claimed to be over a hundred, but she did the gargantuan job of washing, which included the heavy red woolen underwear of the ranch hands. In those days no servant ever left a job except to make *la longue traverse*. On one memorable occasion Smoothy announced that, beginning with the following Thursday, she would no longer preside over the wash house. When asked why not, she placidly remarked, "Next Thursday me die." Since she had no medical history of any import, Smoothy wasn't taken seriously until she failed to show up the following Thursday and, on investigation, we learned that she had summoned the tribe to her shack at a certain hour, stretched out on her cot, and expired as per schedule.

By the time Cleopatra finished with childbearing, there were six children. Two died in infancy; of those who grew up, the first was Fred, who took too much after his father to add any excitement to this record. My mother, Minnie, was also ultra-respectable, a feminine version of her father. Then came Mae, who was too fat to be interesting. Last of all came Nina, a beauty and a blonde with spirit and ambitions which duplicated her mamma's, but Nina brilliantly achieved the career at which Cleopatra had failed and in time caused quite a stir in the night spots of New York, London, and Paris.

It is more than likely that Cleopatra's craving for adventure finally came to be satisfied by drugs. There was gossip in the valley that the family doctor's visits to the ranch were suspiciously regular, considering that his patient was merely "ailing."

Eugene O'Neill would have reveled in Grandma, although she was so little given to self-pity that she wouldn't have provided his particular talent with much dialogue. She never blamed her predicament on Fate, Karma, an outraged God, or even a jubilant Devil, and apparently felt that the best thing to do about the matter was to keep her mouth shut. But, with an apology to Mr. O'Neill, I honor Grandma as a more bona fide heroine than his disgruntled and loquacious ladies.

I cannot even guess whether Grandma went in for morphine, like the heroine of *A Long Day's Journey into Night*, or whether she may have used cocaine. When the latter drug was developed in England it was thought at first to be a harmless tonic. Most likely our respectable country doctor had so considered it himself; even that staid Victorian, Conan Doyle, had allowed Sherlock Holmes to use cocaine as a pick-up after a hard day's sleuthing. But Doyle was so shocked when the drug was found to be habit-forming that he cured Holmes by the instant method known as "cold turkey." Evidently Cleopatra had no scruples and she indulged in a habit without violent results for quite a normal life span.

By the time we grandchildren made our appearance on the scene, Grandma had become a recluse in a darkened bedroom, where our visits were dramatized as special occasions and were fraught with mystery. We could hardly see her in the dim light, but her ailment, whatever it was, only made Grandma look romantic. Dressed in a pale blue wrapper with a wide cape of white eyelit embroidery, she reclined on a divan of Burgundy red velvet. As a coverlet there was a crocheted throw, in the fashioning of which Grandma certainly had no part, for her helpless white hands could never cope with a crochet hook. Her still youthfully brown hair, draped over her ears and confined in a low bun, made her face seem very pale by contrast. On kissing Grandma, we got a delicious whiff of lavender from a cologne called Florida Water, after which we exchanged some brief amenities, were treated to a few jelly beans and dismissed, feeling that we had made a detour into far-off alien territory.

Intriguing as were Cleopatra's faults, they were tame compared with those of her daughter Nina, who on reaching teenage provided the valley with far more fascinating gossip. Two items concerned a family of Austrians that had migrated to the area from that lively suburb of Vienna called Grinzing. They gave a seductive flavor of the Wienerwald to life in the region, introducing accordions, featherbeds, and an appreciation of fun. The family boasted two sons of extraordinary good looks and virile temperament. The fact that they could chalk off a day's work in half the time required by Grandpa failed to impress him. He sternly disapproved of their Austrian levity, so they were strangers to Cleopatra in her dark seclusion, but Nina came to know them both only too well. Neither of the resulting scandals could be straightened out by marriage because both young men were encumbered with hardworking farm wives and a number of offspring.

Bad behavior got Nina a lot farther than it ever got her mamma, for she finally escaped from the valley, even with the assistance of her stay-at-home papa. On a train which bore Nina to San Francisco, where she was supposed to enter a school for girls who balked at becoming ladies, she made her most important conquest; he was a high-powered international confidence man named Horace Robinson. Nina fell in love with him at sight; but the reason why he is important to this story is that, at the age of seven, I was to do exactly as Nina did, and I think that Horace Robinson may have set a pattern for all the men who would ever fascinate me.

Seeing that he was a seasoned man of the world at a period when most young Americans were engaged in hard pioneer labor, Nina's conquest of Horace was outstanding, for she was merely a farm girl, even though a bad one. There's little doubt that the young adventurer could have had Nina for the asking, but he was so enthralled by her blond beauty, high spirits, and love of life that, without waiting to reach San Francisco, he impetuously took her off the train in Sacramento and brought her straight from the depot to the city hall, where they got married.

When the telegram announcing their news reached Nina's father, he couldn't help feeling relieved, even though he knew nothing about the groom. He would have preferred her to have met her husband in a less public place than a train, and later, when he found out that his son-in-law was Jewish, he may have regretted the fact, being a Church of England man. But Nina's mother was completely intrigued, and when Horace was brought home to meet the family Cleopatra even ordered her bedroom window shades to be raised so that she could see him better. I am tempted to describe what she saw by paraphrasing George du Maurier: In his winning and handsome face there was a suggestion of that priceless, irrepressible, indomitable, indelible blood which is like the dry white Spanish wine called montilla, without which no sherry can go round the world and keep its flavor intact.

Horace, in his early thirties, was soft-spoken, urbane, and elegantly dressed, as a big-time racketeer should be. I remember that his wavy black hair gave forth the subtle male perfume of an English preparation called The Guard's Hair Wash. (Horace, as an inveterate promoter, had once thought of introducing it to the New World. But the British firm didn't want it to become common, as, indeed, it still isn't today. Horace was more amused by a firm's not wanting to do business than disappointed over his offer's being turned down.)

Because I was a child when Horace graced our family, I knew very little about his activities and wouldn't know any more today, except that recently I happened across a book entitled *The Marconi Scandal*. It tells of a deal that was pulled off in England, that purveyor to the world at large of so many mighty scandals. This particular one took place just before the First World War and was so notorious that years later it moved G. K. Chesterton to write: "It is the fashion to divide history into pre-War and post-War conditions. I believe it is almost as essential to divide them into the pre-Marconi and post-Marconi days. It was during that affair that the ordinary English citizen lost his invincible ignorance, or in ordinary language, his innocence."

Of course there wasn't the least need for fraud in launching so legitimate a project as Marconi wireless stock; the great inventor himself had nothing to do with the manipulation. I remember visiting Auntie Nina in San Francisco and going with her to one of

Horace's promotion meetings in the grand ballroom at the Palace Hotel. His pitch began with a dramatic account of the recent sinking of the *Titanic*; Horace described the horrors of that event and then told how they had been mitigated by the new wireless apparatus aboard ship, which had saved any number of passengers. Having galvanized his audience with this epoch-making incident, Horace launched into his ballyhoo. "And now, good friends, do you wonder why we need *your* small investments to further a project which has revolutionized the communication systems of the entire world? It is because, sooner or later, this innovation is going to cause *new laws* to be written; laws which may possibly work to the disadvantage of our international requirements. It is at that time, my dear people, that *we* are going to need friends—thousands of good friends—*with votes* which will prevent the passing of any statute which might 'hamper' our 'operations' with the parent company in England." This was said with an air of innocence that, at the same time, made a joke of innocence, and thus he insinuated to his public that *they themselves* could be partners in some vague sort of larceny; a state of mind irresistible to the genus sucker.

At the end of Horace's speech he announced that he had to catch a train in order to board a transatlantic liner which would bear him back to his worthy colleagues in London. Therefore, time being of the essence, he would prefer that stock be paid for by cash instead of check. Baskets were passed around to accept the money, for which Horace's gentlemanly assistants provided stock certificates, and the big heavy California silver dollars came rattling in. There must be homes in every district of San Francisco where those old Valentines lie in dusty trunks, testimonials to my uncle's penetrating charm.

It was many years before our family learned the truth about Horace's way of life and, when I did, my memory of him lingered on with sneaky undertones of admiration. His genius for influencing people could have made him a success at any honest endeavor, but larceny suited Horace better.

It was from Uncle Horace that I learned the first important rule in dealing with members of the male sex. One day, in the disinter-

ested manner of a grown-up trying to make conversation with a
child, he asked me for a kiss, and for some strange reason, seeing
that I approved of him so highly, I rather impudently refused. Perhaps the reason was that to be kissed for the first time by the man
you love is a business of such magnitude as to give a girl pause. But
the moment I turned Uncle Horace down, his attitude, which had
been so purely casual, gave way to one of genuine interest. For he
was accustomed to seduce people by the roomful, and to be denied
by a moppet suddenly made me seem a personality, someone whom
he was challenged to win. Both intrigued and amused, he went to a
jewelry store and bought me a diamond ring. So I was given my
first diamond at the age of seven.

My ring came from Shreve's, the finest jewelers in San Francisco; therefore its good taste was guaranteed, but the diamonds
were as large as possible for a little girl, and they were alternated
with sapphires in an unconventional design. With Uncle Horace's
ring, an *entente* developed between him and me for which there is
no adequate English word. In Italian it is called *simpatia*. Outside
the category of sex, it describes an intimacy which, in a way, is
even closer, for it means "You and I understand each other," a state
much more lasting than infatuation. It has colored my life with
some strange relationships, not always worthy, but never dull.
Many years after I had enjoyed that first *simpatia* with Uncle Horace, I was informed of the Italian word for it, in Rome, by a racketeer named Benito Mussolini.

That Horace and Nina would drift apart was a foregone conclusion. In her mid-thirties she took to a steady diet of gin rickies,
which, combined with a tendency toward nymphomania, finally
brought about a divorce. In time she acquired a nondescript second
husband and settled in Rahway, New Jersey (of all places, for the
woman of the world she had been during her years as Mrs. Robinson).

The last we heard of Horace Robinson was when, years after he
and Nina separated, he returned to San Francisco. A front-page
article stated that Horace was a "railroad tycoon" and had just
come from Moscow on a mission to promote a "Trans-Siberian

Railway." I don't know whether the bona fide railroad was already in existence at the time or was merely a project, but whatever its status, it was grist to Horace's mill.

Horace's income was always that of a millionaire, but he spent it like a multimillionaire, and the front-page article described an incident in which he tossed ten-dollar bills out the window of his suite in the St. Francis Hotel. It was stated that a pretty brunette was standing beside him at the time. He died soon after, no doubt from the wear and tear a life of swindling inflicts on the muscles of the heart.

When at the age of sixteen I found myself in the midst of the silent-film industry, I often thought of Uncle Horace, of how perfectly he would have fitted into the cinema world. Harry Warner would have appreciated Horace and offered him a post of honor selling a product so fabulous that it was beyond any need for larceny—although, as Harry would be the first to say, "it helps."

While Uncle Horace was the first full-scale rogue of my experience, I had started at birth with a pretty fair example in my father, Richard Beers Loos. R. Beers (as he chose to sign himself) was born in Newcomerstown, Ohio, to a family that had originated in France, where the name is not uncommon (there are some Loos Islands in Guinea, which used to be French Guinea), and R. Beers' grandmother bore the obviously French name of Marlatte. In Newcomerstown the Looses were famous for being eccentric, and, since there seems no domestic reason why French people should ever go to Ohio, it's possible one of our forebears decided to settle there just to be different. Exhibitionism was in the Loos blood, but it was conveniently of a type that found satisfaction in minor achievements. A certain uncle of R. Beers boasted hypnotic powers and a legend told that he had once taken revenge on an enemy by causing the man to refuse nourishment to the point of starvation. Another Loos won fame during a flood by floating to his doom while playing the violin on a rooftop. My father first distinguished himself by starting a newspaper at the age of fifteen, but what made him really unique was that, instead of using stock jokes from outside sources as most country editors do, he wrote his own.

When R. Beers had just turned twenty he got word from a friend who had migrated to the West that all of Northern California was in need of newspapers. R. Beers immediately decided to investigate the field. An only son, he deserted his grieving mother and father and took off. After investigating the territory, R. Beers finally chose the town of Sissons, which was a two-day journey by stagecoach from Yreka, where my mother lived. Sissons no longer exists as a name; the town is now called Mount Shasta after the extinct volcano with its perpetual cap of snow that towers above it. Having selected his locale, R. Beers sent East for a small outlay of type and started a weekly which he called *The Sissons Mascot*.

My mother, Minnie, first met R. Beers at a dance in Yreka, to which guests came by stagecoach from all over Siskiyou County. She was on vacation from Mills Seminary near San Francisco, an elegant finishing school for young ladies which flourishes even today. Minnie Smith was only one of many girls who fell for R. Beers at that ball. He was an overnight sensation, a newcomer to the district, witty, outrageous, and with the urbane type of good looks which foretells early baldness. Indulging his talent for exhibitionism, he appeared at the evening's entertainment in blackface, doing a song-and-dance version of "Ta-ra-ra Boom-de-ay." During the following summer Minnie took to paying long visits to friends in the vicinity of Sissons. Finally her pursuit of the young newspaperman became so alarming that her father, already in a hectored state over Nina, decided to send her away to college, which was a radical step in those days. She was removed from Mills Seminary, and her father, with an eye to exposing Minnie to some reputable males, chose a coeducational school. There were very few at the time; the best was the University of Delaware, and it was there that she was exiled. As a coed from the Far West, Minnie Smith was a romantic figure. She was a brunette, excessively feminine, and, as her photographs prove, very pretty, although she never set any great store by her looks and had small interest in the fashions. Even so, and lacking the vitality and gregariousness of her sister Nina, she became a belle. But a term in college did Minnie no good at all. On graduating, she bounced right back to Sissons and married R. Beers

Loos. My mother always called him Harry, a nickname which was the one thing about R. Beers she was never required to share with livelier girls. But Minnie proved to be of sterner stuff than Nina, for she was a one-man woman and, with her marriage, began the lifelong heartache of being in love with a scamp.

&s The first to be born to the young couple was my brother Clifford. I came eight years later, and the third and last was sister Gladys. The *Mascot* prospered well enough to support the family, even after there were five of us. But eventually Sissons grew to be confining to R. Beers. The jokes with which he dished up his news items began to be reprinted in other newspapers throughout the West. At that time the nation's favorite humorist was a syndicated writer named Bill Nye. The Loos witticisms began to be quoted along with Nye's. At length fame went to R. Beers's head and he decided he was ready for San Francisco. My home-loving mother dreaded to make so radical a move, but although I was only four, I remember being as anxious to get to the big town as was R. B.

For some time I had been plagued by a little Portuguese girl of my own age named Johanna, who chose to shadow me with boring adulation. Children are supposed to recall events only back to the age of four. This, then, is the first memory of my life. Our household goods are being packed into crates, I am leaning on the windowsill, looking off at the snow-covered peak of Mount Shasta and muttering to myself, "Never see Johanna any more . . . never have to suffer any more!" Thus was I first aware of the terror of boredom, which to me has always been a more acute pain than a leaping toothache.

Departing from Sissons, the Loos family began peregrinations that ultimately took us from the top to the bottom of California, for we left the northernmost border of the state and ultimately wound up in San Diego on the edge of Mexico. But we scarcely ever took a step for any reason that was really sound.

Once settled in San Francisco, R. Beers launched a career which soon linked small-time journalism with low-grade theatrical ventures. He first bought a weekly called *Music and Drama* with money Mother wheedled out of Grandpa. But after a few issues Pop (as he was now affectionately called by his three children) dropped the subject of music, in which he had no interest, and retitled his weekly *The Dramatic Review*.

Pop's short brush with the world of music had one important outcome in his romance with the American diva Alice Nielsen, who seems to have spent a lot of time in San Francisco between engagements. She must have been quite an episode in Pop's life, because I once ran across a cache of her photographs, some of them from as far away as London, Milan, Vienna, and Budapest. Alice Nielsen was a beautiful blonde and one of the first stars of grand opera who wasn't overweight. She may have fallen for my Pop because, having no knowledge of music, he wasn't impressed by her talent and their affair had none of the restraint of adulation.

Pop's editorial policy for *The Dramatic Review* was to fill it with the pictures of pretty girls which have always been a specialty of San Francisco, and, copying the format of *The Police Gazette*, he arranged expeditions on which he took groups of them to be photographed in unusual locales. I remember a full-page picture showing a number of beauties posed on the engine of a railroad train, one with her arm about the neck of a highly gratified engineer. These jaunts sometimes lasted several days, and while away from home Pop generally took to the bottle. But, to do him justice, he remained a periodic drinker and never lapsed into a full-time dipsomaniac.

In that era the tenderloin of San Francisco, famous as the Barbary Coast, was in full flower, and I fear some of Pop's "cover girls" came from there. The district extended for about five blocks, a dazzling area of cafés, gambling spots, honkytonks, and places for more lusty diversion. Possibly its name had been invented by some world traveler who thought it resembled a certain wicked quarter on the Berber Coast. But sin in San Francisco had a special quality; the Barbary Coast developed its own brand of entertainment and copied no other place. Its honkytonks and sporting houses welcomed colored musicians at a time when they were barred from most white places, so San Francisco heard ragtime at its beginning; appreciated, fostered, and developed it. The raciest of American slang was invented on the Barbary Coast, much of it by an outrageous young man named Wilson Mizner. Generations yet to come will be quoting Mizner without ever having heard his name, although H. L. Mencken's treatise, *The American Language*, bestows full credit on him. It is difficult to give a true impression of Mizner's wit on paper because a great deal of it seems violent to the point of bad taste. But Mizner was no roughneck; he was a gentleman; he was even a "dude." He sent to London for his clothes at a period when such foppery was unheard of in the uncouth West. He was also a man of breeding; the Mizners were direct descendants of Sir Joshua Reynolds, and Wilson's father was an ambassador from the United States to some South American country. Above all, he was extremely handsome; not only did these facts absolve Wilson's humor of vulgarity, but they gave it a unique shock value. To hear that imposing and elegant creature come out with a statement such as one he made about Hollywood during the Fatty Arbuckle scandal produced a rather special effect.

"Living in Hollywood," said Wilson, "is like floating down a sewer in glass-bottom boat."

The burlesque theaters of the Barbary Coast developed several artists who became stars on Broadway; one of them was Blossom Seeley. She appeared on television not so long ago, a sprightly old lady who delivered some of her early song-and-dance numbers belonging to the period of the Bunny Hug. But the most distinguished star to emerge from the Coast was David Warfield. He toured America for years with a serio-comedy called *The Music Master* in which he played an old Austrian piano teacher. There was one moment in the last act when Warfield reduced his audiences to audible sobs. It came in a scene where the Music Master was called on to protect a young girl who was being disowned by her parents; "If *you* don't need her, *I* need her," the old Austrian declared. "If *you* don't vant her, *I* vant her!" In time, that speech became a catch phrase and a joke, but David Warfield's perform-ance has remained a classic in the annals of the American theater. There is no record of where Warfield worked on the Barbary Coast, but the only spot that featured "legitimate" acting was a tiny theater where the drawing-room comedies of Sir Arthur Wing Pinero were acted quite earnestly except that the performers didn't wear any clothes. So the eminent old thespian may have been trained in that naughty and irreverent troupe.

As youngsters we had a lively curiosity about the Barbary Coast, but I was never to see it, for if we children wandered in that neigh-borhood we were quickly turned back by the first passer-by. But when I was writing scenarios at M.G.M., I collaborated on a movie about the Barbary Coast with one of the studio's staff writers, Bob Hopkins. "Hoppy" had been a messenger boy on the Coast in its heyday, when Wilson Mizner was a young dandy in silk hat, white tie, and tails, who gambled with rich suckers for big stakes. Our movie was called *San Francisco;* its leading character was inspired by Wilson Mizner and played by Clark Gable, whose performance suggested much of Wilson's insouciance and illicit charm. Costar-ring with Gable were Jeanette MacDonald and Spencer Tracy, and the film has often been televised on the Late Late Show.

A chain of fond associations developed during the making of that movie. Three of us had the sentimental bond of being fellow San Franciscans. Herb Nacio Brown, who composed some of its song numbers, had played piano as a youth in a honkytonk on the Bar-bary Coast. Our theme song, "San Francisco," was selected by a competition among the composers under contract at M.G.M. and won by young Bronislaw Kaper, who had just arrived from Yugo-slavia, spoke little English, and had never seen the place that was supposed to be his inspiration. However, Broni's tune so character-ized the brisk spirit of San Francisco that it was adopted as a theme song by the city itself. Herb Brown wrote many more important melodies than the ones he composed for our movie, among them

round of applause from those undemanding Maccabees; at any rate the episode put it into Pop's mind that I might become a professional. Not long afterward he telephoned Mother from a saloon near the Alcazar Theatre and told her to bring me right down; that he had suggested me for a part in a play called *May Blossom*, and that by no means was I to let slip the fact that I had never appeared on a professional stage.

Opposed to the idea as Mother was, she obediently took me to the theater, where I was introduced to its manager, Walter Belasco. He was a half-brother of David Belasco, who was in San Francisco at the time, having come all the way from New York to direct *May Blossom*, of which he was co-author. So I began my acting career under the auspices of the great David Belasco himself.

Many years later I made good use of my encounter with that first citizen of Broadway. Come 1926, *Gentlemen Prefer Blondes* was due to open in New York, and Edna Hibbard, the actress who was to play our brunette, was just finishing an engagement in a Belasco play called *Ladies of the Evening*. Unless she was released, we would be forced to put off our opening; so I composed a letter of such barefaced flattery that I was almost ashamed to mail it to D. B.

April 6, 1926

Dear Mr. Belasco,

Many years ago you supplied me with one of the most thrilling memories of my life when you directed me as a little child in *May Blossom*. By all the rules I should be trying to do something for you to repay for that memory—and instead, I am asking you to do something for me. But that is a penalty of genius which can only give, because it needs nothing that other mortals can supply.

We need Edna Hibbard to be free the last night of *Ladies of the Evening*. In view of your integrity toward audiences, I realize how much I am asking of a great sensitive soul. But I love my work enough to be a humble supplicant. And I feel

you love the theatre enough to listen and add one more glorious memory to my future.

In deep admiration and respect,
Anita Loos

Letter from DAVID BELASCO:

April 8, 1926

Dear Anita Loos:

Such a letter as yours is not to be resisted. A man of flint
(and I am not one) couldn't withstand your plea.

Edna Hibbard is yours—take her and thank you for making
such a sweet appeal. It enables me to put business to one side
and act from the heart.

Faithfully,
David Belasco

And it was due to this highfalutin flimflam that we got our brunette.

One engagement I played as a child was at the Tivoli Opera
House, the home of a permanent company which produced the
standard comic operas of that day: *The Mikado, Robin Hood, The
Belle of New York*, etc. The star of the company was a handsome,
robust comedian, Ferris Hartman, whose son Paul, with his wife
Grace, rose to stardom years later in New York. In 1950 they asked
me to appear on a radio program called *Breakfast with the Hart-
mans*, and we recalled fondly our childhood in San Francisco.

My theatrical career was much more active than Gladys's, and
the reason must have been that I was Pop's favorite, so he neglected
her and pushed me. Gladys couldn't have been a worse actress than
I was, and we were equally uninterested in the profession. But the
only time I was ever turned down for a job was once when I was
sent for to play a part with a road company at the old California

Theatre. At the first sight of me the leading lady was annoyed by the length of my hair. "The audience will be gasping over that mop of hair," she said, "and it will completely ruin the scene." I actually didn't blame her, for I hated that hair myself and longed to whack it off (which was just what I did in New York several years later and possibly became the first girl ever to be bobbed and wind-blown).

During our schooldays my mother's main concern was to keep us in respectable neighborhoods. She purposely selected one of our homes because it was across from the Denman Grammar School on Bush Street, which was exclusively for girls. In any ordinary city schoolchildren who were also actresses would have been freaks. But San Francisco was anything but ordinary. It was so cosmopolitan that many of our schoolmates were Chinese, French, Spanish, and Japanese. I was often hard put in my typically Loos desire to be different. There was an occasion when a reporter for the *Chronicle* came to the school to interview students on the subject of our ambitions. I realized I would never be quoted among so many others unless I chose a highly original *métier*. Because quite a number of little girls said they wanted to be actresses, I knew such an ambition was bound to put my interview into the discard, even though I already had a head start on that career. I searched my brain for something which would be newsworthy, a career none of the others could possibly think of. Finally I hit it. I told the reporter I intended to become an architect of ocean liners. So it was *I* who got my picture taken and made the headline.

During this time there were five other little girls scurrying around the environs of San Francisco, getting ready to invade the planet. They were Gertrude Stein, Alice B. Toklas, Elsa Maxwell, Gertrude Atherton, and Frances Marion, who became rich and famous writing movie scripts for Mary Pickford, Marie Dressler, and Wallace Beery. Except for Gertrude Atherton, who remained a San Franciscan all her life, we all went far afield when young, and our paths crossed only when we were grown up. Frances Marion and I, being in the movies, met early, and she became my friend, as did Elsa Maxwell and Alice B. Toklas.

Mother's insistence on a nice home for her children was of small concern to Pop. Although he was quite "elegant" in a tacky way, he was such a superb egotist that he was never to learn he was tacky, and the overwhelming jauntiness of his conceit always forced one to admire Pop, much as an alcoholic who hates water is compelled to admire Niagara Falls. In spite of poverty, our family life was pleasant in the extreme. When Pop *did* happen to be around, he often used to take us to the French restaurants for which San Francisco was noted. In all those places the cuisine was of gourmet quality; a table d'hôte dinner used to begin with shrimp or oyster cocktails made of those small, sweet shrimps or the coppery oysters which are local specialties. This was followed by *petite marmite;* then fish served with some unusual sauce; after which was roast beef, and, after that, either chicken or game; then came salad, ice cream, fruit, cheese, and coffee. And in the interest of economics let me state that such a dinner cost twenty-five cents, except in one favorite place, where it was only twenty.

Sometimes, when Pop was in an expansive family mood, he used to bring delicacies home in the middle of the night, insisting that we children be hustled out of bed for a treat on which Mother looked with silent disapproval. There were any number of food specialties that were known only to San Francisco. One of them was called an oyster loaf and was made by scooping out a loaf of hard-crusted bread, the inside of which was toasted by some baffling process. The loaf was then stuffed with oysters, which were breaded and fried crisp, but they merged with the toast in a gooey, buttery mass that was delicious. Another specialty dear to our hearts was the tamale, which had been imported from Mexico; but the chefs of San Francisco improved on the dry, anemic original and turned it into a delectable package of chicken, olives, and red peppers wrapped in corn husks lined with Indian meal. There was also chop suey, which San Francisco invented *in toto,* and it was so delicious that it was even admired by the Chinese.

Pop's midnight feasts were washed down with lager beer fetched in a bucket from the corner saloon; the bucket, for some reason, was called a "growler," and I loved to go for the beer because the bartender and I were cronies; disloyal to his boss, he taught me to smear the inside of the growler with butter, thus preventing a collar of foam and giving me more beer for my nickel.

There were periods when Pop would be away for several days, hanging out with a colony of bohemian friends who occupied a row of abandoned cable cars parked along the beach. But when he *was* in residence we sometimes enjoyed the very fine company of his pals. One of them was a young girl who wrote poetry; I'm sure Pop liked her not so much for her poems as for the fact that she was extraordinarily pretty. It was a great shock one day to learn that she had killed herself, leaving three lines of poetry which I still remember:

> It is a silver space between two rains,
> The world is drained of color,
> Light remains.

Another frequent guest of ours was a rich Chinese merchant who overwhelmed us children with presents, as is the custom of that race. He was typical of the native-born Chinese of San Francisco, who combine the grace and humor of their race with the alert know-how of the New World. Sometimes our friend called on us wearing an Oriental banker's long coat, for which he apologized, saying that his old-world business associates looked askance at Occidental dress.

Another of Pop's glamorous friends was Willie Britt, a San Francisco-born prize fighter, I think a middleweight champion. He was a charmer and the first matinee idol in the boxing profession. It was Willie Britt who introduced ladies into the audiences at boxing matches.

Two brothers who were journalists on San Francisco newspapers sometimes showed up at our home; they were Wallace and Will Irwin. Wallace was to become known for his *Love Sonnets of a Hoodlum* and for humorous stories about a Japanese schoolboy called Hashimura Togo. Will Irwin's claim to fame was an inspired book about San Francisco before the fire, *The City That Was.*

Another associate of Pop's, then unknown, was Jack London,

whose masterpiece, *The Call of the Wild*, was yet to be written. Jack London wasn't sufficiently housebroken to be taken into the presence of my gentle mother. Pop never brought him home; the time they spent together was in saloons along the waterfront, where Jack was soaking up inspiration for *John Barleycorn*, a book he wrote much later about the horrors of drink. But Jack and Pop had little else in common, for Jack was an intellectual, one of the first Americans to read Nietzsche and Schopenhauer, whereas Pop was an egghead only in a hirsute way.

Pop's acquaintance with Wilson Mizner was sketchy. He was far below Pop's age group, so I never encountered America's most fascinating outlaw as a child, but, seeing that I was an acceptable companion for both Pop and Uncle Horace at a tender age, I like to think that a *simpatia* might have developed between us even then. As it turned out, my fondness for Wilson Mizner came many years later.

Pop's one recreation in the great outdoors came while he was fishing, a sport in which he loved to indulge on the San Francisco piers. I often used to accompany him, although I was interested not so much in the fish as in the passers-by. The San Francisco waterfront was a wonderfully exciting place, international in character and with a strong flavor of the Orient. Ships from every country in the world poured a stream of roustabouts into the waterfront saloons, which even in 1900 were still engaged in shanghaiing. Just to walk the streets bordering the bay was an exciting adventure, especially when the fog rolled in from the sea. The fog of San Francisco was unlike that of other cities: first of all it was clean, and the brisk scent of salt and seaweed made it an invigorating tonic. When fog veiled San Francisco, everything seemed more than usually mysterious and romantic. One day as Pop and I were fishing off the pier in a heavy mist, a voice of delirious beauty rose from quite close by, singing Mimi's song from *La Bohème*. In our sense of isolation, the song seemed to be for us alone, but at its end an invisible audience broke into applause that echoed near and far from every direction. The unseen singer could only have been Luisa

Tetrazzini, who loved San Francisco and sang every year at the Tivoli Opera House.

It was on the San Francisco waterfront that I met an unforgettably seductive creature who was the wife of a captain on a freighter that plied between the California coast and the Orient. She came originally from Vermont, as had my grandma. She had green-blue eyes which made a fascinating contrast to the deep tan of her skin and intensified that peculiarly fierce New England type of sex appeal which, in her case, was still strong although she was weatherbeaten and spare and her hair had turned gray. She took a fancy to me and invited me aboard her husband's ship. Her one great interest in life was sex, and day after day, as we sat on deck outside the captain's quarters, she undertook to speak to me of intimacies my poor mother was too embarrassed ever to mention; but her slant on the subject was so extremely poetic that she never quite got down to cases. One day when I went over to see her, determined to ask for some more explicit details, I found the freighter had pulled out and she was off on another high venture with her husband, who in thirty years had never sailed without her. Since bona fide marriages are so uncommon, I record this as one of the few I've ever run across.

My experience with that captain's wife left me with visions of mysterious bliss which might also be dangerous; for she warned me that a girl could love not wisely but too well, in which case a child might be born disgracefully out of wedlock. Her stories made such a powerful impression on me that from time to time feelings of excitement and anticipation mingled with downright fear used to come over me in waves.

If it seems incredible that a youngster raised on the very edge of the Barbary Coast in a wicked city like San Francisco could have been so ignorant of the facts of life, I can only explain that in those days sex was a private matter that was seldom discussed; there was no movie which dared to treat the subject realistically, and no teleivision to cover sex crimes. (This brings to mind a TV interview I recently heard, when a newscaster questioned a child who had just been raped. "And how did you feel, Mildred, after this experience?" asked the interviewer; after which the little girl added her bit to the data on the subject by answering, "I felt awful.")

During all the time that Mother was left out of Pop's affairs she tried to lead her brood into the ordinary pursuits of an average family. When summer arrived she took us to the old ranch in Etna for our vacation, leaving Pop to his citified pleasures. Then, too, there was an extra occasion when we were all called north for Grandma's funeral and she was finally taken away from the room where she had spent most of her life. While on those visits, we were led into all the activities of a big ranch by our four country cousins; we gathered eggs by the hundreds, romped in the hay, and frolicked in the granary until our clothes were full of wheat. But I was always happiest in San Francisco with my Pop, savoring the *simpatia* I felt for him, trying to imitate the way he made everybody laugh.

It's difficult to remember old jokes, but I can cite a not-so-funny one I happened to get off at a time when Gladys and I were appearing in *Quo Vadis* with the Alcazar Stock Company. We were cast as Christian children awaiting contact with some lions in an off-stage arena. Now it so happened that my poor unprofessional mother had chosen tights for us of a violent yellow hue, and when we showed up in them at dress rehearsal the director was furious because, naturally, we were supposed to be bare-legged. (We might have dispensed with tights altogether, but for even children to have appeared without them in that era would have been disreputable.) While the director was loudly criticizing Mother in front of the whole company, I piped up to suggest that he insert a line of dialogue saying that, owing to the persecutions of the Roman emperor, we Christian children had contracted jaundice. My flippancy so embarrassed Mother that she wasn't even grateful that I caused the director to laugh away his disapproval.

When I was around the age of eight I wrote my first piece for publication. A children's magazine, *St. Nicholas*, had announced a contest in which contributions were to take the form of an advertisement for a floor polish known as F. P. C. Wax. Naturally I

knew nothing about F. P. C. Wax but, with a larceny which might
now do credit to Madison Avenue, I wrote an ad in verse, accompanied by the drawing of a Man from Mars. I can remember that
ad even now:

> The best thing I've seen, said the Man from Mars
> Since I left my abode from among the stars
> Is something my own world sadly lacks
> The earth's greatest boon F. P. C. Wax.

I won the competition. The prize of five dollars was instantly borrowed by Pop, who made a deal that I was to be paid interest at the
rate of 10 per cent a week. When that 10 per cent finally amounted
to more than the loan, I told Pop to forget about the capital and
just come through with the interest. But I was only kidding; I
never expected to get my money back and would even have felt let
down had Pop returned it. Although unaware, I was beginning to
sense the thrill a girl can feel in handing money to a man. This is a
trait in us that has been put to good account by most of the great
lovers of the world: the Don Juans, the Rubirosas, and the Aly
Khans, who never gave gifts to loved ones that were in any way
commensurate with their means; Rubirosa took millions of dollars
in cash from women who loved him. In fact the reason that mother-
love itself is so exhilarating is that it provides so many opportunities
for self-sacrifice. The most powerful love stories share the same
premise; Cleopatra most certainly supported Marc Antony, and the
Queen of Sheba provided Solomon with luxuries which, even as a
king, he couldn't afford. Men, too, can wax downright emotional
over being kept; poems like the Song of Songs will never be written to a gold-digger.

There was an endearing spokeswoman for our sex in the twenties; she was Fanny Brice, that homely young star who sang a song
in praise of giving, called "My Man," and invested it with a poignant ecstasy she could never put into that *chanson* of hollow joy
called "I've Got the World on a String." For sooner or later the
most successful gold-diggers will find themselves nursing an empty
void. It may begin very subtly, when a girl acquires her first

trinket, only to learn that her satisfaction over it is brief. Without realizing that it irritates her as the symbol of a lover who has to bolster his appeal by gifts, she decides that a more expensive present will lead to more permanent satisfaction and goes out after more valuable jewels. Finally she may own as many diamonds as Peggy Hopkins Joyce, without ever having experienced any emotional reward. But Peggy Joyce was a smart girl and she ultimately handed over all her loot to a big handsome Swedish bartender, becoming at last a really satisfied female.

The majority of gold-diggers finish by supporting men, but they generally begin when they are too old, with men who are too young, thus making themselves ridiculous. Lucky a girl like I, who was privileged to start early under unique auspices; for not only did Pop demand sacrifices but he doubled their enjoyment by making jokes about them. Moreover, the *rapport* I shared with Pop set us apart from the other members of the family. I never even had the ordinary *entente* with Gladys which most sisters enjoy. No two could have been more different than we were. Gladys was a heedless tomboy, always in the midst of things, whereas I remained on the sidelines, making impudent comments. Gladys was a blonde with brown eyes like her Aunt Nina, whom she closely resembled, whereas I was a brunette. She was the younger by nearly two years, but she was of normal height for her age, while I was diminutive. By the time I was eight and Gladys only six, strangers used to take us for twins. Mother dressed us alike in fashions which I insisted on choosing myself. About that time I discovered the drawings of Kate Greenaway and forced Mother to copy those quaint dresses for Gladys and me. When Mother used to walk down the street with her blond and brunette "twins," we were looked at. One of Mother's first comments after Gladys died was to say, "People won't look at us any more, honeybunch. Now we'll be like everybody else." My own sardonic reaction was to think: I'll have to find some way to overcome that.

So far as my attitude toward my brother was concerned, I always felt a trace inferior. Clifford was eight years older than I, sober and given to worth-while ambitions, even given a little to snobbism. Many of Clifford's qualities were inherited from Grandpa Smith, and thank heaven for that, because he became the one great comfort in Mother's life and his eminent career in medicine made up for the bewilderment I always caused her.

Clifford was just as much embarrassed by Pop's companions as I was entranced with them. I remember a fascinating friend of Pop's in San Francisco, a dark, handsome young man who was forever trying to break into vaudeville with a novelty magic turn. While marking time, he earned his living in a locksmith's shop. On a certain occasion when a vaudeville act that was to open at the Orpheum Theatre failed to show up, Pop talked the manager into giving his young friend a chance. The latter opened and made good, but at the end of his engagement he asked Pop to help him get rid of a wooden packing case that had been part of his paraphernalia and must be gotten out of the way before anyone had a chance to examine it. So the case was deposited in our back yard. I carefully scrutinized that packing case for a clue which might explain how the young man had escaped from it after being securely nailed in, but I could find nothing unusual. It wasn't long before Pop's "discovery" went on to towering heights in his career, for he was Harry Houdini.

Gradually Pop's disappearances from home became more frequent and of longer duration. There were times when he was traveling in the Midwest as publicity man with some theatrical troupe or carnival company. But he seldom kept in touch with Mother, and when he did it was generally by picture postcard with a boastful message such as, "I am now with the Excelsior De Luxe Street Fair and Carnival Company handling publicity for all the man-eating animals." He seldom thought of accompanying his boasts with money, so Mother was forced to carry on alone. I recall one Christmastime when Pop was far away (nobody knew where) and there was no turkey in our larder. Mother concocted a platter of dressing out of bread, milk, and herbs and, with superhuman cheerfulness, tried to dramatize it so we wouldn't notice that the big bird was missing. However, had Mother been supplied with all the ingredients of an Escoffier, her cookery would have been dull. Although her only interests in life were home and family, she was a poor housekeeper. Mother's chief difficulty was that she was inept and it took her much too long to do a job. She was anything but lazy. Up at six in the morning, she dressed before breakfast for the entire day and never looked at a mirror from the time she completed her artless hairdo. Luckily she was never in straits to clothe Gladys and me, because of the huge boxes of second-hand Parisian finery which used to arrive every so often from Nina. The fact that those dresses came from Paris was of no interest to Mother; their importance to her was that they were scarcely worn and she could rip them apart and make them over with *Ladies' Home Journal* patterns. But the labels of Paquin and Worth caused me chills of delight, and I could hardly wait for the time when I would be old enough to wear Nina's dresses before Mother desecrated them. Those garments may have been the reason for my love of clothes, a love which has nothing to do with status-seeking. I've enjoyed my happiest moments when trailing a Mainbocher evening gown across the sawdust-covered floor of a saloon.

Once or twice a year we had a windfall when Grandpa arrived in San Francisco on business, and, although he chose not to comment on our surroundings, he used to come to the rescue. Suddenly it was Clifford's turn to be well dressed; he was outfitted from head to toe, and we girls got the new shoes which Nina's boxes were incapable of supplying. If Grandpa happened to come to San Francisco at times when Gladys and I were acting, he used to go to see us. He was very easy to please; his admiration was never for our "art" but only for our ability to memorize lines. His most searching criticism was to remark, "You little girls really remembered everything you had to say!" Before he left town, Grandpa always presented us children with ten-dollar gold pieces, which I presume are now resting cozily in Fort Knox.

A time finally came when Pop's behavior reached a new low and, while he was off somewhere on a drinking spree, Gladys, then eight years old, was stricken with peritonitis. She developed such an alarming fever that our doctor called in a surgeon who operated on her right there in our own unsanitary kitchen. The operation over, a cab was summoned, and Gladys was wrapped in a blanket and taken off to the hospital in the surgeon's arms. One of the most poignant remarks I ever heard my mother utter was as Gladys was carried through the front doorway. "Dear, dear," said Mother, "I wonder what her father Harry would say."

I knew that Gladys was going to die, because while we sat waiting for a phone call I picked up a copy of *Life*, which in those days was a humorous weekly, and when I opened it my gaze lighted on a joke concerning death. I put the magazine aside with a shudder. Hours of suspense went by, and I was finally driven once more to open *Life*. The second joke that met my gaze also concerned death. Gladys died in the hospital that same night, and her funeral (paid for with money telegraphed by Grandpa) had been over several days before Pop came home and learned that he would never again see his child, who was a lively little tomboy the day he left us. But even then my mother tried to lighten her Harry's burden of guilt. "Perhaps it happened for the best," Mother told him. "If she had grown up, she might have gone the way of her Aunt Nina."

Pop's behavior in that tragedy should have cured him of his addiction to drink and pretty ladies. It certainly didn't. When he died in Santa Monica, at the age of eighty-four, there were three of them bickering over him at his bedside, two being sprightly mothers of famous film stars. In fact, Pop left a trail of minor scandals behind him as long as he lived. I recall one night during World War II when he was arrested in Santa Monica for leaving the window shades up at night during a blackout. The next morning, when Clifford went to bail him out, Pop commented bitterly, "Sometimes I wish they'd never started this war!" And there was another jail experience, which occurred during Prohibition, when Pop was had up in court over trafficking with a renegade priest for a gallon of sacramental wine. As a companion in that fracas, Pop had Pauline Frederick, the beautiful stage and film star. However, Pop was no snob in the accepted sense, for any female with whom he associated was automatically raised to distinction by that mere fact. During one escapade he was admonished by my brother for his attentions to the occupant of a trailer in a gully near Santa Monica. Pop tried to whitewash the affair by explaining that his companion was a real lady; the proof being that she played cornet in a *ladies'* brass band.

Respectable as my mother was, she could be guilty of the most heinous sadism. I remember a time when the nation was thrown into a state of ecstatic shock by the Hall-Mills murder case, in which the Reverend Mr. Hall had been found dead with the leader of his choir in some lovers' lane. It was a particularly vicious murder with suspicions equally divided between the lady's husband and the Reverend Mr. Hall's wife. My mother shook her head over the scandal. "It needn't have been done in quite that way," said Mother, "but of course they *should* have been put to death for having an affair." In trying to reconstruct her state of mind over her own Harry's romances, I can only surmise that Mother was able to see them as a form of onesided adulation on the part of the lady concerned.

After Gladys died I often found myself the family's chief source of income. In those days traveling companies from New York picked up the children they required in various cities along the route. It was the custom for the advance agent to select and rehearse a child before the company reached town. Sometimes I had one rehearsal with the company before we opened, but more often I didn't. Sometimes accidents occurred, as one did when I was playing little Willie in that grand old melodrama *East Lynne*. Its plot concerned a certain Lady Isabel who deserted her husband and baby boy for another man. Finally latent love for her child overcame Lady Isabel, so she disguised herself with a gray wig and got a job as nursemaid to her own small son. While she was so engaged, Willie was taken mortally ill, and as he lay dying Lady Isabel tore off her wig in an effort to make Willie recognize her. The scene was a heart-wrencher, but, having had no dress rehearsal, I thought the removal of Lady Isabel's wig must signify that the curtain had fallen, so I sat up in bed, thereby making Willie's tragic end a cause for very unfortunate laughter.

On another occasion I took part in a historic theatrical event when the famous stage star Blanche Bates gave Ibsen's *A Doll's*

House its first American production and I played one of Nora's
children. Blanche Bates had chosen to introduce the play in San
Francisco instead of New York because she was married to a prominent San Francisco journalist. *A Doll's House* was a great success
and had a record run there.

At times I was sent off on tour, and Mother would generally
place me in charge of the company's character actress. However,
no sooner did the train pull out of San Francisco, than I switched
over to the male members of the group. The actors used to take me
to saloons after the show, prop me up on the bar, and regale me
with free lunch. I adored this element of theatrical life, although
drinking was never to tempt me. Possibly the circumstances of my
sister's death, when we needed Pop so badly and he wasn't there,
left me with a lifelong distaste for alcohol. I've never drunk anything stronger than coffee.

I was certainly never born to be an actress. Many years later
I got an inkling of the reason why from the ballet master Adolph
Bohm, at a time when Norma and Constance Talmadge and I
thought it might be a good idea to take ballet lessons. We were all
pretty bad, but I was the worst, and one day Bohm blew up and
shouted at me, "Mother of heaven, will you never stop *thinking!*"
Had it been a few years later, I might have thought my little head
off at the Actors Studio and been a success. But those were the
good old days when playwrights did the thinking and the actor
never interfered.

It was during my acting career that I had my first beau. He was a
boy named Harry Pilzer, who happened to be in a play with me at
the Tivoli Opera House. Every night he used to bring me a paper
bag, striped in green and white, which contained a chocolate-cream
mouse with a string tail, and, in payment, collected a brief kiss on
the cheek. The Pilzers later moved to Paris, where I ultimately had
a successor in Gaby Deslys, who was supposed to have been the
mistress of the King of Spain. Gaby was famous for her beauty, her
romances, and her jewels, because at best her talent might only be
described as "posturing." She was a natural blonde with limpid blue
eyes, a sort of Grace Kelly with the ladylike attributes removed.

She was a star at the old Casino de Paris, where she appeared in headdresses taller than herself, dripping with pearls and diamonds. The very carrying of those headpieces was a stunt, and Gaby did it with grace and charm. In Paris, Harry Pilzer became her dancing partner and her friend. She paid him a better price for his affection than the brief kiss he collected from me, for when she died in her mid-thirties she left him her fabulous jewels. Her death was actually a form of suicide, because she could have been saved had she submitted to an operation. But it would have had to be on her throat, and the scar would have marred her fragile beauty.

A day finally arrived in San Francisco when our finances took a sudden upturn. Grandpa Smith died, and overnight my mother became an heiress. It was then that Pop really splurged. But on Mother's insistence he first bought us a slick new house in a district near the Presidio on Union Street; after feeling that *he* had amply provided for his family, Pop proceeded to get rid of the remainder of my mother's inheritance as rapidly as he could. Since he was an expert, it didn't take Pop long; soon everything was lost, and Grandpa was no longer around to fall back on.

At this new low ebb of our fortunes, someone made Pop the offer of a job. It was to manage a theater in Los Angeles, one which featured that exciting new form of entertainment to which the public had just given an affectionate nickname, "the movies." Our pleasant home on Union Street was sold, and we were left with only enough money to provide transportation to Los Angeles for three of us and leave a small fund with Clifford so he might pursue medical studies at Stanford University (the medical department was then in San Francisco, although the university itself was in Palo Alto). So at long last we were through with San Francisco, the lovely, lively, openhearted, amoral city which has lingered on in memory as my spiritual home. We headed south toward the new career which opened up for Pop and which was my first connection with the movies I came to know so very well.

We arrived in Los Angeles on a beautiful sunny morning in that era before smog descended on the city. By this time all three of us were excited over the change of scene, and Pop was eager, as always, to charm a new set of associates. We knew nothing of the theater he was to manage except that it was called the Cineograph, in honor of the movies which were the novelty of its shows, and that it was located on Court Street; so Pop decided we should go there directly and then look for a hotel in the same neighborhood. Our cab left the station and swung into Main Street, the principal artery of the city's large Mexican district. Then, as now, it was a rowdy thoroughfare of saloons, burlesque houses, low-grade restaurants, dilapidated stores plastered with signs spelled out in Spanish, and offices of quack doctors who blatantly advertised a cure for the ailment which I would one day hear Wilson Mizner strip of all its drama by calling it Cupid's catarrh. Mother's morale must have wavered as we rode through that rowdy district. She must have been hoping we'd soon be pulling out of it when almost at once the cab turned into an obscure alley which proved to be Court Street, with the Cineograph Theatre in the center of its one short block. The theater lobby, painted white but very dirty, was decorated with posters advertising a movie, and there were a number of frames filled with grimy photographs of vaudeville entertainers. The movie was *The Life of Christ*, a somewhat incongruous subject to be on the same bill with the show's headline comedian, Fritz Fields, whose photos showed him in baggy pants and a clown make-up with a spangle on the tip of his nose. There were also pictures of a pretty soubrette named Maxine Mitchell, an acrobatic act, and six nondescript chorus girls who wore a minimum of clothing. The theater was closed at that early-morning hour, but loafing about the lobby, enjoying its display of nudity, was a straggling of the Mexican clientele to which the Cineograph catered. From inside the theater came the sound of a wheezy piano sighing out a new torch song, "Melancholy Baby," that had just started to sweep the country from the Barbary Coast, where it originated. Mother must have considered our new environment sordid to the degree it actually was, but to Pop and me it was both colorful and exciting. Those Mexican dilettantes gave the premises a foreign tone, and "Melancholy Baby" fell on my ears as a gusty and sensuous theme song.

As we entered the dark theater the piano player, a handsome, dapper young man, rose to greet us. He introduced himself as the comedian, Fritz Fields, and explained he liked to drop into the theater after breakfast and try out new song numbers. Even in that dim light I realized he bore a striking resemblance to my Uncle Horace, and the fact that such an extraordinarily good-looking young man chose to disguise himself with a tramp make-up made him, in my eyes, very subtly attractive. After exchanging a few amenities with Pop, Fritz Fields directed us to a nearby hotel, warning Pop that, while it didn't particularly cater to family trade, he as a bachelor found it okay. So, with quickening pulse, I learned Fritz Fields was single.

We found the hotel just around the corner on the sprightliest block of Main Street. The lobby, on the second floor, was reached by a long flight of narrow stairs, but once we were there it had as exciting an *ambiance* as my already surging emotion for Pop's headliner required. The clientele was made up of Western cattlemen in town on business, pleasure, or both; commercial travelers of the sort who choose to live near the railroad station; and a sprinkling of vaudeville and burlesque entertainers. Naturally Pop was all set to splurge on a suite, but, with our finances in a riskier state than they had ever been, Mother cautiously held him back and we moved, bag and baggage, into one room, which was to be our home for a long while. That room, although shabby, was spacious, its ceiling high, and its crystal chandelier still elegant as such things were apt to be in old buildings.

Pop and I immediately started to investigate our snow-shop." We learned from a young man who operated the projection machine that *The Life of Christ* was a permanent feature, for the picture industry of that day didn't turn out enough movies to provide many changes of program. Our film, a one-reeler, had been broken and patched so many times that the action was even more jerky than was normal in those early-day movies, and scratches had developed which gave the Holy City a monotonous climate of rain-storm. But we soon learned that audiences never tired of our picture. Week after week they watched, entranced, as the biblical story unfolded, and waited eagerly for a certain moment when a streetcar scooted through the background of ancient Bethlehem and was always good for a laugh.

Aside from *The Life of Christ*, other permanent features were Fritz and Maxine, who did single turns which they changed every week. And the show was always brought to a close with a rude form of *commedia dell'arte* called an "after-piece." Those after-pieces were never written down but passed along ad-lib by the vaudeville comedians of that day. Fritz Fields had a repertoire of them, and as a child of twelve I was put to work as a member of his cast. One of my parts was that of a French maid who provided the exposition. My lines, delivered while wielding a feather duster, consisted of soliloquies such as, "I wonder where the master was last night. The way he stays away from home is really a caution!"

Because there was a limited number of after-pieces, they frequently had to be repeated. But our audiences no more tired of them than they did of *The Life of Christ*. One of ours was titled *The Fellow Who Looks like Me*, with a plot that was simple and basic. The comic's wife is continually hearing of her husband's infidelities; he continually alibis them by claiming that the unfaithful one is "the fellow who looks like me." A climax is reached when the comic suddenly looks into a mirror and, to prove the "truth" of his assertion, pulls out a revolver and shoots at his own image. Curtain. Among standard after-pieces were *The Ghost in the Pawnshop*, *Box and Cox*, *McFadden's Flats*, and others, the plots of which I might have written myself.

Fritz Fields proved to be funnier offstage than on, as many comics are. He became Pop's crony, and they were always disappearing together, but it made me feel deliciously close to Fritz to know that he was off somewhere with my own Pop. Finally a tragic day arrived when I had visual proof that Fritz was romantically involved with the prettiest of the chorus girls. I braced myself to undergo a hopeless love affair, lost my sense of humor, ceased to make bad jokes, and took to brooding. But at any rate there was the bittersweet rapture of being rehearsed by my idol in those afterpieces.

Before long my unrequited passion was to cause me great anxiety. One week our after-piece required that Fritz steal a kiss from the French maid. While it was a mere bit of stage business to him, it put me through almost unbearable ecstasy. I then remembered the warning of that boat captain's wife, that it was dangerous for a girl to love "too well." What if the ecstasy of that nightly stage kiss were to result in a disgraceful motherhood? I got through that affair, however, with my virtue intact.

One summer while Clifford was spending his vacation with us, Pop put him to work in an after-piece. He was tall, dark, handsome, and must have had some talent, for later in life he was often to charm audiences when called on to make speeches. But his first appearance as an actor frightened Clifford for the very perverse reason that he loved it too much. He began to fear that he might enjoy the theater more than the life of a reputable surgeon, which he intended to be. Also he fell in love with the pretty soubrette, Maxine Mitchell, and "Maxie" became equally smitten with him. But throughout all these temptations Clifford remained a true grandson of George Smith and an even more considerate child of his mother. He put aside the frivolous desire to abandon a worthy career in medicine for a riotous one in show business and, the summer holiday over, returned to the dull respectability of medical school.

However, my own honkytonk days were almost over. For one weekend Pop and Fritz Fields were off on a jaunt that left the Cineograph without its manager, its comic, its after-piece, and its two prettiest chorus girls. This brought about Pop's dismissal from that entrancing spot and broke my heart.

After the debacle Fritz Fields left for the East and I never saw him again. For over a year we lived from hand to mouth, with Pop doing intermittent jobs as publicity man for carnival companies working in the Los Angeles area. But I will never be one to deride an adventurous poverty. It was always thrilling to hang out with Pop in booking offices where we exchanged gossip or, in the vernacular, "cut up touches" with Street Fair types, pitchmen, snake eaters, and such. I learned to discriminate between a "high" pitchman who sold such commodities as vegetable knives and spot-removers from a small folding table, and a "low" pitchman who had to spread his wares on the sidewalk. While the high pitchman was socially a cut above a low pitchman, the latter found it easier to get away when the police moved in. Such characters were exciting and, to a certain extent, rather moral companions; to quote George Santayana, "The nimbleness, free spirit and quick eye of the rascal must be admired and the very triviality of his arts will always insure his modesty. If one cheats the world only to laugh at it, the sin is already half forgiven."

Unorthodox as was our home life in a succession of shoddy furnished apartments, Mother always saw that I attended school. School had been pleasant enough before we moved south, but it didn't take me long to develop the snobbish attitude of a San Franciscan toward my Los Angeles schoolmates.

There will always be an abyss dividing Los Angeles from San Francisco. Theirs is a classic feud which has its basis in the origins of two widely different types. We of the north are descendants of argonauts in whom initiative and physical courage were requisites before they ever started their dangerous adventure. But the Angeleño came to his city after the railroad had been built, his trip generally a timid retreat from some community of the Middle West where he wasn't smart enough to make a living. On reaching his goal, this migrant found himself competing with others no smarter than himself, so he was able to prosper and, groggy with the astonishment of unmerited success and titillated by perpetual sunshine, he blossomed forth, manufactured gaudy clothing, freak architecture, rowdy exhibitionist religions, and all the other devices which only a brain devoid of moral stamina and good taste could conjure up.

I sometimes think that if the movies had developed in San Francisco when they moved from New York they might have grown out of their infancy in a fraction of the time it took in the south. I cite the case of burlesque, which on Main Street, L.A., was based on bumps and grinds, while the burlesque of San Francisco stemmed intellectually from such high-toned things as the plays of Pinero. When the movies finally came to Hollywood, I was to be a part of that extraordinary camp of dressed-up gypsies, and perhaps I was able to put a little of the *élan* of my native San Francisco into the scripts I wrote. But before that day arrived I chanced to make a detour into yet another field of writing.

At that period the oracle of the New York sporting and theatrical world was *The Morning Telegraph* and, although Pop and I were in a very low form of show business and as far away from New York as one could be in the U.S.A., we both eagerly read the *Telegraph*. On its front page was a column called *The Town in Review*, which one day announced a contest for humorous anecdotes about life in New York. Undeterred by the fact that I had never been there, I wrote a paragraph, sent it off, and won the contest. Thus continued a pattern which had begun when I won that contest in *St. Nicholas*. No doubt it was beginner's luck, but I usually succeeded with a first effort. It might be followed by failures, but I was able to say I did it once and can do it again, perhaps. After winning the contest, I continued to send short paragraphs to *The Morning Telegraph*, which accepted the majority of them and paid me two and a half cents a word. So that at thirteen years of age I became a journalist on a New York daily.

During this period Pop fell in with a theatrical pair, Ed Meade and Sue Iles, who were looking around Southern California for a location where they could install a stock company. Word now came from San Diego that they had discovered a vacant stable which could be converted into a theater, and they invited Pop to join the venture. By that time Pop was as disenchanted with Los Angeles as I was, so we were more than eager to leave that tawdry old city and head south for one more fresh start in San Diego.

❧ CHAPTER 3

❧ When we moved south, San Diego was only just large enough to be called a city. The principal shopping district extended a mere six blocks on Fifth Street. A sizable park overlooked it from a hill, and the waterfront was close at hand, the harbor bristling with boats: large ones belonging to the United States Navy, and any number of pleasure craft. San Diego seemed both cozy and festive; sailors in white uniforms animated the streets, and the sea air was clear and invigorating. Directly across the bay the resort town of Coronado spread along a sandy strip that ran parallel to the coast for several miles.

The Hotel Del Coronado was a famous winter resort for rich people from the East. I had read fascinating items about it in the society columns, seen pictures of it in the rotogravures. Clearly visible across San Diego Bay, it sparkled in the sunlight, a white structure of the "casino" type with acres of red roof. I could hardly wait to explore a paradise that was so near.

The very first morning I prepared to invade Coronado with Pop as an escort. It was a gratifying experience, for there were several of Nina's Paris gowns to choose from. I finally settled on a black velvet model from Paquin, with a wide band of brown fur around the hem. It was a suitable garment in which a big blond Venus like Auntie Nina could swish into Maxim's in Paris, and when it first arrived Mother wanted to rip it apart, as usual, and make it into a dress more appropriate to my fifteen years. But at this I had balked;

I was grown up now, having attained a height of four feet eleven and weighing ninety-two pounds (measurements which are the same today); so I had cajoled Mother into merely reducing the proportions to fit my childlike figure and, with a hat of the latest "peachbasket" style half covering a homemade marcel wave, I set forth for Coronado in high fashion, accompanied by Pop.

A brisk ten-minute trip by ferry across the bay, followed by a ride in a bumpy little streetcar, landed us at the hotel. But as we entered the grounds I began to feel overawed in spite of my Paris gown; the gardens were so pretentiously well kept that the plants looked snooty. We climbed a broad staircase onto a pompous veranda and entered the hotel. Its lobby appeared to be endless; it was dazzlingly white with panels outlined in gold, and the carpet was bright red, a color scheme which still remains in my mind's eye as the peak of luxury. At the back of the lobby gigantic glass doors opened onto a courtyard where the tropical vegetation seemed so outlandish that it might have been painted by Henri Rousseau.

In my eyes those commanding premises took second place to the hotel's guests, for it was the very height of the winter season and the lobby was filled with rich pleasure-seekers, many of them dressed for yachting, tennis, or polo. I recognized from pictures in the rotogravures the noted young horsewoman "Eleo" Sears, who, it seemed, was an annual visitor from Boston. Her hair, innocent of the marcel wave I had laboriously achieved, was in a rather scraggly pompadour, and she wore a tailored shirtwaist dress of white linen that had practically a man's collar and a necktie. As I watched those sophisticates, my courage rapidly oozed away. My Paquin gown, which less than an hour before had seemed the height of chic, had suddenly become tacky. I now realized I was a victim of provincial bad taste, for in Southern California we followed the styles in the ladies' magazines, which were geared to Eastern climates, and during the warm winter months everybody sweltered in heavy woolen garments. But the Coronado ladies of fashion were properly dressed for a warm climate in linen that was mostly white and didn't even look expensive. I was learning a quick lesson in style: that smart clothes must be dictated by comfort.

Pop, blissfully unimpressed, lost none of his jaunty manner, but, even though nobody paid either of us any attention, I began to suffer the qualms of a trespasser. Finally spotting a tiny sign that pointed the way to the bar, I thought that Pop at least might fit in there, so we followed directions down a broad staircase that was heavily cushioned in red, like the lobby. We entered a large area that was just as overpowering as everything else; there was a glistening mahogany bar, adjacent to which were several immaculate bowling alleys, deserted at the moment. Pop and I sat down at a table where, through enormous windows, we could watch and even hear the pounding waves of the Pacific as they dashed against a rocky breakwater. We ordered drinks and I casually tried to overlook two handsome men in polo outfits and their stylish ladies, who were dressed in crisp white linen. The air was redolent of a perfume that was a favorite with chic women at that time. It was L'Idéal of Houbigant; I knew it, second hand, from the empty boxes Nina used to send with her discarded finery. The boxes were covered with silk in an arabesque pattern of lavender and yellow, and the fragrance of L'Idéal remained on them still. That day in the barroom, its scent was mingled with the tang of the sea, a faint aroma of gin, and that strange sweet incense which pervades bowling alleys, to the credit of clean human perspiration.

Embarrassed as I was by my too opulent Paris gown, I now began to be even more ashamed of Pop, wished he were sufficiently aware of his surroundings to take off the derby hat he sported, indoors and out, for the same reason that other men wore toupées. The derby never fooled anybody because it was either cocked over one eye or perched on the back of his head, leaving a large area of baldness exposed. Why couldn't he have bought himself a real cigar with my money, instead of that spineless stogie? Why couldn't he sometimes make a forthright observation without trying to be funny? Right then and there, in that elegant saloon, was born a desire to get away from the raffish milieu of our home, which up to that time had been as satisfactory to me as it would always be to Pop. I was not aware of the fact, but that was the beginning of the end of the lifelong *simpatia* I had always enjoyed with Pop.

Pop paid for his highball and my Coca-Cola and we then went out to explore Coronado. Adjacent to the hotel was a huge glass-domed building that seemed to be a conservatory, but on entering we found that it enclosed a heated swimming pool where some children of the rich, in charge of their governesses, were making an ungodly hollow-sounding racket. Leaving there, we wandered along the oceanfront, lined by glossy, immaculate villas of families such as the Spreckelses, who owned the sugar industry of Hawaii. Scattered about the resort were slick little bungalows that housed the families of officers stationed at the local naval base, one of which, had I been endowed with clairvoyance, I would have seen as the locale of my honeymoon.

If I have described Coronado at some length, it is because of the part it played in changing my entire life; it was where I first met the "cosmopolites" for whom I forever deserted Pop's dear but tacky companions; where for a few seasons I had my first and last taste of life as a normal young girl; and where I was married for a matter of two days (which wasn't exactly so normal).

But Coronado belonged to the future; our first real home was a four-room apartment on the second floor of a building on Fifth Street, right in the center of San Diego's business district. The one luxury we always seemed to enjoy was space, because we could afford to live only in old buildings, where, of course, the rooms were large. Our apartment was especially repainted for us and I, in my new affluence as a regular paid contributor to *The New York Morning Telegraph*, took charge. I dictated a color scheme that copied the white, red, and gold decor which had so staggered me on my first timid look into the Hotel Del Coronado. From the corner of our living room a big octagonal bay window looked down on Fifth Street and made a perfect vantage point for the first great drama of my life. For early one morning we were startled by newsboys directly beneath the window calling out, "San Francisco destroyed by earthquake," "Entire city in flames," "Read all about it!"

On that agonizing day Clifford was in San Francisco, working as an intern in the French Hospital. Appalled, we rushed down to the street, where we remained most of the day, eagerly grabbing every Extra as it appeared. Our emotions were a mixture of hope and despair; hope because we knew that Clifford's hospital was equipped with fire escapes; despair over the fact that, as a wooden structure, it could so easily burn. The Extras were increasingly alarming; every major building and beloved old San Francisco landmark seemed to have been destroyed. Luckily we were in suspense about Clifford for only half the day, for the Western Union Company did a magnificent job of getting out telegrams. Ours read, "Safe and well, don't worry. Clifford."

For days our only occupation was to follow the news and rumors about the fire. (As loyal San Franciscans, we never called the catastrophe an "earthquake," just as we never desecrated our adored city with the name of "Frisco," and this is the last time it will ever be so called in this record.) Los Angeles had been quick to point an accusing finger at its rival in the north and say the fire was a retaliation by the Almighty for our wickedness. But while the fire was still smoldering San Francisco, with typical insouciance, began to make jokes about its own destruction. In one area where the havoc had been most complete a tall sign advertising Hostetter's whisky was left intact, allowing a certain rhymster to come up with a defense of his city:

> If God hit San Francisco town
> Because we were too frisky,
> Why did He knock the churches down
> And leave Hostetter's Whisky?

Another San Francisco joke concerned that unregenerate matinee idol adored by all females, John Barrymore. He had been playing an engagement in San Francisco at the time of the disaster and the story went that the earthquake had dumped him out of bed, that on stumbling into the street he had been drenched by a broken water main, after which the militia had forced him to help clear away rubble. His brother, Lionel, was quoted as saying, "It takes an earthquake to get Jack out of bed, a flood to make him wash, and the United States Army to put him to work."

On the other hand, we had more tragic accounts of the disaster when letters began to arrive from Clifford. He wrote that as soon as the hospital was found to be safe he had gone into the streets with first-aid equipment. There he had met up with the dying, had treated all sorts of injuries, and, in the midst of the rubble, had aided a hysterical woman to give birth.

Although it seemed that our preoccupation with the fire would never simmer down, it finally did and we were able to put our minds back on show business. Ed Meade and Sue Iles, together with a group of actors they had recruited, were busy converting the stable into a theater, doing most of the labor themselves, and now Pop bestirred himself to sit in the auditorium, his derby tilted over one eye, daintily puffing his stogie as he criticized their work. For a reason I don't remember, Ed Meade named our theater the Rudwin. The stock company was headed by Sue Iles as star, Ed was stage director, Pop the impresario, and I was a sort of utility actress.

One week I played the title role in *Little Lord Fauntleroy*, when I balked at wearing the traditional black velvet suit and lace collar, which to my mind were effeminate, and insisted on a more virile sailor suit. The following week I increased my height with French heels and a tall pompadour and portrayed Lady Barbara, the female villain of *East Lynne*, in which I had once played little Willie. I was paid a weekly salary of fifteen dollars, and my income, augmented by what I was still earning from *The Morning Telegraph*, was sometimes larger than Pop's take as a producer.

A good many of the plays we produced at the Rudwin were pirated from metropolitan stage successes. In far off New York a shorthand expert would sit in an obscure seat at a Broadway show and transcribe the dialogue. Then an agency, organized for the purpose of gypping authors out of royalties, would sell the plays to the vast number of stock companies which existed throughout the United States. Sometimes a *contretemps* would develop out of this plagiarism. Once when our troupe repaired to the local costume company to rent the furs necessary for a forthcoming production of *On the Yukon*, we found the fur supply had been depleted by our rival stock company for *their* forthcoming production of *In Far Alaska*. Beginning to smell a mouse, we set spies to work and learned that we were both playing the same Al Woods melodrama of the Arctic, the real title of which I forget. As a way out of the impasse, I suggested we change our locale to the Congo, which would warrant a sexier type of costume. But, joking aside, our troupe was forced to wear a second choice of ratty old furs and the play was done simultaneously at both theaters, to the bewilderment of local drama lovers.

There was one week when a truce was established between us and our rival stock company. It had chosen to do a play called *The Prince Chap*. In this version of a May-December love story, the heroine was supposed to be eight years old in the first act and twelve in Act Two, and wind up as the eighteen-year-old bride of *The Prince Chap* for the finale. I was the only actress in San Diego able to encompass this entire span, so Pop was approached for my services and, disguised by a blond wig and billed as Cleo Marlatte, a combination of my two grandmothers' names, I was loaned out. The title role of *The Prince Chap* was played by a young actor called Harold Lloyd, who was later to be heard from in the movies.

As soon as Clifford finished his internship and was ready to go into practice, he joined us in San Diego and opened an office. He could afford only a cheap neighborhood, so his first practice was extremely humble. Many of his patients were Mexican laborers with ailments that could tax the ingenuity of any medical man. One major problem was to get them to take baths, but Dr. Loos solved it with a miracle drug of his own invention. It was soft green soap, which he declared to be salve and gave orders for it to be well rubbed into the skin and then removed by water. In many instances it actually worked miracles.

One afternoon a Mexican showed up at Dr. Loos's office complaining of an acute backache which Clifford, taking a random shot, diagnosed as a kidney condition. In a routine manner Clifford prescribed some pills and, when his patient was leaving, told him to report if the backache returned. "Oh, it will not return, Señor Doctor," answered the Mexican, "because the dirty coward that shot

me in the back has gone to Baja California." Dr. Loos quickly recalled his patient, made him undress, and dug out the bullet his
patient hadn't thought worth mentioning.

Clifford's practice was so meager that he begged all of us to drop
in whenever we could, not only to relieve the monotony but to
make the office seem less deserted if a patient did show up. One day
Sue Iles and I put up a joke on the young doctor, one that would
have given him more business than he could have wished for. The
two of us appeared at his office distraught, and Sue announced that
she was going to have a baby, that her career as an actress and her
personal life as Ed Meade's "fiancée" would be ruined unless
Clifford came to her rescue. While Dr. Loos was grappling men-
tally with his Hippocratic oath, we finally broke down and explained that Sue's pregnancy existed only in the role she was rehearsing for next week's melodrama called *Lost in New York*.
From this episode it will be seen that I had progressed beyond the
belief, held at the time of my passion for Fritz Fields, that babies
could be created by any system of remote control.

Since Clifford's office was on the edge of the city's then existing
red-light district, its girls were among his first patients. Naturally
they all fell in love with the tall, handsome young doctor. But it did
them no good, for by that time he was engaged to a young beauty
he had met at a dance at Mills Seminary, which our own mother
had attended. Clifford's fiancée was Anita Johnson of the wealthy
O. T. Johnson family of Los Angeles, a hierarchy with a huge fortune based on Union Oil and large tracts of downtown Los Angeles
real estate. She became the second Anita in the Loos family, in
which her daughter would be a third.

It was in my brother's office that I had my first encounter with
ladies of the evening and decided that the real truth about them
was not that they possessed the "hearts of gold" described in fiction but that they had heads of bone. Their traditional generosity
came from stupid wastefulness, and they were, almost without exception, morons.

Those San Diego ladies of the evening may have given me a slant
on that timeworn profession which I was to capitalize on when I

wrote *Gentlemen Prefer Blondes*. For I couldn't take seriously the lost virtue of a heroine who was too dense to have any kind of emotional experiences at all. The first to let me know there was any novelty in my attitude was H. L. Mencken. "Young woman," said he, "do you realize you are the first American writer ever to make fun of sex?"

While I was acting in Pop's stock company fate gave me a really proper steer into a brand-new line of endeavor. Pop used to run short movies between the acts of our plays; *all* movies were short in those days. I adored those old silent films, knew the particular style of each company—Selig, Vitagraph, Kalem, and, best of all, Biograph, which produced more literate stories played by a more sensitive group of actors. Nobody was aware of the young director, D. W. Griffith, who was solely responsible for the fact that Biograph movies were so much more imaginative and, at the same time, *real* than all the others.

We knew the names of all our movie idols except those of the Biograph Company, which never appeared on film. One petulant and spirited little blonde with corkscrew curls was known and adored only as "America's Sweetheart." I used to search the trade papers for a clue to her identity, but she remained anonymous, even to the trade. (The reason for this, as I later found out, was that the business office feared her identification might result in offers from rival companies, or at least cause her to demand more money than the thirty-five dollars a week she was getting.)

Pop, in booking his films, took all the Biograph pictures, and I would hurry with my costume changes to get down to the dark stage, where I could see them from the reverse side of the screen, with the light of the projector casting a bright splotch in the middle. On a certain night, while entranced by one of those movies, I realized that it had required a script, so I decided to try my hand at writing one. The next morning I worked out a plot, and that afternoon at rehearsal (the company used to rehearse in the afternoon so that I could spend my mornings at high school) I climbed up into the projection booth and searched the film cans for an address where I might send my story. The address I found was:

American Biograph Company, 11 East 14th Street, New York City. I sent my manuscript there, having signed it "A. Loos," which I thought would make me appear a more seasoned author.

Not more than two weeks went by before I received a long envelope with "American Biograph Company" impressively engraved on the corner. With hands shaking like an earthquake, I tore the envelope apart and removed this letter:

Mr. A. Loos

Dear Sir: [*Sir!*]

We have accepted your scenario entitled "The New York Hat." We enclose an assignment which kindly sign and have witnessed by two persons, and then return. On receipt of signed assignment we shall send you our check for $25.00 in payment.

Yours very truly,

BIOGRAPH COMPANY

J. A. Waldon

The New York Hat was directed by the great D. W. Griffith himself and played by a roster of equally nameless stars, who, I found out later, included Mary Pickford, Lionel Barrymore, Lillian and Dorothy Gish, Henry Walthal, and Bobby Harron. That movie was one more of my lucky firsts.

In my choice of a locale for *The New York Hat* there may have been a touch of atavism, for I had placed it in a small Vermont town like the one from which Cleopatra Fairbrother had once fled. The plot concerned a sadistic miser whose wife and daughter were long-suffering victims of his pinchpenny way of life. In the opening scene, the mother was on her deathbed, being visited by a handsome young clergyman (Lionel Barrymore). The dying woman had sent for Lionel in order to hand him a bulky envelope, immediately after which she breathed her last. Lionel found the

envelope to contain a sum of money the woman had saved over
many years, most of it in pennies held out from the pittances her
husband allowed her for food. A letter requested that Lionel use
the fund to provide her child with a few bits of finery such as are
due any girl just budding into womanhood.

Along came the Easter season, when the local milliner displayed
in her window a hat which she had imported from New York. It
created a furor among the ladies of the village and so fascinated
little Mary Pickford that she repaired to the millinery shop every
day to gape at it in awe and longing. On Easter Sunday, who
showed up in church wearing the elaborate concoction? Why,
poor little Mary Pickford! And the gossipy milliner, on being
quizzed, announced it had been purchased by the handsome young
clergyman.

After that disgraceful exposure, suspicions of an illicit affair between Lionel and Mary grew to a point where Mary's reputation
was tottering and Lionel was about to be unfrocked. Naturally,
justice prevailed when he produced the mother's deathbed letter,
which showed up Mary's father as a niggardly tyrant, and Lionel
even went so far as to take a swipe at the entire community for its
evil-minded New England prejudices. Needless to say, a marriage
between Mary and Lionel was indicated. It was through seeing *The
New York Hat* that David Belasco decided to put Mary Pickford
into the title role of his Broadway production *A Good Little Devil*.
The movie is still shown at the Museum of Modern Art in New
York as one of the most popular of Griffith's early films and a
particularly fine example of his direction. It is also run sometimes
on the Late Late Show on television.

A time finally came when the Rudwin stock company followed
the pattern of all Pop's ventures and failed, but all the while my
income kept on growing. With Sue Iles out of work, I wrote her a
vaudeville skit called *The Ink Well*, which she broke in at the
Orpheum Theatre in San Francisco. *The Ink Well* told the story of
a pretty young wife who went to a lawyer's office to engage
him to handle her divorce. The lawyer began by being greatly at-

tracted to the helpless little woman and bitterly indignant toward her husband, whose cruelty had reached a climax when he threw an inkwell at her. But gradually the helpless little woman began to show her true colors as a selfish, idiotic, and irritating female who, step by step, reached a climax of behavior so infuriating that the lawyer picked up *his own* inkwell and let her have it.

The Ink Well was a success on its San Francisco tryout, and Sue was booked over the entire Orpheum Circuit for the following three years. So my pattern of lucky "firsts" now included a "live" show and my first royalties.

Several years after *The Ink Well* had run its course, it had the honor of being plagiarized by an obscure French author, as I learned by chance when I came upon its Gallic version. But such occasions have happened only twice in my career, the second time when a plot of mine was lifted by one of Broadway's most eminent senior citizens—with outstanding success, may I add in justifiable pride.

From the time when our financial stability no longer depended on Pop, my earnings paid our living expenses and helped Clifford during his struggle to establish a practice that would enable him to marry. A certain part of my income found its way to Marsden's Department Store for all sorts of feminine equipment. My first purchase was a bottle of L'Idéal of Houbigant, with its familiar lavender and yellow silk box intact, waiting provocatively to be opened.

Pop, still feeling no more qualms over being supported by a female than his fellow scribe George Bernard Shaw, was never at a loss to amuse himself. He now took up fishing off the wharves of San Diego on a six-day schedule, interrupted only on Thursdays when the *Saturday Evening Post* came out and he spent his afternoons on a couch, absorbing it from cover to cover. Life continued along these pleasant lines for Pop until one horrifying day, while he was fishing off a pier, the United States battleship *Bennington* blew up in San Diego harbor. The awful sight so moved Pop that he took to his pen and wrote an account of it. His description of the blast, the bodies of sailors tossed into the air like rag dolls, and the ghastly human debris accumulating on the water, was a piece of reportage that led Pop back to a journalistic career.

He was offered a job on a weekly newspaper, *The Record*, and went to work dishing up the news with his usual debonair approach. He was more or less faithful to that job except every Thursday, when some sort of mysterious disease used to attack him and he was forced to take to his couch with a copy of *The Saturday Evening Post*. I figure the only reason Pop wasn't fired every Friday morning was that his vibrant personality made him such a great success at luring advertisers.

Having once again succumbed to labor, Pop began to change. Although he would always be a ladies' man, he was outgrowing his lengthy youth and possibly getting a little tired; whatever the reason, his disappearances were less frequent and of shorter duration than before. But our companionship, which might have gained by his new way of life, was gradually disintegrating. I became more and more engulfed in a restlessness which I may have inherited from Grandma Smith, even though there were no mountains around San Diego to hem me in, except the mountains of provincial thought.

School was too easy to provide much satisfaction, even though my teacher used to hold me up as an example. One day, when he had posed the question, "What is the first requirement in finding the number of square feet in a given area?" a number of pupils had failed by answering, "Multiply the length by the breadth," but I had come through with the bored response, "Measure it." Such episodes naturally didn't make me popular with schoolmates, but I accorded them the supreme contempt of not caring in the least. I had reached that obnoxious stage of looking down on my peers.

Any famous visitor to San Diego from the outer world thrilled me to a state of palpitation, and from time to time I had just such exciting encounters. The first "great man" I ever set eyes on was a superb phony named Dr. Cook, who claimed to have discovered the North Pole before that feat was actually accomplished by Admiral Peary. At the time I met Dr. Cook his larceny was as yet undisclosed and he was riding high. We were introduced in the lobby of the U. S. Grant Hotel, where he was an honored guest. I must have sensed he was an impostor, for an understanding established itself between us at once. When we parted he turned to Pop and said, "That little girl of yours is going to get somewhere some day." Dr. Cook may not have conquered the Pole, but he certainly won me, and his prediction lifted my spirits to a state of ecstasy.

Meantime, as a counter-irritant to the boredom of high school, I struck up a correspondence with a far-away gentleman in Belgium, who had been introduced to me by a letter from a lady who was a mutual friend. He sent me a subscription to a French weekly called *Comœdia Illustré*. I devoured my *Comœdia* and began to think I was an expert on the French theater as well as Parisian styles.

My "clothes sense" seemed vindicated one afternoon when Mother and I happened to be passing the U. S. Grant Hotel. I was hampered by an ankle-length hobble skirt of Aunt Nina's which boasted a slit that reached almost to the knee and was the first of its kind ever to be seen in San Diego. At this fateful moment the entire Yankee baseball team, in town for their first Western game, emerged from the hotel, and as one man they whistled at me. Mother tried not to faint. But for me a striving had at length paid off. I felt they saw me as a fellow New Yorker and saluted them, as if to announce that I too had been born in Arcadia.

Such occasions, interspersed with a few trips to the Sunday bull-fights just across the border in Tijuana, Mexico, comprised most of my thrills. The bullfighters had been regular patrons of the Rudwin Theatre, so my presence at ringside was noticed, and it was flattering when those second-rate matadors tossed me their capes to drape over the front of the box. Although I ordinarily shrank from the sight of blood, I found that, on steeling oneself, a strange euphoria took hold that blotted out the poor animals' misery. One really didn't care what happened to them; a very sadistic euphoria, it probably carries soldiers through a battle.

I once thought to escape our low-grade milieu by writing a play.

Knowing nothing of the technique, I got a bright idea. A play which my *Comœdia* commended for perfection of dramatic form was then being done in Paris. It was called *The Typhoon* and had been imported from Budapest; its author was a young Hungarian named Melchior Lengyel. One issue of *Comœdia Illustre* published the complete text of *The Typhoon* as a supplement. It proved to be a melodrama about the machinations of a Japanese spy in France. And it now occurred to me that if I wrote a play, patterned speech for speech and scene for scene on *The Typhoon*, its technique would of necessity have to be correct. But I soon realized that a dramatic form suitable for Lengyel's spy melodrama was too complex for my mild little plot; despair overtook me and I dropped the subject. (Years later I told Lengyel about his abortive lesson in dramatic technique.)

Finally my quest for excitement led me down a new path—to the public library, and it was there I acquired an addiction which became what dope had been for Grandma Smith. I proceeded to read my way through the Carnegie Library. Surprisingly enough, the experience even turned out to be an emotional one. Although I didn't realize it then, I was that type the French call a *cérébrale*; my interest in sex stemmed directly from the brain. I had been in love with both Uncle Horace and Fritz Fields because they were smart and quick on the uptake, and so it was with Pop. But now a much more profound love entered my life. My new hero was Baruch Spinoza, and I still possess the copybook in which I made notes on his philosophy, among them his "advice to the lovelorn," one item of which reads: "Intellectual love is the only eternal happiness."

In looking over that notebook today, I find records of other "affairs" I entered into with famous highbrows, long departed. I was particularly moved by Immanuel Kant, and at the time I first read the *Critique of Pure Reason* it seemed perfectly clear to me; actually I believe it *was*, but a few years ago when I tried to recapture its meaning I could make nothing of it. This may be one of the reasons why I so respect the opinions of youth; ordinary minds tend to be warped by emotional experiences and the mounting prejudices of mid-life, but when the intellect is fresh and uncluttered it is able to see things much more logically.

For all my "erudition," I set little store on institutions of learning. In high school I had just squeaked by with the lowest mark possible for one to graduate in English. I felt it had been given me unjustly by a teacher who had chided me on my bad spelling; to which I answered, "My spelling isn't any worse than Chaucer's." But I had means of paying my teacher back for that black mark. She doted on statistics and required us pupils to fill out questionnaires which were to be checked ten years later, to reveal where our English course had led us. So after hours I sneaked my questionnaire out of her files and tore it up. She'll never be able to take credit for any career of mine, I thought.

My graduation from high school had taken place while the Rudwin stock company was still in operation, an event marked only by the fact that I had had to skip a day's rehearsal to accept my diploma. A graduation gown had little thrill for a girl who happened, that week, to be wearing the elegant garb of a court lady in *Sweet Nell of Old Drury*. It distressed me even to think of college and mixing with the same sort of dull civilians I had had to endure for four years at the Russ High School. To me book learning didn't mean a thing unless it became an ingrained part of life. The majority of Americans don't realize what they're reading (unless it happens to be cheap pornography), hearing (except for rock and roll music), looking at (with the exception of television), or even tasting (unless it be hot dogs powerfully accented by mustard). Recently a British scientist, Dr. Bate-Smith, conducted tests for a firm of beef purveyors and proved that only one palate in ten can taste the flavor of meat. It seems to me that the majority of young Americans might gain by passing up college altogether and spending their time hanging around country clubs, associating with their own kind and forming the business and social connections which are their reason for going to college in the first place. At any rate, a girl like I who never got past high school can take modest pride in making out quite well with the highbrows. I was once asked to preside over a symposium at the Faculty Club of Harvard University, where the professors asked such impertinent questions as: "Where did you gain the sex experiences that are indicated by your writing?" When, kidding on the square, I told them, "From Baruch Spinoza, Immanuel Kant, and George Santayana," of course they laughed, but the next day an item in a Boston gossip column stated, "Anita Loos is catnip to Harvard professors."

The Carnegie Library was now established as a solid barrier in the path that Pop and I had traveled in such happy companionship. My pretensions must have been extremely annoying, since Pop was confronted with rivals of whom he had never even heard and forced to battle with their shadows in the dark. One day he picked up a volume of essays I was reading; they were *The Flower, Fruit, and Thorn Pieces* of Jean Paul Richter and, glancing over a single sentence that covered two entire pages with heavy German syntax, Pop asked, "How does that dunce manage when he has to write a telegram?" It was just the sort of crack I once would have laughed at, but my sense of humor had been warped by teenage "intellectuality" and I cruelly let Pop know that I thought his remark unforgiveably vulgar.

At a very low season of my discontent, a completely new avenue of escape opened up which, astonishingly enough, was due to Pop himself. Every winter, when fashionable visitors left Coronado, a summer resort was erected along the beach adjacent to the hotel. It was called Tent City and consisted of row upon row of green and white striped tents. They were ordinary enough, but facing the ocean was a row of bungalows for the elite of Tent City guests, made of dried palms leaves in the manner of native Polynesian huts, and they seemed to me exceedingly romantic. At the center of the resort was a band shell where concerts were given nightly; there was a big dance hall, as well as several fascinating shops. A weekly magazine called *The Tent City News* was devoted to the activities of the resort, and the editorship was now offered to Pop. The job would require his presence in Coronado for the entire summer season; it meant we would be privileged to live in one of those exotic Polynesian bungalows on the Coronado strand; and that, from there, I might take my first step into the sophisticated world of Coronado, even though it was through the back door of Tent City and at the *un*fashionable season of summer.

&8 From the moment I first began to dream about a more sophisticated life than the one we led in grimy downtown San Diego,
I decided that the quickest way to attain it was through that standard trick which antedates Cinderella: marry a millionaire. And an
exotic bungalow looking out on the Pacific from the sun-kissed
shore of Southern California seemed an ideal base of operations. Its
walls were the burnished gold of dried palm leaves, the furnishings
were picturesquely nautical, the floor was carpeted with fragrant
matting, and "rooms" were partitioned off by chintz curtains of
jungle green. Although neighbors were close by, an illusion of re-
moteness was created by the boundless sea in front of us; traffic
noises were drowned out by its surf, and one breathed a stimulating
air that was perfumed by Japanese matting, seaweed, and salt
water. A girl who couldn't hook a millionaire in such an environment would have to be a gargoyle.

I calculated a first move should be toward the luxurious glass-
domed swimming pool which was an adjunct of the Hotel Del Coronado. So, after annexing a makeshift beau, by name Hughie, I
proceeded to convince him that the ocean was too cold, and day
after day the poor boy was swindled into taking me to that heated
pool, which cost him two dollars per session. But for a long time
luck was against me, for during the summer season the bathhouse
was frequented only by the local Navy set; among them were a
number of philanderers, but, wary of the small pay they got, I

passed them by. Had I known then that the chic young wife of one of them, a certain Lieutenant Spencer, would one day marry a king, I might have paid the United States Navy more respect.

At last luck took a turn for the better, and into that bathhouse came a young stranger who looked both Eastern and rich. There was an air of self-confidence about him which Western men seemed to lack, and on his bathing suit were the letters D.A.C., which certainly indicated no local outfit. That morning, as we sported in the water, Hughie's boorish courtship got a more animated response than usual; he never realized he was merely being used as a device to lure his future rival. The trick worked out well, for the stranger lost so little time in following up my lead that the next morning as I was on display in front of our bungalow, pretending to concentrate on a romance by Lord Dunsany, he hove into view, accompanied by someone he had dug up to provide an introduction.

Hughie's successor proved to be exactly what I was looking for. He came from Detroit, and the letters on his bathing suit meant he was a member of the Detroit Athletic Club. My new beau belonged to the industrial aristocracy of America, and his family bore one of those brand names prominent in ads across the nation. He happened to be in Coronado at the wrong season because he had been sent to San Diego to open a new branch of his father's firm and had decided that exile would be more pleasant if he lived at the Hotel Del Coronado.

To pick a quarrel with Hughie and dust him off was a simple matter, after which my new admirer was induced to leave his habitat for mine. The same ocean which, with Hughie, had been too cold for comfort suddenly became salubrious and warm; no need to be disturbed in that indoor pool by those noisy Navy children. At night my new beau found the Tent City Dance Hall a place for high adventure; its band, in happy contrast to the string orchestra at the hotel, played ragtime. Night after night my suitor took full possession through the purchase of entire rolls of tickets at ten cents a dance. Mother, always the chaperon, approved my choice not because he was rich but for his respectability. What was even more heartening, *he* approved of Mother because she came from a background as "distinguished" as his own. To some extent my beau even had intellectual overtones; he never ceased bragging about the D.A.C. as an organization so *à la page* that its club publication, *The D.A.C. News,* engaged young intellectuals like H. G. Wells, Arnold Bennett, and André Gide to write special articles for it.

But it wasn't long before this new beau was relegated to the category of Hughie, for he had a friend who, more than a millionaire, was a *multi*millionaire. The son of a Western Senator who owned a historic silver mine in Nevada, my Detroiter's friend had motored down to spend a weekend with him. He was big, gentle, clumsy, and guileless, and, with the fascination one feels for opposites, he fell in love with me and stayed on in Coronado.

By concentrating on the job, I might have hooked either of those admirable young men. But, without being aware on it, I had already put a fly into the ointment of my own dreams; it took me years of wasted time and effort to realize that no *cérébrale* can ever be happy as a Cinderella.

That summer in Coronado, good luck (or bad) was on the side of the Senator's son, for the Detroiter was suffering pangs of guilt because of a girl back home to whom he was formally engaged. This proved to be a convenient alibi for me to favor his more important rival. Terrible dramas ensued. There was a duel with bare knuckles on the shore at midnight. But it failed to impress me, because I had already written it as a slapstick farce. It featured a cross-eyed comic named Chester Conklin and was called *His Hated Rival*.

Therein lay my tragedy: I was generally going to laugh away romance. A day came when the Senator's son proposed marriage and a life of bliss on the family estate at Elko, Nevada. But the prospect of Elko, Nevada, caused me inadvertently to show such alarm he must have felt I needed further inducements, for the next afternoon he drove up in a smashing red Stutz roadster he had bought me, as both a bribe and a subtle reminder that we could always go for a spin and get away from Elko. Mother was absolutely horrified by his gift and ordered him to take his Stutz away.

I now feel that Mother was responsbile for the loss of a reward which might have inspired me to be a gold-digger. But I never learned the technique, and when at long last the truth dawned I gave in to being the model for the unrewarded brunette of my major opus: a girl who would always pass up a diamond for a laugh.

It wasn't very long, however, before my simple, generous young suitor plunged me into deep distress. He committed suicide by running his car off the top of Point Loma, overlooking San Diego Bay. The tragedy had nothing to do with my rejection; he was morbidly sensitive about an almost imperceptible limp and felt that everyone despised him as a cripple. I wished he had known that to me his limp had been an attraction; it made me think of Lord Byron and gave a certain poetic tinge to his artless courtship.

But it wasn't possible to mourn for long in the festive atmosphere of Coronado, where there was always a plentiful supply of new beaus. Even so, I couldn't quite bring myself to trap another of them. My problem was that, without realizing it, I was in on the ground floor of a sex revolution: the twentieth century's breakdown of romantic love between the sexes, and the transfer of female emotions from the boudoir to the marts of trade. The subject had first been broached by Henrik Ibsen in *A Doll's House*, and subsequently by the Englishman James Barrie in *The Twelve Pound Look*, but the revolution came to its climax in the United States, where the economic situation was as yet unsolidified. In the same manner, the Industrial Revolution, which should have broken out in England, where abuses were most severe, erupted on the virgin soil of Russia. At any rate, the female hearts of America were beginning to flutter with joy as they flew from homes into office buildings. But American women, even today, are bewildered over the change in their emotional status. Not long ago one of New York's most desirable blondes confided in me that she got more thrill out of a new modeling job than she did out of any beau and in a state of confusion asked, "Is there something the matter with me?"

Are women responsible for what has happened here? Has their

vanity become a stronger emotion than love? Or are men to blame? This doesn't seem so much the case as that American women are supplied with so many technical aids in housekeeping that they have to go outside their homes and get jobs in order to feel that they are needed. Even in Scandanavia, Ibsen's Nora of *A Doll's House* was rich; servants had taken over the housework and the care of her children. And so women's most concrete proof that somebody really *wants* them lies in a paycheck; they cling to jobs as a source of self-esteem, so valuable and sweet that they even seem romantic. Of course, any children involved in this arid circumstance must fend for themselves emotionally until they are old enough to fall in love with their own jobs or to be delinquents.

Deeply as American women have come to cherish their lives-outside-the-home, they began to be outdone during the twentieth century by American men, who, having lost communication with womankind, became sentimental joiners of any kind of club—political, athletic, or business. Men began to sublimate the affection they used to feel for hearth and home into a tender passion for the products they dispense, whether they be turbine engines, porous underwear, or sox with a two-way stretch. If they ever quit work, it means retirement from life itself. I once knew a steel tycoon who sold his foundry in order to spend more time with his wife, children, and many grandchildren, but, his goal achieved, he plunged straight into a nervous breakdown, went beserk, fell to the floor, and pounded on it with clenched fists, sobbing, "That plant of mine was my baby! I have deserted my baby!"

American men actually fall in love with the candidates they support and with champions in the fields of baseball, golf, and prizefighting. They find as much ecstasy in a Kiwanis Club rally, a political convention, or a National League baseball contest as men used to feel over a lovers' rendezvous; the American male has come to have a deeper zeal for his own kind than he does for women. It may well be that he distrusts his sentiment for the opposite sex; wasn't there a professor in Vienna who proved such feelings to be neurotic? But Damon can love Pythias without fear of taint because the attraction is based on strength, not weakness, and there's nothing to be ashamed of, even if it gets out of hand and becomes a little bit sexual.

We Americans of every period have had our gimmicks, and we certainly let Professor Freud provide us with the gimmick of his generation. The type of man that belonged to our pioneer heritage, the "Shakespearean" man, the "biblical" man who sustained his dignity even under trivial circumstances, disappeared from the American scene during the depression of the thirties. Even in the theater there were no Edwin Booths to carry on the traditions of *Hamlet* or Francis Wilsons to play our own virile patriarch, Rip Van Winkle. Our typical stage Americans have been two bumbling clowns, Jack Benny and Bob Hope, whose jokes are directed against their own unimportance. I feel now, however, that the Freudian influence is in its decline. The astronauts who are emerging as today's heroes don't climb into their rocket ships from any analysts' couches. It may well be that to establish a man on the moon is a *grandeur de folie*, but if it brings grandeur back into play once again, never mind. And if American men and women realize once again that human beings are worthy to be loved, they may again find satisfaction in loving each other. In the theater, Eugene O'Neill's *Electra* and Edward Albee's *Tiny Alice* may be replaced by Rosalind, Portia, and Lady Macbeth, who was loved even as a murderess because she committed her crime in the grand manner and with none of the sleaziness of that nasty-minded old Viennese professor.

In my own case I had a special sex problem to solve, and it taught me very early to keep my mouth shut about my literary career. When I first mentioned it to a beau, he thought I was lying. It was only too easy to prove the truth by producing a few letters of acceptance. They caused an even more unfortunate reaction; my beau didn't *want* to believe I was an authoress; it turned me into some sort of monster; I no longer seemed to be a girl. So I decided my literary life belonged to a secret world where I could be alone with my plots and those exciting vouchers signed by the scrawl of an unknown man named Griffith.

During those years of girlish maladjustment I underwent criti-

cism from a source other than a beau. My accuser was Grandma
Loos, who had come to join us from Newcomerstown after the
death of Pop's father. She was a mean, suspicious old lady and she
confided to one of our neighbors that I was "a bad lot." "The child
keeps getting money from somewhere," said Grandma Loos, "but
she never does any work." For in Grandma's mind a typewriter
was some sort of decadent toy.

In spite of her harping over my morals, Grandma baffled me by
copying the way I dressed. At that period, through a study of the
better fashion magazines, I had learned that young ladies of royalty, from the Edwardian English to the Imperial Romanovs, all
wore sailor suits, and Grandma Loos, dressed like the Czarevna
Tatiana with ribbons streaming from her hat, cut quite a caper.
Had she joined our family after I entered my movie phase,
Grandma undoubtedly would have been one of that army of gay
old ladies who tramp Hollywood Boulevard in tight slacks, golden
sandals, and platinum hairdos, collecting autographs—one of which
might have been my own. But, ahead of her time, Grandma felt out
of place and she finally returned to Newcomerstown. A little later,
when she died, we learned she must have had a "sneaker" for her
evil grandchild; instead of leaving Pop her estate, which stacked up
to about $4000, she willed it all to me. Had I lived in a real world
instead of one of vague illusions, I would have used the old girl's
bequest to get to New York; Grandma's will even provided a hint
for spanning the distance, for its executor was an attorney by the
name of Brooklyn Bridge. In fact, the whole episode might have
come straight out of one of my slapstick comedies.

That $4000 was of major importance to the Loos family, which
didn't often come upon such a stack of money all at once, although
by this time my movie writing was bringing in quite respectable
earnings. I still have an account book with a record of those early
scripts; between the years of 1912 and 1915 there were a hundred
and five of them, of which only four were never sold. I first submitted them to the Biograph Company and when, rather infre-
quently, one was rejected it went on to the Vitagraph, Kalem, or
Selig Studios and found a ready market.

I never kept copies of those scenarios, but I remember one called *A Girl like Mother*, the heroine of which was a young lady who was having trouble in landing her beau because the young man was hell-bent on marrying *A Girl like Mother*. So a plan crossed our heroine's mind, which was to look up her intended mother-in-law, study the woman surreptitiously, and then give an imitation of her. But in looking up "Mother" our heroine was given a wrong steer by a hated rival, and for quite a while she studied a woman of the type that could only be called a "tramp." As a result, her imitation was catastrophic. She must have landed her victim at the end, but I don't remember that part of the story.

There was a melodrama, *Saved by the Soup*, in which my heroine was a beautiful spy in the United States Secret Service. While at a swell (or should I say "swank"?) dinner party, she overhears some news which that very night is going to bring about the destruction of the U.S.A. It may already be too late for the heroine to save her native land. However, at this juncture luck steps into the script, for our quick-witted little spy glances into a dish the butler sets before her, sees that it contains alphabet soup, and immediately spells out "Call the cops" on the edge of her plate. The butler loses no time in sounding the alarm; the famous Keystone Kops are summoned, and, during a wild chase in which pies contribute their custard to the shambles, the U.S.A. is saved.

Another drama had a more romantic angle and was called *Nellie, the Female Villain*. In this script Nellie is a girl from the Far West who on her arrival in London is invited to an aristocratic ball. She reaches there only to learn that her Western attire is provocative of japes from the high-class ladies of British nobility. But Nellie was not raised in Texas for nothing. Stationing herself in the entrance hall, she looks over the girls as they arrive, chooses a victim who wears a Paris gown, shoves her into the ladies' room, pulls out a gun, makes her disrobe, puts on her dress, and then emerges to become belle of the ball. Also, may I add, that very night she lands a royal duke for her affianced husband.

Frequently I came through with more serious plots. One of these, *The Wild Girl of the Sierras*, brought me a check for $100 (prices were going up!). Another was *The Little Liar*, a real heart-wrencher that starred Mae Marsh and provided her with a death-bed finish. It came to be seen by the American poet Vachel Lindsay, and out of that screening developed one of my own real-life romances.

There was also a tragedy called *Stranded*, for which I received $300 (prices were beginning to soar). I wrote *Stranded* especially for the aging Broadway star De Wolf Hopper, who had just married a beautiful willowy young brunette named Hedda. The plot concerned a ham actor who had always wanted to play Shakespeare, but nobody would give him a chance. Finally, during a tour of the Wild West, he becomes the innocent victim of gun play in a saloon. And while he lies dying on the barroom floor (in the midst of a goodly crowd), he grasps the opportunity to recite, "Friends, Romans, countrymen, lend me your ears," et cetera. Seeing that nobody has the heart to stop him, the poor old boy gives the only Shakespearean performance of his career and dies at the end, a happy hambone.

Trashy as those old plots were, they were acted with a gusto which has disappeared from Hollywood and explains the cult of the early films which exists at the present time. Mack Sennett, the Daddy of all slapstick farce, W. C. Fields, and Mae West were all satirists whose motivations grew out of basic truths in human nature and had a spirit that is even akin to that of Molière.

The plots I wrote in the beginning were pretty contrived, but as my experience with life broadened I began to dredge real situations and real people from it. Inspired by memories of my Detroit beau, I wrote a picture for Douglas Fairbanks called *American Aristocracy*, which was a satire on the big names of United States industry such as the Fords, the Heinzes, so important to the world of pickles, and the Chalmerses, who were touchingly proud of the underwear they manufactured. Eventually every experience became grist to my movie mill; I dished up Pop's cronies and my brother's increasingly important friends, and even began to make fun of the rich who had so overawed me on first acquaintance. I had always thought that the leisure classes led exciting lives; only to learn that

the majority of them are so lacking in vitality that, without an Elsa
Maxwell to tell them how to waste time, they aren't even capable
of giving a cocktail party.

It was in Coronado that I met two characters who supplied the
inspirations for Henry Spofford, the hero of *Gentlemen Prefer
Blondes*, and his mother. They belonged to a Philadelphia family of
obtuse and delightful morons, but when I chose that young man
for my hero I advanced his mental status and made him a halfwit.
"Henry Spofford's" mother was astounded that any girl could have
a brain in her head, and it occurred to her that a girl like I might
inject a vitamin of intelligence into the Spofford bloodstream.
"Mrs. Spofford" used to parade me in front of "Henry's" sex-free
gaze and, removing the hairpins from my long mop of hair, bid him
to heft its weight. She declared that "Henry" was always whisper-
ing sweet nothings concerning me; but he must have whispered
them into *her* ear, for he never bent mine. It was only too apparent
that he had little interest in girls, or even boys, in spite of which he
would have been easy for me to snare. But I decided that "Henry
Spofford" was one more rich beau to laugh off and forget, and later
on I allowed the heroine of *Gentlemen Prefer Blondes* to capture
that prize.

During those days of early girlhood I was a heavy trial to
Clifford, who was as snooty about my film activities as any beau
and generally sided with my beaus against me. Clifford became a
confidant of one worthy young man, who used to apply to him for
sleeping pills to lull him into forgetfulness of my neglect. I have a
record of their alliance in an old love letter:

Little Devil—

I don't know what I'm going to do, dear—it's mighty hard
to work all day and think of others being with you. I meant
to get some sleep stuff from Clifford but forgot it until it was
too late. I'm off for a walk down the strand—wish you could
come with me—*no*, I don't either. I've got to fight this out
alone—I love you.

But that young man's letter left me cold, for I was getting others that packed a stronger emotional wallop, such as:

Dear Madam [I was "Madam" now, as I had taken
                    to putting my full name on scripts]:

We enclose check for $35.00 in payment of your scenario, "The Deacon's Whiskers."

Yours very truly,

T. E. Dougherty
BIOGRAPH COMPANY

Finally a time came when, out of deference to Clifford, I tried to take seriously a rich playboy who happened to be his brother-in-law. The young man had written me:

I have the blues yet about leaving you. I think about you all the time. I have a bid to a dance tonight but am not going because I will feel bum [*sic*] to think that you will not be there. Please learn to wear the ring. Write often and lots of XXX

Your loving Sweetheart

As I was just about to give in and "learn to wear the ring" of a "loving sweetheart" who used the word "bum" as an adjective, something happened that canceled out the whole deal: a letter that was more poetic in my eyes than any mash note Abelard ever wrote to Héloise.

New York
January 6, 1914

Dear Madam,

I shall be in Los Angeles on Tuesday, January 13th, for a short stay, so if you happen to be in that city I would like to have a personal interview with you at the Biograph Studio, Georgia and Gerard Streets.

Trusting you will favor me with a call, and wishing you a very prosperous New Year, I remain,

Very truly yours,

T. E. Dougherty

Dougherty's letter came from the business office of the Biograph Company in New York, but by this time the studio itself was permanently located in Hollywood, a mere two-hour train trip from where we lived. It seems highly apathetic of me not to have thought of invading that studio until Dougherty's invitation arrived. But we were completely settled in our little rut: Pop satisfied, as always, with being a big shot in a small world; Mother so timid that any move at all required superhuman effort; and I aimlessly wasting time among people with whom I was disenchanted. But all of a sudden I was overcome by a desire to meet those shadowy characters who acted in my screenplays. I talked Mother into agreeing to the trip—chaperoned, as always, by herself. Leaving Pop happy, no doubt, to enjoy a couple days of freedom, we took off from San Diego to enter a world of the most fabulous mummery ever devised by man.

We arrived in Los Angeles and checked in at an obscure hotel, and the next morning I telephoned Dougherty at the studio. I was told to come out right away, that both he and Mr. Griffith would be pleased to meet me. This being my phase of copying the stark good taste of royalty, I put on my best white sailor suit (they used to be called "Peter Thompsons," probably after some dress manufacturer), and my hair, in a pigtail tied with wide black taffeta bows, seemed the essence of girlish refinement. But although I was a teenage femme fatale in Coronado, in the flashy locale we were about to enter I must have seemed a schoolchild of about twelve in the charge of a rather meek governess.

As our streetcar entered Hollywood that morning, we found it the same dilapidated suburb it had been when we lived in Los

Angeles. Our main purpose in ever going there had been to ride to the end of the line and take lunch at the old Hollywood Hotel, a rambling edifice painted the same dun color as the hills, with a veranda where elderly seekers after sunshine, mostly from the Middle West, sat in big red chairs and rocked their uneventful lives away. Across from the hotel was a shoddy business district; there were a few bungalows interspersed with vacant lots, and that was all. Nobody dreamed a day was close at hand when that one word, Hollywood, would express the epitome of glamour, sex, and sin in their most delectable forms.

There was no reason why Hollywood should ever have been named in honor of a shrub that can exist only in a cold climate. But according to legend a couple had come there from England in early days, built a fine house, and as a memento of their homeland planted a slip of holly in the garden. Before it had time to wither in the hot, dry air, they had caused the name Hollywood to be painted on the front gate, and from there it gradually overspread the whole community. Thus was Hollywood christened with a name as spurious as anything that was ever to come out of its studios.

Mother and I got off the streetcar under the blinding sun and betook ourselves to the Biograph Studio. It consisted of a row of one-story buildings that were scarcely more than sheds; on a center door was painted BIOGRAPH COMPANY—MAIN OFFICE, the sight of which speeded up my already rapid circulation. But now Mother, ordinarily so timid, forged on ahead of me. She must have sensed that she was in danger of forever losing her honeybunch, and wanted to investigate what sort of world it was that might gobble me up.

We came into a long narrow office partitioned by a counter, behind which two minor employees in their shirtsleeves were engaged in desultory conversation. One of them asked what we wanted, and Mother said that Miss Loos was there to see Mr. Dougherty. Polite, but not very interested, the man gestured toward a bench, told us to take a seat, and then disappeared through the back doorway. Presently a large pleasant Irish-American in a summer-weight suit emerged and, mistaking Mother for his authoress, approached her genially.

"Well, Miss Loos," he said, "it's nice to meet you after all this time."

"But I'm Anita's mother," she corrected him. "*This* is Anita."

Dougherty turned a look of blank amazement on me and said nothing at all. At the time my first scripts, signed A. Loos, had come in, it was thought for a while that their author was a man. It had been something of a surprise to learn that those none-too-refined slapstick comedies were written by a female. But that I appeared to be a child was such a shock it took Dougherty a long moment to regain his breath.

"Do you mean it's *you* who wrote those stories we've been buying?" he finally asked.

"Yes, Mr. Dougherty," piped up little Anita.

At which moment the door opened and the movies' first real genius entered from the back lot. Up to that time David Wark Griffith had been merely a name scrawled on my vouchers; most of my correspondence had been with Dougherty, who seemed the more important of two unknowns.

Tall, bronzed, and rangy like a cowboy, Griffith was in his shirt-sleeves and wore a battered straw sombrero tied under his chin with a black shoestring; the ridiculous get-up didn't detract one bit from his enormous distinction. Griffith must have been in his early thirties, but he had an authority that seemed to deny he had ever been young. His highly arched nose belonged on some Roman emperor; his pale eyes, in sharp contrast to the tan of his complexion, shone with a sort of archaic amusement, as if he were constantly saying to himself, "What fools these mortals be!" But that morning it was Griffith's own turn to be fooled, for he passed right by me and advanced to greet Mother.

"You're shaking hands with the mother of your authoress," Dougherty spoke up. "It's *this* little lady who's been writing our scenarios."

Turning to look at me, Griffith's expression went blank, as had Dougherty's, while I was still so impressed by his Jovian dignity

:hat I could only stammer I was pleased to meet him; after which there didn't seem to be anything more for either of us to say. And then Mother, for the first time in her entire life, boldly spoke up to save her child.

"Good-by, gentlemen," she said. "Come along, Anita."

We walked out of that office, with Mother feeling we had escaped from a nest of hobbledehoys. I knew it was my childish appearance that had stunned them into silence; but, even so, to be allowed to leave after so brief a welcome made me feel bitterly frustrated and disappointed.

We had gone about half a block toward the streetcar line when we heard a booming voice call, "Miss Looze!" (Griffith would always pronounce our name "Looze" and drag it out as if it were in two syllables. He had his own pronunciation for words, an affectation which in him seemed natural. Griffith never did or said anything in the same manner as ordinary people.) Not sure the summons was for us, we turned and saw Griffith standing on the sidewalk, beckoning with his long arms for us to come back. Even under that ridiculous sombrero he looked so compelling and fateful that Mother's hackles must have risen; she must have known that this might be good-by forever to her little girl. But, like an invincible magnet, Griffith pulled her back, with me in tow.

Without any explanation of his strange first greeting, Griffith invited us onto the lot. What we saw in the glare of that raw insolent sun was startling. On the unroofed stage was an ancient pavilion of great splendor; enormous braziers were filling the air with incense, and the set was teeming with characters dressed in biblical costumes. Prominent among them were dancing girls wearing little more than beads, their faces dead white, with black smudged eyes and violent red lipstick. Their semi-nude state was a shock, even to me, for, as I have said, when Gladys and I played in *Quo Vadis* we had modestly worn tights. Griffith demanded a chair for Mother and a high stool for me, from which I could oversee the entire stage. Sitting in that place of honor next to Griffith's camp chair, I had my first experience of movies in the making, while Mother tried to look at the shocking spectacle without actually seeing it.

The picture was *Judith of Bethulia*, a daring innovation; for it was to take four reels in the telling, and up to that time two reels had been the limit of any film. The scene that day involved Holofernes' seduction by Judith. I recognized both the stars, although I still didn't know their names. Holofernes proved to be Henry B. Walthall, and Judith was Blanche Sweet. She was small, fragile, blond, with a compact little face and a highly arched nose. Blanche Sweet seemed rather unsure of herself, as did all Griffith's young actresses; he wanted no positive traits to prevent them from being passive instruments on whom he could improvise.

Many of Griffith's actors were in fact not actors at all, for he picked people up whenever he was impressed by their looks, as the great Italian film directors were to do later on. Frequently a mere bit player supplied Griffith with an unforgettable scene. There is a close-up in *The Birth of a Nation* of an uncouth Union soldier gazing soulfully at the frail Southern belle, played by Lillian Gish, in a way that will be stamped forever on the memory of anyone who ever saw the picture. Griffith had a cameraman with an amazing control of that apparatus; a slovenly, uneducated German-American named Billy Bitzer, who gave the Master any effect he desired without protesting that there was no possible way to do it.

While Griffith was directing Blanche Sweet that day he stepped onto the set from time to time to demonstrate some tactics of seduction, which he did with a sense of fun that prevented any harm to his male dignity. Sometimes he put his arms about the semi-nude Miss Sweet and whispered in her ear, obviously to save the young actress the embarrassment of his criticism's being overheard. But to Mother those embraces looked like sheer license, and she felt more and more that we were in an anteroom of hell.

When time came for the company to troop off for lunch, Griffith invited Mother and me to the corner drugstore, and there, in the seclusion of a booth, he proceeded to quiz me, with Mother sitting by in stony silence. I told him of having inherited an aptitude for writing from my father and also mentioned my experience as an actress; on hearing this, Griffith's eye lit up, putting Mother instantly on the alert, but I was too engrossed to note the danger signal. Expanding under the attentions of that remarkable man, I confessed to the cramping effect of my home life and explained that my only escape from boredom was the library.

"What do you read?" asked Griffith.

I proceeded to sound off with some intellectual name-dropping: Plato, Montaigne, Spinoza, et al. It was obvious that he was as lacking in education as I was, but I had had more time to read, and now the great man began to pick my small brain for scattered bits of information. I had recently discovered Voltaire, and Griffith wanted to know something about him. But Voltaire's cynicism, as expounded by A. Loos, didn't necessarily convince Griffith, and he remarked with a benign smile that the human race might possibly be nicer than that arch pessimist conceded. In return, I felt perfectly at ease to criticize Griffith's own preferences. His idol, it appeared, was Walt Whitman. I impudently argued that Whitman was hysterical. "Hysteria has no place in great writing," said A. Loos. "Shakespeare is never hysterical, neither is Goethe. Walt Whitman is as uncontrolled as Ella Wheeler Wilcox!" Griffith laughed and was probably as much amused by my impertinence as I was intent on trying to set him straight.

I can't say I fell in love with Griffith that day over a sandwich in a corner drugstore, but our session provided the sort of cerebral excitement that makes the bohemias of the world, the Greenwich Villages and Sohos and Left Banks, so much more sexy than any other places. Our discussion continued so long that finally the studio's efficiency expert, a little man who bristled with *lèse-majesté*, barged in to tell the Master that if he didn't get back to the set he'd never finish the day's schedule. On our way to the studio Griffith said to me, "I think we'll have to get you out of San Diego."

"To Hollywood?" I asked.

"Yes," said Griffith, "and then New York. I think you belong in New York, Miss Looze."

New York! Now had I really and truly found *simpatia*.

Back on the set, the first thing Griffith did was to send for the wardrobe mistress. "This is Miss Anita Looze," he told her. "She's going to play a part in the scene I'm shooting tomorrow. So arrange a slave girl's costume for her."

Turning to Mother, he added, "If you bring the child to the studio about eight, she can be ready for a nine-o'clock call."

Mother nodded in assent, I thought.

I spent the remainder of the day watching the Master in a fever of delight. There in the harsh sunlight, with Griffith presiding like a pagan deity, Blanche Sweet continued to debauch Henry Walthall; he succumbed to her wiles, and the slave girls rattled their beads in a way that emphasized their nudity, until finally the sun disappeared and there wasn't light enough to photograph them. I said good-by to Griffith until the next day and left the studio in an aura of rosy bliss.

No sooner had we reached the sidewalk than Mother spoke. "If we hurry," she said, "we can catch the evening train to San Diego."

It was some time before I was able to comprehend what she had said. "You mean I'm *not* to go back to the studio tomorrow?"

"No," said Mother.

"But what will Mr. Griffith think of me?"

"He didn't ask whether or not I wanted you to be a movie actress," said Mother. "If he had, I'd have let him know it was out of the question."

We were back on the streetcar before I composed myself sufficiently to put up a plea. And when I did I learned more about my mother than I, in my sole absorption with Pop, had ever known before. She disclosed that she had always been unhappy over the life into which her Harry had taken her.

"I'm miserable when I'm around the theater," Mother said. "I don't know how to talk to those people. I make mistakes and they laugh at me. When they do, you take sides with them and laugh at me too. I've never gotten over the shock of seeing your little face made up with rouge. It didn't seem so dreadful inside a theater, because things look 'softer' under the electric lights. But today those dancing girls were showing their naked bodies in the bright sunshine."

"It was a scene from the Bible!" I argued.

"There are passages in the Bible it's more modest to skip over," Mother said. And then she issued her ultimatum. "I'll never let you go back into that studio."

As I reacted in dazed silence, Mother brought up a matter so distasteful to her that it took great effort; she confessed to a constant worry over my heredity: Grandma Smith's addiction to drugs, my father's periodic weakness for drink, Aunt Nina's loose way of life; the fact that I had respect for almost nothing, that the things which impressed other people only made me laugh. Mother said she felt my only salvation was to marry one of the nice young men I went about with and settle down to the responsibilities of normal life. Up to that moment I had seen Mother only as a gentle and complaisant female, with no opinions of her own about anything; but now her anguish was so disturbing that she almost convinced me. Almost—but not quite.

Mother dragged me away from Los Angeles without even a phone call to excuse my failure to report to Griffith the next day. I was bitterly resentful, but just the same I still harbored a strong feeling of guilt over the agony I was causing her. And on the train going back to San Diego I put my brains to work to figure out some means of solving both her problem and my own. Since, to her mind, marriage was synonymous with safety, I decided to brace myself and enter that haven; but a marriage altar would be merely the first station on my road to freedom. To achieve it I'd have to change tactics, concentrate on some likely prospect, and, this time, really go through with it. That solution was along the lines of my most contrived movie plots, but perhaps it was as valid an excuse for matrimony as most people ever have. Then, too, I was in a hurry.

The summer season was near its close in Coronado. It had been an excellent showcase for the wares I had to offer, but soon we would have to move back to the obscurity of San Diego, a fact which meant I would have to work fast. While looking the field over for a prospective bridegroom, I kept brooding over Griffith, wondering if he had forgiven me for running out on him. For a few weeks I was too timid to write another script, which I feared might be returned with one of the insulting rejection slips devised for amateurs. I finally decided to try my luck with a slight half-reel comedy that might give a rather casual note to the situation. Never at a loss for plots, I dashed one off at white heat. It was called *Only a Fireman's Bride,* and I sent it on to Dougherty. It brought an immediate reply which said, in part:

> I hailed your script as one would receive advance news of the prodigal. What have you been doing all this time? Please don't answer this question if it is embarrassing. All I have to say is that Mr. Griffith would like to receive manuscripts from you and to welcome you to the studio whenever you happen to be in L.A.

Dougherty's letter was all I needed for a return to bliss. And I now got busy on the real-life plot calculated to take me back to D.W. Griffith for keeps.

It seems axiomatic that, in every urgent marriage, the victim is generally brand-new; too aware of the faults of people we know, we pick on somebody whose shortcomings stand a chance of being easier to endure. So, in looking over the field, I separated the men from the boys and purposely chose a boy. The others were either young men of substance which gave them a certain authority, or they were launched on careers which could easily have gotten in my way; what I needed was a "straw husband" whom I could dominate.

Poor little Freddy (or was his name Frankie?) had been hanging around in the background while I stalked more notable prey. He was almost as young as I was. Moreover, he belonged to the entertainment world, as his father conducted the band which gave concerts in Coronado. At any rate, both father and son were sufficiently bohemian not to be disturbed by my movie career, and, best of all, there would be no problem of a mother-in-law, as Frankie's father was a widower.

Pop deplored my forthcoming marriage, having felt I was much too "smart" ever to enter that degrading institution. Clifford, having recently acquired a wealthy socialite wife, thought I was making one of my periodic lapses into the rowdy, while Mother's relief at my imminent escape from sin was diluted by anguish over the metamorphosis of her virgin child into a woman.

The day before I was to enter into the larcenous arrangement, I began to sense my own stupidity. For years I had been earning enough money to plunge into the great world on my own, and now I had finagled an escape by an archaic method that belonged back in the generation of my poor helpless mother. But, beginning to sense that her feelings about marriage as a refuge were mixed with dread, I partly took her into my confidence, told her I feared I was about to make a mistake, and suggested calling the wedding off.

"But we can't do that, honeybunch," said Mother. "I've already ordered the cake!"

The wedding took place in the chapel of the small Episcopal Church in Coronado. Among the guests were members of the wealthy family to which my brother was allied, but that class had ceased to impress me, for I had learned, to my disgust, that they were merely human. I had worn several wedding gowns on stage that were more elaborate than the girlish job of cream-colored chiffon chosen by Mother. My memory of the service itself is vague, but once it was over I glanced at Pop and, suddenly stabbed by his awful look of disillusionment, I rushed to whisper a quick bid for his forgiveness, couched in the kidding mood of our old-time intimacy. "Don't worry, Pop! This wasn't legal; I had my fingers crossed." But it was too late for a joke to bring me absolution. Pop was crushed.

That was the beginning of a nightmare honeymoon. The worthy Episcopal clergyman who performed the ceremony got Frankie and me aside to advise that we keep away from the frivolities of Coronado, which might tamper with the sanctity of our family life. "*Family* life!" Why did he have to inject *that* note into the proceedings? Our party left the church and proceeded to a private dining room in the Hotel Del Coronado for a wedding supper, during which not even the champagne could lessen my distress. There was to be no wedding trip; my bridegroom had rented a furnished bungalow in Coronado, to which we retired. To climax my disenchantment, I felt that night that married life was not only a clumsy, much overrated business but an urgent reason for ending my predicament before that dreadful complication at which the clergyman had hinted had any further chance of setting in.

However false my marriage vows, I really had chosen the right bridegroom, for the next day, when I asked if he would take the ferry to San Diego and buy me some hairpins of a special type, he was quite agreeable. No sooner had he left than I rushed back to Pop and Mother in Tent City. In one quick breath I told them, "I'm leaving Frankie right now! Today! I'm going to catch the afternoon train to Los Angeles and report to Mr. Griffith tomorrow morning."

Pop, still hurt to the core, was noncommunicative, but I had fully expected Mother to put up an argument. I found myself completely mistaken; she had lain awake all night agonizing over the virginal qualms she thought her child was undergoing and was relieved to the point of tears at having me escape from more of the same. She agreed at once that I return to the movie studio as a choice between two evils. It seemed I was now equipped to combat the sins of Hollywood, for I had lost my virtue quite respectably. Mother further assured me that from then on she would always be present to chaperon me. There was also a vague plan that Pop could follow us to Hollywood when his job ended at the close of the summer season.

While Frankie was searching for me all over Coronado in order to turn over a box of hairpins, Mother and I caught the afternoon train to Los Angeles. The following day we went back to the studio, where I announced to Griffith that we had decided to move to Los Angeles so as to be near my place of work. And, to give my statement a touch of drama, I mentioned in an offhand way that I had just left my husband. Griffith was surprised I hadn't told him I was married when we first met, so I explained that the ceremony had taken place only the previous day. He looked clear through me with his searching quizzical eye and asked, "Why did you run out on the guy?"

Not wanting to let him know that he was directly involved, I took refuge as usual in a joke. "After he promised to take me to New York," said I, "I found out he only had money enough to get to Omaha."

Griffith grinned and turned to Mother. "I'm glad she's married," he said. "From now on those plots of hers may be a little better." Thus did the great man set Mother's mind at ease and let her know he'd never try to turn me into a movie actress. He had sensed her feelings on that score the day she whisked me away from the studio, and he never brought the subject up again. He was probably wise, at that. A teenage iconoclast with the effrontery to criticize Walt Whitman was no passive instrument on which the Master could improvise.

CHAPTER 5

🍂 The scenario department at the old Biograph Studio occupied one of the sheds at the front of the lot. It was headed by Frank Woods, a shaggy old boy with a mop of white hair. Because of his paternal manner, everyone called him "Daddy," but he was the only member of the force who was allowed a nickname. Griffith insisted on the most formal behavior throughout the studio, but he realized that no familiarity could undermine Daddy Woods's homespun distinction.

Frank Dougherty, who was my first mentor at the studio, escorted me to Daddy's office and turned me over to him, and Daddy proceeded to quiz me not only professionally but concerning my entire background. His questions indicated that he didn't consider authors very smart, and when he drew forth an account of my overnight marriage it did nothing to disprove his theory. At any rate, he took full charge of my career, personal as well as professional.

Daddy was a realist who had spent most of his life in the magazine field, and he regarded writing as a commodity, along the lines of groceries or hardware. He decided that I should concoct material for the roster of stars as their needs came up. I would get a regular salary of fifty dollars a week, which at the time was opulent; in addition I was to be paid extra for any script that was accepted. As far as I know there were no other Hollywood authors working on salary at the time, so I was possibly the movies' first staff writer.

Daddy felt it would be safer for me, as a runaway bride, to work at the studio, where I could be protected in case Frankie showed up and tried either to whisk me away or even to shoot me. In order that an alert could be sounded in case Frankie appeared, Daddy asked me to describe him to his staff, which he summoned. They were his reader, Mary O'Connor, and his film cutter, Hetty Gray Baker, both of them distinguished gray-haired spinsters. They bristled with interest over my peril. The description of my irate husband scarcely made him seem like Frankenstein; but because their department was far removed from the excitement of the lot, my situation became a welcome break in their daily routine. They nicknamed me the Brat and, in their virginal state, ascribed a fascinating wickedness to me that I only wish I had lived up to.

I was soon to meet another important adjunct to Daddy's staff: his wife, Ella. No sooner had the matter of my safety been established than he phoned Ella and asked her to find an apartment for Mother and me. It seemed odd that she wanted to know my birth date, but Daddy didn't tell the reason, and I didn't ask him. It turned out that Ella was an amateur astrologer and that she spent a large part of her time casting horoscopes for everyone at the studio. Ultimately I came to wish that Ella Woods had never cast my horoscope, because it turned out to be so uncannily correct that it has given me a disturbing belief in all sorts of mumbo jumbo. Even now I eagerly turn to the horoscope in one certain newspaper, my faith unshaken by the fact that the horoscopes in two other dailies never seem to jibe with it or with each other. During the New York newspaper strike of 1962, we true believers were forced to stumble through five long months without any guidance from the stars. However, I ventured to phone my newspaper's city desk one morning and asked the editor for the day's prognostications. He complied but, after tersely reading my horoscope, he said, "That's it for today, madam, but don't ever again call the city desk about that hogwash!" Rebuffed, I gathered that the city editor of the *Journal American* didn't share my faith in its astrologer.

At any rate, Ella Woods consulted the stars and discovered the right apartment for us on Crown Hill Avenue. It was furnished, ready for immediate occupancy, and in a district so obscure that a Pinkerton detective couldn't have tracked me down. Every morning I cautiously set out for the studio on the same streetcar line that had carried Mother and me there that first fateful day; once on the lot, I could breathe easily.

Did I feel no guilt over deserting my husband without even a note of explanation? I'm afraid my compulsion to get away from home was too strong for me to give Frankie much thought. He had known me so short a time that he couldn't possibly have missed me very much, but at the same time his pride must have suffered a jolt. He was too boyishly incompetent to organize a search; he had no job, nor indeed any profession, and was solely dependent on a father who, being a matinee idol as well as a band leader, was too engrossed in his successes with the ladies to be impressed by his son's failure with the mere snip he had chosen to marry. Pop removed himself from the scene of confusion by going on a fishing trip, but Clifford, who was to be my comfort and ally every time I committed a stupidity, put his usual tact to work and actually convinced Frankie that he didn't know my whereabouts (of which he was perfectly well aware) but that he would help to find me.

At first Frankie thought that I had run off to New York. He knew how much I longed to go there, and had promised that one day we would make the trip together. He began to bombard *The Morning Telegraph* with telegrams and letters asking for information about me, naturally without result.

For a little while the entire studio enjoyed a game of cops and robbers to "protect" me, but the game had lost its novelty before my husband finally tracked me down, came to Los Angeles, and took to haunting the studio. Then Daddy Woods stepped into the breach and talked him into giving up the chase. I don't know how he did it, or what was said, but Frankie disappeared and it was so many years before I encountered him again that when I did I was surprised I even remembered what he looked like.

My whole first year at the Biograph Studio was spent in concocting plots for its secondary units, while I eagerly awaited the day when the first thrilling intimacy I shared with Griffith would be resumed. But he was too deeply involved in his own affairs to pay me any attention at all. The aftermath of *The Birth of a Nation* had been serious and bitter; there was no question as to the film's artistic merits, for it had caused the movies to be recognized for the first time as art. But the picture had come to grips with the race issue and it was producing riots in the movie theaters of both North and South. In addition to which problems, Griffith was preparing his next film, a picture calculated to surpass *The Birth of a Nation* in both grandeur and sociological importance. So my dreams of a close association with the Great Man went glimmering.

In those days the one girl D. W. ever appeared with outside the studio was Lillian Gish, although none of us even dared whisper that their association was anything but platonic. Nobody had ever heard D. W. address Lillian except as "Miss Geesch," mispronouncing her name as he did mine. Lillian was the personification of all the heroines D. W. ever created, so sweetly childlike, reticent, and timorous that even then her type of girl belonged to a far-distant past. The two made an extremely romantic-looking pair. I remember seeing them enter the grand ballroom of the old Alexandria Hotel in Los Angeles one night, when D. W. looked like one of his own Southern aristocrats of *The Birth of a Nation* and Lillian, in her pink ball gown and black lace mitts, was so breathtakingly beautiful that for a man not to be in love with her seemed inhuman. Astoundingly enough, D. W. seemed almost inhuman; he was of Welsh extraction, and the Welsh are a very peculiar breed, poetic, unpredictable, remote, and fiercely independent. For such a man to be in love must be terribly frustrating, because his deepest instinct is to be a loner.

However, far off in D. W.'s background there was a wife he had married in New York when they were both very young. Her name was Linda Arvidson and she had been an unsuccessful actress in the theater. For a short period she appeared in Griffith's early films, at which time, in his passion for mystery, he made every effort to keep their marriage a secret. After a short term in the Biograph

Company, Linda Griffith abandoned her career and retired to a home which D. W. had purchased in the small Southern town where he was born. As far as any of us knew, she never came to California and must have been as content with their equivocal arrangement as was D. W.

Many years later D. W. arranged for a divorce and married a very young girl who was reticent, vague, and typical of all the heroines ever created by Lillian Gish. However, by that time the Great Man had drifted into obscurity, and the isolation he had once loved so fiercely had turned into stark loneliness.

Not long ago Lillian and I were reminiscing about Griffith's strange detachment, and she told me that during the many years they were so close she had never presumed to call him anything but "Mr. Griffith." It was only a short while before his death, when he was in deep trouble and Lillian had become his only friend and the confidante of his child-wife, that she had ventured to call him David.

Because D. W. so loved to be mysterious, none of us at the studio had the least idea what his new picture was about. But he had caused a stage setting to be built on Sunset Boulevard in full view of the street, and it drew hordes of sightseers all day long. The set represented ancient Babylon and was colossal to a degree that no modern spectacle has yet surpassed. (It formed the background of a notable experience in the life of Lorelei Lee, the blonde whom gentlemen preferred, and Lorelei's diary tells of a battle scene in which thousands of extras took part and she was "the girl who fainted when a gentleman fell off a tower.")

Griffith's day-by-day activities in the studio made no more sense than Lorelei Lee's. There would be weeks when his actors were understandably in Babylonian costume; but then suddenly a new cast of characters started to mill about in modern dress; then came a troop wearing garments of seventeenth-century France, and there was one sequence where a young actor was made up as Christ.

Interspersed with their jobs on regular program pictures, all the actors on the lot were working in Griffith's new film. Sometimes the same stars were acting in two different periods. There was a scene in which Constance Talmadge as a sort of Babylonian flapper was riding in a chariot, one arm around a lusty charioteer, at the same time gnawing on a raw onion. Then, the very following day, Constance would become a court beauty of a romantic era in France. The beautiful but meagerly talented Seena Owen was obviously a princess of Babylon; Mae Marsh and Bobby Harron were young people from a modern slum. But there was no dialogue to provide even the actors with a clue to what they were doing. Daddy Woods, who wrote the script, and possibly Lillian Gish were in on D. W.'s secret, but it was perfectly safe with them.

Bemused though we all were with the Great Man's activities, we had our own jobs to do on pictures being filmed by several run-of-the-mill directors. I was permanently busy on plots for one of the movies' first slapstick comediennes. Her name was Fay Tincher and she was under contract to turn out one-reel subjects at the rate of two a month. I was also providing more lengthy scripts for other stars. Most of all I was reveling in the activities of other young people on the lot; for us the excitement of that fantastic playground far overshadowed our work. My particular pals were Mae Marsh, Constance Talmadge (whom we called Dutch), and Dorothy Gish. We spent a lot of time giggling about our betters and playing practical jokes that were all the more entrancing because they had to be kept so strictly under cover.

There was only one romance among our special group; Bobby Harron was in love with Dorothy, but they were both so young that the affair was rather on the callow side. Every man on the lot was infatuated with Dutch, and she flirted with them all but never wanted to be serious, while Mae and I, for the time being, were looking for love in some sort of "artistic" form that was far removed from Hollywood. When not up to nonsense, we were given to aesthetic pursuits; we read poetry and, in an attempt at sculpture, messed about a bit with Plasticine. Only Lillian had sufficient appreciation of the films to take them seriously; to the rest of us they were an easy way to make a living, too much fun to be exactly honest. And most of us suspected they were a fad without any future.

All our silly group were in awe of Lillian, even her sister Dorothy. We considered her too earnest about her career and too much in the confidence of the great D. W. to be good fun. Prompted by jealousy, we used to joke about Lillian as "teacher's pet." But it was dangerous to make light of anything in the studio, and one frightening day when Mae Marsh was overheard calling the Great Man "Griff" she was treated to a bit of Jovian ire that reduced us all to a wilted state of guilt.

Most of us who worked at the old Biograph Studio have drifted apart through the years, but Lillian and I became New Yorkers and she is now one of my most valued friends. Lillian has never married; much of her youth was spent in looking after an invalid mother, whom she and Dorothy loved, nursed, pampered, and treated almost as a doll. When, after years of self-sacrifice, the death of their mother removed that obstacle to marriage, Lillian preferred to continue the even tenor of spinsterhood.

Many men have been profoundly in love with Lillian. One very prominent admirer sued her out of revenge for being jilted and forced Lillian to go through the embarrassment of hearing her love letters read in court. Joseph Hergesheimer, the novelist, fell under her spell and expressed his ardor in print. The love letters Lillian inspired from George Jean Nathan, one of the most sardonic writers of his time, include such tender passages as to confound most of us who believed George Jean to be a Don Juan. Long her devoted suitor, he realized he had no chance of marrying Lillian while her mother lived, but when, after Mrs. Gish died, Lillian still refused him, George Jean was close to suicide. When he ultimately found a young actress who approximated Lillian's reticence and fragile charm, he married the replica, just as D. W. had done when he acquired his child-bride. Men have always been marrying Lillian *in absentia*, while she has gone serenely on her way.

That Lillian was never recognized by the general public as a sex symbol is because her appeal isn't the least bit vulgar and is certainly not to be measured by Hollywood standards. But in real life she has always been more desirable to men than all the publicized movie vamps, the Clara Bows, Jean Harlows, and Kim Novaks. Havelock Ellis describes Lillian's type, in one of his works on sex, as the irresistible siren, with an extraordinarily gentle exterior, under which lies a character of stainless steel.

Lillian's character finds expression in her flaming patriotism. She is ready to speak out in public whenever an opportunity arises and loves to remind Americans of the ideals we used to have when we were known for our integrity and pride. She will even go to Washington when she feels that somebody down there deserves to be scolded. She is as fiercely American as Walt Whitman, as purely American as Grandma Moses; both have influenced her enormously. As a girl, Lillian played Whitman's eternal mother in *Intolerance*: a frail young woman seated beside an "endlessly rocking" cradle. And in later years she became a close friend of Grandma Moses—a real distinction, for Grandma had little truck with city folks. The magnificent old lady even consented to have Lillian portray her in a televised account of her inspiring life story.

In short, Lillian has more spirit than any other blonde I ever knew; had she cared for diamonds (which she doesn't), she could have been as dangerous to men as Lorelei Lee. One of Lorelei's observations comes right from Lillian's gentle lips: "I think that bird-life is the highest form of civilization." At the time she uttered that remark I laughed over it. But lately I have come to feel that Lillian was right.

Lillian and Dorothy became exceptionally close after their first Hollywood phase, possibly because they never tried to live in the same house. Dorothy's early plan of one day marrying Bobby Harron was ended by his sudden death in a manner that may have been suicide. He shot himself, and, although it could have been an accident, it appeared otherwise, for Bobby had that type of Irish gloom which can be as deep as any Irish love of fun, and he had a motive in the sudden rise of Dick Barthelmess, who was alloted roles which previously would have gone to Bobby.

Dorothy, some time later, married the actor James Rennie; but the marriage was of short duration and ended in divorce. She has lived contentedly for years in a New York hotel with an inseparable canine friend of humble lineage named Rover. Unlike Lillian, Dorothy has small interest in acting; financially independent from her film career, she is always turning down comedy roles in Broadway plays for which she pretends she is not equipped. But this is so obviously an excuse that I'm sure the real reason is that she prefers to baby-sit with Rover.

In those Biograph days Mae Marsh was as important a star as Lillian Gish, but Mae during her early twenties married a Los Angeles newspaperman, Louis Lee Arms, and gradually drifted away from the movies. The marriage has been an outstanding success, and today Mae lives with her husband in Laguna Beach, California, where, many times a grandmother, she leads a serene domestic life and is prominent in the civic life of the community. Mae sometimes writes poems and has them published.

The fifth member of our teenage group, Constance Talmadge, was to leave the Griffith ranks and move to New York, where her career became closely connected with my own, and we were destined to travel a long way together in silent films, as in due time I shall report.

While Griffith was involved in the mysteries of his new film, he entered into other activities that were not connected with it. In advance of his time he realized that the movies, in order to improve, had to recruit talent from the New York theater and, while on business trips there, he raided Broadway. At that time "film" was a nasty word to legitimate actors; even the importance of *The Birth of a Nation* had not broken down the barriers of snobbery that Broadway had erected around Hollywood. But Griffith succeeded in placing a few stage notables under contract by offering them a lot more money than they could ever earn in the theater.

Griffith's most charming importation was a Broadway juvenile with the stage name of Douglas Fairbanks. (Born in Denver, Doug came of a family named Ulman.) He was darkly handsome, of irrepressibly high spirits, and an ardent believer in the strenuous life

as preached by his idol, Teddy Roosevelt. It is quite likely that
Douglas agreed to go to Hollywood because of the opportunities to
lead a strenuous outdoor life there. But, after bringing young Fairbanks to the studio, Griffith tested him and found one serious de-
fect: Doug couldn't act. The company had protected itself by op-
tions in Douglas Fairbanks's contract, so it wouldn't be stuck with
him for long. Doug, on his part, soon began tugging at the leash to
get back to "civilization." Married to an Eastern socialite, Beth
Sully, he was quite frankly a snob. They had a toddling little son,
Doug Junior, who would grow up to be a swashbuckling star of
films himself and, like his father, marry a young woman prominent
in society.

Whiling away his time around the studio, Doug Senior worked
off surplus energy by training with several prizefighter hangers-
on, but his dissatisfaction with the movies did not let up, nor did his
restlessness. Doug never walked when he could run, he never used
stairs when he could jump, and his favorite method of taking a seat
was to step over the back of a chair. Contemptuous of the movies,
he counted the days until he could get back to Broadway.

Another of D. W.'s New York importations was a stage star in
his early forties named John Emerson. Emerson's career on Broadway had begun with small parts in the company of the distinguished star of high comedy, Minnie Maddern Fiske. Later he had
joined the ranks of Charles Frohman, who both artistically and
financially was the most important Broadway producer of that
time. While with Frohman, Emerson had acted with eminent stars
such as Billie Burke and Maude Adams, and he finally reached stardom himself in a play which he wrote in collaboration with a now
forgotten dramatist. It was called *The Conspiracy*, and in it John
Emerson played a crotchety old amateur sleuth who stumbled onto
the solution of a murder mystery. Emerson and Fairbanks had been
friends in New York, where they were both members of the
Lambs Club; they had much in common, principally their nostalgia
for New York, except that Emerson was genuinely interested in
the movies; in fact, he was one of the first members of the legitimate theater ever to take them seriously. So, when Griffith had

approached him to make a film of *The Conspiracy*, Emerson was
intrigued not only by the idea of acting in the picture but with the
thought of ultimately becoming a director.

It was not long before Griffith was sorry he had ever imported
Fairbanks and Emerson. Douglas, as a non-actor, was of no use to
him at all, while the chief attraction of Emerson's *Conspiracy*
turned out to be a little fifteen-year-old girl named Bessie Love,
who played the part of a slavey. (She had a long career as a star in
silent films. It might also be of interest to note that, in 1962, Bessie
Love played old Lady Spofford in the London production of *Gentlemen Prefer Blondes*.) No sooner had Emerson finished the film
version of his play than he began to plead with Griffith to let him
try his hand at directing a comedy with Douglas Fairbanks as star.
No amount of warning deterred Emerson; he felt he could make
Doug's personality triumph over his small talent for acting.

Finally, at a time when Doug's option still had several months to
run, D. W. decided to pacify both him and Emerson until option
time, when he could rid himself of them both, once and for all. He
told Emerson to go ahead and see if he could find a comedy idea
for Fairbanks. Delighted, John Emerson betook himself to Daddy
Woods's files in search of a script. There he ran across dozens of
my stories, many of which had not been filmed. Emerson read his
way through them with increasing satisfaction and then sought out
Griffith.

"I've found a gold mine of material for Fairbanks!" he told
Griffith in a fever of discovery. "A lot of stories by some woman
named Anita Loos."

Griffith was not impressed. "Don't let that material fool you," he
said, "because the laughs are all in the lines; there's no way to get
them onto the screen."

"But why couldn't the lines be printed on the screen?" Emerson
asked.

"Because people don't go to the movies to read," Griffith answered. "They go to look at pictures."

Bewildered by the fact that Griffith had bought so many of my
stories, Emerson demanded to know his reason.

"I like to read them myself," said Griffith. "They make me laugh."

Emerson ventured that this seemed an argument in his own favor and he begged permission to try out a story of mine called *His Picture in the Papers*, which had been inspired by the growing American absorption with publicity that has reached its apotheosis today on Madison Avenue. Griffith grudgingly told Emerson to go ahead but suggested, "You'd better talk to Miss Looze; she might help you." Emerson was interested to learn that the author of those scripts was right there on the lot. He had never happened to run into me, for he belonged to the older group at the studio, whereas I was lost among the young fry. Griffith sent for me and, at a time when I had so recently freed myself of a first husband, I was introduced to the man who would be my second. Not that marriage was on my mind at the time. It was too soon after my escape from it even to dream of a divorce, in which I would have had small aid. Both Mother and Pop felt that the status quo was a safeguard against my wandering into that dubious field again. However, Pop's influence in my affairs was steadily on the decline. Soon after we were established in Hollywood he had joined us there, but, bored by activities in which he had no part, he had accepted a job to edit a weekly newspaper in nearby Santa Ana, where he could more thrillingly sow his oats.

That day when I repaired to John Emerson's office to discuss his projected movie, his reaction to me was typical of others'; he was amazed that any creature who looked fourteen, at the most, could have so profoundly ironic a slant on life. As for me, I wasn't very much impressed. Emerson's stardom on Broadway meant little to any of us in Hollywood. True, he was quite handsome; he was tall, his dark hair was turning attractively gray, and he had the somewhat romantic air of a semi-invalid. John Emerson lived under the constant threat of pernicious anemia, but even so I gathered he was overly concerned with his health; he had an abnormal dread of drafts and, being completely without self-consciousness, went about the studio with such adjuncts as a rubber cushion to sit on, woolen scarves in that California heat, an endless assortment of pills, and a valet who was constantly on call to supply those ignoble props.

To me the idea of making a film with the untried Fairbanks didn't seem too attractive. I had already written pictures for such top-flight stars as Mary Pickford. Mae Marsh, who had attained the heights of stardom in *The Birth of a Nation*, was at that moment making a story of mine called *The Wild Girl of the Sierras*. In short, I was a veteran of the movie industry while John Emerson was a novice, and, when the two of us went to work on a shooting script, it was up to me to teach him how to put it in proper technical form. I did realize, however, that the "old boy" had a different sort of movie in mind from any in my previous experience; he insisted I include an unusual amount of dialogue and put in all the gags I could think of, whether or not they could be photographed.

Emerson and Doug had a hilarious time shooting the picture, while I was busy at other things and paid little attention to them. But after the film had been put together, with its dialogue told in copious subtitles, Emerson dragged Griffith into the projection room along with Doug and me to take a look at it. *His Picture in the Papers* was in five reels, and during its entire running Griffith sat in rigid silence. When it was over he dismissed it briefly by saying, "If you'll cut out those subtitles, Mr. Emerson, and edit your film down to two reels, we'll see what can be done about releasing it." The three of us were deeply disappointed, because we had thought it funny. But the film was carted off to the stockroom, where it lay neglected on a shelf while Emerson busied himself preparing a movie script of *Macbeth*, which he felt would sufficiently impress D. W. to make him overlook *His Picture in the Papers* and assure his option's being taken up. I continued to devise mild little stories for the young girl stars, and Douglas returned to sulking out the time he had to wait to be released from Hollywood forever.

The sequence of events concerning Doug's comedy now jumps to the Strand Theatre in New York. The Strand was one of the first of the old motion-picture "cathedrals." Its high priest was a colorful old character called Roxy, which was short for Rothafel.

Roxy was looked on with affection by his audiences, whom he used to treat as if he were a fond parent providing the kiddies with a treat. Standing in the lobby, Roxy greeted people as they came in, exchanging views on his programs, and he also loved to make intimate little curtain speeches. It seems unjust that an individual as important to the entertainment world of Manhattan as Roxy was could be forgotten as he is today.

One week, which was fateful to the lives of three of us in silent films, Roxy had booked a film which failed to arrive at the theater. As show time drew near, the situation got serious and Roxy called the film exchange in a panic. He was assured that the movie was en route to the theater, obviously held up in traffic. However, a substitute would be rushed right over, which Roxy could screen until the regular feature arrived.

Before the show started, Roxy felt called upon to square himself with his patrons and, most of all, with the critics who were there to review his new show, so he proceeded to make one of his cozy little speeches, announcing that his feature had been unavoidably delayed and while waiting for it his patrons would be regaled by a substitute which he would pull off as soon as the feature got there. Now it so happened that, through some fluke, *His Picture in the Papers* had been shipped to the New York exchange, where it was placed on the shelf and forgotten, as it had been in Hollywood. At any rate, it was the substitute that was rushed over to Roxy. No sooner had the opening titles appeared on the screen than the audience began to laugh. By the time the first reel had run its course, the theater was fairly rocking with laughter. One subtitle I remember came at a point where the villain had blown up a factory, wrecked the police station, cut the main artery leading from the power station, and destroyed communications through an entire city. At which juncture the villain declared, "I will have to resort to violence!"

When the delayed feature finally arrived at the theater, Roxy didn't stop Doug's film. He later told me that had he done so the audience would have booed him. The next day *The New York Times* published a review which said, in effect, that motion pictures had grown out of their infancy, satire had reached the screen. *His Picture in the Papers* wasn't replaced on Roxy's program, business reached a record high, and Douglas Fairbanks rose to stardom in a single week.

Griffith was always ready to admit when he was wrong. He immediately took up Doug's option, and Doug never went back to Broadway. Neither did Emerson. That picture also changed the course of my career; I was put to work writing another picture for Doug, with subtitles to be a main feature of it.

One day, when strolling across the lot, I was brought to a halt by hearing that thrilling, imperious voice call out, "Miss Looze!" It was the first time the Great Man had summoned me since I joined the studio, and I could hardly control my excitement as I approached him.

"I'm running my new picture tonight," said D. W., "and I'd like you to see it with me. You're to write the subtitles."

The news was so stupefying that I could make no comment.

"A car will pick you up after dinner," D. W. concluded. "And tell Mrs. Looze you may be kept at the studio rather late."

The streetcar that took me home that afternoon should have been a jet plane, so anxious was I to break the staggering news to Mother; it meant at long last I was to work with D. W.; I was to be considered as a serious writer; an even greater honor was that the studio's mystery film was to be revealed to me in the company of the Great Man himself. Hardly inside our front door, I called to Mother, "I'm going to see the picture tonight—Mr. Griffith's new picture! He's sending a car for me right after dinner."

"Oh dear," said Mother, "do you *have* to go back?"

That night I sat alone in the projection room with D. W., the first viewer ever to see *Intolerance*. I must be honest and say I thought D. W. had lost his mind. It is difficult to realize in these days of non-sequitur film technique what a shock *Intolerance* provided. In that era of the simple, straightforward technique for telling picture plots, Griffith had crashed slam-bang into a method for which neither I nor, as was subsequently proved, his audiences had been prepared. The story of *Intolerance* jumped back and forth between four different periods of time with nothing to tie the pieces together except its theme of man's inhumanity to man. That the scenes in themselves were visual poems of great beauty was easily recognized, and it was true that each period had a thematic unity with others; also, toward the end a tremendous crescendo was achieved by a mass "run to the rescue," which in the Babylonian period was shown as a chariot race; in the Huguenot episode, the heroine was saved in the nick of time on the Eve of Saint Bartholemew; and the modern story concerned a reprieve that was on its way to stop a miscarriage of justice on the gallows. But when the film was over I sat a moment in stony silence, which I could only explain to the Great Man by telling him I had been moved beyond words. Actually, he was so absorbed in his film I doubt he realized my bewilderment.

At any rate, I went to work writing the subtitles for *Intolerance* and for weeks went about the studio nursing that mighty secret. I spent every day alone in the projection room, running the picture over and over and fitting it with words. D. W. bade me put in titles even when unnecessary and add laughs wherever I found an opening. I found several. At one point I paraphrased Voltaire in a manner which particularly pleased D. W.: "When women cease to attract men, they often turn to reform as second choice." Recently, when *Intolerance* was shown at the New Yorker Theatre on Broadway, that subtitle cribbed from Voltaire was still getting a big laugh.

The importance of subtitles to those silent films having been established, Daddy Woods sent for me one day and said, "Anita, Mr. Griffith wants you to title every picture we turn out. Would you agree to do them at twenty-five dollars a reel in addition to your regular salary?" I was stunned. Titling pictures had all the fascination of doing crossword puzzles but was a lot more fun. I told Daddy I couldn't possibly accept money for indulging in such an exciting pastime. But Daddy insisted, and in time the $25 a reel stretched to $1000 a reel for titling feature films. There was one job I later did on a soggy drama of Norma Talmadge's for which I was paid $6000. I turned it into a comedy by transforming a mean old father into a spurned lover. It was still far from being a success, but audiences had a better time laughing over it than they would have had taking it seriously. And it even made a profit.

During my job on *Intolerance*, John Emerson demanded my aid on his project of filming a Shakespearean play for the first time in Hollywood history. Unabashed, I went to work on *Macbeth*. That old film has disappeared completely without leaving a trace; film, alas, is fragile. Even so, it was hailed as a big step forward in the art of the cinema. But in that era moviegoers were no more Shakespeare fans than they are today, even though the subtitles of A. Loos came to their rescue and cut the Bard of Avon down to size.

ᴥ§ CHAPTER 6

ᴥ§ B y the time John Emerson was ready to turn a camera on *Macbeth*, the movies had become such a sound investment that the New York banks which financed them made no complaint about the high salaries paid to stars, and Emerson had a choice of some illustrious talent for his cast. Macbeth was to be played by the foremost English tragedian, Sir Herbert Tree, and Lady Macbeth would be that impressive lady of the British stage, Constance Collier.

Steeped in Shakespearean tradition, Sir Herbert and Miss Collier were inclined to look on their Hollywood venture with amazement, and Constance later told me that the day they were introduced to me as the Shakespearean authority who had prepared their script, it was like meeting Alice in Wonderland. They had been impressed, however, by John Emerson's understanding of his job and, on reading the screenplay, discovered I hadn't actually tampered with the material, so they relaxed. But Constance then undertook to investigate me as one of Hollywood's quaint conceits, and a friendship began which lasted until her death in New York many years later. If I were asked what friends have given me the greatest satisfaction in life, Constance would be near the top of the list.

Although she was my elder by many years, Constance and I shared many things in common. We always agreed that our greatest achievement in life was the fact that we had won the devotion of two wonderful alter-egos; Constance's was her companion, an English lady, Phyllis Wilborne; mine is Gladys Tipton, who is very basically American, for she is part Cherokee Indian. The desire of those two to stand by us through many years is almost unheard of in shifting and slippery times like these.

Another point Constance and I had in common was that we both took our own careers in hand when we were children. Constance was a precocious fourteen when she sneaked away from her home in a dreary London suburb to present herself at the Gaiety Theatre and ask for a job. Her beauty was of so statuesque a type that the management, without suspecting her youth, engaged Constance for the chorus of respectable and respected Gaiety Girls who were a famous London institution. The Gaiety chorus was a recruiting ground for British peeresses, and Constance had many an opportunity to marry into a grand family. But she was a *cérébrale*, like I, and the love of her life was the great caracaturist, essayist, and wit Max Beerbohm. It is an accepted fact that the devastating effect Constance had on the male sex inspired the satirical novel *Zuleika Dobson*, which is Beerbohm's masterpiece.

Constance's career as a Gaiety Girl was short, for her acting talent soon emerged and she graduated into the legitimate theater, where she became a leading lady for such stars as H. B. Irving and Gerald du Maurier; she played the Queen in John Barrymore's production of *Hamlet* in London.

I was able to see a great deal of Constance, for after the filming of *Macbeth* she remained in our country except for infrequent engagements in London. For many years her New York apartment on West 57th Street was a focal point for the most interesting social life the city had to offer. Unlike the majority of actresses, Constance was alert to everything that went on in the world—politics, the arts, scientific affairs, social and sporting events. She had a faculty of bringing together such divergent types as Eleanor Roosevelt and Zsa Zsa Gabor; she was a wise and witty confidante in every major scandal.

I remember a Sunday afternoon when Zsa Zsa Gabor barged in

on one of Constance's tea parties wearing an eye-patch because of a black eye supposedly given her by Porfirio Rubirosa on the very day before his marriage to heiress Barbara Hutton. But, seeing that Zsa Zsa's grievance was being dished up in the newspapers as a publicity stunt and the "black eye" was conveniently hidden by the eye-patch, none of us believed that the suave and sophisticated Rubi had socked her. However, presently a long-distance call came through from Rubirosa in Palm Beach, where he was on his honeymoon. In a frenzied voice that rang throughout the parlor Rubi asked Constance if she knew where he could track Zsa Zsa down and further mar her fatal prettiness. We listened, spellbound, as Constance explained that Zsa Zsa had left for Budapest; after which Constance brought Rubi back to a sense of duty by sending her regards to his bride and hung up on the sex-starved bridegroom. An unspoken apology for having doubted Zsa Zsa went up from all Constance's sophisticated guests; I don't remember who they were that day, but they might have included Bernard Baruch, Elizabeth Arden, Leopold Stokowski, Kate Hepburn, Mike Todd, and John Barrymore. The incident was one of those moments of truth so often experienced at Constance's, bringing a realization that life is far more diverting than one dares believe.

Because she couldn't find enough classical roles in the movies or on Broadway to keep her busy, a large part of Constance's time was spent in coaching. Among her pupils were many important stars: Kate Hepburn never attempted any role before studying it with Constance; Helen Hayes went to her for advice when she acted in Shakespeare; and during the many years Constance lived in New York there was hardly a Shakespearean production on which she wasn't consulted, not only by the leading actors, but on all matters of production.

And there was one memorable occasion when Constance was approached for advice by none other than Mae West. Mae, at the time, was appearing at the Latin Quarter, doing a night-club act with a group of chorus boys she called her "muscle men," one of whom, Mickey Hargitay, she particularly favored. It had struck

Mae that, as she had thoroughly explored burlesque, it was time she tackled another area of the theater, so, with Mickey in tow, she went to see Constance.

Mae confided in Constance that Mickey was loaded with talent, that she wanted to give the kid a break and would like Miss Collier to dig up something out of Shakespeare along the lines of a nightclub blackout.

Constance thought Mae's request over and suggested a scene between Hamlet and his mother. Now nothing was further from Mae's mind than to play Mickey Hargitay's mother, so she was rather deeply hurt. Quick to realize her *faux pas*, Constance informed Mae that some scholars held a theory that Hamlet was passionately in love with his mother. This angle of the mother-son relationship soothed Mae's feelings to a certain extent, and she remarked, "Oh! Well . . . that figures!" But before Mae's Shakespearean career could get off the ground, Mickey must have been tempted by the more expansive bust measurement of Jayne Mansfield, for he ran out on Mae and married Jayne. So the loss to Shakespeare became Miss Mansfield's gain—for a while.

I learned some valuable hints myself from Constance Collier, on how to grow old without tears. She realized that plastic surgery in itself has no power to make we girls adorable; that a firm character is much more important than a lifted face; that no person of any sex was ever more enticing than Winston Churchill as an old man, which didn't mean that one needed to have Churchillian wit, but only his interest in life as an unfrightening miracle. Or, if one is unequipped to be jovial as was Winston, one can easily dodge the mounting loneliness most people fear by being outrageously entertaining. Elsie Mendel was an arresting old fraud when nearing the century mark, Bernard Shaw an entertaining grouch at ninety-eight. Mae Murray's antic senility diverted her public and, more importantly, herself, until the day she died as she had lived, magnificently self-enchanted. Constance Collier managed to combine some of the traits of all those four charmers. She was far too old for the schoolgirl affair she had with Britain's foremost caricaturist of World War I. When the idyl was wrecked by gossip columnists

who tipped off the betrayed wife, Constance's grief was un-
bounded, not for her lost love, but for the more human reason that
she might not be asked to Her Majesty's next garden party.

If ever good health fails me and I'm tempted to use it as an alibi
for turning sour, I have only to remember Constance Collier's stub-
born interest in living. Her health was racked in early years by
diabetes; her life saved only in the nick of time by the discovery of
insulin, which she had to take every day. There was a long period
when we all knew that she was going blind, but if Constance ever
mentioned the fact at all, it was only to Phyllis.

A day finally came when Constance was able to make a graceful
exit from the world which had been, for her, a magnificent stage
setting. One morning when I phoned Constance for our regular
eight-o'clock exchange of gossip, the call was answered not, as
usual, by Phyllis, but by one of Constance's socialite friends, Andrea Cowden. Andrea told me she had had a frantic summons from
Phyllis that morning, that in an almost incoherent state of shock,
Phyllis told of having entered Constance's bedroom and found that
she had died in her sleep with a smile of deep contentment on her
face. Later on, when Phyllis and I were able calmly to discuss Constance's sudden death at a time when she seemed so full of high
spirits, we came to a conclusion about its cause. On the day previous to her death, notice was served on Constance that her apartment house was to be turned into an office building, she would have
to move. To find a vacant apartment in New York that was capable
of housing her massive Victorian furniture, the countless photographs and mementos of her extraordinary life, would be practically impossible. Constance thought of a better move to make, and
so she simply made it.

At the time I met Sir Herbert Tree in Hollywood, he was accompanied by his daughter Iris, a tawny blonde who greatly resembled the Du Maurier drawings of Trilby. I was in awe of Iris,
who, although only in her teens, was already recognized as a poet.
Today Iris lives in Rome; she played a character based on herself in
the Fellini film *La Dolce Vita,* and declaimed her own poems in

that unforgettable scene of an evening in Rome's top-level bohemia.

Hollywood was greatly excited by Sir Herbert's presence on our
lot, but we were also a little bothered because nobody knew how to
address him. We began by calling him Sir Tree, which didn't sound
right. Finally Daddy Woods went to Sir Herbert for information.
"Why not call me Herb?" he suggested jauntily. Griffith would
never have approved, and we were finally instructed on the correct
use of his title. But Sir Herbert soon posed other problems that had
nothing to do with protocol, for when Emerson began to shoot his
scenes Sir Herbert insisted on speaking every word of Macbeth's
long speeches. This would, naturally, have been a terrific waste of
celluloid, as no movie audience would sit still to watch an actor
mouth several hundred feet of silent film. Emerson finally found a
way around the dilemma, which was to have the cameraman pull
his crank from its socket so that he could grind away while Sir
Herbert gave forth with those long-winded speeches. Then, on a
signal from Emerson, the cameraman returned the crank to its
socket and filming commenced again. Sir Herbert's reactions, when
he finally saw the movie and learned that so much of his Art was
missing, are still among the mysteries of the past.

But it wasn't long before Sir Herbert provided the studio with
another and more delicate problem. He was noted for having an
unceasing interest in the ladies. In England he had fathered a number of distinguished illegitimate children, but in Hollywood Sir
Herbert began to favor the undistinguished young ladies who were
available as extras. A crisis developed when Pasadena's most eminent hostess was inspired to give a dinner in Sir Herbert's honor.
He would never have dreamed of accepting the invitation until
Daddy Woods stepped in and begged him to make the sacrifice; for
Pasadena had held the movies in such contempt that the occasion
might serve to bolster relations between the two cities. Unwilling
to waste an entire evening among Pasadena socialites, Sir Herbert
asked if he might bring along a lady. When Daddy agreed, Sir
Herbert set about making his selection from the extra bench. Daddy
Woods was nonplused, for none of those young ladies could ever

have been assimilated by Pasadena. At length Daddy persuaded Sir Herbert to settle for one of the waitresses at the corner lunchroom for whom Sir Herbert showed a penchant, a girl whose sex appeal was so moderate as not to bring turmoil to Pasadena. Ella Woods took her into the wardrobe department, put a damper on her taste, and got her properly rigged out for the occasion. The young waitress's awe of her surroundings restrained her conversation to a safe minimum, and she managed to get in and out of Pasadena society without disaster. But not Sir Herbert. He endured boredom until time to leave, when, indicating the whereabouts of his companion, the hostess gestured toward the rear and said, "I believe she's 'round behind." "Ah yes," remarked Sir Herbert lustily, "but *aren't we all?*"—with which he gave his hostess a slap on the behind that finished Hollywood's chances to break into Pasadena society for many another year.

But Sir Herbert's antics in Hollywood were mild compared with those of less distinguished members of the movie colony. The focal point of their misbehavior soon came to be the old Hollywood Hotel. Mother, Pop, and I had taken up residence there, where we looked on its entrancing turmoil with delight. The hotel was still on the outskirts of town, although flashy new buildings were now encroaching on it from every direction. At any rate, it was an ideal base for a swelling population of actors who were undergoing a period of ease never before known in the history of that insecure profession; they were working under contract all year round, eating punctually three times a day, and basking in winter sunshine heretofore reserved for the rich. Their jobs required a minimum of study: they didn't have to learn lines, and their evenings were free. Pessimists were saying the movies wouldn't last, which was all the more reason to make hay while that California sun shone.

The full brunt of policing the Hollywood Hotel fell on the shoulders of a gaunt old lady named Miss Hershey, who owned and operated that bouncing hotbed of frolic. In pre-movie times the worst offenses of her boarders had been to order more items from the menu than were permitted on the American plan. At mealtime old Miss Hershey used to patrol the dining room, counting the dishes in front of each diner, sternly removing an extra bird-bathtub full of peas or a second entree, and scolding the elderly waitresses for cooperating in such acts of insubordination. As Miss Hershey's eyesight, even through spectacles a quarter of an inch thick, was none too good, the offenders used to get away with many an extra dish of spinach or mashed turnips right under her nose. But now movie actors were smuggling strong drink into the dining room and becoming hilariously loaded. Their worst offenses, however, were not taking place in public; guests of opposite sexes were sharing rooms indiscriminately, sometimes for a mere few hours. Miss Hershey rapidly began to disintegrate.

One star of the silent movies who was the first to be labeled "the girl next door" changed rooms with the mobility of quicksilver and the same lack of direction. Miss Hershey would tap on the little star's door the last thing at night, and if she was not in her own bed Miss Hershey would go snooping for Diana (which I shall call her in case she lives a respected life somewhere as "the grandma next door"). Miss Hershey seldom tracked Diana down, for the poor old lady wasn't born to be a house detective. But one night she caught Diana in some variation of *flagrante delicto* and ordered her to leave the hotel. It was a stern command; not only was the hotel an actor's dream come true, but the only other lodging places were distressingly humdrum. Diana walked out at dawn, carrying one small piece of baggage, having left the remainder in the room of some accommodating lover. But scarcely an hour later she reappeared at the reception desk, where, assuming the cultured accent of a Boston schoolma'am and introducing herself under a pseudonym, she asked Miss Hershey for a room. Miss Hershey, unable to focus through her thick glasses, obliged and summoned one of the bellhops, all of whom were more than fans of the little star. And, crossing the lobby in triumph, Diana whispered to occupants of chairs along her line of march, "I'm in again!" Out on the veranda word passed from one rocking chair to another. "Did you hear the good news? Diana just put it over on Miss Hershey!" For a startling disloyalty now emerged on the part of Miss Hershey's ancient clients; they actually began to side with the movie outlaws *against* her. It was the first time in their lives that they had ever participated in scandal or had something more intimate to talk about than the California weather. All of which might indicate that censure is based on envy and that the prudish can be mollified by being allowed to share in the fun. When even Mother came to know the sinners of filmdom at close quarters, her sense of fun almost stretched into a sense of humor and turned her into a sophisticate.

Later on there were two movie beauties at the hotel whose behavior was just as circumspect as Mother's. One was Tallulah Bankhead, who would sit on the veranda and allow Mother to show her a new crochet stitch with as great an interest as if she intended to spend her life crocheting tidies. However, Tallulah was born a lady and, no matter how much she has outraged the conventions, she chooses her victims with impeccable taste and affronts none but the phony.

And there was the prettiest girl in the hotel, a brunette named Virginia Rappe. Virginia could have been successful as a film actress, but she was not much interested in her career. A quiet, if not a lazy girl, Virginia was in love and preferred to spend her energies on that diversion. Her lover was one of the Mack Sennett directors, so Virginia, left with nothing to do all day while he was busy at the studio, would sit on the veranda with Mother, rocking and talking the banalities that were dear to Mother's heart.

Another of Miss Hershey's guests was the slapstick comedian Fatty Arbuckle. Off screen and on, Fatty was a clown and not a very good one, his comedy being of the type which relies on fat, in itself, being funny. He invented one gag which all but drove poor old Miss Hershey mad. Sitting in the dining room, Fatty would fold his napkin into a long narrow strip, place a pat of butter in the center of it, and then, by bringing the two ends together and abruptly jerking them apart, he would flip the butter clear up to the ceiling, where it would cling until heat caused it to melt and drip on the diners below. Virginia Rappe disapproved of Fatty almost as much as did Miss Hershey, and she seldom exchanged banter with him, but a day came when the two were to be connected in Hollywood's most shocking and repellent murder.

From time immemorial there had been a dance every Thursday night in the lobby of the Hollywood Hotel. Miss Hershey provided a string quartet of lady musicians who could be counted on for refined selections: no Charlestons, no Bunny Hugs, sometimes a restrained Fox Trot, but more often waltz numbers such as Over the Waves. In the pre-movie days those balls were attended by lady and gentleman guests who danced with arthritic dignity. But now, seeing there were no other places of diversion in the area, Miss Hershey's Thursday evenings were patronized by the film folk. And while poor Miss Hershey watched from the sidelines, jittering with affront, those movie actors purposely made a sport of being caught in "lewd" dancing and getting ordered off the floor.

There were two young ladies of the film set who were of great comfort to Miss Hershey because of morals so lofty that they wouldn't even dance with men; they danced only with each other. Miss Hershey thought it sweet when they snuggled together and, if forced to reprimand a couple of neckers, she'd tap the gentleman on the shoulder and say, "Why can't you two dance respectably like Gertrude and Isabel?"; for innocent Miss Hershey had never heard of the Isle of Lesbos.

One Thursday evening we were electrified by the appearance, fresh from her wedding ceremony, of Mae Murray, then the most glittering of all stars of the silver screen. She had just married Jay O'Brien, an internationally famous gambler and playboy. We all stopped dancing to applaud the glowing bride as she made her way toward the broad staircase on the arm of Hollywood's first socialite bridegroom. But it is dismal to report that a brief two hours later the bridegroom booted the bride down the selfsame staircase, out into the night. What happened between those honeymooners in the bridal suite is a mystery still, and the bride, who wrote her autobiography in the terms of a book-length Valentine, might have produced a best-seller if she'd only leveled with her public and told a few fascinating truths, such as how she came to be bounced out of that particular wedding bed.

There was one period when the hotel was depleted of some of its glamour, after the revelation that a certain blond bathing beauty, instead of being over the age of consent required by the laws of the state, was a mere fifteen years old. One day the company which employed her called a meeting of male personnel to explain that any of them who had enjoyed the little lady's society had stepped into the shadow of San Quentin prison. It was advised that all guilty males should cross the border into Mexico and remain there until the heat was off. But so many of the personnel had to expatriate themselves that the entire company was forced to transfer operations to Tijuana, Mexico, and for over six months the famous Keystone Kops chased malefactors around on alien soil.

That scandal was a private one and it never got into print. But Hollywood was soon slated to produce worldwide headlines about a sex tragedy so revolting that it might have come straight out of a novel by William Faulkner. One weekend a number of film people went on a jaunt to San Francisco, among them Virginia Rappe and Fatty Arbuckle. The group checked into the St. Francis Hotel, and during their holiday a drunken party developed in one of the suites. To what extent Virginia drank too was never revealed. But apparently she had always been on Fatty's obscene mind, and he took that occasion to have his way with her, not normally (which in view of her feeling about him would have been shocking enough), but in an especially revolting manner. Virginia died in frightful agony, and Hollywood's most loathsome scandal broke into headlines in every newspaper of the world.

The members of that drinking bout all scurried for cover, but Arbuckle was too fat to hide. He was brought to trial, and the higher-ups of the film colony, frantic with insecurity, spent hundreds of thousands of dollars on lawyers and bribes. Ultimately Fatty was released through the same sort of legal abracadabra by which the wealthy have always been able to escape penalty for crime. The scandal not only ended Fatty's career but it had a lingering aftermath in Hollywood, which for years went under the misapprehension that a film star could be destroyed by notoriety. But Fatty was the only one that scandal ever harmed. From the early days when Mary Miles Minter was the central figure of a murder mystery, down through Liz Taylor's snatch of two other

women's husbands, guilt has only made film idols more delectable
to their fans. The women's clubs, composed of replicas of poor
Miss Hershey, can mumble and bumble to their heart's delight, but
they can't shorten the lines at the box offices.

The underworld, quick to take advantage of any new field, very
soon moved in on Hollywood and set up headquarters in a suburb
called Vernon. Movie actors quickly deserted the Hollywood
Hotel as a playground and ventured out to the Vernon Country
Club. While losing the fun of putting things over on Miss Hershey,
they more than made up for it by the thrill of outwitting revenue
officers. For hanging around the bar at the Vernon Country Club
were pushers of dope. They had an easy time converting those
simple young drunks into drug addicts, and among their first victims were two stars of first magnitude, Wallace Reid and Mabel
Normand.

Mabel and I first became friends when Mack Sennett had borrowed me from Griffith, feeling that I might add a feminine touch
to one of Mabel's scenarios and, at the same time, keep it rowdy.
Mabel was a natural clown. She adored making herself look ridiculous and, when required to fall off a motorcycle at top speed or be
dunked in a mudhole, she never allowed a stunt girl to take over.
But cooperative as she was with the gags I devised for her, I found
Mabel to be the studio's chief headache. It took an all-out effort to
get her to work in the morning. I remember the company's sending
a car for Mabel one day when an expensive mob of extras caused
time to be of the essence. The driver honked at Mabel's front door,
she scrambled out of bed, picked up a hat en route to the window,
and poked her head out. "I'm just leaving in my own car, Mack!"
she called down. And as the studio car drove away, Mabel scam-
pered back to bed and took a snooze that cost the company many
thousands of dollars.

There was one time when Mabel was sharing a dressing room
with Mary Garden, that majestic lady of grand opera, who was
making her debut in the cinema. The diva's love interest, on screen
and off, was an elegant and sophisticated Greek, Lou Tellegen, who
later distinguished himself by being married for a short while to

that idol of operatic fans Geraldine Farrar. The *entente* between Lou and the diva he was then courting was coyly romantic and expressed in such elegant clichés as, "A penny for your thoughts!" or "How goes it today, lovely lady?" Lou also did a great deal of hand-kissing, and everything between them was as sentimental as all getout.

Now it so happened that one day, when I was with Mabel in her dressing room, there was a tap on the door and Lou called out in dulcet tones, "Are you there, lovely creature?"

Mabel, mimicking the coy manner of Lou's lovely creature, replied, "Yes indeedy."

"May a devoted slave come in?" ventured Lou.

"Not at the moment, dear," his lady answered. "I'm on the chamber pot!"

There was a silence now, fraught with horrible suspicion on Lou's part that his inamorata had been making fun of his delicate wooing all along. We heard Lou's footsteps as he retreated down the corridor, and the great lady never found out what put a snag in her romance.

Lou Tellegen's life had a tragic end, for he killed himself, characteristically, because of wounded ego. When he was found dead of a pistol shot in a room at the Hollywood Knickerbocker Hotel, clutched in his hand was a torn gossip column which had branded him as a has-been.

One of the strange manifestations of Mabel's cocaine addiction was a frenzy for writing letters. She would write to anybody; she used to send long chatty accounts about nothing at all to salesgirls whose names she didn't know—addressing them, for example, to "Saleslady in Stocking Department." I destroyed the letters I got from Mabel, perhaps subconsciously because they were so disturbing.

Mack Sennett, who was Mabel's employer throughout her entire career, adored her, but he was a busy man and found it impossible to go along with her irresponsibility. Their protracted love affair broke up, but she depended on Mack for orientation in the world where dope had made her so unsure and, as a friend, he never failed her. Mabel later on became the sweetheart of one of the cinema's most distinguished producers, who tried his best to straighten her out. But in her love for laughs she was constantly turning her beau into a figure of fun, and the poor man finally gave Mabel up.

Mable Normand died young, as many dope addicts do; toward the end she was in a Los Angeles hospital, and my brother Clifford was her doctor. Mabel knew that for her the chips were down, and she begged Clifford to let her go home to die. But she was too far gone to be moved, so Clifford had a screen brought from her house and placed about her bed, where, thinking she was in her own room, Mabel died in peace.

Mabel's fellow addict, Wallace Reid, was of a far different caliber. When Wally died of his addiction there were not many of his peers who mourned him, in spite of his thousands of fan clubs. He was tall and handsome, with immaculately kept blondish hair and a flair for wearing Ivy League clothes. But when he took to using heroin Wally also adopted a few gangster methods of behavior, one of which was blackmail. He used to hide out during the shooting of a scene and send word to the director, "If you want to bring this picture in on schedule, it'll cost you a thousand dollars to get me on the set." The money would generally be sent to Wally, and he would come out of hiding to give a convincing performance of an upstanding, clean-cut, clear-eyed, square-shooting American hero of the type that was his specialty.

About the time of the Arbuckle affair, Elinor Glyn moved in on Hollywood. She was among the first of the novelists to discover that the end of the rainbow was in the film capital, and in her case the pot of gold rested on the Paramount lot. In those days Elinor's books were considered extremely "broad." Her best-seller, *Three Weeks*, was based on adultery, but she handled the subject in so dainty a manner as to make D. H. Lawrence's *Lady Chatterley's Lover*, with its identical plot, a sewer of clinical realism. But Elinor was not content with merely putting elegance into her plots; she was hell-bent on bringing refinement to the film colony. She checked into the Hollywood Hotel and at once got on the right side of Miss Hershey, for Elinor was an aristocrat, while her sister,

Lady Duff Gordon, not only boasted a title but operated a dress salon in New York where, under the name of Lucille, she catered to the upper classes of both our country and her own. Elinor never allowed anyone to forget she was lady to the core, but for all her pretensions to a Mayfair background she belonged, body, heart, and soul, to Hollywood; in fact, had Hollywood never existed, Elinor Glyn would have invented it. Her appearance was bizarre; the make-up she wore might have been scraped off the white cliffs of Dover, and it provided a startling contrast to her dyed red hair, green eyes, and mouth of vivid crimson. She jangled with long earrings, economically set with second-rate gems.

Elinor's first move in Hollywood was to establish a "salon," and on Sunday afternoons she invited us all to her suite in the hotel for tea (tea!), during which she lay on a tiger-skin rug, wearing Persian pajamas in the pastel shades made famous by her sister Lucille, and recited poems of Shelley and Swinburne, to which, for good measure, she added Ella Wheeler Wilcox. Quoting from the latter, Elinor would declaim, "Smile and the world smiles with you, weep and you weep alone," doing so in lugubrious tones that precluded any attempt at smiling.

We all knew that Elinor's salons were merely her own particular form of publicity, but the movie group was generally hung over from its Saturday nights at the Vernon Country Club and too groggy to indulge in more active pastimes; besides, there wasn't anything else to do of a Sunday afternoon. But those literary sessions would bog down about seven p.m., when the Vernon Country Club opened and life in the raw could begin again.

Sometimes Elinor herself attended the rowdy sessions at Vernon, where the limelight shone bright and, trailing chiffon, she could face a newspaper camera at every turn. Her alibi for being there was that she must acquaint herself with the entire Hollywood scene in her quest for an actress to play the heroine in *Three Weeks*. It was a difficult search, for the stars had to be of a refinement that would give her slide from virtue a certain element of surprise. And, in Elinor's terminology, none of our stars were people of "race."

One evening I myself happened to be at Vernon and ran into Elinor. She was surrounded, as usual, with fastidious young men, but I was with Joe Frisco. Joe was as successful a vaudeville comic as he was a failure at the race track; along with which he was the favorite philosopher of show business and the underworld. Among Joe's pearls of wisdom was his comment on the California climate: "Sometimes it's hot and sometimes it's cold; a man never knows what to hock." I adored the soundness of Joe's logic; one day when I was lunching with him at the Brown Derby he ordered apple pie and, when informed there wasn't any, he briefly remarked "Fake it!" As a *cérébrale* I cared for Joe deeply, but I was smart enough to hide the fact because Joe's heart belonged to horses.

The night Joe was introduced to Elinor he gave her some expert advice on the problem of her search for a lady. "Leave me get this straight," said Joe. "You want to find some tramp that don't look like a tramp, to play that English tramp in your picture. But take it from me, that kind of tramps don't hang out in Hollywood."

Joe was wrong, however; there was a lady or two in the area, one of whom was a Mack Sennett bathing beauty named Madeline Hurlock. But Miss Hurlock was much too on to the Hollywood racket to take it seriously; she occupied an obscure furnished room where she lived respectably on her salary and gave no thought to Elinor's search for a lady like she. Today Miss Hurlock is prominent in Anglo-American society, the widow of the distinguished playwright Robert Sherwood. She is the only known survivor of the Mack Sennett bathing beauties; beauty combined with lack of brains is extremely deleterious to the health.

Elinor Glyn's search at length ended in victory; the lady of "race" she found was Eileen Pringle. Eileen had culture. I shall never forget the night she trapped us in her parlor and put us on the rack by declaiming sections of that grand old cornball called *The Spoon River Anthology*.

Three Weeks was a smash hit at the box office and it made a star of Eileen Pringle. From then on Paramount gave Elinor *carte blanche* further to invade the field of sex. She proceeded to discover a little brunette named Clara Bow, who managed to be, at

one and the same time, innocuous and trashy. As such, Clara justified a tag that Elinor put on her, one which archly stated that Clara
Bow had "It." The It girl and I were supposed to look alike and
sometimes on leaving the Brown Derby I was mobbed by her fans,
for whom I graciously signed Clara's name in autograph albums.
But that was the extent of movie glamour in my life, for D. W.
took it for granted that we of his organization were above such low
diversions as late nights at the Brown Derby or at Vernon, so we
mostly followed his hint and rose above them. Moreover, he kept
all of us hard at work. Whereas the other studios had rather sloppy
discipline, we were required to be on our jobs early in the morning, and we rehearsed in the enervating sunlight and listless air until
we were glad to go home and rest at the day's end.

By this time the stars were moving out of the Hollywood Hotel
and beginning to live in their own private houses with servants,
most of whom were their peers in everything but sex appeal—
which pinpoints the reason for the film capital's mass misbehavior.
To place in the limelight a great number of people who ordinarily
would be chambermaids and chauffeurs, give them unlimited
power and instant wealth, is bound to produce a lively and diverting
result. Baby Peggy's town car was painted baby blue, and the windows had lace curtains expecially woven in Nottingham with her
initials. One famous star honored her mother with a dedication in
letters of gold on the door of her Cadillac. It read, "To Mother,"
but when the car was delivered she felt the painter had left too
much space between the words and was all for having him do it
over. "Let it alone," I advised. "If you two have a fight, there's
room between the 'To' and 'Mother' to have 'Hell with' painted
in." And that was as "sick" a joke as anyone ever got off in those
halcyon days.

Just to live in daily contact with Griffith was a notable experience. Sometimes I sneaked onto the set while he improvised scenes
which were to become classics in motion-picture art. Even his
affectations, of which he had any number, became poetry when he
transposed them onto film. One favorite scene that D. W. filmed
over and over, practically without variations, showed a teenage

heroine being chased around a tree, bush, table, chair, bench, or bed, by either a hero with honorable intentions or a villain bent on harm. Lillian Gish and Mae Marsh must have run miles around the prop trees and furniture of the old Biograph lot.

Despite his genius, D. W., like his idol Whitman, never became a worldling and he had a naïveté about sex in particular which sometimes took an incredible turn. One day, when John Emerson was rehearsing the scene in *Old Heidelberg* where the prince and his sweetheart (played by Wally Reid and Dorothy Gish) were saying good-by forever, Dorothy bypassed the kiss, but as this is generally done in rehearsals Emerson thought nothing of it. However, while the camera was grinding, Dorothy's farewell to her lover turned out to be a chaste brush on his cheek, and Emerson called a halt. He got Dorothy off to one side and asked why she didn't kiss Wally on the mouth with a proper show of feeling. Dorothy argued that Mr. Griffith had made it a rule that she and Lillian were never to be photographed kissing any man on the mouth. Unable to believe such a statement, Emerson went to D. W. to ask if it could be true. It was indeed, and no argument of Emerson's could break D. W. down. So in order to simulate the passion of that heartbreaking good-by kiss Emerson had to resort to a trick camera angle.

Then there was an occasion in one of D. W.'s own short subjects when Lillian was playing a role obviously inspired by Sarah Bernhardt. A certain scene showed the famous French actress in pretty close contact with a lover. When the picture was being titled, D. W. ordered me to insert one to the effect that during the filming of the love scene Miss Gish's mother had been present on the set. But Daddy Woods talked D. W. out of that bit of chaperonage.

But in spite of such ingenuous prudery, D. W.'s attitude would sometimes take a wild curve into the outrageous. There was a time in London when one of his actresses had deserted the films for a while to star in a play of Zoe Akins. On a bitterly cold winter night Zoe went backstage after the show to pick the young star up and take her to a party. As she was getting into her evening gown, Zoe found that she intended to face the frosty winds without any un-

derwear. Zoe was horrified at the danger to her health and also, no
doubt, to the box office in case she caught pneumonia. But remon-
strating got Zoe nowhere; the little lady primly quoted a theory of
Mr. Griffith's that underwear was a detriment to a girl's sex appeal.

Sometimes D. W.'s imagination proved to be impractical, and he
would contrive a sequence that had to be discarded. I remember
one day when every girl on the lot was rigged up in a trailing white
robe and a pair of outsized wings. The girls were then hoisted high
into the air on wires to produce the effect of flying angels. In no
time at all most of the angels got seasick, and the scene ended in a
welter of very embarrassing nausea.

But almost always D. W. made use of the raw human material he
found at hand with enormously telling effect. Just outside the entrance to the studio there were several benches on which ordinary
Los Angeles loafers of both sexes used to sit all day, hoping to be
summoned inside for jobs as extras; the directors had only to step
out the front door, run an eye along the benches, and select faces
and bodies with which to fatten up their scenes. There was never a
professional actor among that riffraff, and sometimes Griffith
would inquire about someone's normal occupation. The answers
were varied in the extreme; I was present once when a certain
character informed D. W. that he was a wheelwright. "Come with
me!" said D. W. "I've got everything in this picture but a wheelwright."

There was one fateful morning when an undiscovered genuis
turned up on the extra bench. John Emerson was about to begin
filming *Old Heidelberg* when, on his way into the studio, he suddenly stopped in amazement at the sight of a man who conveyed
the very spirit of Heidelberg itself: rigid posture, shaved head,
monocle, saber scar on cheek, everything. When Emerson approached to ask the man's name, he rose stiffly, snapped to attention, and with the salute of a Prussian officer answered, "Von Stroheim, sir."

"Do you know anything about Heidelberg?" Emerson asked.

"I am a graduate of that university, sir," said Von Stroheim.

"Come on in!" Emerson told him.

That was Erich von Stroheim's first entrance into any studio and his introduction to an art of which he was to become a master. Emerson started him off as technical adviser on life in the university town, but before long Von was playing an important role in the picture. By the time the film was completed, Von's wide general culture had made him so indispensable that Emerson engaged him permanently as his assistant, in which capacity Von remained until his genius could no longer be held down and he went on to fame, first as a star and then as a director who was to rank along with Griffith himself.

While he was Emerson's assistant, Von Stroheim's ingenuity came into play in every department. One time he designed a magnificent parquet marble floor for the great hall of Macbeth's palace, but when Emerson arrived on the set, ready to shoot the scene, he found that Macbeth's palace lacked its floor. D. W. had spotted it and ordered it to be moved during the night to grace a Huguenot sequence for *Intolerance*.

I recall another device of Von's that was not so successful. To play the three witches in *Macbeth* Emerson had selected actors with a special aptitude for female impersonation, as is usual in productions of *Macbeth*, and Von conceived the idea of making sparks fly from their fingertips. An electrician rigged up a gadget which sent sparks flying in all directions, but unfortunately the current proved too strong, and before it could be turned off three gaunt young female impersonators were screeching curses that Shakespeare would have gratefully plagiarized could he have heard them.

Von Stroheim in real life was as great an actor as he ever was on film. Like D. W., he made a fetish of being mysterious; nobody knew how he happened to have left Germany or why; his own accounts of his past were vague and probably as fictitious as was his claim to have graduated from the University of Heidelberg. He posed as an Austrian, but on the surface no character was ever more Prussian than Von. He delighted in being subservient to everyone above him and tyrannical to anyone beneath. As an assistant director, he gloried in being feared by the unfortunate extras under his jurisdiction. But it was all too phony to be really sadistic. At heart Von was as good as gold.

At a later time in New York, Emerson engaged Von to act in a picture the locale of which was Berlin during World War I. The war was then in progress, and it was a hazard for Von Stroheim, with his Prussian looks and mannerisms, even to appear in public. But when not needed on the set Von, dressed in the Prussian uniform of the movie's villain, would stalk over to the Plaza Hotel, engage one of the fiacres stationed there, and ride arrogantly through Central Park, accepting the jeers of American patriots along his way with an imperious twist of his monocle. For, along with his ability to shock, Von gloried in a perverse sex appeal that prompted some press agent to give him the sobriquet by which he came to be known: "The Man You Love to Hate."

As a director Von created such masterpieces as *Greed* and *Foolish Wives*, which early foreshadowed Bergman's *Wild Strawberries* and Fellini's *La Dolce Vita*. Another movie, which Von himself wrote especially for Gloria Swanson, was brought to an abrupt end after only a reel or two had been filmed by the withdrawal of its multimillionaire backer. The picture was titled *Queen Kelly*, and a description of a certain scene which Von managed to photograph before the production was halted will prove how far he went beyond the limits of that era's sophistication.

A troop of Prussian cavalry is filing down a German road under command of a captain who, although not played by Von, had all his *savoir vivre*. Along the same road marches a file of schoolgirls from a nearby convent, dressed in uniforms of virginal white. Two nuns in charge of the girls are powerless to prevent their gaping at the dapper soldiers and, as Gloria reacts, overawed by the elegant captain, she becomes the victim of one of the most unfortunate accidents that can happen to a female; her panties fall down. The captain, calling a halt, laughs in sadistic glee over the contretemps. Now it so happens that the girl, being of fiery Irish temperament, goes berserk with indignation, picks the garment up, and hurls it into the captain's face. But immediately Gloria regrets the gesture, for the captain confiscates the garment and smugly tucks it into his tunic. In the sequence which follows, Von had exploited to the limit Gloria's attempts to retrieve her panties. The shot where they are finally returned to her would have been shocking enough had the captain done it in a simple gesture. But with a gleam of appreciation shining through his monocle, he raises the garment, kisses it, and savors the moment deeply before returning it to the lovely owner.

Von's shooting of that scene was merely an expensive self-indulgence, for even in those days before censorshop the studio itself would never have outraged public opinion by including it in the picture. It has taken over three decades in time and the talents of Fellini and Tony Richardson to get away with episodes that match those of Von Stroheim's outrageous imagination.

Von Stroheim's private life was a long series of tragic incidents. When he was very young and had just arrived in America, he contracted an unfortunate marriage with a girl who could in no manner be a companion to him. To the end of his life Von remained both legally and financially loyal to his marriage vows. Long after it was apparent that their relationship could never be anything but a protracted irritation, Von's wife suffered a horrible accident in a fire which scarred her face beyond any help from plastic surgery. Later Von met the pretty French girl whom he was to love until he died, and he went through years of anguish because of that hapless first marriage. For underneath Von's bombast was a pathetically masculine lack of courage.

As an artist Von Stroheim suffered the same rejection by Hollywood that was accorded to Griffith. Von's great talent could no more be restrained than a raging torrent; he undertook projects that ran into twenty or more reels of film, and, although it was understandable that he might be considered a financial risk, he was regarded as dangerously insane, repudiated, and allowed to go broke. When unable any longer to find jobs, Von decided to look for work in France, where his genius had never been in doubt. His friends made up a sum of money to see him through the period of change, and we all felt bereft when he took off alone for Paris, burdened with the heavy responsibility of supporting the family he left behind. The money we gave Von was a gift which nobody wanted him to return. But one Christmas day, several years later, Von's eldest son appeared at my door to deliver a holly wreath to which was attached Von's check for the amount of my gift, together with a touchingly dignified note of thanks. And that was at a time when he was making only a modest living in Paris.

Von worked as a featured actor in French pictures, but his talents were too special for many roles to be forthcoming. He was honored as a director, but the French picture industry was too poor to finance his elaborate productions, and he finally resorted to publishing his screen material in the form of novels. Among my prized possessions are two books of Von's: *Paprika* (in English) and *Poto Poto* (in French), both equally overwritten and unreadable. *Poto Poto* bears an inscription Von wrote the year before his death: "For Anita who is such a wonderful friend that she *bought* this copy. With all my love, Erich."

Von was as shocking in his novels as in his pictures, and he was in the vanguard of all the modern writers of four-letter words. But his stories failed to sparkle with the philosophy and wit of either his movies or his conversation. He was trilingual and had equal facility in German, French, and English.

On my yearly visits to France I always used to visit Von at a home he established in the small peasant community of Maurepas, about forty minutes outside Paris. The interior was always dimly lighted and it had an atmosphere of such heavy-footed *gemütlichkeit* that one felt it belonged in the Black Forest of Germany. The dun-colored, pockmarked plaster walls were hung with sabers and guns arranged in patterns, together with some German officers' tunics, and over the huge fireplace of the living room was a collection of enormous beer steins. The housekeeping was in charge of the chic and pretty Frenchwoman, an actress and journalist, whom Von had met soon after his arrival from Hollywood and had wooed in a manner characteristic of him. She had come to Von's hotel to interview him for some theatrical publication when, early in the interview, Von interrupted to pose a question of his own—in effect, to ask the young lady whether she enjoyed being made love to, phrased in those old Elizabethan terms which are still written on fences. The young journalist, after a moment of shock, replied, "*Mais oui, Monsieur.*" "Then," asked Von, "what are we waiting for?"

She never left Von on that or any subsequent day, and her devotion made up for much of the defeat he had suffered in his marriage. She nursed him through the last four pain-racked years of his life. She still lives in the house at Maurepas, and when in Paris I go out there and together we visit Von's grave in the village cemetery. I am happy to report that it is as impressive as Von himself could have wished, for it is covered by a black marble slab which bears his official recognition by the French government. While he lay dying of cancer, Von was visited one afternoon by a delegation sent out to Maurepas to decorate him with the *Légion d'Honneur.*

Such dramatic recognition as Von enjoyed was denied Griffith, who died poor and in obscurity, abandoned, except for Lillian Gish, by all the stars he developed. Fortunes were made by those Biograph stars, but not by D. W., who gambled all his substance on pictures which brought no financial return. After having been for years so far ahead of everyone else in the industry, D. W. was incapable of marching with the times. It is strange that, while frail little Lillian has been alert to everything that goes on in the world of the theater, the Master himself slipped back, so weighted down by the sentimentality of his youth that, even after working on tragic locations in two world wars, he was still unable to free himself of the romantic naïveté that graced life when his career began.

Unable in his hypersensitivity to accept defeat, D. W. took to drinking. Long after he was forced to give up his film activities he tried to make a comeback in New York. He was then living at the Astor Hotel, which is devoted to a commercial clientele, and he was able to hide his misfortunes among its transient guests. One day D. W. sent for me, and while we were sitting over lunch in the grillroom he outlined a plot he had concocted and asked if I would write the script. It was soap opera, pure and simple, and concerned the horrors of drink. Although it was not at all my cup of tea,

D. W. was at the end of his tether and I undertook the job, hoping against hope that once the camera began to turn inspiration might pay D. W. one more visit. I begged him to get Jimmy Durante for the leading role, thinking that Jimmy's robust clowning might remove some of the character's naïveté. D. W. was intrigued, but he finally settled for a straight leading man, whom he directed with old-fashioned bathos. It was the last picture the Master made and it dissolved into a mass of maudlin sentimentality.

But D. W. and Von Stroheim, through all the trials of their separate careers, remained men in the noblest sense to the very end of their lives. I am grateful to them both for having provided me with the assurance that men can be both human and divine.

CHAPTER 7

◆§O ne day Griffith sent for me to come to the cutting room, where I found him working on the final version of *Intolerance*. Preoccupied, looking through long strips of film, and, in his usual manner of understatement, D. W. told me he had decided to use me in the publicity campaign for *Intolerance*. "Those 'learned' remarks of yours, coming from the mouth of a flapper, ought to amaze the gentlemen of the New York press."

In one brief statement, D. W. made my whole life up to that moment seem to be merely a dull prelude. Trying to swallow my excitement, I asked what my duties would be. Griffith answered that Daddy Woods would line up interviews for me, that I could talk about anything I liked. "Whatever you say may startle the newspapers into giving us a little space." He brought the matter to a close by saying, "You must be ready to leave in a few days"; and that ambiguous "you" left it open as to whether his plan included Mother. Playing safe, I took it for granted that she was to be left behind, so poor Mother was to suffer the most violent shock since my marriage when I rushed into our suite at the Hollywood Hotel, exclaiming, "Mother! I'm going to New York with Mr. Griffith!"

"Oh!" gasped Mother. "When do we leave?"

I let her think it was Griffith's decision that I go alone, which was pretty sneaky, but to be repressed by Mother in New York would have ruined everything, and I had reached that point where youth simply had to be served. By this time my most ardent dreams about New York had come to center on one particular hero, the *enfant terrible* of American letters: H. L. Mencken. Mencken edited and wrote for the monthly magazine *Smart Set*. It had started out with a policy of printing short stories based on sophisticated themes, but when it fell into Mencken's hands the title became a misnomer, for his objective had nothing to do with smart fiction; Mencken's main idea was to kick the naïveté out of American manners, art, and politics, which he did in words of his own invention, calling his fellow countrymen "boobus Americanus" and "the booboisie." Mencken was loud in his praise of Schopenhauer and Nietzsche, who were having a tremendous impact on all we young intellectuals. Along with Mencken, another idol of mine was his sidekick, the *Smart Set*'s ribald drama critic, George Jean Nathan, who was bent on getting the plays of Ibsen and Strindberg off the shelves of libraries and onto Broadway.

Odd as it may seem, Broadway had no part in my girlish dreams of New York. To me acting seemed a pointless exhibitionism that could be excused only in females, in whom vanity is not unbecoming and may even be cute. I've known very few actresses who couldn't be tricked into a bad play, providing they might wear a nun's outfit. Sometimes the matter of making a first entrance in a riding habit can turn the trick. But actors, to my poisonous little mind, were merely trying to escape nonentity in the prefabricated situations of the theater. At any rate, I found the conversation of show folk to be artless shop talk in which only their sincerity was commendable, for they do honestly adore one another; how else can they justify their mass cowardice in hiding out from life?

Two actors I later came to admire were John Barrymore and W. C. Fields, but they both had a very sour slant on their means of livelihood; they were men first and actors only because of the irresistible salaries they attracted. Also, I have honestly admired a few actors who, like Charlie Chaplin and Marlon Brando, try to be thinkers but, as it generally turns out, they mistake their notions for ideas, which doesn't make them the political theorists they claim to be. I rather doubt if Charlie, in particular, ever read a book. That he was exiled from the United States for trying to be

other than the world's greatest clown is vastly unfair. Those emotional half-thoughts of Charlie's could never have harmed anyone.

The summation of my dreams about New York, then, was of
evenings I might spend with Mencken and his cronies, listening to
first-rate thoughts at first hand. Not that I planned to agree with
them on every count; for instance, by this time I had come to have
reservations about Ibsen's *A Doll's House,* with its theme that men
had turned womenfolk into mere toys. I knew far too many
women who were supporting men, from the waitresses at the
Hollywood Hotel up to most of the top film stars, to be fooled by
Ibsen. If there was a doll in our house, it was Pop. I longed to give
George Jean Nathan an argument that his avant-garde playwright
belonged back in the Victorian era.

I tried to justify my desertion of Mother with the knowledge
that she was very pleasantly located in the Hollywood Hotel,
where she had become a sort of mother-at-large to all the film girls,
who, heaven knows, needed a mother and came to mine in their
emergencies—generally after it was too late for anything but her
tears of sympathy. Pop, as the hotel's most popular cavalier and
jester, would be too occupied with a full-time audience to miss me.
But it must have taken Mother a long while to overcome the suspicion caused by my eagerness to get away from home. Like most
extremely innocent people, she was obsessed by sex—not as a diversion (God forbid). She saw all females as constant objects of attack, while at the same time she never trusted me and wasn't at all
sure I wouldn't be ready to cooperate in that sort of shady deal.

Her misgivings were increased by the fact that I had begun to
get publicity of the soapy type generally inspired by film actresses.
Very soon after I entered the films, *Photoplay* magazine had
sprung into being almost without gestation, and when its publisher
and his editor first visited Hollywood from the main office in Chicago they chose to "discover" me. The fact that movies were actually written instead of being ad-libbed on the set, and that one of
the authors was young and, for a writer, rather toothsome, made
me seem a sort of West Coast Aspasia. Articles about me began to
decorate *Photoplay,* together with photographs. One effusion,

headed "The Soubrette of Satire," read, "Next to Mary Pickford, Edna Purviance and Neysa McMein's cuties, Anita Loos ranks right along as a leading cause of heart disease."

Following this sort of blurb, the fan letters came tumbling in. They were generally scrawled on bits of grubby paper that had been used to wrap up groceries and, after the first novelty of getting mail from strangers wore off, I never looked at them. The fact that any exist today is due to an overly efficient secretary who put them in a filing case that was shipped to me in New York many years later. But Mother studied those fan letters with an ever-mounting suspicion, and she sensed rapine in every line.

Chicago

Dear Anita,

If you would like to have a nice little fellow hug you up and give you all the loving your sore heart needs, just write me and I will be your man.

Lester Libbey

Tokyo, Japan

Dear Miss Loos,

I confide sufficiently that you will permit me to write that I am longing for you very much.

Masao Kato

Los Angeles

About two months ago I was in the ante-room of the Griffith Picture Corporation, when you came in with Mae Marsh . . . you with your romantic girlish figure that reminds me of a Bedouin, Italian or Spanish Gypsy.

While such ardent prose may have justified Mother's fears, she failed to realize and would never understand that any temptations to go astray would always be limited by my mental snobbery. Even the love affairs common at the studio would have been too basic for my taste. Steeped in the poetry of Byron, Pushkin, and Heinrich Heine, I dreamed of a lover whose sardonic attitude would complicate the whole affair; one who would whisper bittersweet things to me like those which Heine used to pour into the ears of his Mathilde in Montparnasse.

And about this time the movies began to be noticed by a man of literary stature, the poet Vachel Lindsay. Before he espoused our cause, films were considered so unimportant that even such theatrical trade papers as *Variety* (in which they now take up the major part of every issue) relegated them to a few obscure pages at the back. But Lindsay took to eulogizing the silent movies in such high-class journals as the *Atlantic Monthly* and the *New Republic*. The first of his articles to mention me was brought to my attention by Daddy Woods, who ran across it in the studio's press department. Lindsay wrote, in part, "*The Wild Girl of the Sierras*, of which Anita Loos is the scenario writer, appealed to me more than any other film of that year."

I had only vaguely heard of Vachel Lindsay as being a sort of American Bobby Burns who wrote in the vernacular of the Midwest, but I was so staggered by his attention that I bought a book of his poems, read them with delight, and sent him a fan note in care of his publisher. Very soon came a reply: "Be sure I have watched all your work with great interest and I keep you well in mind."

At last a letter from a stranger that was worth the reading! I answered Lindsay at once, and our correspondence grew apace. Then one momentous day Mae Marsh came to me jittering with excitement over a poem Lindsay had sent her, inspired by her performance as *The Wild Girl:*

> She is madonna in an art
> As wild and young as her sweet eyes,
> A frail dew flower from this hot lamp
> That is today's divine surprise.

Mae was so transported by Lindsay's words that she felt she ought to write him a note of thanks. "But," said Mae, "I wouldn't know what to say to such an intellectual gink." The upshot was that she begged me, as an authoress, to come to the rescue. After I had written a letter expressing Mae's heartfelt thanks, a regular correspondence between the two was inevitable—one in which I was forced to continue as Mae's ghostwriter. I thus developed into a small female Cyrano de Bergerac, sending the poet some much more emotional thoughts on life and love than I ventured in my own purely intellectual correspondence with him. Mae copied my innermost thoughts in her own handwriting, and Vachel's replies became increasingly ardent. In no time at all he was falling madly in love with Mae.

If I had been jealous of Mae's romance at first, the fact that I was able to enthrall the poet in the terms of her own Irish whimsy flattered my ego as an author. Moreover, Vachel's romance with Mae didn't seem to interfere in the least with our own hightoned correspondence, and as A. Loos, I even felt a little bit superior to Mae. And may I here suggest that Platonic friendship can definitely hold its own against the sex urge, that it is more enduring and, in my case, has provided several associations that ended only when their heroes died.

During the early phase of our correspondence with Lindsay, Mae and I were both anchored in Hollywood, while the poet, when not at his home in Springfield, Illinois, seemed to be in the Midwest, giving recitals. But Griffith decided that Mae was to join in our hegira to New York and, after I had casually mentioned the fact to Vachel in "Mae's" next letter, his answer was more ecstatic than usual. It appeared he was to be in New York for a poetry reading at the same time. They were actually to meet.

Instantly Mae was seized by pangs of self-deprecation; would she be as delectable to her poet in the flesh as she was in those camera effects that erased her freckles? And might not her ad-lib dialogue serve to give away the ruse we had perpetrated? I had little anxiety on that score, being aware of how uncritical is man concerning the utterances of a blonde.

When we boarded the Santa Fe, bound for New York, in company with D. W. and Daddy and Ella Woods, Mae and I nursed in secret the idyl into which she was heading. At that time young people indulged in romantic speculations about love for which the word today is "corn." Sometimes I believe that today's keen interest in the past stems from an atavism for that twittery indulgence; to us, romantic love encompassed the best there was in the way of thrills. But then, we had no space ships.

Our trip, as a first venture outside my native state, was as exciting as I had anticipated. While the train was speeding from Los Angeles to Chicago, Mae and I remained glued to the windows of our drawing room, fascinated by Indian bucks loafing in front of their huts, watching their squaws hang out the wash or tote firewood. Our awe for the vastness of the desert was mitigated by giggles over the way we looked with icebags strapped to our heads like turbans. For in the days before air-conditioning those icebags provided the only means of counteracting several hours of unbearable heat while crossing the Mojave. With the desert behind us, the endless plains dotted by tacky railroad stations were diverting, and what a sadistic pleasure to lie cozily in bed, eating a hot breakfast and watching unlucky fieldworkers in the frosty morning air, their breaths as visible as fog. We had no personal adventures, and even Mae was never recognized; for in those early days movie personalities seemed so remote it was difficult for the public to realize they might actually be encountered in the flesh. No fellow passengers flirted with us in the dining car; they were Westerners and too lacking in assurance to pay strange girls any attention. Western men seem to lack not only gallantry but even interest. It is rather revealing that in all the Western movies cowboys seem to caress only their ponies.

But our situation took a dramatic turn when we boarded the Twentieth Century Limited in Chicago for the last lap of our journey and we encountered our first male New Yorkers. For they looked Mae and me over with sophisticated candor; we were treated to gallantries in the dining car and observed on the observation platform, and extremely urbane gentlemen tried to pick us up.

One middle-aged charmer tapped at our door and, addressing me, asked, "I beg your pardon, but are you by any chance Spanish?" On learning that I wasn't, he deftly bypassed his reason for asking and launched into affable generalities. (*N.B.* That old boy remained my friendly admirer until he died; he showered me with such respectful gifts as flowers, books, candy, and visits to the opera.) At any rate, the success Mae and I enjoyed on the Twentieth Century Limited augured well for even more romantic adventures once we landed in New York.

In Vachel's letters to Mae he had outlined plans for their future rendezvous; he would time his New York stay to coincide with ours and intended to put up at the old Brevoort Hotel on the periphery of Greenwich Village, a locale romantic enough to harbor any poet. At that time the Village was a *real* bohemia, where living was cheap, and its occupants were bona fide artists, poets, and playwrights who were romantically poor. During our first preparations for the trip, Mae, as a would-be sculptress, had suggested that we too live at the Brevoort. Of course we were both too prosperous to belong in the Village. My own salary was $250 a week at a time when every dollar was worth five of the kind we have today. Mae earned even more. But I had set my sights on the Hotel Algonquin because Doug Fairbanks, commenting on my addiction to the *Smart Set* magazine, had informed me that the Algonquin was the meeting place of the highbrow set to which Mencken and Nathan belonged. Thrillingly enough, Daddy Woods sided with me, as the Algonquin's central location on West 44th Street would make us more available to the press. So Mae and the Brevoort lost out.

Long before the Twentieth Century reached its destination, Mae and I were in our coats, hats, and even gloves. We stood gazing entranced at the big suburban apartment buildings as they came into view and were increasingly excited by the swarming streets of Harlem; then the train plunged into a tunnel that seemed endless and finally slid to a scarcely perceptible stop. New York at last.

Oblivious of my own group, I walked the length of Grand Central Station, through swarms of people who looked as if they were hurrying toward some exciting goal; there was none of the leth-

argy of Southern California, where nobody seems to have a destination worth getting to. The porters who ushered us through the
confusion made comments that were worth listening to. The driver
of the taxi into which we were bundled entertained us with observations on politics, philosophy, and the humanities in the enchant-
ing accents of Brooklyn. I've scarcely ever met a Brooklyn taxi-
driver with whom a *cérébrale* like I couldn't fall in love.

On reaching a suite at the Algonquin, I immediately set about
doing something I'd had in mind for years but had been forced to
postpone until I could get away from Mother. Before even starting
to unpack, I phoned down to the barber shop and asked for a loan
of the barber's scissors. Then, with hands actually trembling in excitement, I proceeded to whack off my hair, becoming one of the
very first girls of our century ever to be "bobbed."

Any change in a girl's hair-do produces a psychological effect
which it must be difficult for men to understand. Just as Samson
lost strength by getting his hair bobbed, girls gain theirs through
the process, a fact which must also have been discovered by Joan of
Arc and by Madame Casimir Dudevant, a suburban French house-
wife who cut her hair, took the name of George Sand, and started
life on a grand scale with Alfred de Musset and Chopin. About the
same time that I bobbed my hair, Irene Castle, then an obscure
American ballroom dancer working with her husband in a Paris
café, happened to cut hers too. What had prompted the two of us
to do it? As Irene told me later, she had never even seen a bobbed
head; neither had I. Perhaps fate was mystically getting us ready
for the stepped-up life of the flapper, so soon to take over on the
world scene. At any rate, thousands of girls saw pictures of Irene's
page-boy bob in the fashion magazines and rushed to follow suit,
and the trend of the twenties began. As a salute to the new mood,
Scott Fitzgerald wrote "Bernice Bobs Her Hair." My own short
hair instantly made me feel secure, free, and capable of taking on
the New York press. Sitting in the parlor of that Algonquin suite,
my feet missing the floor by a good sixteen inches, I held my shorn
head high and proceeded to give forth on D. W. Griffith, *Intolerance,* and culture in general. The discovery that those New York

reporters knew even less than I served to put me into the category of a charlatan, which I greatly relished. At any rate, my *entente* with the press was most sympathetic and I dated a number of those boys socially.

When the interviews were published they were sometimes accompanied by photos; Mother inevitably learned I had bobbed my hair and she wrote me in short but eloquent terms, "Oh, Anita!" But across the three thousand miles that separated us I was able to take the accusation in stride.

After *Intolerance* had been launched, with much confusion on the part of both audiences and the press, in spite of the "salons" I had held for it, D.W. decided to take advantage of a season mild enough for outdoor filming and remain in the East for a while. Mae sent for her family and, feeling that I had established my authority, I wrote Mother to join me. Her presence would supply an excuse for us to try out living in a furnished apartment as bona fide New Yorkers. Scarcely had we found an apartment, when word came from Vachel Lindsay that he would soon be at the Brevoort.

Mae's great moment was at hand. However, the first rendezvous with Vachel created a problem. The rather large Marsh family had moved into a flat on a teeming block of Riverside Drive which at best could only be called commonplace. Worse than that, it was overrun by Mae's noisy and nosy sisters and nieces; they wouldn't know how to behave in the presence of a poet who, gauged by the bittersweet tone of his letters, must be a cross between Lord Byron and John Barrymore. But I was once again able to come to Mae's rescue. The apartment Mother and I occupied was decorated in the august style of fake Louis XVI, with a parlor that was lighted by no less than seven floor lamps with shades of sexy red. I later realized that our West Side neighborhood was suspiciously transient and my landlady must have been in a wanton line of business. But Mae agreed that my parlor would be the ideal setting for a love affair destined to go down through the ages.

This, then, was to be our plot; when Vachel phoned Mae, she would invite him first to take tea at her girl friend Anita's apartment. Under this arrangement, I would come in handy during early lulls in the conversation and, once the ice was broken, I would disappear "to do some work," after which their tête-à-tête would proceed. Mae could then arrange for subsequent meetings in romantic little bistros of Greenwich Village, and Vachel might even come through with some artistic double date for me.

On the day of the rendezvous Mother was shipped off to Rahway for a visit with my alcoholic Auntie Nina, who was living there with her second husband. Before teatime Mae and I spent hours on a decor that featured a number of heavy cut-glass vases which we had filled with long-stemmed American Beauty roses. We softened the light effect by putting pink bulbs in all the lamps, and the air was perfumed with incense especially imported from Chinatown. Mae's freckles had disappeared under a coat of make-up, and as a gown worthy of the occasion she chose a green and gold Fortuny robe of the crinkled type which clung to her slim figure and even trailed a little bit. With her red-gold hair drifting in waves to her shoulders, Mae moved through the rosy atmosphere like Mélisande.

Our stage had been set long before Vachel was due to arrive, and waiting for him was a sort of delicate agony. But when our poet finally entered the scene, he broke every rule laid down by dramatic unity. He clashed violently with the background we had provided, and from head to toe he failed to conform. He resembled neither Byron nor Barrymore. His reddish hair was full of cowlicks which he had apparently never even tried to control. His shoes were made for his favorite form of travel, which was tramping. The most accurate image I can conjure up of poor darling Vachel is that of the red-headed ventriloquist's dummy called Mortimer Snerd.

He was a hurricane of activity; he seldom sat, he paced. He never spoke; he shouted, he bellowed, he roared. What he said was poetry, but nevertheless he roared it. The *ambiance* we had created put no damper on him; I doubt if he noticed the pink lighting and I'm sure no whiff of that incense permeated the pure breath of his nostrils. For no matter what locale Vachel entered, he always dragged the spirit of the cornfields with him. Disappointed in her lover as Mae was, she was even more embarrassed. Without any resources to meet the situation, she hadn't a word to say, and in her panic she made an unrehearsed excuse to go home and left me with Vachel on my hands.

I now feel that Vachel Lindsay's roaring bumptiousness was the camouflage of a tremendously sad man. Anyone as sensitive to physical beauty as he must have flinched at the sight of every mirror. Certainly he was lonely and avid for companionship; at any rate, he clutched at mine. That afternoon the transfer from Mae to me was so instantaneous he seemed scarcely to notice her departure.

The following two weeks we saw each other every day; we tramped through Central Park or, even better, roamed the byways of Greenwich Village; on all our outings Vachel never stopped extemporizing poetry. I didn't find an opening to confess the literary trick with which our friendship had begun, and I doubt if Vachel ever suspected it, so unaware was he of what went on outside his own overpowering thoughts. Finally, when forced to return home to Illinois, Vachel spoke of carrying me off to a cottage in Springfield, where we would live the classic American life within the confines of a white picket fence. So our Cyrano-de-Bergerac beginning might have had a romantic end, except that I couldn't measure up to my own dreams of living with a poet. There he was, one of the best of them, asking me to marry him, and I could only hedge and change the subject like the victim of that ancient jape, "Be careful what you wish for or you might get it." The upshot of his proposal was an evasive answer on my part that sent Vachel on his way confused. Our correspondence continued, but the lonely poet, only too used to having girls turn him down, touched only obliquely on romance. He always left a door open, but I was never tempted to enter in. The year following Mae's marriage, Vachel wrote me:

I do not know the exact stage of Mae Marsh's adventure, but hope her garden has blossomed by this time. By her account, we are to look for Castor and Pollux, Damon and Pythias, or something else in pairs. I think I will suggest Vachel and Rachel, if it is that kind of a pair.

After I myself married, Vachel's blessing read:

Be sure I send you my most fraternal Godspeed in your thrilling adventure. I feel very communicative indeed, for no one, not even me, knows what I may say. Look out! May Santy Claus come to see you every Christmas and George Washington every Fourth of July. May St. Valentine appear ever and anon through the whole year, and may all the other Saints bless you and keep you. . . . I wish I was married.

Poor Vachel never ceased falling in love, as a poet should, and sometimes he reported his romances to me:

I just saw the most beautiful red hair on a lovely 16 year old Tom-boy girl in Noo Orleans; a girl with a kind of a Kate Greenaway finish. I have written her a poem, and since she is only sixteen I'm not going to send it to her. [N.B. Those were the days before Lolita.] I will send it to you confidentially.

> What her Best Young
> Man Should Say To That
> Golden Haired Girl Over There
> If He Has Any Nerve
>
> You are a sunrise
> If a star should rise instead of the sun.
> You are a moonrise
> If a star should come instead of the moon—
> You are the Spring—
> If a face should bloom

Instead of an apple bough—
You are my girl,
If your heart is as kind
As your eyes are now.

In one of his last letters to me Vachel wrote:

I am home and take up two months of letters this morning—
yours the first.
"He who lives more lives than one, more deaths than one
must die."
I hope that you will think of me just as a person—unoffi-
cially as it were, once in a while. You have your picture on
my wall so I see you every day.

Vachel was always searching for the pioneer maiden with whom
he could live out his own version of the American dream. I failed
him, as Mae did, and most of the others. But I believe the great
tragedy of his life lay in the failure of the American dream to live
up to its rugged past. And when he felt that our native spirit was
losing its stamina, he lost his joy in living. I had a hint of this as
early as August 1920, when he wrote me, "I know I am a poor
thing, but take me as I am and do it at once before it is too late."
"Before it is too late"; how prophetic those words became in the
face of Vachel Lindsay's suicide.

A few years after the poet's death, I happened to be visiting the
Houghton Library in Cambridge, Massachusetts, with its curator,
Professor John Sweeney, and noticed a vitrine with a collection of
letters written by the poet Keats. I commented on the fact that I
too possessed some letters from a poet. Professor Sweeney was so
interested that I forthwith promised to send them to the library as a
gift, and there they now repose, an obscure hint that we Americans
have strayed too far from our hardy beginnings.

During the first New York summer I made some progress toward one day calling the magical city my home. Several lifelong
friendships began during my early peregrinations into Greenwich

Village with Vachel Lindsay; one of them with Hendrik van Loon, the historian. Van Loon's books, written in an informal, chatty manner, and illustrated with his own rather unprofessional sketches, still provide a very painless briefing on world history, particularly for young readers. Hendrik was a typical Hollander, big, rugged and unkempt, with tousled brown hair and an air of always feeling awkward. I treasure the first mash note he wrote me:

Miss,

A perplexed young man went to his spiritual advisors and asked for counsel.

He said that he was very bashful in this big city and had met a very beautiful young lady made of solid gold and subtle little ideas. Could he take her out for dinner?

Hendrik and I corresponded throughout his lifetime, his letters illuminated by the type of casual sketches that illustrate his books. We always planned a trip to his native Holland, where he was to have been my guide. It never took place, to my regret.

In Greenwich Village I also came to know Max Eastman, the Daddy of socialism in the United States, and the editor of *The Masses*. Affluent though I was, I became a cover girl on *The Masses*, and a favorite model for its far-to-the-left staff artist, Frank Waltz. Never having had a mind for politics, I brought my theories on the subject into focus during my friendship with Waltz and Eastman. They were (and still are) founded on the fact that whatever party happens to be in control, its personnel tends to be human and will be affected by blondes, bribery, and attempts at tax evasion. My radical friends used to think I was cute and laughed at my views, which I promised to revise the next time the United States produced an Abraham Lincoln. In the meanwhile, I preferred not to tamper with a capitalism which, at the time, was producing some very delectable rogues.

I was able to invade another area of New York that was much more elegant than the Village. It was located on Park Avenue, which was just being penetrated by the smart set, and its first citizen was Frank Crowninshield, the editor of *Vanity Fair,* unofficial host of the city, and wonderful gentleman of the arts. Crownie's magazine, together with *Smart Set,* had an enormously civilizing effect on the United States; but while Mencken's policy was to boot our native land into an awareness of culture, Crownie's was to lead us there with a gentle, properly gloved hand. In spite of Crownie's association with writers, artists, and assorted bohemians, both at home and in Europe, he always retained the stuffy conservatism of his Back Bay Boston family.

I had been brought to Crownie's notice by submitting from California a short article to his magazine; titled "The Force of Heredity and Nella," it was accepted and only recently reprinted in *Vanity Fair: A Cavalcade of the 1920s and 1930s,* edited by Cleveland Amory and Crownie's nephew, Frederic Bradlee. As soon as Crownie learned that one of his new contributors was in town, he phoned to invite me to lunch. When we met, I found him to be a slender and elegant gentleman of middle age, which he couldn't possibly have been, but, as an American, Crownie was too soigné ever to have seemed young. His hair, clothes, and even his pale benevolent eyes gave a chaste impression of grayness.

My lunch date with Crownie was at old Delmonico's, an occasion made unforgettable by the entrance of the most ravishing blonde of that decade, Gaby Deslys, in the company of an exquisite foreign-looking gentleman. She wore "ropes" of pearls, as they were then called, and they were so enormous that one could almost hear them clank. Mademoiselle Deslys was a friend of Crownie's (as who in all that glamour spot wasn't?), and he rose in homage when she neared our table in an aura of perfume. Seeing Crownie in company with someone so childlike, Gaby treated us to the fond smile one might turn on an indulgent uncle giving his little niece a treat. After she passed by, Crownie proceeded to defend Gaby's reputation and assured me decorously that any rumor connecting her with King Manuel of Portugal was a lie. But Crownie's gallantry made one rather skeptical; how could anyone less than a king come through with pearls like those? During luncheon

Crownie entertained me with inside, but highly proper, stories of other of his youthful French connections: Pablo Picasso, Bébé Bérard, Cocteau, and Colette.

When we parted that afternoon Crownie asked if he might make me a present of a dress. It arrived the next day and proved to be adapted from the uniform of a French schoolgirl, with a white collar of the type called "Claudine," after Colette's naughty teenage heroine. In spite of Crownie's warm paternal attitude, there was a brief moment after his gift arrived when my antennae picked up a thought wave which no doubt emanated from poor Mother: "You'll have to 'pay' for that dress." But nobody ever had to pay darling Crownie for a single one of his daily acts of generosity.

On that first visit to New York my pursuit of Mencken never reached a culmination, and it was then I learned that he spent little time in the city, that his home was in Baltimore and he came to New York only when editorial duties required his presence. But I did catch sight of him one day across the lobby of the Algonquin. My first impression of Mencken was of his arresting masculinity; he was smoking a big cigar which he held, like Pop, at a jaunty angle; aside from that sign of maturity, Henry Mencken looked like a young farmhand who was dressed in his best, with too much starch in his shirt and too high a collar. His boyish appearance made him all the more fascinating, for it aroused a girl's motherly instincts.

In view of Mencken's desirability, it is odd that, to a certain extent, he resembled Vachel Lindsay; both men, while scrupulously neat, paid small attention to grooming; their hair was full of cowlicks, of which a tuft or two always stood on end. But Mencken's pale blue eyes had the permanent expression of an impudent schoolboy, and one felt that he was in full control at all times, while Vachel always gave an impression of floundering. That I never met my idol on that occasion was largely my own fault, for as a bachelor he greatly fancied the opposite sex and was the essence of gallantry. But the very excess of my adoration made me bashful, and my opportunity slipped by. Neither did I meet

George Jean Nathan, who, a blatant Don Juan, occupied a love nest at the Royalton Hotel across the street from the Algonquin.

However, I was initiated into that celebrated group called the Round Table, which assembled for lunch at the Algonquin every day. At its center was Alexander Woollcott, drama critic, humorist, and later radio commentator; another of its bright lights was Franklin P. Adams, who wrote a daily newspaper column signed F. P. A.; the reigning queen of the Round Table was the artist Neysa McMein, who painted cover girls for magazines, *Cosmopolitan* in particular.

Crownie had introduced me to Neysa soon after my arrival in New York. She was a magnificent young creature, a Brünnhilde with a classic face, tawny hair that scorned a brush or comb, and a style of dress for which her inspiration could only have been a grab-bag. But all New York knew she was the heroine of a succession of romances with extremely prominent men. When Neysa invited me to her studio I accepted, but I confess to being critical of her; to me Neysa's unkempt appearance seemed phony and even a little conceited; it was as if Cinderella had purposely gone to the ball in rags, knowing they'd make her all the more a sensation.

I found Neysa's studio in a rundown old building on West 57th Street. Its big main room was a pale yet dirty beige and, although sparsely furnished, it gave an impression of being cluttered because of a jumble of coats, overshoes, sporting gear, and bundles. That day the studio was occupied by a number of Round Table regulars, but by the end of the afternoon I dismissed them as being without interest, except for Dorothy Parker and Herbert Bayard Swope. I thought the others very naïve indeed. Although self-styled intellectuals, they were concerned with nothing more weighty than the personal items about themselves that were dished up in gossip columns; their conversation was a rehash of easy forms of exhibitionism in which they had recently indulged, such as parlor games and croquet tournaments; the latter seemed to have been punctuated by childish fits of temper, which I figured were more assumed than real, probably trumped up for any audience they could capture, most particularly each other.

As a group, they behaved with that overly casual air which is an attempt of the unsophisticated to appear at ease; Neysa made some offhand comment on the fact that she was wearing one brown and one black shoe, the mates of which had been left that morning in a certain gentleman's apartment. Another manifestation of their self-consciousness lay in hobbledehoy bad manners, at which Woollcott excelled. He was just as unkempt as Neysa, but fat, fuzzy, and fussy to boot. The others seemed to take pride in the ill-tempered cracks they inspired in Woollcott. It was a contradiction that his drama columns bubbled over with praise for a constant succession of his rather schoolgirl type of crushes. Having learned that George Jean Nathan had termed Woollcott "The Seidlitz Powder of Times Square," and that the appellation hurt, I was predisposed to look down my nose at him.

Woollcott, however, unleashed one of his enthusiasms in my direction. It happened that the subject of modern art entered the conversation, by way of a comment I made about one of Schnitzler's plays then running on Broadway. I mentioned that the heaviness of its decor smacked more of Munich than of the Vienna of its correct locale. Raising his eyebrows in interest, Woollcott asked when I had been in Munich, and I told him never. That an American girl had heard of Munich, even as a locality, staggered him. "How do you happen to *know* about Munich?" he asked. I remarked that one of the mainstreams of the new art movement then flooding the world had its source there. This was a fact which should have been known to anyone engaged, as was Woollcott, in commenting on the *mores* of his day, but Woollcott simply couldn't get over my "erudition." He proceeded to usher me through the group that afternoon, burbling, "This child *from Hollywood* knows all about modern art!" The group was duly impressed by its oracle, and perhaps I should have been gratified, but I knew next to nothing about modern art, and the fact that Alex knew even less gave him a place on my own private dunce list from which he was never ousted.

Dorothy Parker was small, dark, and fragile, with a sharp, pretty face and an air of being almost too sensitive to what went on about her. Although a permanent member of the Round Table, she was no dolt; she seldom spoke, and when she did her remarks, although bitter, were not snide and they were cleansed of offense by their wit. That day there was a comment on a telegram Dorothy had just sent two friends on hearing of their marriage, after they had been living together for some time. It merely read, "What's new?"

When I was introduced to Dorothy, she greeted me with an almost caressing enthusiasm that was the reverse of the self-consciously casual air that permeated Neysa's salon. But I sensed that her overfriendliness could only be a sardonic comment on the fact that she had no belief at all in friendship and knew herself to be a lone wolverine. I doubted that she found any true companionships among members of the Round Table, and felt that she had given in to their advances on the theory that she might as well be with them as elsewhere. At any rate, its members provided endless cues for her brilliant sarcasm, which they no more resented than they did the crude insults of Alex Woollcott, doubtlessly considering the barbs to be a fair price to pay for the honor of being accepted by the two of them.

I failed to make contact with Dorothy on that or any other occasion, and we never became friends; I was overawed by her brilliant mind and had no desire to be a target for her irony. Let me quote a Parkerism of several years later, when both Dorothy and I lived in Hollywood. At that time the darling of the entire film colony was a movie star who was backed by a man of great wealth. He had caused an elaborate bungalow to be built at the studio to serve her as a dressing room. It was of Spanish style, and in a niche over its front door was the statue of a Madonna, which inspired the following jingle from Dorothy:

> Upon my honor
> I saw a Madonna
> Standing in a niche
> Above the door
> Of a prominent whore
> Of a prominent son of a bitch.

One may easily gather that Dorothy's presence anywhere tended to produce an atmosphere of tension.

At the time I first met Dorothy she was in love with the youthful newspaper reporter and budding dramatist Charlie MacArthur. Her crush was as fervid as it was ill-advised, for, up to the time that Charlie fell in love with little Helen Hayes, he was not to be pinned down by any one girl. Charlie, together with his fellow wit Bob Benchley, covered New York like an impecunious Harun al-Rashid, taking in every phase of its swarming life, even the Round Table. In time Dorothy learned that Charlie was carrying on an affair with another girl, and I always wondered whether Charlie might have been the inspiration for Dorothy's poem "Résumé":

> Razors pain you;
> Rivers are damp;
> Acids stain you;
> And drugs cause cramp.
> Guns aren't lawful;
> Nooses give;
> Gas smells awful;
> You might as well live.

A really informed member of the Round Table was Herbert Bayard Swope, for many years executive director of the *New York World*. Swope possessed an encyclopedic brain and he remembered everything he had ever read. I hung on his words with almost as much interest as he did himself. When Herb ran out of breath, he had a trick that insured against loss of attention; he would come out with a resounding conjunction, hold up his hand to stop anyone from cutting in, and then, refueled by fresh oxygen, continue his magnificent monologue. Herb Swope looked like an orator; his enormous frame was impressive, his halo of red hair arresting, and his voice stentorian.

From my early position as a distant onlooker at Mencken, Nathan, and their cronies, it seemed significant that, although they

The only thing wrong with this picture is that an authoress like I never learned how to type.

My sole preparation for a career was to buy a fountain pen and a large yellow pad: no dictionary or grammar required. Some day I'll give a course on how to succeed in literature without any learning.

Grandpa George Smith was hum drum, but Grandma Cleopatra pr vided the family closet with fascinating skeleton.

My mother, Minnie, was an earth-bound angel. . .

... which may have been the reason why Pop was a scamp.

But don't be fooled by Pop's female attire. His single lifelong preference was for the ladies.

My first contact with ESP was provided by a lady of
the Klamath Tribe of Indians named Smoothy.

My birthplace looked like a movie set for a D.W.
Griffith film of homespun American life down on
the farm.

When I was three, Pop put me to work advertising his weekly newspaper, thus instituting my lifelong joy in working for the men I've loved, for free.

My sister Gladys was generally mistaken for my twin because, although she was blond and two years younger, we were of an identical size.

My brother Clifford was to be the family pride; he became a distinguished pioneer in the practice of group medicine.

Cleopatra's sister Ella flashed her blond sex appeal on the early-day miners of Virginia City, Nevada. (*N.B.* I left Aunt Ella out of the book; I doubt that she inspired the name of that virgin outpost.)

But Aunt Nina's blond sex appeal got her as far as Paris, France.

Uncle Horace was an international racketeer on so grand a scale that he even took in Imperial Russia. He was the first and last gentleman who ever bought me diamonds; and I was only seven.

In the publicity campaign for a stage production of
Quo Vadis? Gladys and I were featured as a snack
for a man-eating lion, but it is all too apparent that
he had already been stuffed with sawdust.

When I played in *Little Lord Fauntleroy* I broke
tradition by disdaining the black velvet suit and lace
collar, which, in my opinion, were prissy.

I wrote many scripts for Fay Tincher, the popular comedy star of silent films, with such titles as *Nearly a Burglar's Bride, Saved by the Soup, Laundry Liz, The Deacon's Whiskers, Only a Fireman's Love.*

Fay's interpretation of the title role in *Nellie, the Female Villain* brought out every one of that character's dimensions.

The first movie I wrote, *The New York Hat*, was directed by D.W. Griffith, with Mary Pickford, Lionel Barrymore, and a cast of such distinguished extras as Lillian and Dorothy Gish.

Movies were so disdained by the intelligentsia that we never realized D.W. was a genius; but nevertheless we breathed a rarefied and somewhat disturbing air when in his presence.

Nobody who has seen *The Birth of a Nation* will ever forget Lillian Gish's brief encounter with a Confederate soldier. He was an obscure extra named Walter Freeman, a passive instrument on which D.W. extemporized.

Culver Pictures, Inc.

OVERLEAF:

A set for *Intolerance* provided the background for an incident in *Gentlemen Prefer Blondes*, when Lorelei Lee fainted as a gentleman fell off a tower.

Culver Pictures, Inc.

One of the still pictures I studied for inspiration when I wrote subtitles
for D.W.'s *Intolerance.*

The movie version of *Macbeth* starred Sir Herbert Tree and Constance
Collier. D.W. can be seen on the sidelines, but the film was directed by
John Emerson, with subtitles co-authored by A. Loos and W. Shakespeare.

This picture is 100 per cent publicity. Mabel Normand was never like that.

Movies can be made or ruined in the cutting room. It was one of the first places my husband put me to work for him.

For a while Mae Marsh got terribly artistic and took to sculpture.

patronized the Algonquin dining room and bar, they kept away
from the Round Table. So, after realizing that I'd never meet my
hero in that coterie, I ceased accepting their invitations. In fact, my
association with the group was of so little moment to me that there
is small need to mention it, except that several years later it gave
rise to an interview with Alec Woollcott that stands out as one of
the most astounding psychological demonstrations I ever witnessed. I hesitate to write about it; in the first place it's so incredible that nobody will believe it, I can hardly believe it myself. Sec-
ondly, it shows poor Alec in a pitifully embarrassing light. But
what actually happened was that he phoned one morning and, taking me completely by surprise, asked if I would come to tea some
day at his apartment. I had just written a derisive piece about the
Round Table and Alec in particular, and felt that his only possible
motive for seeing me was to demand an apology. This was pretty
disturbing, although Woollcott had sounded extremely cordial. At
any rate, there was no excuse to decline his invitation, so I set a
time for our rendezvous. I found Alec alone, and for a while he
spoke in generalities, which he presented interrupted to say that
there was something he wanted to show me. It proved to be a faded
old photograph of some youths in a college play. Alec, his hand
shaking, indicated himself as a character dressed in girl's clothes.
Suddenly floodgates of emotion opened up, and Alec burst out
with the statement that he had always wanted to be a girl. As I was
reacting to his confession rather quizzically, Alec reached an outlandish climax in which he declared, "All my life I've wanted to be
a mother!" I had no idea how to take the disclosure; was he joking,
or tight, or what? Sensing my bewilderment, Woollcott grasped
my hands in both of his and proceeded only to add to it. "Now that
you understand me better, do you think we can be friends?" As his
guest, there seemed only one polite answer, which was an evasive
"Why not?"—after which I made the quickest possible escape.
From then on I'm afraid I avoided Alec even more assiduously than
before. Whenever we met, it was by chance, and the poor soul
never again mentioned that lamentable tête-à-tête.

When time came for D. W.'s troupe to return to Hollywood Mae was completely satisfied and, her curiosity appeased, anxious to get home. But I left New York stubbornly intent on getting back there. The only way to manage it was to make Ella Woods's giddy prophecies for me come true.

✤ CHAPTER 8

✤Soon after our return to California, Daddy Woods suggested to D. W. that I stop my other activities and devote all my time to writing for Doug Fairbanks. He had now zoomed to the top of the industry, his fame equaled only by Mary Pickford's, although before long Charlie Chaplin would share their worldwide acclaim and they would become a powerful triumvirate. Movies were still, as Vachel Lindsay put it, "today's divine surprise," but now they had begun to affect the daily existence of people everywhere; those of us who were creating them led lives as they had never before been lived in show business, and our jobs were so colored by fun, success, and the discovery of exciting new techniques that we worked in a constant state of euphoria.

In addition to a professional crew, Doug acquired a group of stooges, for he was the innovator of the Hollywood institution of the "yes man," without which no movie mogul to this day ever functions. Prominent in Doug's retinue were two prizefighters, Spike Robinson and Bull Montana, who drew salaries for sparring with the boss. Spike behaved with the ponderous dignity of an ex-champ, but Bull Montana was as gentle as a lamb. He had cauliflower ears, a cauliflower nose, and also a cauliflower brain which supplied the troupe with low comedy that was almost Shakespearean. Another important member of our group was Doug's valet, Buddy, a bright young man of sepia color who took a large part in all our fun.

It's hard to remember how those early Fairbanks scripts ever got written. Seeing that typewriter desks and chairs are designed for full-grown people, I never learned to type; it was more pleasant to curl up on a chaise longue in my room at the Hollywood Hotel and scribble my plots on a big yellow pad. The only thing that required serious thought was a basic theme; once I hit on it, the rest was child's play. After finishing an outline, I would be driven to the studio in one of the company limousines, the elegance of which I never got used to. We held our conferences in Doug's dressing room. It was equipped with a punching bag, electric horse, and boxing gloves and looked like a gymnasium. Interrupted by Doug's boisterous clowning with Spike and Bull, and the appreciative guffaws of Buddy, I would read my script aloud.

In deference to Doug's idol, Teddy Roosevelt, the action always had to conform to "the strenuous life," and my heroes always had to be on the move. Sometimes I attempted a love scene that would have required Doug to calm down and be sentimental for a moment, but he invariably broke it up to say with a grin, "I can't play that, Nita! Hell—I'm no actor." So my most seductive love scenes had to be interrupted by an abrupt and sometimes unaccountable bit of action, requiring Doug to jump onto a chandelier or swim upstream over a waterfall. Doug was so lacking in fear that, no matter what the risk, he never allowed a stunt man to substitute for him. But on one occasion he turned coward in the presence of us all. It was during a scene where my hero had to deflate an automobile tire by sticking a hatpin in it. John Emerson shot the action several times, but Doug bungled every take just at the point of sticking the pin into the tire. Finally he broke down and confessed. "I can't do this," he said. "I'm scared." We all thought Doug was kidding, but he was actually afraid the tire would blow up and blind him, so John had to make use of the first and last stunt man Doug ever required.

Sometimes the idea for a film would come from an outside source, such one that was mailed in by a young reporter Doug had encountered in Chicago. His name was Ben Hecht, and his plot was flippantly scrawled on the back of a used envelope. It concerned a young man who had been rejected by his sweetheart and was bent on suicide. Being too cowardly to do the job himself, the hero hired a mob of gangsters to shoot him by surprise from ambush. No sooner was the deal made than the sweetheart relented and agreed to marry the hero, from which point it was up to me to concoct his frantic endeavors to track down the leader and cancel the deal. The movie, titled *Double Trouble*, was a huge success.

We never ceased playing practical jokes on each other. I remember running across a novel one day of the *Elsie Dinsmore* or *Pollyanna* variety, written for retarded teenage girls. John and I sent it to Doug with a note which read, "On the surface this book doesn't look like material for a picture, but it has the germ of an idea that Nita might develop into something exciting. Our option runs out tomorrow, so you'll have to read it tonight. Hate to rush you, but the situation is pressing." The next day Buddy reported he had been forced to stay up all night supplying the Boss with black coffee so he could wade through a book that only a moron could stomach. It wasn't until Doug reached its soggy end that he realized he'd been had.

It was a natural conclusion that any joke would be avenged, and a chain reaction of pay-offs went on and on. I'm afraid the Fairbanks unit was going through an epidemic of swelled heads; however, Doug was so beguiling that Griffith let him get away with any amount of rowdy behavior. But while our blissful hilarity was invading the decorum of the Griffith studio, dark clouds had begun to gather, and one day the storm broke over my own head. I was told that D. W. wanted to speak to me and, excited as always by a summons from the Master, I joined him on the open lot. I can't remember that D. W. ever had an office; the entire studio was his office; he was too active and restless ever to sit down at a desk. Pacing back and forth and speaking in an offhand manner that must have covered great anguish, D. W. stated that the New York banks which financed his pictures had decided to withdraw their backing and liquidate his company.

As I reacted, stunned by the bad news, D. W. proceeded to tell me that his contract with Doug was nearing an end and that the banks had now arranged for Doug to have his own company and make pictures apart from him. I was deeply shocked by what I took to be Doug's treachery to Griffith, who had brought him into the movies and was responsible for his entire career. But D. W. went on to say that the new arrangement was going to benefit me very much, since both Doug and the banks were anxious to keep the Fairbanks unit intact, with John Emerson to direct and me to write the scripts, for which I would be paid double my present salary. When D. W. finished telling what he apparently felt was to me good news, I could only speak up timorously to ask if I might remain with him. D. W. was both surprised and touched, having taken it for granted that I'd welcome the opportunity to go with Doug. D. W. assured me that there would always be a place for me with him but that it could only involve the writing of subtitles; that it would be a great mistake for me not to go with Doug, who was so ideal an instrument for the expression of my ideas. I indulged in one of the few emotional moments I ever allowed myself and told D. W. that neither money nor ambition meant as much to me as working close to a man of his genius. I remember that D. W. grew misty when I said that, but just the same he grinned his Jovian grin and asked what caused me to consider any man a "genius" who had so little appreciated my work that he allowed it to be buried in the files of Daddy Woods's office. He reminded me that I owed a debt of loyalty to John Emerson, who had fought to make my stories into films at a time when nobody else recognized their potentialities. "I don't know what John Emerson would do without you," said D. W. Still wavering, I explained my feelings about Doug's betrayal, and Griffith proceeded to put my mind at ease on that score, explained that Doug had turned down the banks' offer until D. W. himself advised him to accept it. D. W. rationalized that he had never taken any satisfaction in Doug's success because he had been able to contribute so little to his pictures. He added that Fairbanks would always dominate any studio in which he worked, and the Jovian smile again came into play as D. W. remarked that it wasn't in his nature to play second fiddle.

I let D. W. convince me that I should go with Doug, but it would

be the saddest good-by of my youth when the time came to leave. I
never knew the magnitude of D. W.'s own tragedy until it was explained to me years later by Lillian Gish. It appeared that, following the public's cold reception of *Intolerance*, the banks had summoned Griffith to New York, where they put him on the rack for
not letting them know what he was "up to" when he made a film
which, in their words, was "an act of criminal folly." The accusation staggered D. W., seeing that the profits still being earned by
The Birth of a Nation could wipe out any losses on *Intolerance* and
still leave them with enormous gains. The ruthlessness of his backers so wounded Griffith that he offered to pay them a million dollars and take *Intolerance* off their hands. The banks accepted with
brutal eagerness, and Griffith incurred a debt that crippled him
financially for the remainder of his life.

After breaking with Doug, Griffith went East to find new backing and produce pictures far from Hollywood. Years went by during which I scarcely even saw him; show business is like that, so
absorbing that when one phase of it is over there's little time to
take a backward look. And no sooner was Doug established in a
new studio than our activities took on further speed and hilarity.
The same Eastern backers who had condemned D. W. for not letting them know what he was "up to" never even asked what we
were doing, for Doug's pictures were pouring streams of gold into
their banks. Doug imported a pal from his native Denver, a young
socialite and playboy named Al Parker, whom he made his general
manager. Al was not only a companion in all our fun, but he also
learned how to manage. (He is now prominent in theatrical London and married to the beautiful stage star Margaret Johnston.)

Our cameraman was Victor Fleming. Vic had been a taxi-driver
whose cab was stationed just outside the front gate, from which
position he worked his way inside the studio as an extra. He was
tall, handsome, and engaging and might have become a successful
actor, but Vic's interest lay in the technical side of movie-making;
after mastering the camera, he argued John Emerson into trying
him out as assistant director. John was again a stepping-stone for a
noteworthy career, for among the many features Vic was to direct

were *Gone with the Wind* and *Mutiny on the Bounty*. When Vic became assistant director, our camera was taken over by Oliver Marsh, Mae Marsh's brother, a mere curly-headed boy but so expert at his job that he made it seem like play.

The film colony was small in those days and studios were not so insular as they became later on, owing to the enormous distances between movie lots. The over-all leader in most of Hollywood's fun was Sid Grauman, the bright young showman who managed Hollywood's two largest movie houses, one being the still existent Grauman's Chinese. Sid's theaters were inherited from his father, who, having started in San Francisco, had followed the movie tide and gone south. Sid, when little more than a boy, had taken charge of the family business and increased its holdings. He looked like the Mad Hatter, small and wiry with an enormous nose and a halo of fuzzy red hair. Sid was far ahead of his time in the fine art of advertising, discovering as he did that vast wealth could be earned by idiocy. His showmanship was never confined to the screen itself, for Sid devised stunts outside his theaters that caused crowds of tourists to gather on the sidewalk and gape in wonder. When exploiting *Intolerance*, he set up an armed guard, dressed in the period of Belshazzar, to parade on the roof of his theater. What they were supposed to be guarding was beside the point; the fact that they were on the roof twenty-four hours of the day suggested danger from afar, which so excited the yokels that *Intolerance* had a longer run at Sid's theater than in any other spot of the United States. His most famous tour de force survives: the footprints left by movie stars in the cement outside the gaudy entrance of Grauman's Chinese.

Sid's principal adherent was Jack Pickford, Mary's kid brother and one of the most devastatingly attractive characters I ever knew. His boyish charm and good looks could easily have made Jack a successful movie star, but he neglected his career and preferred a life of pleasure, generally financed by his idolizing but at the same time disapproving sister, Mary. There is no male quite so provocative as one who lives off some adoring woman (a theme appreciated by Colette when she wrote *Chéri*). Jack Pickford's career in the world of pleasure had begun in New York when, at the tender age of fifteen, he had been taken in charge by Ziegfeld's most delectable showgirl, Lillian Lorraine, and initiated into what every young man ought not to know, which included an overindulgence in alcohol. Jack was doomed. At a time when most boys are having measles, he was contracting cirrhosis of the liver and doctors were warning him that alcohol would be as deadly to him as cyanide, a prediction which didn't interfere for a moment with his love of laughter, ladies, and liquor. I have known very few drunks who were good company; Jack Pickford heads the list. He indulged in that profligacy of time, health, and money that I have seen in several others who died very young. Carole Lombard and Jean Harlow had the same outlaw spirit of fun, and so had little Mary MacArthur, the daughter of Helen Hayes and Charlie.

As a child I myself had a precocious sense of humor, about which one of the wisest men I ever knew threw a scare into me later. He was Viscount D'Abernon, a close friend I made in England on my first trip there, in the twenties. Lord D'Abernon used to counsel me so seriously about my health that one day I asked the reason why, and he rather frighteningly explained that a too sharp sense of humor in the very young may indicate their lives will be short and they thus have an ingrained perspective on the futility of serious schemes. Perhaps, in my case, curiosity about those schemes has kept me going.

Along with Jack Pickford's nonchalance went a matter-of-fact acceptance of death which must be the only healthy attitude toward it. The last time I was with him was in the bar at the Savoy Hotel in London, where he was drinking, as usual, against the grave warning of a Harley Street specialist. Presently Jack began to chuckle. "I've just played a joke on one of these British tailors," he said. "I've ordered five new suits that he'll never collect on because corpses don't pay bills!"

Jack and Sid Grauman, except for their love of jokes, couldn't have been more different. Jack was always involved with girls while Sid, a mamma's boy, had no interest in any other woman. Sid never drank, and during the daytime, when Jack was sleeping off the previous night's hangover, Sid was in his office cooking up schemes to publicize his theaters. Sid worked equally hard at concocting practical jokes, and the reason they succeeded was that all his publicity stunts seemed so foolish that one couldn't differentiate between them.

Some of Sid's jokes required the most elaborate preparation. There was one time when, in his role as an impresario, he announced the discovery of two fabulous nature dancers who were destined to take their places along with Isadora Duncan and Ruth St. Denis. Sid said that he had signed the team to an exclusive contract and that he wanted his friends to witness a demonstration of their art. In order to present the dancers in a proper setting, Sid organized an all-night picnic on the beach at Malibu, with a gaudy arrangement of tents for sleeping and dining. There were about thirty guests, who comprised most of the film elite of the period; among them Jack, Mary, and Lottie Pickford, Doug and Beth Fairbanks, and Bebe Daniels. During the evening there was an undertone of drama in the air, for Doug and Mary were covertly involved in the beginning of their epoch-making romance. Another famous star was desperately in love with Jack Pickford, and I myself had begun to dream about a December-May idyl with John Emerson.

When time came for the main event of the evening, Sid ordered us to a semicircle of beach chairs that had been set up facing the ocean, and proceeded ceremoniously to bang on a big Oriental gong. As a hush settled over the audience, two earnest young homosexuals in sketchy garments of ancient Greece leaped from behind a big black rock and, in the moonlight, flung themselves into a routine of posturing which emphasized the most unfortunate mannerisms of their type. Sid's build-up had been so earnest that it was a long moment before we realized the two unsuspecting little things had been sacrificed to give Sid's guests a Roman holiday.

Another of Sid's victims was Jesse Lasky, for whom we had a fondness based on his excellence as a butt for jokes. Jesse was the first of the early producers to take the art of the films seriously. He was given to making speeches in defense of the movies to any organization that would sit still and listen. On one occasion Sid, having acquired some letter paper from the Pasadena Chamber of Commerce, invited Jesse to deliver an address to its members. Jesse arranged for the affair to take place in the big projection room of the Paramount Studios, and on the night in question Sid and Jack Pickford filled all the seats in the room with dummies borrowed from the prop department; after which they arranged the lighting so that it shone in Jesse's eyes and prevented a clear view of his audience. Jesse made a scholarly entrance, flicked his pince-nez glasses and, although a little disturbed by the lack of applause, launched into an earnest defense of our industry. As Jesse continued, his audience applauded not; he attempted jokes at which they failed to laugh. The more silent their reaction, the harder Jesse strove, until he was fairly breaking out in perspiration. When he had had enough of our joke, Sid turned the lights on full. It was a long time before Jesse forgave any of us.

Throughout the excitement of life in Hollywood, Doug, John, and I never lost our distaste for it. In those days a trip to New York took five days each way, but during our two weeks' layoff between pictures we thought nothing of spending ten days on a train in order to be in New York for four, to breathe the brisk Eastern air after a term in the flabby *ambiance* of Southern California. On those trips Doug would travel with an ever-increasing "gallery," and our progress on the Santa Fe Chief was one long triumph. By this time the public had become aware that movie stars were tangible entities. Doug held forth at stations along the line, standing on train platforms like a Presidential candidate and haranguing his public along the lines of conduct laid down by Teddy Roosevelt, advocating a strenuous life of noble purpose flavored by the pure love of a man's first, last, and only helpmeet. Little did Doug realize that his championship of Teddy Roosevelt would soon bring on nightmares in which his hero's famous big white teeth would loom up and bite him.

&2Sometimes, when nostalgia for New York became acute, I managed to contrive a plot like that of *Manhattan Madness*, which required New York exteriors, and we would go East for several weeks to film them. While working in New York we were without shame in exacting the use of locations; in one of my plots a Fifth Avenue mansion was required as the home of a debutante whom the hero was wooing against the wishes of her family. The action was to show Doug being turned from his loved one's door, and John Emerson had selected an impressive town house, in front of which, without asking anyone's permission, he ordered Oliver Marsh to set up his camera. Oliver proceeded to grind away while Doug bounded up the steps and rang the bell. When a dignified butler answered, Doug blithely asked if Mrs. Hossefrosse was at home and was politely informed that he had come to the wrong address. Whereat Doug, finding the butler's behavior too mild, brashly put up an argument, during which the butler suddenly noticed spectators gathering around our strange-looking crew on the sidewalk and irately slammed the door in Doug's face. The scene was exactly what we required; the butler fitted his role better than any hired actor, and, moreover, the price was right. Those were the days of carefree and economical movie-making. And when viewing the old silent films one senses an intangible spirit and spontaneity in them that are missing in the elaborate concoctions which Hollywood developed later on.

In New York I had no opportunity to meet Mencken, for whom I would still have relegated John Emerson to second place. I also saw little of the New York friends I had made previously, since I was required to serve as a member of Doug's court. Once in a while, however, I spent time with a Chicago journalist who came to New York frequently on business. Our romance never reached a culmination because he had long been involved with New York's most famous nightlife figure, Texas Guinan. If he had ever married Texas, it would have been quite honorable to divorce, but to desert a sweetheart who lived in the white light of publicity would have subjected her to the wrong kind of scandalous headlines. Actually I think we were both glad of an alibi; my sentiments for John Emerson were on the rise, and I fear my beau thought Texas capable of taking a pot shot at him. At any rate, we were resigned to our fate and indulged in that favorite diversion of lovers in New York: wandering through off-beat neighborhoods, enjoying a vicarious thrill at being a part of the teeming life of the city.

Doug's entire troupe lived at the Algonquin Hotel, where he found no difficulty in being its most prominent guest, but he shared the New York limelight with one other celebrity, the musical-comedy star, Elsie Janis. Elsie and Doug had been friends from the time when he was a mere Broadway juvenile, better known around the Lambs Club than he was to audiences, while Elsie was already the toast of New York. Her first hit show had been *The Vanderbilt Cup,* in one scene of which she was disguised as a racing driver in boys' clothes, which always suited her better than girls'. Elsie's greatest talent was for imitation; she used to sing "Sonny Boy" in the manner of Al Jolson, accomplishing that mass-hypnotism of audiences which is a sure test of stardom.

Together with her mother, Elsie instituted a running celebration at their Park Avenue apartment in honor of Doug's spectacular rise to fame; parties went on every night after the theater, based on the theme "We knew him when." All New York's theatrical celebrities showed up at those affairs; it was there I first met John Barrymore; his distinguished sister Ethel; their uncle, that monocled and mustached old aristocrat of the theater John Drew; and New York's favorite comedian, Raymond Hitchcock, then starring in *Hitchy Koo*. The group was a cut above that of the Round Table, in so far as their amusements were not contrived but spontaneous and there was plenty of wit on display, but I was only an amused onlooker of what I took to be their exhibitionism.

Elsie Janis was always romantically involved with whatever leading man happened to be playing opposite her, and at that period he was Walter Pidgeon, a youth whom Elsie herself had discovered. He had an exceptionally fine voice, of which most theatergoers are unaware today, for Walter chose to give up singing in order to play the nonmusical roles which made him a star in both the theater and the movies. We all felt that Ma Janis's morbid possessiveness was ruining Elsie's chances with Walter Pidgeon, just as we realized that Ma was squandering her daughter's earnings on things for which Elsie had no use nor even any liking. I remember an occasion when Tomboy Elsie appeared wearing a pair of exotic black pearl earrings which by rights should have belonged to Theda Bara. Elsie was much more at ease when, during World War I, she dressed as a doughboy in olive drab and entertained soldiers at the front— adored as a pal by all of them.

Poor Elsie was forced to pay a big price for her mother's extravagance. By the time Ma Janis died she had spent all Elsie's earnings, but much more tragic was the fact that she left her daughter a legacy of dependence on her for everything. Then in her forties, Elsie was unable to cope with the simplest functions of daily life or even to formulate opinions and, without Ma Janis to push her on, Elsie's career foundered and she drifted into marriage with a nondescript and obscure young man who was never born to be a husband. They settled in that haven for misfits, Hollywood, where Elsie landed infrequent jobs in the movies, generally as technical expert on films that dealt with World War I. In the absence of an anchor, Elsie floated into spiritualism and developed a behavior which, to anyone but a Hollywood spiritualist, seemed insane. I remember visiting Elsie one afternoon in her scrubby little garden when she spoke to a butterfly that hovered overhead. "Hello, Mother dear!" she said. "That butterfly is Mother," Elsie informed me. "She often materializes as a butterfly, to remind me that she's always near." Mothers really ought to take thought, while alive, as to what will happen when the umbilical cord they failed to cut will be attached to a ghost.

Doug felt that it was wise not to become identified with any particular leading lady, so he acquired a new one in each picture and we had a steady succession of pretty actresses, none of whom ever developed into full-scale stardom on her own. But in his private life Doug was equally fickle, and it may just as well be faced that he was an ardent ladies' man; Doug rationalized that, because he neither smoked nor drank, he had a right to some sort of folly. Presently, however, one of his romances, which had started as a mild flirtation the night of Sid Grauman's picnic at Malibu, began to get out of hand. The girl in question was, of course, America's Sweetheart herself, Mary Pickford. Mary had tried marriage, while in her early teens, with a sardonically attractive young leading man of the films, Owen Moore. Although he was of the same Irish-American extraction as her own, the experience had been disastrous, for Owen resented Mary's being the more important and, in order to demonstrate his male superiority, took to belittling his wife. Mary, flirtatious, petulant, and adored on all sides, refused to accept Owen Moore's abuse, and they soon broke up. Because they were Catholic they eschewed divorce and got a separation; but Doug, following in the footsteps of Teddy Roosevelt, considered himself married for life.

Never has anyone squirmed with guilt over a love affair as did poor Doug. What made it particularly embarrassing was that he had just gotten out a book of advice to the youth of America in which his ghostwriter included a chapter on the sanctity of the marriage vows. "Marry early and remain faithful to the bride of your youth," that book recommended, and it was on the counters of every five-and-ten-cent store in the U.S.A., ready to testify to Doug's perfidy.

Before long I found myself pulled into Doug's plight. My involvement was first manifested by my being unaccountably cut by

Beth Fairbanks. Finally, when her slights became more apparent than usual, Doug took me into his confidence. "I hate to tell you this, Nita," he said sheepishly, "but I've had to use you as an excuse in order to be with Mary." In effect, he had told Beth that I insisted on his coming to the Hollywood Hotel to work with me on the script. Beth was convinced that Doug was carrying on an affair with me, and with an eye to policing the two of us, she insisted that I work at their house in the future. From then on Doug and I, trapped in the Fairbanks library, pretended to work, with Doug's thoughts on Mary and mine on John Emerson, while the air between Beth and me crackled with ice.

At the same time I formed a friendship with Doug Junior that was warm and cozy. Junior was a mere eight years old, but we were the same size, so, feeling that we were the same age, he was always dragging me into the nursery to play with him. One evening when I had been snared into some childish game, Junior's Mummy and Daddy came in to get him ready for bed and Doug Senior, launching into a domestic act, was proceeding to undress his son when Junior spoke up to ask, "Daddy, are you going to undress Nita, too?" Beth froze into a pillar of outrage, and, guiltless though I was, my blushes did nothing to cancel her suspicions.

Any love affair that had to be conducted secretly in the glare of the Hollywood limelight was bound to have its suspense, and Doug would often joke about it to me. One such incident concerned a scheme he'd worked out for keeping midnight trysts with Mary. As a lover of the great outdoors, Doug took to sleeping on an upstairs porch from which he could easily slide down an Ionic column to the ground; after that it wasn't difficult for his car to leave the premises without any noise, for the garage was at the top of a steep incline; all Doug had to do was to push his car into the open and silently coast downhill. But after a date with Mary, Doug's return home wasn't quite so simple. In order not to be heard by Beth, he had to turn his motor off at the foot of the hill and push the car all the way up to the garage. Athlete though he was, the chore at that late hour rather took it out of Doug. Also, his climb up the Ionic pillar wasn't nearly as easy as the slide down, and on reaching the porch he was not only exhausted but very hungry. It appeared that Mary, absorbed only in romance, never thought of providing him with a snack, so Doug was wont to have a piece of cake and a glass of milk left on his bedside table in case, as he told Beth, he "woke up hungry in the night." On the night in question, Doug wolfed the cake down in the dark, undeterred by its rather strange Oriental flavor; then he tumbled into bed exhausted and went to sleep. The next morning Doug discovered the reason why the cake had tasted as it did; the crumbs that remained on the plate were a creeping mass of California red ants, and Doug must have swallowed several hundred of them.

It took more than an army of red ants to conquer love, but Doug and Mary were forced to play a twenty-four-hour-a-day game of hide-and-seek to keep their romance a secret. Sometimes John Emerson and I would sneak off into the hills with them on horseback. Mary would tuck her telltale curls into the top of a slouch hat, and Doug would pull down a sombrero to cover his famous face. If other riders approached us, it amused Doug to carry on a line of dialogue purposely to be overheard. "I saw that new Fairbanks picture last night," he'd say, "and is he a show-off!" "He couldn't be any worse than what's her-name—you know—Mary Pickford," Mary would pipe up; there was no need to disguise their voices, for those were the days of silent films.

It was inevitable that sooner or later Beth found out who her rival really was, but even then she pretended ignorance, hoping that Doug would get over his infatuation by seeing too much of Mary. But this never worked out because the public never allowed them any privacy. Sometimes Doug was able to appear with Mary openly, as he did on platforms and balconies during bond-selling tours of World War I, but in order to be alone with Mary, Doug had to sneak up back stairways of hotels, dodging elevator operators and other personnel en route.

There was a certain period, however, when Beth's hopes of getting Doug back seemed to brighten, for she had a powerful ally in Doug's snobbishness. He used to talk this problem over with me in my role as confidante. "Gee Nita, I'm crazy about Mary," he'd say wryly, "and it would be swell to marry the Queen of the Movies, but what about that family?" It bothered Doug that Mary, who adored her family, loved to joke about its being shanty Irish. Doug felt that Mary's real name of Gladys Smith might have allowed her to claim a proper, even if modest, British ancestry. The Pickford antecedents were obscure. Mary's father had disappeared before Ma Pickford ever left her native Canada with three small children.

Ma Pickford was plump and jolly, and she had an even more humorous slant on the Pickford clan than Mary's, for she was nearer by one generation to the bogs of Eire. As a Mother Machree she was delightful, but nobody would ever interest Ma Pickford in making the Social Register.

Society would have taken Jack Pickford to its heart had it been given the chance, but he went his reckless way, making unfortunate headlines for the scandal columns. As a Harlequin of our gypsy world of show business, Jack had no right ever to have married. But he did marry a Pierrette of a wife who was one of the most delectable blondes ever to graduate from the Ziegfeld Follies into film stardom. Her name was Olive Thomas. While she and Jack were in Paris on their honeymoon, Jack failed to show up at the hotel one evening, and Ollie, in a fit of jealousy, took poison. Jack was tracked down at one of the Paris night spots and dragged back to the hotel to find his bride writhing in agony. The poison she took was of a slow-working type, but nothing could save Ollie. Her convulsions endured so long that, before they ended, the heavy odor of decay permeated every corner of the honeymoon suite. The only serious remark I ever knew to come from Jack was when he went home to Mother Charlotte after Ollie's burial, wept for a moment, and said, "That's the first time I ever had to watch anybody die." Poor Harlequin! Poor Pierrette!

Jack's behavior was always an embarrassment to Doug, but he felt that the greatest hazard to his social eminence was Mary's sister. Lottie was a counterpart of Jack, enjoying life to the limit—and, incidentally, she died quite young, as did her brother. Like Jack, she had made a halfhearted attempt at a career, which never really clicked. Lottie, a brunette, was not nearly as pretty as Mary, and she was further hampered by a keen lack of interest in work. Once in a while Mary prevailed on Lottie to knuckle down to a job; one was in a serial on the order of Pearl White's *The Perils of Pauline*. When Lottie signed her contract, however, she failed to notify the firm that she was pregnant, and during the latter part of the serial she had to be filmed peeking over the tops of furniture or hedges. Lottie's carelessness in that deal put her on the blacklist of Hollywood producers; not even the valuable name of Pickford could keep her career going against such hazards.

I never knew Lottie as well as I knew Jack, but I once employed a maid who had worked for her and volunteered an over-all picture of Lottie which makes me regret to this day that I neglected knowing her better. Lottie's ex-maid, although a complaisant, workaday type, boasted an elegant trumped-up name which, if memory serves me, was Cherice. Cherice informed me that Lottie used to worry a lot over Mary's disapproval. Although anything but a snob, Mary was earnest, hard-working, an extremely clever businesswoman as well as an actress, and a fervent Catholic. She kept a close watch over Lottie's social activities. "And," said Cherice, "when they all heard Miss Mary's car swing up the gravel path, boy oh boy, did they put their clothes back on!"

There had been an effort to camouflage one of Lottie's several undistinguished husbands by boasting that he was a mortician. "But he wasn't no mortician at all," said Cherice. "He wasn't nothing but a bootlegger, and that swell hearse he drove didn't have nothing in it but booze."

All the while that Mary's prospective groom was wrestling with his snobbism, Mary had her own reasons to hesitate over their marriage; for her church threatened to turn its back on Mary if she divorced. But no obstacle could cause the two natural-born flirts to waver in the belief that their love was going to last forever. And finally Doug said to me one day, "Why shouldn't I divorce? Caesar did it! Napoleon did it!" Having granted his qualms a historical stature, Doug finally decided to take the great step, as did Mary. When the Catholic Church disowned Mary, she found solace for her strong religious needs by turning to Christian Science. She even took to her pen at one time and wrote a tract that answered all the problems which beset the human race. She called it *Why Not Try God?*

Immediately the Fairbankses' divorce decree was final, Beth gamely jumped the gun on Doug and beat him to the altar. Her second husband was Jack Whiting, a debonair Broadway comedian whom she had first met in the entourage of Elsie Janis. This gave Doug some justification for his own second marriage, although by the time it took place his ever-expanding fame proved that no defection from the ideals of T. Roosevelt could ever harm Doug's reputation.

When at long last the marriage of the King and Queen took place, Doug, always a stickler for the right thing, caused it to be performed with such dignity and restraint that I can't remember the details. A tighter knot was never tied, and now Doug began to formulate all his own rules of conduct. He proceeded to have cards engraved that were to be mailed to hostesses before any social event. They read:

> *Mr. and Mrs. Douglas Fairbanks*
> *beg leave to inform* _____ _____
> *that it is their desire*
> *to be placed next to each other at table.*

And so, with the bridegroom giving hints on etiquette that Emily Post never dreamed of, there began a honeymoon that Doug and Mary felt would last their whole lives through. It didn't.

Even before their marriage I was witness to an episode suggesting that their epic love affair was built on pretty shaky ground. One evening, during the time that Doug was still trying to keep up a show of marital devotion to Beth, we had all gone to the premiere of *Intolerance* at the Los Angeles Civic Auditorium. It was the first of those revels which later came to be a movie institution; the street in front of the theater was a mass of hysterical fans; film stars were crushed as they left their cars; Doug and Mary arrived in two different parties and were separately acclaimed. The next day at the studio Doug, smoldering with anxiety, took me aside to ask, "Do you think Mary got more applause last night than I did?"

After a few years of unrelenting togetherness, the Fairbankses' marriage finally lost its sheen, and they were both impelled to find a means of *not* sitting next to each other at table every night. There was always a convenient excuse that work forced them to be in different locations, and one time, while Mary was filming in Hollywood, Doug betook himself to the French Riviera. There fate ordained that he should meet a devastating English beauty, Sylvia, Lady Ashley. Doug was an instant victim of Sylvia's blond allure, which was right in line with the irony that seemed to dog his footsteps, for their encounter took place at a dinner party where Sylvia occupied the very chair that, in Doug's moral code, rightfully belonged to Mary.

At the time Doug first met Lady Ashley, John and I had already known her for several years. We were introduced in England, where we had gone to produce our comedy, *The Whole Town's Talking*, which had just finished an eight-month run on Broadway. The play required an actress of outstanding beauty for a minor role, and somebody recommended a young woman named Sylvia Hawkes, whose ash-blond, loveliness had just flashed across the London scene. She was reputed to be the daughter of a London greengrocer and she had no theatrical training, but all John required was one look at Miss Hawkes and he instantly handed her the role.

Our farce was tried out in Liverpool, and the opening-night audience included a number of swells who came up from London for Sylvia's debut. She was showered with floral tributes and with telegrams, one of which was signed Edward P. (as the present Duke of Windsor then wrote his name). But Sylvia's stage career was soon brought to an end by her marriage to a peer of the realm. That brief alliance ended in divorce, but during two subsequent Hollywood marriages Sylvia would always cling to her title, and she was always addressed and referred to as Lady Ashley.

Sylvia was partial to marrying titles: two were English (Lords Ashley and Stanley); one Russian, Prince Dmitri Djordjadze; but the two greatest were kings of Hollywood, Douglas Fairbanks and Clark Gable. I never felt that Sylvia had the least gram of snobbery; her need for a title was basic and legitimate; she was so ravishing that she could feel at ease only with an aristocratic mate.

Doug would have preferred his love for Sylvia to remain a romantic interlude, but her spell was potent and as a titled lady she supplied the dimension of snobbery which meant so much to Doug and so little to Mary. Before long he began to feel that nothing short of marriage could give this new saga its proper conclusion. But once again the danger of bad publicity brought on a chill of apprehension. Doug's career had survived one broken marriage on the excuse that his love for Mary was comparable to Romeo's for Juliet, Dante's for Beatrice, Abelard's for Héloise, but could it possibly survive two?

Doug and Mary had been so publicized as historic lovers that all the combined press agents of Hollywood might not be able to erase the image. Finally Doug decided that the better part of valor was to cut and run. Unbeknownst to Sylvia, he boarded an ocean liner and started to beat it back to America's Sweetheart. But when Doug's liner docked in Marseille, who was on the pier but his British loved one, she having grabbed a pioneer commercial plane of the period. Poor Doug was always victimized by his own Rules of Right Behavior. The news of Sylvia's flight to join him broke out in headlines which compromised a titled lady in every country of the civilized world; the only way for Doug to set himself right with the British peerage was to marry the girl.

Newspapers brought the bad news to Mary, and she read it with a modicum of resignation; there was no question that their marriage had become a bore to them both. At the same time, Mary felt that the reason for its break-up had been Doug's social pretensions, and on that score she was bitter. Then, too, she was uncertain as to what effect one more scandal might have on *her* career. The divorce went through, however, and the Kingdom of Hollywood had to be divided in two parts. Mary continued to receive the homage of the film colony at the royal estate of Pickfair, and obeisance was given to the new queen, who was formally addressed as Mr. Fairbanks's wife, Lady Ashley.

Hollywood was now beginning to realize how dearly the public loves scandal. But, alas, one of Doug's principles of conduct had results which were actually fatal; he was too ardent a devotee of physical fitness. During his last year Doug and Sylvia lived just down the highway from my house on the ocean front in Santa Monica. I had recommended to Doug my masseuse, a Swedish woman who, being blind, had an insight beyond material vision. One day Mrs. Adkins told me that Doug was in an extremely precarious state of health. I thought she was mistaken, for, as usual, Doug was bursting with vigor, his skin a dark tan, his muscles like iron. "But Mr. Fairbanks is overtrained," Mrs. Adkins argued. "He's so muscle-bound that no amount of massage can work up any circulation." Mrs. Adkins was right. Doug died almost without being ill, and our gallant Hollywood mentor, guide, philosopher, and friend was no longer around to set the movie colony straight on etiquette, celibacy, monogamy, and the strenuous life.

CHAPTER 10

✑ John Emerson, who was so much wiser in the ways of the world than I, used to tell me over and over again that he never had been nor ever could be faithful to any one female. But I'm sure his major attraction for me was the fact that he was hard to get, and, with the arrogance of youth, I thought I was different from all his other girls; to prove my point, I wrote a story titled "The Heart That Has Truly Loved," which made bold to state that true love lasts forever. Its soggy plot dampened the pages of *The Woman's Home Companion*, and so completely can the printed word fool the most intelligent cynic that John was actually impressed when he read it.

I worked every other angle I knew to trap the unfortunate man. I had already made myself necessary to his career; one after another of the pictures I wrote for John was a success. Conversely, the movies he made without me were all failures; one in particular, a story of India which starred Mary Pickford, was the only failure Mary ever had. Then, too, I was a Galatea to John's Pygmalion; having rescued my stories from the files in which they were buried, he was proud of having "created" me. On another level, I was contributing to his intellectual life; John had great respect for learning, but at the same time very little application to it. I read constantly, applying myself to weighty subjects, which I then relayed to him. But the most devious trick I played on John was to undermine his other sweethearts by wisecracks; he once complained to me bitterly, "You ruin my girl friends for me. I begin to see them from *your* angle, and dammit, I prefer to be fooled."

I was also tremendously "tolerant" of his many sweethearts. My most serious rival was the famous Broadway star Emily Stevens, a red-haired beauty in her mid-thirties who had the racy wit of a seasoned woman of the world. I still remember a comment Emily once made when we were casting a movie. "You begin by choosing Ethel, John, and Lionel Barrymore," she said, "but by the time rehearsals start, you're grateful if your actors aren't albinos." On another occasion, when a group of us were seated around and about the Brown Derby and making detailed plans for a trip which we knew we'd never take, the bored Miss Stevens spoke up and asked, "Why don't you people describe your *return* from that voyage?"

Emily's rivalry, however, failed to halt a devious snippet like me. I recall one time when she was in Los Angeles with a play, and I arranged to attend to some of John's studio duties so he could see more of her than would otherwise have been possible. I knew very well that my "consideration" would make John say to himself, "Obviously the little thing is in love with me, and yet she hasn't the slightest grain of jealousy"; in this way I so intrigued John as to destroy his concentration on a sweetheart who was much more worldly-wise than I.

Something else in my favor was the fact that John was so busy working with me that he had no time to spend on the mature women who were his first choice. As a matter of fact, I had assumed a maturity myself through looking out for his health; a hypochondriac to begin with, John actually was a semi-invalid. Threatened with pernicious anemia, he was marking time for word to come from the eminent New York surgeon John Erdmann that he had perfected an operation for removal of the spleen which was to be the first cure for this disease in medical history. Erdmann, who had been experimenting for nearly five years, was not yet satisfied with results, and while John was waiting I had an opportunity to nurse him, supervise his diet, and keep tabs on time to take medicine. John had a disarming selfishness that amused all of us; he found nothing ungallant in saying, "Buggie, the draft where I'm sitting could give anyone pneumonia; will you change places with me?"

John's dread of being seriously involved with any girl was not without reason, for he had gone through a disastrous first marriage. At that time he was in Sandusky, Ohio, studying for the ministry under his real name of Clifton Paden. His wife was an assistant instructress at the college, older than he by several years. He once described her to me as being spare, beautiful, and prematurely gray-haired; she may somewhat have resembled Katharine Hepburn. However, very early in the marriage a revelation broke over the bridegroom; he saw himself in a true light and realized that his religious fervor was based on a desire to stand up and perform in front of a lot of people. In all honesty, he didn't want to be a preacher; he was eaten up by a desire to act. He decided then and there to give up the ministry, go to New York, and study for the theater.

At the time of their separation, John's wife was still deeply in love with him. She must have had great understanding and tolerance, for, realizing that his theatrical career would turn her into an encumbrance, she simply bowed out. After their divorce, Clifton Paden moved to New York, where he enrolled at the American Academy of Dramatic Art, changing his name to John Emerson, which he felt was more impressive than the one with which he had been christened. John finished his course brilliantly and on graduating was offered a job on the faculty. As a teacher at the academy, he made use of every possible contact to find an opening in the theater and, with his qualifications of charm, intelligence, and good looks, it wasn't long before he stepped into a job on Broadway. From the beginning John associated with first-rate talents; he was actor and stage manager with the star Minnie Maddern Fiske; became an assistant to Clyde Fitch, who wrote the first American comedies of manners; and graduated into becoming a director for Charles Frohman, the foremost New York producer of that era. While with Frohman, John worked with such exciting actresses as Billie Burke and Clara Bloodgood. John's career in the New York theater provided him with a charming way of life. His reputation as a Don Juan intrigued the actresses with whom he associated, and his frail health brought out mother instincts that are a valuable asset even to romance.

In 1914, when John attained stardom in *The Conspiracy* and Griffith offered him a contract to go to Hollywood, better girls than I had failed to snare him. But I was determined to get him by hook or crook; and that was how I finally landed him, by crook. I made use of the durable lie that I was going to marry somebody else. John needed me in so many different areas that this threw him into a panic and turned the trick. So, having started with the resolution to steer clear of exhibitionists of all kinds, actors in particular, I went out of my way to marry the most ardent example I've ever known. The results, quite naturally, were both tragic and comic, together with a thousand combinations of the two, but they were far from dull and I certainly achieved my one great ambition, which was never to be bored.

Pop, who had always boasted I was too smart to marry again, was as disgusted by my project as he had been the first time, while it threw poor Mother into despair. She always considered me too fragile to be subjected to the abhorrent intimacies of wedlock and was certain that my first twenty-four hours of married life had been sufficient to keep me from ever again entering that state. Thus she wrote her own scenarios, ascribing to me the only emotions of which she herself was capable—a pallid sort of sentimentality combined with a fierce possessiveness with which she would have entered a pit full of hissing snakes. The only thing that could break down Mother's opposition to my marriage was that John might harm my reputation, so she finally helped me get a divorce. The lawyer, Martin Gang, was very young but very capable and is now one of Hollywood's notable legal lights. His plea of incompatibility was not contested (by that time nobody even knew where Frankie was), and the interlocutory decree was handed down in a matter of minutes, after which I would have to wait a year for the final decree that would permit my becoming Mrs. John Emerson.

But there were other than domestic changes in store for me. After I had written all Doug's movies for the first exciting two years of his career, things began to go badly between him and me.

Doug had developed a fierce self-sufficiency that made him dislike depending on anyone but himself for anything. The situation reached a climax when the *Ladies' Home Journal* published a picture of me seated on a movie set in the type of camp chair always reserved for the privileged; the underlying caption called me, in effect, the little girl responsible for making Douglas Fairbanks a star. Doug had an honest basis for resentment; that I was the first to write his own personality into a film was true enough, and that he was no actor Doug freely admitted. But he didn't need me; his unusual talents would have come to the fore in either the theater or the films without outside help from anyone.

Another change had come over Doug; Hollywood had become his kingdom, and he had grown to love it. This hadn't happened to either John or me. We determined to end our affiliation with Doug, move to New York, and produce pictures there. Our parting from Doug was achieved with a semblance of good feeling, and later on we became real friends once more; Doug even tried to get us to work with him again. But John and I, financed by the Paramount Company, left Hollywood for good, as we believed, to produce comedies in the East, while Doug remained in the film capital, took to writing his own scenarios, and replaced John with Vic Fleming as a director.

Again in New York, I longed to have a permanent home, which would be the first of my roving life; John supervised the search and chose an apartment for me that was a far cry from the one with seven floor lamps in which I had so unconsciously fascinated Vachel Lindsay. John's taste smacked of New England; he had even adopted the surname of the great Boston moralizer. The apartment he decided on was in the conservative Murray Hill district. It was all done up in pseudo-Chippendale with a grandfather clock in the hall and copies of red chalk drawings by Michelangelo in heavy mahogany frames. Taking a cue from those surroundings, I led a life that Ralph Waldo himself would have approved and spent as much time as possible in the nearby public library. But the fashions which might have provided me with a career had I not drifted into show business used to take me far afield, to patronize a

little dress shop in the Bronx which had just been discovered by
some fashion scout—truly a case of beating a path to a new mouse-
trap, because the shop was up an obscure flight of stairs and had no
windows on the street. It was run by a pretty curly-headed blonde
named Hattie Carnegie, who seemed little more than a child. We
were the same size, and sometimes I would buy Hattie's dresses
right off her back.

World War I was in full swing when we started working in
New York. The war itself was to make little mark on me. The only
male of military age in our family was my brother, who, as a major,
was safely in charge of an Army hospital in Texas. On looking
backward, it seems to me that war years in general are colorless;
events too painful for human acceptance are taking place, and time
itself becomes like those disks used in experiments on color; divided
into the primal colors, a disk is made to whirl so fast that it takes on
the dun gray of battleships and gun barrels. I had my own private
war to endure, the life-and-death struggle of John Emerson against
a disease which by this time was clearly gaining on him.

While keeping in close touch with Dr. Erdmann for word that it
was safe for John to undergo an operation, we started work on our
first independent movie. It was filmed at a small studio in the East
Fifties and starred a small and dainty blonde, Louise Huff, whose
acting career was cut short soon after by her retirement into a
marriage with a prominent New York industrialist, Edwin Still-
man. Costarring with Louise was little Ernie Truex, who is still a
valuable asset to Broadway. Our movie was a satirical comment on
the bombast of the Prussian war effort, and it was while playing in
that film that Erich von Stroheim spent his lunch hour, dressed in a
Junker uniform, driving around in a fiacre to the derision of by-
standers, savoring the first thrills of being the Man You Love to
Hate.

Following our separation from Fairbanks, we all went through a
period of floundering; not having Doug's athletic prowess to take
into account, the comedies John and I made became merely illustrated subtitles, and although Doug, as his own script writer, was
able to contrive any number of gags, they lacked the basic satirical

themes I had contributed to glue them together. I recently saw on television a picture Doug made following our break-up. It was called *Till the Clouds Roll By* and is pretty much of a jumble. However, in those war years the worst pictures made money, ours as well as Doug's. And it wasn't long before his keen sense of showmanship led Doug into the new field of cloak-and-dagger melodrama. Such movies as *The Three Musketeers* and *The Mark of Zorro* not only climaxed Doug's career but added greatly to the prestige of Hollywood.

And may I here remark how few people realize that Hollywood, as a world center of the movie art, was the chance by-product of two wars. Before World War I, the best films were made by such artists as Max Linder in France and Asta Nielsen in Sweden; in Italy scenarios were being written by the poet D'Annunzio. European production, however, was abruptly curtailed by the war, and Hollywood, in its isolation, enjoyed full freedom to experiment with the new art form. After World War I, Europe was a long time developing the wealth necessary for the most costly form of art expression ever devised—even more expensive than the cathedrals of the Middle Ages. But no sooner did movie production again get under way in Europe than it was slapped down by World War II. Hollywood, still far from the firing lines and backed by enormous wartime profits, continued to stamp its ingenuous charm on the world at large. Today movie production is at its best in Italy, France, Sweden, England, and Russia, and since World War III will spare no single area of the earth, it is clear that Hollywood's heyday can never be restored. Its first brilliance, however, is not to be contested; the naïveté of Griffith is just as great art as the decadence of Bergman or Fellini. And today's finest movie talents all confess the debt they owe D. W. Griffith as a master.

A day finally came when Dr. Erdmann reported an impressive backlog of successful operations for removal of the spleen, and he felt that John could safely risk surgery. So we interrupted our work and took time off for John's operation. In those days removal of the spleen was so drastic a procedure that it had to be immediately followed by an extensive blood transfusion. In John's case the results were spectacular; not longer than five minutes after the transfusion, I sat at his bedside and saw the parchment color of John's skin turn to pink. I held a mirror up to his face so he could see the miracle for himself. It astounded John; life seemed to begin all over again for him and, taking my hand, he spoke to his nurse. "Aren't I lucky at my age to have such a darling little sweetheart?" That was possibly the finest moment in my life with Emerson.

The trouble with such blissful occasions is that they cost too much, and the bill we would both be required to pay for them was already being run up. Its first items seemed so small I couldn't take them seriously. One day just after my first script for Doug was finished, John came to me and asked that I allow him to share credit for its authorship. I was surprised, but I had had an early schooling in male vanity from Pop, so, without giving the matter a second thought, I agreed. How could a movie plot seem important to a girl who was impressed only by great writing? I had no pride in authorship because I never thought that anything produced by females was, or even should be, important. It is horrible to think what sort of monster Shakespeare might have been as a woman; even Proust and Oscar Wilde, who were the next thing to women, are fairly ridiculous as people. The only authoresses I ever respected were women first of all, like my friend the playwright Zoe Akins. That they happened to take up writing was beside the point.

Had I been on my guard about John, I would have recognized another warning that appeared while he was editing the first film I wrote for Doug. "Buggie, it's rather undignified for a man of my experience to take second credit as author of this picture. Do you mind if my name comes ahead of yours?" I agreed with merely a smothered giggle; the credit title read, "by *John Emerson* and Anita Loos." I failed to realize that John suffered from a very dangerous pathological insecurity. When, after our marriage, he first heard himself addressed as Mr. *Loos*, it hit his egotism with a bang that reverberated as long as he lived. Had I been a *femme fatale*, I couldn't have destroyed him more thoroughly. Yet through it all, John loved me, was amused by me, depended on me, and then, alas, he envied me. And until the day he died he resented me.

Salvation for poor John was right at hand, had I merely continued to write his scripts and married his best friend. While John was in the hospital and I was keeping an impatient vigil at his bedside, waiting for my final divorce decree, I met Rayne Adams. He was an architect and, in appearance, rather like John: the same medium height and spare, professorial good looks; his dark hair, like John's, had begun to go gray. But there the resemblance ceased. Rayne's eyes reflected a state of permanent amusement when he looked at me; there was none of the alarm that used to streak across John's face, an intent gaze which meant I was being summed up as a curiosity, a look which in time became abnormal and frightening. Although Rayne was in his late thirties, our age difference wouldn't have mattered so much because there were compensations. While he was a gentle misanthrope and no smart aleck, Rayne had a healthy disrespect for all the things that impressed John Emerson. He never took my writing seriously and considered it, as I did, a rather crooked means of earning money.

Aside from Rayne and John being friends, they shared an unusual relationship, for after John's first wife divorced him she had married Rayne Adams. The trio became close companions—one of those involved situations which develop in worldly circles. And when, after little more than a year, Rayne's wife died, it seemed only to strengthen the bond between the two men.

Rayne came to the hospital every day while John was convalescing, and I thought it was to visit him. Rayne was preparing to sail overseas for the Red Cross, an assignment for which he was sacrificing his career, but his eagerness to join the war effort was untinged by the rampant chauvinism of wartime. He looked on war as a calamity for which no one nation was more responsible than another, and he was going off to France in the spirit of a fireman rushing to a conflagration in which his favorite locale was threatened. Rayne was to be stationed in Paris, which he knew and loved, having studied there at the Beaux Arts.

During Rayne's student days in Paris he had perpetrated an elaborate trick on the concierge at his lodging house—one which I have heard ascribed to other pranksters but, knowing Rayne, I think the idea may have been his own. One afternoon, while passing by a pet shop, he noticed a tank full of turtles. Rayne proceeded to buy six in graduated sizes. He then made a present of the smallest turtle to his concierge, who affectionately placed it in a fountain that decorated his conciergerie. Rayne then stealthily proceeded to change the turtles, each time substituting one of a larger size. The concierge and his wife, *bouleversés* by the rapid growth of their turtle, became famous throughout the *arrondissement;* a steady succession of people came every day to check the phenomenon. After the turtle reached its peak in size, Rayne reversed the process, and the turtle gradually began to get smaller until it disappeared altogether. Possibly a vague *souvenir* of that miracle persists in the *quartier* to this very day.

One evening during John's convalescence, Rayne and I left his stuffy hospital room for a breath of fresh, unmedicated air and, while strolling along Second Avenue, Rayne suddenly asked if I didn't find it strange that he came there every day. I hadn't given it a thought; Rayne was too much an oddball to make anything he did seem unusual. He then supplied the reason: "I come here on account of you."

I stopped in amazement; it hadn't crossed my mind that he didn't know of my feelings for John; now I realized he took them to be a matter of our collaboration on movies. As I was standing on the sidewalk, incapable of speech, Rayne gestured toward a light in one window of the hospital and said, "Do you see that light? It was in that room my wife died." (*John's wife too! And in that same hospital!*) "And because she died," Rayne said, "I can ask the one girl I ever loved to marry me." The proposal seemed so fantastic I still couldn't believe that Rayne meant me; he finally had to tell me so in that three-word statement which is our main reward for living. The situation packed more punch than any I had ever dared to write: the widower of John's ex-wife now wanted to marry John's sweetheart. It gave a girl a very healthy respect for soap opera, which I have never lost. I had to tell Rayne that I was going to marry John, and he appreciated the humor in that mishmash of coincidences, motives, and sentiments as greatly as I did. And there on the corner of Second Avenue we laughed grimly about them in the dark.

Before Rayne left for France I gave him $500, with instructions to spend it on hats for young Parisiennes who had been deprived of millinery because of the war. Rayne later sent me thank-you letters from those girls, and Elliot Paul wrote about my war effort in his book *The Last Time I Saw Paris*.

After Rayne was established in Paris he used to joke about his feelings for me in letters:

Anita dear,

. . . You write concerning an altercation with John—but if it eases you at all, you are free to consider yourself married to me. It doesn't do any harm and you can have the thrills, anytime you wish, that come with infidelity.

Today the reasons why I couldn't fall in love with Rayne have become obvious: he gave me full devotion and required nothing in return, while John treated me in an offhand manner, appropriated my earnings, and demanded from me all the services of a hired maid. How could a girl like I resist him?

❧ While John and I were getting ready to resume production on those static movies which might well have ended in disaster, a good Samaritan loomed up to save us. He was Joseph M. Schenck, one of the most powerful figures in show business at that time. Joe and his brother Nick had risen from the slums of New York, to which their parents had come as Russian immigrants. The two brothers started careers in the entertainment world by developing Palisades Amusement Park in New Jersey, across the Hudson River from New York, and from this beginning they went on to acquire the national chain of movie theaters which still goes under the name of the Loew Circuit. Joe Schenck had entered into the production of movies for a personal reason: to further the career of the beautiful, sultry Norma Talmadge, whom he had rescued from obscurity and married. Among the films Joe produced for Norma were *Camille*, *The Eternal Flame*, and *Smilin' Through*, and they established her as the foremost dramatic star of silent films. Meanwhile, the career of Norma's sister, Constance (known to all of us as Dutch), had sagged. Dutch's one claim to fame had been the role she played for Griffith in *Intolerance*, but after she left Hollywood and accompanied her sister to New York, no further opportunities arose for Dutch's talents as a lovely clown.

On a certain day that turned out to be momentous for John and me, Joe Schenck sent for us and told of a dilemma he was in with his mother-in-law, who was known throughout the film world by her nickname of Peg. It seemed that Peg was hectoring Joe about Dutch's professional eclipse and insisting that he give her some attention. "So I'd like to turn Dutch over to you," Joe said to John, "and have Anita do the same sort of thing for her that she did for Doug Fairbanks; write her into some films that will satisfy Peg and get the woman off my neck." Joe's offer was tremendously attractive; to produce movies for Constance Talmadge would bring us great financial reward; they would be booked over the entire Loew Circuit, and last, but not least, we would benefit by Joe's flair for showmanship. Seeing that Dutch and I had been together on the Griffith lot, I felt I knew her potentialities; it would be a challenge to make use of them.

A third and youngest sister in the Talmadge family was Natalie, whose nickname was Nate. All three girls were unique in that they took small interest in film careers. Nate was dark and she resembled Norma without being a beauty; having no equipment for the movies, she was perfectly content to live a life of ease. Norma's stardom seemed rather to bore her, while Dutch, a dedicated playgirl, spent her time giving the runaround to a legion of earnest suitors. The one ambitious member of the group was Peg. It was she who had prodded Norma into stardom, using the same energy she was now exerting on Dutch. Then in her early forties, Peg looked older; years of poverty as a young woman had left her with a placid acceptance of graying hair and matronly heft, but along with them went a ribald sense of humor that ultimately worked its way into the character of Dorothy, the girl friend of Lorelei Lee in *Gentlemen Prefer Blondes*. Several of Dorothy's cracks are direct quotes from Peg Talmadge.

Greatly as I loved and was amused by Peg, we had our little differences. The first movie I wrote for Dutch was *The Virtuous Vamp*, its title being supplied by Dutch's persistent young suitor, Irving Berlin. The plot concerned a teenage heroine's hot pursuit of a forty-year-old hero who had a resistance to sex that bordered on paralysis. Peg objected to Dutch's role, declaring that never in her life had Dutch run after any man, that she spent most of her time giving them the go-by. I argued that a movie in which the heroine took up precious footage running away would merely result in a chase; the only way I could put Dutch's talent for comedy to use was to invent devious schemes for her to hook the hero. Peg appealed to Joe to have me rewrite my script, but although he cowered under her attack, he told John to go ahead and shoot the picture as written. The hero was played by Conway Tearle, whose mature good looks made him eminently desirable. The picture ended with his stand-off-and-touch-me-not resistance going down to triumphant defeat. Immediately *The Virtuous Vamp* was released, Dutch's stardom was established. Vachel Lindsay wrote of it in *The New Republic*: "The picture is pure Greek in its spirit of epic comedy." Peg was still unconvinced, but she had to admit that the film had added a second star to her family.

Thus began a series of comedies for Dutch in which her career paralleled Norma's and one success followed another. Our pictures were filmed under the happiest circumstances; because the entertainment empire ruled by the Schenck brothers was centered in New York, we worked there instead of in Hollywood. Our productions were a family matter, in which Joe's main interest was to keep his mother-in-law happy. One day Joe sent for John and me to come to his office. "Look, folks," he said, "when I put Dutch into your hands, it was only to satisfy Peg. I never expected to make money on the deal. But the pictures have turned out to be gold mines, so I want you two to have a little bonus." He handed John a check for $50,000.

Norma's appreciation of Joe was pretty shallow; she resented the fact that he always remained an uncouth product of the New York slums. When Joe was a mere child, he had been put to work in a Bowery drugstore that catered to dope addicts; cocaine and heroin were kept openly on the counter and the little boy was ordered to dispense them as if they were bicarbonate of soda. That early contact with vice seemed only to strengthen Joe's sturdy temperament, but he came to know every element of the gangster world, from its lowest ranks on up to the top echelons that were graced by His Honor Jimmy Walker, the Mayor of New York himself. Until meeting Norma, Joe had been vastly content with a bachelor life that provided him with the prettiest girls in show business, and he was lusty to the degree that he sometimes patronized several of them at the same time. When he first met Norma she was an obscure movie actress just beginning to cause a stir at ringside tables in the city's night spots. Joe fell for her all the way, possibly because Norma was coolly indifferent to him. Together they looked like Snow White and an overgrown dwarf; Joe's figure was portly, he was beginning to go bald, and he suffered a cast in one eye that gave him a permanent squint. But these were only surface faults; in every other way Joe was most engaging; he had the subtle masculine allure which so often accompanies power, and he used his power with the greatest consideration for others. Although he had little native wit, Joe cheerfully rose above its lack by repeating over and over the wisecracks of his Broadway cronies, in speech that always kept the accents of his Russian peasant origin.

After their marriage Joe installed his girl-wife in a vast Park Avenue apartment with white wall-to-wall carpeting, gold furniture, and pictures that were copies of Watteau at his sexiest. Norma's bedroom had an outsized bed with an ermine throw, a mountain of maribou cushions, and a telephone covered by a fancy doll. The apartment boasted every item of an opulent love nest, except the one which only Norma could supply, and that was love. Joe longed to have a child, a son in particular. Norma never sensed she was cruel when she used to declare quite primly, "I think it would be wrong to have a baby. What if it looked like Joe?" But Norma did allow Joe the privilege of adoring her, showering her with jewels, and establishing her as the most idolized film star of her day.

It is incredible that the movies made by Norma and Constance Talmadge have disappeared so completely. Photographs of both girls can always be found in albums dealing with the history of the movies, but their films are never seen either on television or in movie theaters devoted to the past. Possibly the blame rests in the girls' own lack of vanity; had Norma shown more interest in her movies, Joe would certainly have taken every means to preserve the negatives. When he was curator of films for the New York Museum of Modern Art, Richard Griffith told me that he had been able to find only one of Norma's films: a copy of *Smilin' Through* which he unearthed in Czechoslovakia, but it is so tattered that it can't be screened. Of Constance's *Virtuous Vamp* there is no trace. When the museum tried to get Schenck's assistance in tracking the picture down, Joe was an invalid unable to function.

At the time when Norma's and Dutch's careers were at a peak, movies were still so new that the public-relations contingent hadn't moved in and begun to devise fake images to which their victims were forced to live up. Movie stars were allowed personalties of their own. Norma was a moody girl, strangely restless, unable to bear solitude, yet even in the midst of people she always seemed remote. Her pensive type of beauty gave an impression of romantic sorrow, but as I came to know Norma's lack of resources I realized she was always bored, and in her boredom lay the seed of the same tragic end that overtook Mabel Normand.

After several pampered years as Mrs. Schenck, Norma fell in love with Gilbert Roland, a darkly handsome young actor who played opposite her in movies. I think Norma was only mildly in love with Roland, but she was definitely out of love with Joe. By that time he had given up all hope of happiness in his marriage and become an affectionate guardian of his wife. Refusing to accept the offer of gangster friends to rub out his rival, Joe arranged for Norma to get a divorce, after which he practically oversaw her marriage to Gilbert Roland. Joe then resumed his bachelor ways, but he never married again; he had learned a lesson about which he was touchingly realistic. I was present once when Joe was advising a pal who was bent on purchasing a flashy Long Island estate. "Why do you need it?" asked Joe. "To entertain friends." "Look," said Joe, "roughnecks like you and me have to buy our friends, and that kind ain't worth the money."

Norma's marriage to Gilbert Roland didn't last long; petulant, as always, she soon sought another divorce, this time in favor of George Jessel, a youthful crony of Joe Schenck's. Jessel was then a matinee idol who had recently won stardom in a play called *The Jazz Singer*. He was a fine dramatic actor; one of the few occasions I ever heard an audience break into audible sobs was when George, as the jazz singer, justified having deserted a career of cantor and defended jazz as a sort of incantation that sprang from the very soul of the American people. In addition to his stage career, Jessel was a popular night-club monologist, singer, and wit. He still functions as a time-honored after-dinner speaker, TV comedian, and master of ceremonies, scarcely looking any older than when he married Norma. Their marriage broke up before World War II, and Norma then acquired a fourth husband, who was an obscure physician. She may have married a doctor for a very grim reason; at any rate, while her husband was away serving in the Navy, Joe felt called on to resume his unhappy post as Norma's guardian. Joe understood her tragic problem all too well because of his boyhood apprenticeship in a Bowery drugstore. When the war was over, Norma retired with her husband to a remote community in Florida, where she died, tortured by the most crippling type of arthritis.

Constance, a brown-eyed blonde, is one of the few genuine *femmes fatales* I have ever known. Not to be in love with her would almost make a man seem abnormal; but no woman could be too jealous of Dutch because she had a sense of humor about sex that made her laugh off the majority of her suitors. They included the foremost bachelors of show business; to name only a few, there were Irving Berlin, Richard Barthelmess, and Irving Thalberg. The importance of Dutch's beaus meant as little to her as did their adoration. I can remember a time when we were on location in California, and the boy genius Irving Thalberg used to pace a Beverly Hills sidewalk night after night, his gaze fastened on the light in Dutch's window. And where was Dutch? Having left her lamp burning to make Irving think she was studying a script, she sneaked out the back door to join a movie clique that spent its free time in clowning. Dutch only wanted to be where the laughs were.

I was sometimes required to listen to tales of woe from Dutch's neglected beaus. One who is now world-famous determined to commit suicide because she was beginning to take seriously a young Greek man-about-town, a tobacco magnate named Pialogiou, whom Dutch married later on, *en première noce*, for a very short term. I sat at the bedside of that rejected suitor all one night, giving him all the arguments I could muster against suicide. At any rate, he survived and made a socially historic marriage later on.

Dutch, like Norma, soon divorced her first husband; her second was Allie MacIntosh, a British aristocrat and chum of the then Prince of Wales. As the dashing Mrs. MacIntosh, Dutch gave up her movie career for good and moved to London, where she was pursued (but unfortunately bored) by all the best people. I recall lunching with Dutch one day in the elegant grill room of the Savoy Hotel, when suddenly her eyes filled with tears and she launched into a heartrendering confession: "Buggie, I'd give anything in the world for just one hour at Dinty Moore's with Marty Herman!" Now Dinty Moore's was then, as it is today, a hangout for lusty males who appreciate Irish stew and corned-beef hash; as for Marty Herman, he wasn't even a beau; he was merely the red-haired, freckle-faced, wisecracking brother of Broadway producer Al H. Woods, who was himself no Lord Chesterfield. Personally, I was fond of *both* the British aristocracy *and* Marty Herman, but I understood Dutch's plaint and realized that her London days were numbered.

After divorcing MacIntosh, Dutch took as a third husband a Chicago playboy and millionaire whose first and last claim to fame was that he had annexed Dutch; just as his brother had earned headlines for having married one of the playful Dolly Sisters. Dutch enjoyed her husband's way of life until his persistent jealousy began to spoil her fun and she once more sought relief in a divorce.

Dutch's fourth husband, of whom she is today the widow, was a

very correct gentleman who occupied a seat on the New York
Stock Exchange. Theirs was a happy marriage, for her husband
gave Dutch full freedom, understanding her for what she really
was. Indeed Irving Berlin's summation of Dutch as a virtuous vamp
had the same basis of truth that underlies all his lyrics.

Once Dutch was happily married, she severed the last frail connection with her movie past and spent her time providing comedy
relief for a group of all-night cardplayers and doing a charity job
for the blind. Although she was never the least bit mercenary, everything she ever touched turned to gold; Dutch's career in silent
films had made her independently rich, and in time she became
heiress to Norma's considerable fortune. Three of Dutch's husbands were men of wealth, but all four were enormously attractive,
and in no case did she marry for money.

In a family as domestic as the Talmadges, the fact that Nate was
without a career made her the most important member of the clan,
because her future was unresolved and required more attention.
Peg kept an eye on the horizon to find Nate a satisfactory husband,
and she finally settled on Buster Keaton. The marriage produced
two sons, but while they were still toddlers Nate, like a true Talmadge, got a divorce. Nate never married again, and although Buster had annexed several wives, his only offspring are by Nate. She
now lives in Santa Monica, as obscurely as if she had never been the
wife of the movie clown who is second only to Charlie Chaplin; in
fact Buster is sometimes rated above Chaplin by more selective
connoisseurs. The two Keaton sons were ultimately provided with
jobs in the technical branch of the film industry. And who was
their benefactor? Naturally, Joe Schenck.

Peg Talmadge never allowed success to go to her daughters'
heads; her stock admonition to Norma and Dutch was, "Now girls,
don't get the idea you're important because you make faces in
front of a camera." They both took Peg's advice to heart, and
when fans approached Norma to ask, "Ain't you Norma Talmadge?" she'd give them short shrift: "I am not that common

movie girl, so please go away." And it was Peg's own humorous
acceptance of the facts of love that kept Dutch from being serious
about it. When Dutch came home from a date with a beau Peg
would ask, "Did he make free?" "Free? Why, Peg, he kissed the
face off me!" "Did you like it?" Dutch's report, enthusiastic or
indifferent, would be a true one. Peg was no fool; the breath of
scandal never touched Dutch; no homes were broken, and she was
never forced to betake herself to an analyst's couch.

Peg always made fun of herself as relentlessly as she did of her
daughters. I remember a birthday party we gave Peg in their luxurious five-room suite at the Ambassador Hotel. That day we barged
into Peg's bedroom to surprise her with gifts, of which those from
Norma and Dutch were very expensive. While contemplating her
loot, Peg began to laugh. "What's the joke, Peg?" "It's a joke on
me," she said. "I just remembered how I used to go to Coney Island
before you were born and ride that bumpy roller coaster, trying to
get rid of you rich little bastards."

For a long period after I joined the family there was no evidence
of any Mr. Talmadge, although rumor had it that when Nate was a
babe in arms Daddy left their flat in Brooklyn one night, ostensibly
for a short snort at the corner saloon, and never came back. Peg
went through years of struggle trying to feed and clothe her
brood, until word got around Brooklyn that a movie studio was
paying girls the incredible sum of five dollars a day merely to pose
for the films. Peg escorted the fifteen-year-old Norma to that gold
mine, where her loveliness very quickly landed her a job; from
which time on, Norma supported the family in comfort.

As Norma's and Dutch's fame and wealth increased, it was
thought that Daddy Talmadge must have shuffled off this mortal
coil, else he would have shown up to claim a piece of that pie in the
sky. Fred Talmadge did not materialize. But one afternoon when
Peg and the girls, dripping with mink, were rolling through Central
Park in their Cadillac, Peg suddenly buzzed for the chauffeur to
back up. Then, gesturing toward a ragged character who was hud-
dled on a bench trying to keep warm, she remarked, "If you girls

care to know who that tramp is, he's your father." Peg would have ordered the chauffeur to drive on without an exchange of amenities, but the girls were curious and Dutch insisted on bouncing out to greet her long-lost Dad. She briefly introduced herself by saying, "Hello, Fred. How'd you like to meet your family?" At which Fred glanced up, took in the Cadillac, the chauffeur in uniform, and the acres of mink, and grunted a casual "Hi." The girls, and even Peg, approved such nonchalance and, scooping him up, they took him to a hotel where Fred was supplied with all the necessities.

I never heard where Fred had been before the time of that encounter, and it's possible the family never asked any questions. They were realistic enough to know that there's not much variety in a tramp's life, so they probably let sleeping dogs lie. But along with their largess to Fred, Peg insisted on his taking a job at the studio. He was not grateful. One day I saw him balancing on a stepladder as he tried to tie paper leaves on the bare branches of a prop tree. "This is a hell of a job for an able-bodied man!" commented Fred. As there was a friendly *entente* between us, I agreed. But presently Fred disappeared into the cozy limbo of saloons that graced Third Avenue near the studio; from that time on he kept contact with his family not as a nuisance, but only for his weekly check.

In spite of their touch-and-go relationship, an affinity existed between Fred and the family; Peg and her husband might have been blood relations, so closely did he resemble her in a matter-of-fact insouciance. But years later, when Fred died, Peg's sense of humor broke down and she wrote me from California:

Dear Bug,

The gang are cooking Thanksgiving dinner and I told Norma I would write you about the funeral. There were hundreds of set pieces and a Hawaiian orchestra played "Aloha." The girls went down to see Fred at the undertakers two and three times a day—they were wrecks, he looked about 35.

The Talmadges, all in all, were the most engaging family I've ever known, and our several years of work and play together were sheer delight. But the amalgam that bound us together was Peg and when she died we girls lost contact with each other. The last time I saw Peg was in Hollywood, where Dutch's studio was then located. I had been in Europe for several months, during which my friendship with Peg was carried on in frequent letters. I knew she had been ailing but I was stricken almost inarticulate with shock when I saw the ravages that disease had made on her. But Peg herself carried on in gallant trivialities except for one brief moment when she suddenly gasped, "Oh, Buggie, I'm scared!" The confession was so awful I could find no response except to pat the thin narrow shoulder that had once been sturdy enough to carry all the family burdens. Peg is buried in the small Hollywood cemetery in the center of town, far from the noted glamour of Forest Lawn. Naturally the arrangements were made by Joe Schenck.

Joe remained the head of the Talmadge family as long as he lived, and he bore the sorrow Norma caused him with a benign cheerfulness that was his attitude toward grief of any kind. There came a period when Joe was forced to serve a jail sentence because of some sort of corporate tax snarl. It was generally believed that Joe took the rap for a friend who, had he been convicted, would have had to be separated from his small children. Joe wrote me from his prison cell, "Dear Buggie, don't you worry about me. I'm just fine."

During a certain period when I was living in California I sometimes used to lend Joe my Santa Monica beach house when I went away on trips. And it was on my return from one of them that a servant I had left in the house happened to remark that Mr. Schenck had a deep affection for the child of his confidential valet. The little girl lived on the premises with her parents, and I was informed that Joe showered her with as many Paris dresses, ermine muffs, and jewels as any movie child in Hollywood had. So that, unknown to any of his associates, Joe at long last achieved a touch of the family life for which he had been so eager.

This small bouquet of words is quite insufficient to express the fondness and gratitude I shall always feel for Joe; it often strikes me that one of the best Christians I've ever known was a Jew. If Hollywood ever wants to film a supercolossal epic of its own, it couldn't do better than to settle for the private life of Joseph M. Schenck.

ↅ When, at long last, my year of waiting for a final divorce
decree ended, John would have liked our wedding to take place in
his family church at Clyde, Ohio. But the Episcopal Church refused to marry us because I was divorced. Of course John had also
been divorced, but the stain had been removed by his wife's death;
ecclesiastical reasoning I still can't fathom. However, we settled
for a strictly comedy wedding on the big estate Joe and Norma
Schenck occupied in Great Neck. The ceremony was to be performed by a New York judge who was a semi-gangster member of
the Jimmy Walker administration. I would be attended by my
friend Frances Marion, who wrote Mary Pickford's screen plays
and was my "chaperon" in a summer home we shared together with
John at Great Neck. John's best man was to be Joe Schenck, and
from the day of our wedding one of Joe's stock jokes would be to
tell how John had been too nervous to make responses, which he
was forced to supply, so that actually I was married to Joe. The
wedding guests would include all the Talmadges and Buster Keaton,
then just beginning to pay court to Natalie.

A certain apprehension overshadowed the wedding day. John
had forgotten to provide a ring until the morning of the event and,
because it was Sunday, he was forced to go into New York and
scour Broadway for a pawnshop that happened to be open. There
he bought a second-hand platinum ring set in diamond chips,
doubtless a relic of some unhappy marriage.

Added to that disturbing incident was the fact that Mother refused to come East for the wedding; by this time she was resigned
to my outlaw way of life, but it made her so uncomfortable that
she preferred not to witness it. Pop was against marriage even as an
institution, and he wanted no part in any wedding of mine. Also
absent from what should have been a family affair was my brother,
Clifford. I tried to think that his excuse of being too busy to leave
home was valid, for during the time I had spent dishonoring poor
Mother Clifford was adding distinction to the family. He had been
putting into practice a plan he invented together with Donald
Ross, another young doctor, whereby people might pay for their
medical services in small monthly installments. Los Angeles had
taken to the idea with enthusiasm; it was being copied in other
cities of the United States, and from that beginning was born the
system which is epitomized today under the title of Blue Cross.

Yet another cause for disturbance on my wedding day was a
letter from Rayne Adams:

June 20, 1919
Paris

Anita dear,

I am sending you a suitable wedding gift, a book with a
chapter devoted to "Jesus in the Bridal Chamber." In the
opinion of this writer, most brides do not enter that chamber
with their thoughts fixed sufficiently on Jesus. But I am also
sending you a much better gift, which is my wish that you
and John may be happy forever and ever.

That comic love letter touched me enormously. (Note to Rayne
at this late day: If only you'd written to ask me for money, I might
have backed away from that unlucky altar.)

But the ominous mood of my wedding day was soon dissipated;
the twenties had started off with the manic illusion that America
had won the war and peace was here to stay; the postwar boom
began and everybody was having a fling at being rich. Elevator

men used to talk about the market instead of the weather. "Good morning, folks, did you get in on Kreuger and Toll yesterday?" I never bothered about the market, but John was handling all my money and, like all the others, we were getting rich.

Nobody dreamed the world was heading smack into the epoch of mass terror that grips the sixties, and that the generation which had been smart enough to crack the atom would begin to jitter over what it had done. While it's true that previous ages have had their science-fiction bugaboos, nothing so terrifying has happened since the 1820s, when mankind invented the railroad, only to realize that the human body couldn't stand a speed of fifteen miles an hour; that lungs would collapse, blood spurt from eyes, ears, and mouths; trains would become mass hearses running amuck, the mere sight of which would drive onlookers to commit suicide and thus depopulate the earth. The same dire result had also been achieved in the fifteenth century, when there were plenty of eye-witnesses who saw the Devil, in Person, unloading sackfuls of a new commodity called Gun Powder straight from Hell, to do away with humankind. Of course, it's possible that science has finally turned the trick and that today one single crackpot with a bomb no bigger than a suitcase can blast the world into nothingness. But in the twenties there was nothing to fear. Small wonder that we of the sixties have developed a cult for those happy, happy days.

In New York the pungent brew of Mayor Jimmy Walker's administration was being distilled, and Jimmy was seeing to it that every con-man worthy of the name had a brimming glassful. Jimmy's was not the undercover graft of the sixties, where malefactors in high places delegate crime to businesslike murderers, blackmailers, and pushers of dope. Jimmy was right out there in the open, a comforting assurance to the lowliest panhandler that eminence need not prevent a man from being human. Even the scandals of that day had a wholesome virility, as in the case of the Mayor and our friend the chorus girl Betty Compton. Jimmy could have had his pick of girls from Broadway or Park Avenue, for, aside from the prestige of his job, he was extraordinarily handsome and possessed the racy wit and quiet charm of a first-rate gangster. Betty, a bobbed brunette, was pretty in a vulgar way but otherwise quite mediocre. However, she must have been a change from Jimmy's dowdy wife. I only met Mrs. Walker once, for Jimmy scarcely took her anywhere. The occasion was a cocktail party, and one look at the poor woman supplied a reason for Jimmy's desertion; awareness that her forlorn state was dished up daily in the gossip columns had given Mrs. Walker's face a look of permanent indignation not to be recommended as a beauty aid.

In spite of Jimmy's grace and aplomb, he was so jealous of Betty that he sometimes lost control and pulled off a good old Irish rantan. I remember an occasion when a group of us went to Philadelphia for the opening of *The Band Wagon*, which starred our pals Fred Astaire and his sister Dellie. After the show Jimmy and Betty had a violent quarrel, climaxed by Betty's locking His Honor out of their hotel suite. The Mayor of New York was reduced to roaming the halls of the sedate Barclay Hotel dressed only in a pajama jacket that was too short for proper coverage.

The Talmadge girls and I ("girls" being a generic term that included Peg) fitted quite naturally into a deluxe group who were kept by rich friends of Joe Schenck, girls of a type that can't exist today, when the Treasury Department sticks its nose into every expense account and frightens gentlemen into impotence. Although Norma, Dutch, and I were working girls, we had as much fun as the ones to whom having fun was an occupation. Even when Norma and Dutch were filming, they didn't bother with any such nonsense as the "interpretation" of their roles, and there was no dialogue to learn. My own job was a matter of rising early and getting it out of the way; no preparations were required from any of us except John, which was all to the good and kept him from realizing to what extent I was spending my time on trivialities. Although cerebral activities may have helped to land my man, now that he was safely hooked it was time to celebrate with a little light diversion.

The girls and I did a great deal of shopping. Wherever shopping tours started, they generally ended at the dressmaking establishment of Madame Frances, where the most prominent kept girls bought their clothes. It occupied an elegant old white stone residence in the East Fifties, where Madame Frances held court as high priestess of our lively sect. The Madame was no beauty; her reddish hair was too frizzled, her blue eyes were too sharp, and her figure was too sturdy, but, as is so often the case, her romantic successes were even more spectacular than those of her beautiful clients. She had the one quality which, as an attraction to men, far surpasses beauty: a robust love of life. Aside from making money out of the rich, Madame Frances was a sexy godmother to any number of Cinderellas. She could spot undiscovered talent as expertly as did Flo Ziegfeld, and when her antenna picked up a girl of humble circumstances who was worthy to wear her dresses, Madame Frances would stake the girl to them, send her out into the nightspots with an escort, and then present the accumulated bills to the first rich admirer the girl attracted. The system didn't seem the least bit gross; in those days money was undefiled by taxes and so alluring that it brought out feelings of romance in girls. Had they ever left their love nests to wander with their keepers in Central Park, there would still be scores of trees bearing on their bark the tender legend "Baby Loves Daddy."

Once Madame Frances told me of a case in which she had failed to recognize potential sex appeal. A nondescript and poorly dressed little creature had wandered into her salon and timidly announced that she would like to buy some clothes. The saleswoman, having no heart to send the child on her way, asked Frances what to do. Equally kindhearted, Frances approached the girl and diplomatically told her the price of her dresses. "That's all right," she said, and forthwith opened a shabby pocketbook which was crammed with thousand-dollar bills. Now torn between curiosity and suspicion that the girl might be a thief, Frances proceeded to wait on her. The girl paid thousands of dollars in advance for clothes and furs and departed as modestly as she had come in. She became one of the shop's chief clients, although she was never seen in nightspots and wore her clothes with no more distinction than that of a child dressed in her mother's finery. Overcome with interest as to who was paying the bills, Frances struck up a friendship with the girl and sometimes used to go to her Park Avenue apartment for tea. The apartment was not only luxurious but in excellent taste; however, the girl remained silent on all personal issues and there was no photograph in evidence that might be a clue as to her keeper. Frances never solved the mystery, but the girl must have been kept by some man of very great wealth indeed. It was situations like this that gave the twenties their audaciously romantic flavor; inspired Scott Fitzgerald, for instance, to write stories like "A Diamond as Big as the Ritz."

The cost of a Madame Frances creation was high ($250 for an evening gown used to be a wild extravagance). I myself was barred from being a regular client. I admired Frances's dresses and could well have afforded them, but John happened to be a parlor pink, and in order to make good with him I pretended to be above caring for fashion. To carry out the bluff, I was forced to wear cheap clothes which I generally found in children's departments. I didn't even own that uniform for prosperous New York females, a mink coat, which I could have bought with a mere two weeks' salary.

Madame Frances's clothes were extremely feminine; she drew heavily on lace and ribbons and specialized in pastel shades. She exploded that false theory of the Theda Bara school that men are seduced by girls who dress in red or black. Frances knew as well as Ziegfeld that men's desire is more quickly provoked by the colors worn by little girls when they, as little boys, experienced the first thrill of romantic love. The one occasion when I dared John's resentment and ordered a dress from Frances, I told her I wanted a more sophisticated shade than baby blue or pink. She had an instant solution: "I've got it, dear! A nice sexy beige."

Well, what about sex in the twenties? In the light of today, it was pretty tame. How could any epoch boast of passion with its hit love song bearing the title "When You Wore a Tulip, a Bright Yellow Tulip, and I Wore a Big Red Rose"? As regards pornography, when it existed at all it was so humorous as to cancel out lust; there was none of the realistic smut required by the dirty mind of the sixties. Four-letter words were barred from popular books. The most scandalous popular novel of those years, *Three Weeks*, was written in vague and highfalutin terms that would cause any teenager inured to the obscenities of today to yawn. D. H. Lawrence's *Lady Chatterley's Lover*, which went into physical details in well-written prose, was banned so successfully that few except the *cognoscenti* had a chance to read it.

The real-life assignations of the twenties took place against such naïve backgrounds as *thés dansants*, where the most violent clutch was that of a tango, or in cozy corners where seldom did anything more sinful take place than the snapping of a garter. Little was needed to satisfy those males whose eroticism was unconfused; there was none of the frenzy of the Freudian era, which leads people to suspect they have a sex craving for a mother, father, sister, brother, or maybe even a canary, and are thus either driven erotically mad or else deprived of any sex gratification at all.

Beginning to be childishly smug about my situation as a bride, I begged John for a more pompous establishment than our chaste Early American apartment in Murray Hill. We shopped around and discovered a brownstone residence on Gramercy Square, its main attraction being that along with the lease went a key to the gate of Gramercy Park. But our dream of hours to be spent in the greenery went the way of many others, for not once during our year of residence did either John or I bother to use that key. Possibly we were both too insecure about our marriage to relax and enjoy such simple blessings. I'm sure our neighbors on Gramercy Square were putting John down as a sugar daddy; otherwise how could the mere child that I seemed to be occupy such elegant quarters? All my group were so young and foolish that when we tried to keep house, as I did, we were only playing at it, as I was. We never gave a thought to the fact that we didn't appear to be "respectable."

But it wasn't long before my ego as a matron and householder was reduced a peg or two by a pact on which John insisted; we were to spend every Tuesday evening apart, do anything we wished, and no questions asked. Much as I hated the idea, I tried to pretend I liked it, but I was so possessively in love that any evenings spent away from John were lost time. When finally I became resigned to these separations, it was because John claimed I was a more interesting companion to him on Wednesday mornings than if we'd spent the previous evenings together. In my eagerness to entertain him, I reported all my innocent diversions, but John never revealed where he spent his free nights, with whom, or what they had been up to. I later found out that, rather pathetically, he sometimes used to take his dates to the same plays we had seen together and would entertain them, second-hand, with cracks I had made, so that actually I was helping to entertain my own rivals.

Married as I was to the love of my life, it soon became apparent that my most exciting experiences had nothing to do with our being together. John's chief diversion was the theater, which we attended nearly every night; on Sundays we went to movies or, less frequently, concerts. Never having been a theater- or music-lover, I was bored by those evenings, and I would sit beside John with my mind wandering. My good friend Henry Sherek, the English raconteur and theatrical producer, once put my own feelings into words: "Everyone in the theater thinks it is the whole of life, whereas it's really a reproduction." I even regarded the time-honored theory that love for the theater is an admirable trait as being pretty fatuous; it seemed an alibi for people who were too listless to manufacture situations and dialogue in real life.

Sometimes, under the aegis of Frank Crowninshield, John and I met up with New York society. Crownie used to recruit guests for parties given by Condé Nast, the publisher of *Vogue* and *Vanity Fair*, in the ballroom of his luxurious Park Avenue apartment. Among Condé's guests there was always a fresh supply of the girls with whom New York was filling up, girls on their own whose families were far in the background, as mine was. Most of them were headed for careers in the theater or as professional beauties.

A new age of adventure for girls was coming into focus. Park Avenue debs were revolting from boredom and, if sufficiently adventurous, they got in with the underworld. The American Prin-

cess Dorothy di Frasso earned distinction by making good with
the mobster Bugsie Siegel. He was by far the most fascinating
young man around New York in those days; tall, dark, and rather
Italian in appearance, he probably looked and behaved more like a
prince than the real one Dorothy had annexed as a husband. Bugsie
resented his nickname, which was always used by newspapers.
Dorothy called him Benjamin; to us he was quite awesomely "Mr.
Siegel." Bugsie's only visible means of support developed later on,
when he moved to Beverly Hills and opened an elegant barbershop
which was patronized by film stars who paid five dollars for a hair-
cut. Even at that unheard-of price, the shop was always crowded
with the elite of Hollywood, and unless a gentleman "belonged" it
was difficult to arrange an appointment. Bugsie's romance with the
Princess continued until he was murdered by a bullet, shot through
the window of his Hollywood mansion by a gangster whose identity has never been revealed.

My husband dated some of the pretty girls we met at Condé's,
while I, seeing that the guests included some fascinating rogues,
quickly found my own level in the ballroom. I forget most of the
social registerites, except one innocuous young man, Caleb Bragg,
and I remember him only because he had a lisp and used to bore
everyone with unbelievable praise of his secretary, a girl named
Ethel Zimmerman, who he claimed could "sing like a bird." He was
always trying to get a Broadway producer to audition her, and it is
now pretty apparent that he succeeded. Her stage name is Ethel
Merman.

When the Talmadge girls and I wanted to be really festive, Harlem was the place to go. Its living quarters, although less congested,
were probably as dingy then as they are now, but every block was
a pleasure zone and Lenox Avenue a permanent carnival. Nobody
wanted to stay indoors; tenants spilled over into the streets, where
jazz was in the air; new rhythms were being extemporized that were
giving America its first serious standing in the world of music. At
Small's Paradise and the Savoy Ballroom the Charleston and black
bottom were danced not as we did them, with a main thought to-

ward showing off; the strut of Harlem was expressing an apotheosis of the human body that even our own high priestess of the dance, Isadora Duncan, admitted she could never achieve.

At that time colored people realized that their instinctive sense of values was more elegant than ours, and they were tolerant of us. But, because the white race failed to segregate its bedrooms, colored blood has been adulterated and our unhealthy traits of doubt and humility are showing up more and more in the colored bloodstream. As this insecurity mounts, it is going to be responsible for ever-increasing peril.

During the 1920s the dope industry, with which the white race has so tragically darkened Harlem, was a minor problem; there was none of the mass addiction which today requires mugging and murder. It seems to me that dope-pushing might be reduced by registering addicts and allowing them to supply their needs openly and at a low cost, as is done in England. That the method is not even tried here makes it seem as if the main profits from pushing dope must be enjoyed in very prominent areas of Washington, D.C.

I learned something about the undercurrents of the Harlem of those days from a maid I had named Clara. She was about twenty-eight, statuesque, attractive, and with a skin so light that there seemed no incongruity in her bleached blond hair. She was given to spells of moody silence, which I used to dramatize as sadness over not being entirely white. One day I ventured to ask Clara if she had ever thought of "passing." "Why, Miss Loos," said she, "I wouldn't be white for anything in the world!" I asked why not. "Well, take those Schencks," she explained. "Mr. Schenck's great big Cadillac stands in front of his office all day long. If one of us colored folks had an automobile like that, we'd be going on a picnic every day. No ma'am! I wouldn't ever want to be humdrummy like that!"

Clara informed me that her friends who had passed did so in order to hold down jobs which were available only to white girls. Because Harlem addresses and telephone numbers were a giveaway, a system had been worked out whereby colored people could use those of some white district. The owner of a Madison Avenue linen shop supplied his address and phone number to a number of Clara's friends, who could check in for mail or messages. But when work was done, Clara assured me, they could hardly wait to get back to Harlem.

It was rather humiliating to find out that Clara's moody silences were just plain boredom over the "white" behavior of my circle of friends. At the same time, I began to wonder if the good old American ideal of working when it isn't necessary might not be the ethic of a grubworm. I am even more certain today that the Negro race has a sense of values which makes ours seem pretty benighted. A motive for celebrating can frequently be that someone is broke and needs to be cheered up. The "rent parties" of the twenties were devised for this reason; a large number of guests made small contributions; landlords were appeased, a good time was had by all, and poverty became an occasion for rejoicing.

On the frequent excursions the Talmadge girls and I took into Harlem we were usually escorted by beaus who were approved by Joe Schenck as being harmless to Norma. One of them was a Jewish boy who seemed to be a permanent fixture on the sidelines at the Savoy Ballroom; generally alone, he appeared to be hypnotized by the music. Sometimes we used to comment on the fact that Georgie Gershwin never seemed to have a girl, and one night I made bold to ask him about it. Moodily George told me the reason: he had had an unhappy love affair with a girl he could never forget. I asked if another boy had come between them. "No," answered Georgie, "she liked me well enough, but she moved to Chicago." The fact that George's lonely state could have been alleviated by a ticket to Chicago made me feel he was pretty lacking in temperament.

Of course the love of George's life was music, and his affair with her made history. But just before he died in Hollywood, George did fall in love, possibly for the first time. The girl was then the wife of Charlie Chaplin, so George's feelings for her must have had sad overtones, but only Paulette Goddard knows how love affected that man of genius, and Paulette refuses to talk. Possibly George's own comment was expressed in the last song he wrote for a Sam Goldwyn musical, "Embraceable You."

On John's Tuesday nights off I began inviting my girl friends in for the evening, and it wasn't long before Joe Schenck took advantage of these parties to keep Norma safe from the wolves, while he played poker with a group of film and theater magnates. His regulars were Sam Goldwyn; the Warner brothers, Jack and Harry; Sam Harris, the theatrical producer; his partner, George M. Cohan; Irving Berlin; and Flo Ziegfeld. Sometimes, when I went to the Schenck apartment to pick Norma up for an afternoon's shopping, the hallway would be acrid with smoke from a game that was still in progress. When Norma dutifully ventured in to give Joe his first kiss of the day, we caught an inspiring glimpse of those big-shot gamblers in their shirtsleeves, intent on stacks of poker chips which might represent half a million dollars. A time came later on when they used to allow the pretty daughter of the stage star Richard Bennett to join them, because Connie Bennett played poker like a man.

As our Tuesday-evening parties caught on, their ranks began to be swelled by other "Tuesday widows" recruited from Broadway and Park Avenue. Those "cat parties" rotated among our various homes: my own; the suite occupied by Peg, Dutch, and Nate in the Ambassador Hotel; the brownstone house on Riverside Drive of our chorus-girl friend Marion Davies; the apartment of a Ziegfeld Follies beauty who was admired by young Vincent Astor. Our parties, while exceedingly gay, were enlivened only by youthful high spirits, giggling, gossip, soft drinks, or, at most, the type of sweet concoctions that are mildly flavored with gin. We cherished an escape from the coquetry required when men were around, while the opportunity to take those same men apart and catalogue their faults was very refreshing.

Little did that coterie of girls realize there was an inspector among us; I realized it least of all, possibly because *I* was the inspector. Unconsciously I was taking the measure of them all and

learning a lot; I learned that, contrary to the supposition that bitch-
iness generally exists among pretty girls, they have an unusual
kindness toward one another. In the first place, they share the bond
of special persecutions which average young women never need to
suffer—the revulsion that comes from being mauled by practically
every man they meet. Then, too, pretty girls are forced to listen
while males who happen to be in their liquor make absolutely ap-
palling declarations in words of four letters; they learn too early
that married men are cheaters and that those who don't cheat aren't
real men. Among the more opulent type of showgirls there is an
almost apologetic sense of being freaks of nature, which indeed
they are. But possibly the biggest fly in the beauty ointment is the
fact that most men who chase after pretty girls are only trying to
attract attention to themselves. Men worth having are thus inclined
to be wary, so that pretty girls are often forced to content themselves with second-class citizens. Sometimes in their efforts to
annex real men they make tragic mistakes, as did poor little Marilyn
Monroe.

Yes, pretty girls have an unusually deep sympathy for one another, a feeling that they stand together with the whole world of
men lined up against them. They are as capable of producing female versions of the Damon and Pythias mystique as were Lorelei
Lee and her girl friend Dorothy.

One of the prettiest girls in our set and of that era was Marilyn
Miller; I shouldn't wonder if it was she who introduced the name
of Marilyn into the nomenclature of our country. A doll-like
blonde, but a thoroughly trained singer, ballet dancer, and comedi-
enne, she was the bright particular star of the Ziegfeld Follies.
From childhood Marilyn had been so disciplined by a grim Prussian
father that she had never learned to play and she had no life of her
own, although Flo Ziegfeld loved her passionately and she was the
idol of all stage-door Johnnies. The exhaustion of giving eight performances a week and the tyranny of her singing and dancing
teachers kept Marilyn on a treadmill, but sometimes in the dead of
night she was able to sneak away from the family flat on Riverside
Drive, hail a taxi, and show up at our cat parties. Ill at ease, she

added little to our laughing sessions, although we went out of our way to include Marilyn in the fun. (Ultimately she escaped from home by means of marriage to an unimportant young actor. But the vitality of her sparkling stage presence was purely a matter of technique and all on the surface. Like that other famous Marilyn, she died young.)

One regular guest at those cat parties was the lively teenage blonde whose stage name was Marion Davies. She was the daughter of a Brooklyn judge of Irish extraction, by the name of Douras. The judge had allowed Marion to scamper off to Broadway and take a job in the chorus of *Lady, Be Good*, a musical revue running at the Liberty Theatre on West 44th Street. Marion was placed at the end of a chorus line of beauties, the other end being occupied by Justine Johnston, a more classical type of blonde whose story is one of the most incredible I've ever known. This was brought home to me years later when Julian Huxley, the noted British author and scientist, first planned to visit Hollywood. As a friend, I had written to ask him whom he wanted to meet in the film capital, and his reply had mentioned Charlie Chaplin and Justine Johnston. Mr. Huxley (now Sir Julian Huxley) had no information about Justine Johnston except that she had just earned worldwide recognition for her part in developing the first cure for syphilis in medical history. When Huxley met Justine her slim figure had the same allure as when she was one of the most desirable showgirls in Manhattan. Her blond hair had turned white, which gave her beauty an extraordinary shock value, and Huxley gained an impression of glamour that even outdid that of Hollywood.

When Justine and Marion Davies first took to frequenting our cat parties, Marion's chief admirer was the middle-aged and wealthy publisher of the *Brooklyn Eagle*, and she had only just met William Randolph Hearst, the greater and richer publisher who would soon be launching her as a film star.

When Marion joined our group she had just had her first date with Mr. Hearst. He had invited her and Justine Johnston to a party at a studio in the West Forties which he kept purposely to entertain bohemian friends. Marion, who was always modest to an absurd degree, thought she had been asked merely as Justine's chum, and that night, when W. R. began to pay her special attention, she became terribly self-conscious and confused. In order to gain composure she drank too much champagne and before long realized she was going to be sick. Too embarrassed to ask such a great man the location of the bathroom, Marion sneaked into an empty study, where the traces of her sad condition were hidden behind the cushions of a cozy corner. From such a humiliating and absurd beginning there grew the most enduring love story of our entire era.

During one of our late sessions in my Gramercy Square house we girls happened to be rummaging through a closet and ran across a dictaphone with a number of cylinders. On testing them out, we found they recorded a series of pompous sermons delivered by a character who happened to be my landlord, a middle-aged scion of a prominent Knickerbocker family with strong church affiliations. Finding those recorded sermons prompted me to tell the girls about an incident that occurred the day I went to the old boy's office to sign the lease and he made a pass at me which somewhat reduced his stature as a churchman. The occurrence gave Marion an idea to pay the old rascal back; to shave his sermons off the cylinders and replace them with risqué jokes, of which we had a goodly collection handed down from Wall Street admirers. (One day I should like scientifically to explore the reason why so many dirty jokes emanate from Wall Street, whose denizens are not noted for wit.) One recording we made that night was a parody on "The Merry Widow Waltz," and the lyric was sung by Marion to music played by Dorothy Norman, a brunette whom Ziegfeld allowed the distinction of playing a piano solo in the Follies. The lyric goes as follows and can be sung by the present reader, if he so chooses:

> She wears a chiffon nightie
> In the summer when it's hot.
> She wears her woolly panties
> In the winter when it's not.
> But often in the springtime,

And sometimes in the fall,
She slips between the sheets
With nothing on at all.

With the innocence of the twenties, we considered it to be a
wicked song, but, even though mild, it must have provoked something of a shock in anyone who ran the cylinder expecting to hear
the voice of my landlord come out with, "Dearly beloved, I come
before you on this Sabbath day with a warning against the sin
of . . ."

While the other girls of our set were committed, by husbands,
beaus, or keepers, to spending their free evenings with their own
sex, I was left to do exactly as I wished. And if I had John to blame
for night after night of unwilling theater attendance, I had him to
thank for some Tuesday evenings spent in the companionship of
extraordinary men. I would never have entered into those friendships had my husband resented them, but he made a great issue of
our forming attachments of our own, which he vaguely indicated
were to be platonic. But ironically, when John advocated my seeing other men, he failed to realize that they might prove to be more
important than he was, and when such turned out to be the case I
must have rubbed salt into his already wounded male vanity.

❧ CHAPTER 13

❧ When, after years of anticipation, I finally met Mencken, it was difficult to remember that he had ever intimidated me. I can't even recall when or where our friendship began because it now seems as if I had always known him. I am hard put to describe Menck's enormous charm; based on extreme masculinity, at the same time it never seemed to be quite that of a grown-up. There was always something of an outrageous small boy about Menck, one whose habitat was country lanes, barns, and little red school-houses. Along with his homespun appearance, innocent blue eyes, and straight brown hair that was normally short in back but long enough in front for a precise and rather countrified part down the middle, went a sophistication that made the typical New Yorker seem pretty shallow.

Menck's writings had caused him to be a "matinee idol" on every college campus, but his attraction didn't end there. I knew any number of Ziegfeld Follies beauties who went about carrying copies of his *Prejudices* under their arms on a chance of running into its author in that circuit of the West Forties that included their theater and his hotel. Had Menck wished he could have enjoyed all the success of which his elegant confrère George Jean Nathan boasted and Scott Fitzgerald wrote. I'm sure Menck owned a large collection of gift neckties from lovelorn females, together with endless handkerchiefs initialed by hands that would never have taken up a needle for any but a sexy reason.

At the time I met him Menck was a bachelor in his early forties; he made his home in Baltimore with his mother, occupying the house where he had lived from infancy. He spent no more time in New York than the few days each month required of him as co-publisher with George Jean Nathan of *The Smart Set*. His preference for Baltimore was because, in his own words, "it bulges with normalcy." "The charm of getting home," Menck said, "is the charm of getting back to what is inextricably one's own—to things familiar and long loved, to things that belong to me alone and none other. No conceivable interior decorator could give me the peace and comfort of my own house."

As I was curious about Menck's life in Baltimore, I used endlessly to quiz his cronies about it. His house was described to me as one of a long row of brick structures of the Federal type, which on the inside was anything but typically American. The décor smacked of Menck's Teutonic background and of the Lutheran ancestors in whom he took great pride; there were portraits of a succession of professsors at the University of Leipzig, the first of which had been painted way back in medieval times. It was easy to visualize the old-world charm of the life Menck led there with his mother. I've always felt that the Germans are able to combine the tender emotions with expert housekeeping as no other people can. At any rate, the word *Gemütlichkeit*, which expresses that combination, doesn't exist in any other language; it has been best described by the French writer Giraudoux as "a sort of dynamic energy which persists among Germans, even when scattered onto other continents. From it rises not only the music of symphonies, but also the aroma of sauerkraut." The Mencken kitchen was famous for such *heimisch* items as *Knackwurst* and *Apfelschnitten*, for *Baumküchen* at Christmastime that were as steeped in sentiment as any wedding cake; for cookies that looked like valentines. Music, too, formed an integral part of Menck's home life. Every Saturday night he held forth in his parlor as pianist for an all-male group of amateur musicians, most of whom were scientists or professors at Johns Hopkins University. They drank beer from steins and banged

My chief requirement in writing scripts for all those first Fairbanks movies was to find a variety of spots from which Doug could jump. This is one of his jumping spots in *American Aristocracy*.

Wallace Reid played the typical upright American hero with a modicum of native equipment.

Wallie's was a face that launched a thousand slips, one of which was a then un-American drug addiction. In the terminology of Wilson Mizner, Wallie was a "user."

Culver Pictures, Inc.

One of my best-loved impostors was Erich von Stroheim, a tender-hearted lamb who staggered about in wolf's clothing.

The Museum of Modern Art Film Library

Von's favorite disguise was that of a sadistic lecher straight out of Krafft-Ebing: the man you love to hate.

Culver Pictures, Inc.

Fashion was never out of my mind. I tried to appear dignified and tall, but the wolfhound was a giveaway. I should have gone around with a Mexican chihuahua.

But I triumphed in trying to copy Fritzi Scheff, the operatic star. The day I met her she gasped: "Good heavens, child, you look just like me when I was a girl in Vienna!"

For my Pola Negri phase, the demi-monde's most famous couturière, Madame Frances, chose a color she termed "a nice sexy beige."

A girl could buy hats in Holly-wood that came all the way from Paris.

This was the formal outfit that slew George Jean Nathan.

The day Buster Keaton married Natalie Talmadge my husband and I tried to provide an example of painless domesticity; Buster's expression indicates he was not impressed.

D.W. Griffith and Joe Schenck completely broke down my vaunted lack of respect for everybody.

The Museum of Modern Art Film Library

This was the hairdo on which my angelic mother insisted.

I took a pair of scissors and whacked out the first recorded boyish bob of the twentieth century; one which Mme. Lanvin copied on one of her manikins the day she saw me in Paris.

This picture of "marital felicity" was shot in Vienna when my mind was 3000 miles away.

Vachel Lindsay wanted to trap me behind a
picket fence in Springfield, Illinois.

Sherwood Anderson was "Swatty" to those
who knew him; he and John grew up together
in Clyde, Ohio. From there they took opposite
directions. The one I preferred was Swatty's.

Constance Talmadge, an idol of the silent films, has been largely forgotten because nobody bothered to protect the negatives of her films from disintegrating into dust.

Culver Pictures, Inc.

Constance's film *The Goldfish* indicates that she never studied with Stanislavski, but this never lessened her impact on movie fans.

My first movie for Constance was titled by Irving Berlin *The Virtuous Vamp*, a name that suited her both on screen and off.

The Museum of Modern Art Film Library

Norma Talmadge was a figure of romance all over the world, but I never knew any girl who was less to be envied.

The men I most cared for outdid each other in their jaunty irreverence. Henry Mencken, in a priest's garb, wrote on this picture: "Sister Anita, pax vobiscum, Brother Heinrich."

I loved the vaudeville comic Joe Frisco, but Joe was in the toils of the race track and his heart belonged to horses.

Wilson Mizner was inveigled by Darryl Zanuck into attending a studio costume party as a monk. It gave Wilson an opportunity to go Mencken one better; he sent me this picture inscribed "*Pox* vobiscum."

There have been many famous Lorelei Lees, from June Walker, who first played her on the stage, to Ruth Taylor, who was the Lorelei of silent films, to Carol Channing of the stage musical and Marilyn Monroe of the musical film, but to me none was more satisfactory than Chester Conklin.

Dear miss foot.
Here is your Lorelei
I have changed a little
but I'm still a good girl.
Love and kisses
Chester Conklin.

out the melodies of Schubert, Brahms, and Bach, making up in masculine fervor what they lacked in proficiency.

Menck's loathing of the infantilism that had overtaken American thought was exceeded only by his reverence for the maturity of our pioneer ancestors. He claimed that nobody could live the good American life amid the "glittering swinishness" of New York. "The New Yorker," he declared, "is a vagabond. His notions of the agreeable are those of a vaudeville actor. He is extremely 'in the know' and inordinately trashy. What makes New York so dreadful," wrote Menck, "is the fact that its people have been forced to rid themselves of the oldest and most powerful human instinct— the love of home." And by "home" Menck meant a small house with a bit of garden. I used to look on Menck's summation of the typical New Yorker as one of his ribald jokes but, in the light of the sixties, I find that his description was, on the whole, a compliment. To be "in the know" has now been reduced to the two-letter preposition "in"; it means that a person is so insecure as to be constantly on exhibition, but at the same time playing a mere super's role in a production that any self-respecting vaudeville actor of the twenties would have turned down. While few New York homes of the twenties boasted gardens, many of them had both a parlor *and* a dining room which were rather large; ceilings were high, and there were even fireplaces.

Recently I had a revealing experience about the life of New York in the sixties; it took place when our neighborhood grocery store had to be torn down to make room for a new cell-block of apartments. One day I asked our grocer where his new store would be located and learned that he was going out of business. I remarked that this seemed foolish when the population of our neighborhood would soon be enormously increased. "That doesn't mean a thing," he told me. "These new apartments are so small they don't require any housekeeping; most women have office jobs these days; at mealtime they order sandwiches from a delicatessen or eat sitting on stools in a drugstore. Every time a big new apartment building has gone up here, my customers have decreased."

One result of these cramped quarters is that home life is forced out into the streets. Holidays and special family occasions must be celebrated in theaters or restaurants; romantic intimacies have to be indulged in at discothèques, where there is too much noise for any spoken endearments. Typical New Yorkers express themselves in gyrations which are bald and primitive, with no originality at all—except in Harlem, where the gyrations were invented and remain spontaneous.

But to give the sixties their due, they have developed one civilizing new element which would have delighted Mencken; it is the great number of shops where paperback books are sold. There is one in my own apartment building that is open seven days of the week, twenty-four hours a day. While it's true that many paperbacks are reprints of current pornography, there is an extraordinarily large range of authors; books by Pushkin, Hawthorne, Walter Scott, Victor Hugo can be bought very cheaply, so there is reason to hope that the typical New Yorker may not succumb to a mass softening of the brain.

On my first date with Mencken he took me to dinner at Luchow's, of which he was a devout patron, for it was during Prohibition and Luchow's provided genuine Würzburger beer disguised in teacups. But neither Menck nor his group ever examined any drink too closely and, as our friendship progressed in the various speakeasies of Manhattan, I found that they all drank freely of bathtub gin, whisky colored with creosote, and beer that was needled with ether. I sometimes wonder how much lusty health was ruined, how many deaths accelerated, by Prohibition; and how many first-rate minds were lost to the U.S.A. in exchange for Mrs. Carry Nation, whose contribution to progress took the form of smashing beer barrels with an ax in small neighborhood saloons.

One of Menck's favorite playgrounds was a Rathskeller in Union Hill, New Jersey, which boasted a secret pipeline to a Munich brewery. He took a boyish pleasure in the long cab ride to Union Hill. The Rathskeller looked like a scene in one of Grimms' fairy tales, for it was patronized by a colony of midgets who lived in the neighborhood, and the beer steins they hoisted were colossal in contrast to their tiny bodies. There I would sit, sometimes the only female in the company of Mencken, Joseph Hergesheimer, Ernest Boyd the Irish-born essayist, and theater critic George Jean Nathan, listening to the most rousing talk I've ever heard about politics, art, music, philosophy, and life in general.

Menck took immoderate glee in roaring out insults at fellow Americans. He invented the term "Bible Belt" for that portion of our country where the mental climate is produced by "Methodists, Baptists, and other vermin of God." Menck's nickname for our Southern states was "The Sahara of the Bozarts" (meaning Beaux Arts), which one day would be my reason for making the moronic heroine of Gentlemen Prefer Blondes a citizen of that nadir of intelligence, Little Rock. My book was certainly an offshoot of Mencken's point of view, just as a gadget can be produced by the important theory of a scientist.

Henry Mencken was one of those rare monologists who could also listen. But no bore was ever allowed the opportunity to start an argument. "You're probably right!" he used to say, graciously bringing all such stupidities to an end. Menck made a big issue of being sacrilegious and a foe of monogamy, while at the same time his attitude toward true believers was one of full-scale respect. In his day intellectuals were steeped in the ideology of Schopenhauer and Nietzsche and it was the fashion to be sacrilegious. One time Menck sent me a photograph of himself in clerical robes, which it must have taken some effort to fake. On it he wrote: "Sister Anita, pax vobiscum. Brother Heinrich." His equally irreverent crony Ernest Boyd, being spare and of pale complexion, with red hair and a pointed beard, loved to make a joke about his own resemblance to the paintings of Christ. When Ernest lived in Dublin he had even posed as Christ for the window of a church. He sent me a photograph of it on which he wrote: "Anita, what a friend you have in Jesus!" Another ribald character, Wilson Mizner, whom I later came to love, was once inveigled into going to a costume ball dressed in a monk's outfit. I still treasure his photograph, on which Wilson wrote: "Pox vobiscum."

Although the three men were different in other respects, they all had a swaggering wickedness, and it was for this I first loved them. But I never loved them less when I finally came to realize they were not as tough as they pretended and could be easy victims of the tender emotions they made fun of and struggled to deny. None of them could ever hold out against a vapid blonde, a nostalgic perfume, or a schmaltzy melody; they were all in constant danger of softening of the heart. Menck proved to be a vulnerable and even a religious man when, after his mother died, he knelt in front of an Episcopal altar in Baltimore and married Sarah Haardt, a plain-faced schoolmarm who was no longer young, the antithesis of all "we" girls who believed Menck when he pretended to be "beyond good and evil." And in time I came to realize that my poor mother's clichés were uncommonly sound; a man worth marrying generally chooses a wife he can visualize as his mother. It is of no small significance that, in the sound psychology of Tin Pan Alley, the height of sex appeal is expressed by the term "red-hot mama."

I was far too cagy to let Menck know the depth of my feelings for him, but today, as I look through the letters he wrote me, I can accuse him of a subtle type of come-on that kept our romance very actively alive. "I can imagine nothing more lovely," he wrote, "than seeing you again and kissing your hands." "What became of you last Monday? I sat guarding the beer keg all day and you didn't show up." "You are a handsome gal, as well as a gifted authoress." "Are you in New York? I hope to be there toward the end of the month. I crave the boon of witnessing you." After the publication of *Gentlemen Prefer Blondes* Menck became a trace more definite and wrote me in the vernacular of my heroine: "A woman with a husband who lolls around with actresses deserves to take a look at a handsome man once in a while and if she sends him a pitcher of herself and he gets mashed on it, no one has any call to remark on it, if he behaves like a gentleman. . . ."

But Menck was a man of honor in the most old-fashioned sense; the fact that he sometimes spent time with both my husband and me made him feel obliged to consider John a friend. He never wrote me without sending his respects to John. But even in 1934, after his own marriage, Menck wrote me in Santa Monica: "Don't you ever come East any more? I can imagine nothing more lovely than seeing you again and kissing your hands."

While Menck's infrequent visits to New York limited my dates with him, I got to know other men of importance, and without realizing it I began to usurp John's place with the chum of his boyhood, a novelist who was just coming into fame. Sherwood Anderson and John had been childhood friends in Clyde, Ohio, where they were born. About the time John entered college to study for the ministry, Sherwood (or Swatty, as I must call him, since we never used any but his nickname) had enlisted in the Army and gone to that feeble little skirmish we pulled off in Cuba and pompously called the Spanish-American War. On Swatty's return from war he had gone back to Clyde, taken a job in a washing-machine factory, married, settled down, had two children, and seemed on the surface to be an ideal washing-machine salesman—ideal, that is, up to one evening when, just like Fred Talmadge, the father of Norma and Constance, he failed to come home to supper. Swatty's absence was so unusual that consternation gripped his family. When he failed to show up for days on end, it was even feared that Swatty might have been run over by a train or otherwise met with a fatal accident. But he had simply walked away from home and turned tramp in pursuit of freedom to write. Previous to this, although he spent many evenings poring over the novels of Dostoevski, nobody, not even John, ever heard Swatty say he wanted to write.

For several years Swatty lived as an itinerant laborer, during which time he wrote his short-story collection *Winesburg, Ohio*, and managed to get it published. The first news that either his family or John had of him came from book reviews in which critics hailed Sherwood Anderson as a new force in American literature. John wrote to Swatty in care of his publisher; Swatty answered, saying that he had settled in Chicago, where he was trying to make a living as a writer of advertising copy, but without much success. John sent for Swatty to come to New York and be our press agent. The job was only an excuse to help him out, for Swatty was incapable of writing the provocative trash required by newspaper columns; I doubt that a single one of his items ever got into print. But, hanging around us, he became more my friend than he had ever been John's.

Mencken respected Swatty, as he did all writers who were honestly wrestling with the truth, even though he was a little quizzical over Swatty's particular brand of it. In fact, no two men could have differed more than Swatty and Mencken. Swatty was monumental, big-boned, rugged, and he had a shock of graying hair that served to accent his leonine appearance. But poor Swatty was as impressed by New York as Menck was contemptuous of it. I remember a confidence Swatty made soon after he arrived: "Nita, I'm not going to let New York get me down. When I walk along the streets, I brace myself to look everyone right in the eye!"

There was one element in Swatty's writing that I failed to appreciate: he considered the most inconsequential victim of a nervous or mental disorder to be more important than any normal human being. I feel this was caused by his attempt to copy Dostoevski. In Swatty's accounts of life in a bustling Midwestern town, he ascribed to our energetic people a passivity that is characteristic of the Russians and not at all true of our efficient makeup.

This phony Russo-American slant on life was not confined to Swatty alone; in fact I remember discussing it with Aldous Huxley one day when we were walking home from a matinee of a Tennessee Williams play. Aldous made a wide gesture which took in an entire district. "Look at this busy area," he said, "and figure the tremendous amount of healthy, organized effort required to run it twenty-four hours a day, from its high-powered executives on down to the scrubwomen. Surely the problems of these coordinated people are more dramatic than those in the play we just saw; problems based on the active business of living and not on the erratic misfortunes of a peculiar minority."

I believe that the antithesis of *Pollyanna* is just as inartistic as that idiotic Glad Girl is herself; that the real American belongs to a coordinated breed which produces astronauts; that even such science-fiction characters as Superman, the Mighty Hercules, and Astroboy, are more real than the heroes of Tennessee Williams, Arthur Miller, and sometimes even Faulkner, whose guilt over the discovery of a sex urge makes them all so childishly morbid. Mark Twain, when dealing with his moronic poetess in *Tom Sawyer,* didn't try to make her anything more than an amusing goon. Arthur Miller would have given her all the importance of Lady Macbeth.

I feel that sex aberrations, such as those described by the French stylist Jean Genet, are deeply rooted in the author's own character and reveal a poetry that nature never lacks, even in sex-riddled tramps. But I don't believe in depravity that is trumped up on a typewriter. The American critics, however, have been impressed by what they mistake for truth; our literature has been influenced by their praise and it began to lose a sense of normal American mankind as we find it in Mark Twain. Out of this trend there developed a school of writing that reduced the American scene to the status of a bowl of worms and then reported their convolutions from the viewpoint of one of the worms.

Such fiction has been widely read for its shock value and the novelty of seeing four-letter words printed elsewhere than on fences, but although it has a certain value as comment on the adult infantilism of its day, I doubt that much of it will ever join the classics. The nearest that Dickens ever came to an indecent episode is the one in *David Copperfield* when Little Em'ly is skipping about on top of a parapet and Dickens states, in a veiled comment, that it would have been better if Em'ly had slipped and fallen to a death which, in that day, was preferable to "dishoner." Thackeray's raciest incident describes Clive Newcombe kissing his beautiful cousin Ethel while going through a tunnel in a crowed train; Trollope, even in dealing with the very naughty Lizzy Eustace, merely allows her to be embraced in broad daylight while a scandalized gardener looks on. But with all their Victorian restraint, those old best-sellers are still hot items in the paperbacks, because their characters are just as alive as the reader. In order for people actually to relate to an unbalanced school of thought, they have to be equally off base, and, as an optimist, I doubt that the reading public will ever develop a majority of such weaklings.

The callow attitude of American fiction showed a tendency to disappear when Edward Albee, although dealing with a set of amoebic characters, chose to look on them not through the eyes of an amoeba but through those of an eagle—an American eagle, may I add, giving him a very low curtsy for the classic spirit of his *The American Dream*. But in his recent works Albee himself fell into the trap that was first baited by Freud and when he defected our literature might have sunk back on the analyst's couch where it lay dying, had it not been rescued and once again put soundly on its feet by Truman Capote. While Capote's *In Cold Blood* is based on the atrocities of two degenerates, he treats his material with the superhuman sanity of genius.

A time finally arrived when John's work as a director of Constance Talmadge light comedies failed to satisfy him; he yearned to play to larger audiences than those on his movie sets and decided he could find them in quasi-political activities. His theories slanted toward the extreme left, while my own followed those of my adored Mencken toward the right. Menck had no truck with the welfare state; I was with him once when he let out a blast at a panhandler that was awful to hear. "Goddam it," he said, "I'm paying ruinous taxes to provide you bums with leisure! I'd like a little leisure myself to spend on the Greek philosophers. Beat it!" But even though I sided with Menck, I saw no reason why John shouldn't be sincere, and I respected his theories. And there now came an opportunity for him to put them into practice. The New York theater was full of injustices; chorus girls were required to buy the stockings they wore on stage; actors were forced to rehearse for long stretches without pay. The Actors Equity Association decided to brave the producers and demand reforms; having once been an actor, John stepped into the situation on the part of Actors Equity. The arguments which ensued that spring presaged an actors' strike in the fall. While it was gathering steam, John decided we should take a trip to Europe, which was to be my first.

One of my fondest dreams had been to see Paris under the guidance of Rayne Adams, who had remained there as a permanent resident after the war. Rayne had written me a description of the Left Bank hotel where he lived; it was easy to visualize through having known the quarters he occupied in New York. They were in a bohemian hotel on East Tenth Street, by name the Albert. I still recall that a feature of Rayne's living room was an electric-light bracket at which he used to toss his neckties; some of them stuck to it, and on Rayne's wall-bracket they looked good. I sometimes wondered if, in the zany surroundings of a Left Bank attic, Rayne might forget his allegiance to John and resume his comic courtship of me; even speculated whether, in those circumstances, infidelity might lose some of its importance. But one day a tragic cablegram put a stop to all such speculations. Rayne had been taken to a hospital for what should have been a simple operation for appendicitis and had suddenly died. So we were never again to share our impressions of life, love, and literature, but even today I never pass the old Hotel Albert without thinking of Rayne.

Before our departure for Europe, Joe Schenck offered John a five-year contract to supervise productions for both Norma and Constance Talmadge. However, Joe had decided to transfer his operations to Hollywood, which would mean our living in a place we disliked. Worst of all, it would remove John from the battleground of the forthcoming actors' strike. Seeing that we were financially independent through John's investments in the stock market, he decided to retire and devote his life to helping the downtrodden, and I thus entered the world of the earnestly liberal rich. We sailed on the *Paris* with Dutch, Peg, and Nate Talmadge in tow. Swatty was left behind, for by this time, as a virile man of letters, he was earning big money by giving readings to ladies' clubs; he also began a masochistic career of divorcing and marrying one woman after another. He had shed his Ohio wife and was taking on a rawboned bride, appropriately named Tennessee. I failed to appreciate Tennessee, but during the years she spent as one of Swatty's manifold wives she provided some of the inspiration for his novel *Many*

Marriages. At the same time, she never interfered with the platonic friendship I enjoyed with Swatty, and for that I was grateful to Tennessee.

Before we sailed for France, John decided that his socialistic activities required a press agent, and he engaged a young man named James Ashmore Creelman, who belonged to Swatty's family. Uncouth though Swatty was, he had some socially prominent relatives in New York. Young Creelman's father was a gentleman journalist and close friend of Theodore Roosevelt. He had fought in Cuba as a member of the elite Rough Riders and had written the official account of their exploits for *The New York Times*. Young Creelman's mother, who was beautiful, cultured, and a connoisseur of painting, was engaged by Henry Clay Frick to select the collection which is now housed in the Frick Gallery in New York. John included young Creelman in our European holiday, and as long as he lived he was my shadow, with John's acquiescence, for "Ash" must have reduced some of John's guilt over neglecting me. I'm afraid I took Ash for granted and failed to appreciate his devotion. He was merely one of a collection of weaklings I seemed to attract; some of them had tragic endings, of which I absolve myself; except for John Emerson, I was merely an innocent bystander.

CHAPTER 14

The first time I saw Paris, I discovered it with the same gusto as does any American tourist. I remember the boat train slowly making its way through those exciting old-world neighborhoods on the wrong side of the tracks. Looking out the window that morning, we saw numberless little girls on the sidewalks and I remarked that we must be in the vicinity of a school. But it seemed an unusual hour for school to be out and as we puzzled over these children it finally dawned on us that they weren't children at all; they were grown women wearing the first knee-revealing skirts in the history of fashion. We were actually looking on at the beginning of a clothes revolution that was going to affect women all over the world, changing the rhythm, culture, and even the moral tone of every generation up to now.

Those short dresses already worn by hoi polloi on the wrong side of the Paris tracks all stemmed from the enterprise of a newcomer in the fashion trade, a gamine named Coco Chanel, whose name as yet we hadn't heard. (In this winter of 1965, Chanel is still an influence in fashion; her designs have changed very little since the twenties. It would be too great a sacrifice to pass up the rejuvenating effect of short skirts and skimpy jackets which help women not to look their age.)

In days like these, when fashions are duplicated on the bargain counters of New York a few days after their origin in Paris, it's hard to realize that it used to take a style several months to cross the Atlantic, and when the Talmadges and I arrived in Paris wearing New York clothes we found ourselves incredibly dowdy. The Talmadges felt they could endure the situation until they might buy some Paris dresses. I couldn't. My first act on reaching the hotel was to call a valet and order him to remove a good two inches off my skirts. The result was so rejuvenating that, having looked all of sixteen on my arrival, I might now have passed for twelve. The effect was heightened by a new hair style devised just before I left New York. I took manicure scissors and thinned my page-boy bob into tousled locks so that I appeared, to coin a phrase, "windblown."

On our first morning in Paris we girls ventured forth to inspect the dress collection at Lanvin's. Since none of us had ever been in such a place, we were overawed by its regal entrance. We were further disturbed when a *directrice* on guard at the door wanted to know who had invited us. Dutch announced that we had merely stumbled in from the street, and the woman, smiling icily, led us to some uncomfortable gilt chairs across a salon so chastely elegant as to chill our spirits even further. The few clients who happened to be there that morning were French; to our envious gaze they seemed entirely at home. They paid us no attention, in spite of Dutch's sparkling blond beauty. We looked on, spellbound, as the manikins showed the dresses, but had no idea how to go about buying anything. Our feelings of insecurity increased when a *vendeuse* approached and, addressing me, said, "I beg your pardon, mademoiselle, but Madame Lanvin wishes to know if you would step into her office."

We girls exchanged glances, convinced that I was going to be asked to take our group away because we had crashed. Nevertheless I summoned the courage to swish my short skirt into Madame's office. She was seated behind her desk, a motherly type, in a black dress that made no pretensions to chic. She graciously asked my name, which of course meant nothing, and then said, "Mademoiselle, would you permit my designer to make a sketch of your head, so that one of my manikins can show your coiffure while modeling the dresses?" I was almost dumb with amazement over the request, and at the same time no end relieved that we weren't going to be thrown out. I eagerly agreed to pose, whereat Madame sent for a young man who sketched me then and there. When I returned to the girls and reported what had happened, they were as astounded as I. But, at the same time, my adventure made us bold enough to summon a *vendeuse*, try on dresses, and purchase any number of them.

Although I would have adored to investigate Paris with my husband, he preferred much of the time to go it alone, searching adventures which I'm sure were innocuous enough but would have been dulled by the presence of a childish-looking wife. I think he spent his time showing the city to American tourists he picked up, most of them nondescript young girls who made him feel important. He had purchased an enormous English touring car and hired a chauffeur, and after breakfast he would bid me good-by, step into our car, and disappear, leaving Ash Creelman and me to our own devices and the mercy of Paris taxicabs.

During those first days in Paris I experienced the same ecstasy over its famous landmarks as does every American, but I had an advantage over most sightseers; I had met many of the international café-society set in New York, and we were ushered into a few holies-of-holies. One of them was the salon of Gertrude Stein, into which Ash and I were introduced one evening by the youthful Mexican caricaturist Miguel Covarrubias and his pretty brunette wife, Rose. Gertrude Stein then lived in the little jewel box of a house she shared with Alice B. Toklas, at 27 rue de Fleurus. Every Saturday night a mixed group of intellectuals paid tribute to our compatriot; among them were even some of the French, whose love for Americans is generally confined to our dollars and our jazz. At those Paris evenings Gertrude held forth, an imposing figure, enthroned in the enormous chair required by her weight. Gertrude's clothing had no more style than your grandpa's flannel bathrobe; she wore a loose shirtwaist and skirt, her ground-gripper shoes seemed equally comfortable, and, with her hair sensibly cropped like a man's, she had the air of having found the amiable contentment of a Buddha.

Gertrude's atelier at the rue de Fleurus was a storehouse of paintings by Picasso, Cézanne, Matisse, and other impressionists, Fauves, and Cubists, whom Gertrude had collected at a time when hardly anyone else recognized their worth. Most people were shocked by the eccentricity of those radical art schools, but in my eyes Gertrude made the pictures look almost normal. I should have been impressed by some of the famous painters who were at the house that night, but they were lost in the confusion. I was equally unimpressed by American writers I did recognize. Coming from our unsophisticated New World, they were a jejune lot; among them were Ernest Hemingway and Scott Fitzgerald, who spent their time freewheeling around Paris, their attitude being "Look, Mom, I'm an author!" I respected Gertrude as the most manly of the lot, and I took an instant liking to her companion, Alice B. Toklas. Small, dark, and with a girlish hairdo that ended in bangs, Alice had that certain feature which adds piquancy to a woman, provided she is cute to begin with—a mustache. In Alice's case it was very black, an arresting contrast to her feminine accomplishments of needlework, housekeeping, and cookery. But it seemed to me that by rights the mustache should have been on Gertrude.

When I had first heard of Gertrude Stein, she happened to be an idol of Swatty's, and we used to argue about her literary style; rightly or wrongly, I couldn't concentrate on her writings. Swatty explained her book *Tender Buttons* in this fashion: one should look on it as one looks at the palette of a painter, appreciate the words merely as words, and pay no attention to the context in which she placed them. When I paraphrased Swatty's summation of her art to Gertrude, she approved it highly. "Anderson understands exactly what I'm getting at," said she. "Words which in a dictionary are dead, immediately spring to life when I put them onto paper."

Many years elapsed before I again saw Gertrude's fabulous collection of paintings; in fact it was after her death following World War II. The pictures were then hanging in a cavernous flat Alice

Toklas occupied on the Left Bank behind a butcher shop. I went to tea there in company with that true Parisian, the American writer Tom Curtiss, who was then drama critic for the Paris edition of the *New York Herald Tribune*. The state of Alice's health was grim; a crippling arthritis had resulted in curvature of the spine, and she could barely manage to hobble with the aid of two stout canes. Her hair had turned iron-gray, but her mustache was still black, and it seemed more prominent than ever against the pallor of her skin. She wore a dark gray flannel skirt and a loose jacket required by her ailment, but with feminine coquetry, sported a flamboyant black hat of the type called Merry Widow. It was trimmed with willow plumes, and Alice must have treasured it since the Gay Nineties when it was in style.

During our visit that day, Alice's arthritis brought up the subject of a cure I had undergone the previous year at Acqui Terme, an isolated spa in northern Italy. I had gone to Acqui suffering from the form of arthritis called writer's cramp, for which I had had endless cortisone treatments by specialists in New York, London, and Paris, to no effect. But after two weeks of the radioactive mud treatment at Acqui I was able to discard a splint that had disabled my right arm for more than a year. When I mentioned the fact to Alice it was more or less by way of making conversation, because she appeared too feeble to make a trip to that rather remote place. But she took me so seriously that she managed to get to Acqui that same summer. At the end of her two weeks' stay Alice wrote me in gratitude: "I have just strapped my canes to my umbrella and am *walking* to the station."

Although Alice's income had always been meager, she had one magnificent luxury, the paintings Gertrude left her. There was a clause in Gertrude's will stating that, if pressed for money, Alice might sell a painting. The sale of a single one of them would have provided all the creature comforts she lacked but, as she told Tom and me, the sight of the paintings every morning when she waked up gave her pleasure enough to carry her through the day, no matter how great her pain.

During the winter months Alice was forced to leave Paris because her flat was without central heating and her health couldn't support the damp and chill of the Paris winters. At these times she found hospitality and warmth in a convent on the outskirts of Rome. One year, on returning home, Alice was appalled to find that nothing remained of her dazzling Picassos, Cézannes, and all the others except pale spaces on the grimy walls where they used to hang. Gertrude Stein's heirs, to whom the pictures will go on Alice's death, had secured an order from the Paris authorities to confiscate them. The shock of finding her paintings gone without any warning took so heavy a toll of Alice's health as to alarm her many friends. Foremost among them is the composer, Virgil Thomson, who immediately flew to Paris from New York to give Alice aid and comfort. It became apparent that Gertrude's heirs actually had an excuse for removing the paintings from the apartment, where they were unprotected from both theft and mildew, and that they were far better off in the storage house where they had been placed. When I dined with Virgil not long ago, he reported that Alice was resigned and cheerful and that her situation had been improved by her moving to a heated apartment, the cost of which is borne by the Stein heirs.

My Paris adventures were not all as exalted as those among the art-lovers. We spent some of our nights at galas at the Pré Catalan or Les Ambassadeurs, which featured the elegant ballroom-dancing teams of those days; besides Irene and Vernon Castle, there were Maurice and Florence Walton, Leonora Hughes and Clifton Webb. Since they all moved in our set, we became friends. The fact that the delectable Leonora Hughes made a joke of having started out as a telephone operator in Brooklyn gave her great pazazz. Another ballroom dancer among that group was Barbara Bennett; the two other Bennett girls, Constance and Joan, were in Hollywood carving golden careers for themselves in the movies. Barbara, a brunette, was just as pretty as her blond sisters but, lazy and fun-loving, she had none of their will to succeed. There were evenings when we had to pull Barbara out of bed to get her into her dancing clothes, with Barbara as limp as the fringe on her Charleston dress. But once out on the town Barbara wouldn't go home until time for the morning sun to smack her down. She lived only to laugh. We used to run into her in Montparnasse after her professional stint was over, dancing for free at Jimmy's Bar, Bricktop and Zelli's—places which featured loud music, crowded dance floors, and no air, just as in the discothèques of today. Barbara's domestic life consisted of a single marriage to the Irish tenor Morton Downey. It was of brief duration, and, like two more famous girls of the same laughter-loving type, Carole Lombard and Jean Harlow, she died young.

The most elegant place in which to greet the Paris dawn was a night club called Le Jardin de Ma Sœur. It occupied an ancient town house with a lush, well-kept garden where we dined and danced out of doors, weather permitting; when the rain came down, activities moved inside. The proprietor was a tall and dashing young Irishman, Captain Edward Molyneux, who had had a heroic career in World War I. In those days the Captain was, as he is now, an arbiter of Paris fashion; his famous dressmaking house supplied clothes for all the royalties and theater luminaries of Europe. The Captain's assistant in that night-club enterprise was a bouncy young woman, Elsa Maxwell, who was just starting on her unique career of supplying energy to an apathetic group, the idle rich. Because we girls were adept at dancing the Charleston, Elsa welcomed us as pace-setters in the new craze, and we frequently danced the summer nights away in the lovely *ambiance* of the Captain's Paris garden.

The best of our Charleston partners in those days were handsome playboys from Argentina. We girls used to get many of our beauty hints from them: the name of a cologne they all used, Carnaval de Venise; their English hair dressing was The Guards, which made me quite nostalgic for the Uncle Horace of my childhood. There was a famous quartet of Argentinians, Macoco, Camillo, Pancho, and Basualdo, who belonged to families of wealth and were free to live for the gratification of their whims. Leonora Hughes married Basualdo and retired to the Argentine, lost to our gay world, but a decoration to the fashionable life of Buenos Aires, where she is related by marriage to half the chic population of that city.

Paris was full of gigolos who found working conditions there at their best. I remember sitting with several of them one halcyon afternoon, innocently taking tea in the garden of the Ritz, while they compared cigarette cases and cufflinks given them by rich females. We girls helped them to appraise their romances in terms of dollars and cents. It was then I began to learn how niggardly our American women are in keeping men. It appears that being stingy helps our countrywomen to feel loved for themselves alone and gives their vanity a boost. My rich compatriots were even known to lock their boy friends in their bedrooms to keep their loyalty intact.

But none of those young men in Paris ever had it so hard as a retired actor in his early thirties, by name Jack Dean. He was married to the baby-faced, blue-eyed little blonde Fanny Ward. She was then crowding sixty, and the energy she spent on holding back the clock ought to have aged Fanny beyond her years, but she was younger in spirit than any of us. (In *Gentlemen Prefer Blondes* I wrote of Fanny: "When a girl is cute for fifty years it really gets to be historic.") Fanny's career had begun spectacularly in her native London when, in her early teens, she appeared in musical comedy and her pert blond beauty devastated the smartest young men in England. An early marriage placed Fanny in a family so correct that today her great-grandchildren are among the most conservative members of the British court, but her subsequent marriage to Jack Dean was as enduring as her indestructible youth. She was financially independent through the generosity of her first husband, so that she and Jack could live the rich, full lives of international playboys and -girls. They also spent some time in Hollywood, where Fanny starred in a few silent movies, playing soubrette roles when she was already a grandmother. Fanny's need of Jack covered many areas; for one thing, she never submitted to any beauty treatment without first trying it out on Jack. At a time when certain misguided beauty experts first used injections of paraffin to fill out hollows and erase wrinkles, Fanny made Jack submit to the treatment for an unfortunate lack of chin. The result was disaster, for, instead of the clean-cut square jaw that Jack had been promised, the wax melted and ran down until he developed not merely *one* but *two* double chins. Nothing could be done to remove the wax, and from that time on Jack was known among us as Chin-Chin. Jack's mishap was illustrated by the wicked French caricaturist Sem in a sketch which showed Fanny as a chortling babe-in-arms, with Jack nursing her at one of his bountiful chins.

During the Paris season Fanny and Jack used to live at the Claridge Hotel on the Champs Elysées, which today houses the Lido night club. It was never exactly elegant, which couldn't have bothered Fanny less. She wanted to be where the fun was. One morning, when we stopped at the hotel to drop Fanny and Jack off after a breakfast of onion soup at Les Halles, Fanny was impelled to stop on the curb and demonstrate a Charleston step. Looking on from the front of the hotel was a scrubwoman doing a job with a mop and pail; she was about twenty-eight and as haggard and worn as French scrubladies can be at that age. Leaning on her mop, she reacted to Fanny's capers with a nostalgic murmur. *"Ah, jeunesse!"* said she.

As nobody ever expected Fanny to be wise, nothing she ever did surprised us. One afternoon I dropped into the Claridge to pick her up for lunch and found Fanny kneeling on the floor of her bedroom, in the act of cutting up a chinchilla coat that was spread out before her. "Look, Nita," said Fanny proudly, "I'm remodeling my chinchilla. Just think of all the money I'm saving!" It hadn't crossed her mind that to sew chinchilla required a special technique that poor longsuffering Jack Dean could never master.

Fanny went far beyond being an optimist; she was a Christian Scientist of such faith and determination that one day, when in the throes of a violent toothache, she declared to me with tears of pain streaming down her cheeks, "God is love. God is health. God is good. God damn it to hell, there's no such thing as pain."

With such a heritage it's small wonder that today one of Fanny's descendants is a valued prop to the British throne. Her grandson Patrick, Lord Plunket, is Deputy Master of the Queen's Household. His august presence at court can be no better described than by quoting New York's witty gossip columnist Suzy Knicker-bocker: "The 42-year-old Lord Plunket is loaded with charm. He has the widest set of friends in all the royal circle, plays a good swing piano and even does the shake at the Ad Lib Club—without lowering for an instant his role as a courtier. What does one expect when Patrick's grandma went on and on for what began to seem like forever?"

Some of my most durable friendships began during those frivolous weeks in Paris. I took an instant liking to Elsa Maxwell's handsome, stately companion, Dorothy Fellows Gordon, nicknamed "Dickie." Dickie loved to laugh and she remained more or less in Elsa's background, preferring better company than that of Elsa's overprivileged friends; unlike Elsa, Dickie never had any fish to fry, as the saying goes. And in Elsa's surroundings we witnessed some pretty hilarious manifestations of the human comedy. Together with Dickie, I indulged in a favorite pastime, which was to take long walks with which Elsa's fat little feet were unable to cope. During the many years of our friendship, Dickie and I have walked miles along the Seine, in Chelsea, in Beverly Hills, and through offbeat neighborhoods of New York.

Different as Elsa and Dickie were in temperament and background, they shared an intense devotion. It began in London, when Elsa was on the first lap of her career. As yet she had not discovered that her personality in itself was an inexhaustible medium of exchange, so Elsa then worked for her living. She had first earned her livelihood by playing piano in her native San Francisco. Later she got a job as a traveling accompanist for a beautiful young singer named Marie Doro, who in time became a famous star of musical comedy. When an opportunity opened up for Marie Doro to sing in England, she took Elsa with her. The British upper classes were captivated by Marie's beauty, talent, and charm; she was frequently asked to sing at soirées of the rich, and it was as her humble accompanist that Elsa Maxwell made her first connections with a society to which she would one day be a combination of queen and court jester.

After Elsa rose high in the world, her clothes were specially designed for her by such artists as Molyneux and Mainbocher, and she became the world's most stylish stout, but in the beginning she was downright frumpy. She scurried about Mayfair dressed in a dun-colored suit topped off by a brown derby worn at a rakish angle, in the manner of Al Smith. Elsa's situation was fraught with both pathos and injustice; she realized she was invited to parties only because Marie needed her at the piano; the injustice lay in the fact that she loved fun much more than did those British party-givers.

When Dickie Gordon first met Elsa she was a teenage orphan in an eminent family. Finding Elsa to be livelier company than her stuffy relatives, Dickie took to neglecting home ties, and finally, when Elsa left for South Africa on a concert tour with Marie Doro, Dickie ran away to go with them. From then on, Dickie and Elsa spent their entire lives together and were separated only by Elsa's death in 1963. Not that they didn't have disagreements. For long stretches Elsa was bitter about two of Dickie's suitors (both aristocrats, one British, and the other a Spanish duke), and Dickie pulled no punches over a very great number of Elsa's schemes that were ill-advised. At any rate, the two engaged in running battles which only accented their devotion to each other.

When Elsa was in charge of Le Jardin de Ma Sœur she must have felt the need of it as a background, but once she zoomed into prominence she discarded all help and singlehanded organized the greatest one-woman show on earth. She was among the first to discover the mines of purest gold that lie hidden under mountains of nonsense. An entire industry has grown up since Elsa's revelation; in New York it occupies a good part of Madison Avenue, where in the name of "public relations" solid wealth is created out of childish banalities. Elsa was also a pioneer in the discovery that perquisites are rapidly supplanting cash, that high taxes have brought on a latter-day form of barter which may deprive money of any value except to coin-collectors. That Elsa never needed money was more than a boast; it was a new reality. Naturally there were occasions when a sheriff might close in because of a bill which demanded

ready cash, and in those extremities Elsa had to evolve it by a special form of osmosis she invented: the debt would be shuttled to
her nearest rich friend; if the first one failed to come through, Elsa
would go on down the list. In dire extremities she would make use
of social climbers of such low degree that they actually needed
help to get into café society; there were also a profitable few who
set their sights on café royalty.

From the time I first met Elsa, she always toted an outsized pocketbook crammed with telegrams, letters, and press clippings that
connected her with the famous. I feel that Elsa's megalomania did
her great injustice, because people were prone to think she was
exaggerating, when actually she wasn't. Finally she extended her
activities by writing a gossip column, and came to have some influence in world affairs. I was to learn how great an influence at a time
when she and Dickie spent several weeks as my house guests in
Santa Monica. It was during a presidential campaign, and I was as-
tonished by a number of long-distance calls to Elsa from no less a
personage than the Republican candidate for president, who
phoned to beg Elsa for her backing. But it is to her credit that,
disapproving of his policies, Elsa gave him small encouragement.
Elsa never truckled to the great, and in fact one of her best gimmicks was to force important people to woo her, an art at which
she was impishly clever. When planning one of her parties, she
would leave one or two socially impeccable characters off her list,
at the same time inviting a few who were exceptionally low-grade.
In this manner would Elsa cut celebrities down with a two-edged
sword; they were not only rejected, but marked as inferior to the
outstanding nobodies whom Elsa *had* invited. The situation made
for bewilderment, consternation, and word-of-mouth publicity for
Elsa in all the gossip centers of Christendom: at Maxim's, Le Pavil-
lon, Claridge's, and Mike Romanoff's. Elsa used to twist VIPs
around her finger until they had no more dignity than pretzels, and
I have seen her laugh over her Machiavellian schemes until the tears
rolled.

In matters of character and attainment there were enormous
differences between Elsa Maxwell and Gertrude Stein, but they can

both serve as inspiration to anyone who feels too fat or homely for success; their careers were more exciting over a longer period than those of any beauty I ever knew. Social climbers used practically to batter in their doors; only the cultured ever succeeded with Gertrude, but Elsa wasn't choosy. How did those two attain such eminence? Merely by cultivating their own native aptitudes. Gertrude's interest was in art, Elsas' was in publicity, and those inclinations, pushed to the utter limit, brought fame and fortune to them both.

A more serious character who drifted briefly into my life in Paris was a distinguished Swedish professor of philosophy who looked me up to ask about the movies. At that time the word "Hollywood" was just coming into prominence as a synonym for glamour, enchantment, and the allure of far-away California, but very few people ever took an interest in the inside workings of the industry, realized that movies had to be written, or thought of me as a writer. I had never thought of myself as a writer, and, while I loved to work on plots, I looked on them as crossword puzzles— frustrating when they failed, but rewarding when dramatic unities began to unfold which indicated they were going to work out. That Swedish professor chided me on the levity with which I viewed the movies; spoke of them as folk-art; gave Hollywood credit for revivifying the decadent culture of Europe with pure and childlike fairy tales. I didn't agree with him then and am still incredulous that today's silent-film buffs think along the same lines as the Swedish professor.

Among the girls John picked up in his wanderings around Paris were two who were both cultured and witty; ultimately they became my own valued friends. They were Janet Flanner and Solita Solano, then budding journalists; Janet's brilliant career has continued without a break, and for years she has written the pungent letters from Paris for *The New Yorker*, which she signs Genêt. Solita, on the other hand, became a disciple of the mystic Gurdjieff, who until his death held forth in Fontainebleau and whose disciples have learned a very peculiar method of finding happiness by doing what appears to be nothing at all. I never met Solita's idol, to my own loss, for according to the review of the recent book *Boyhood with Gurdjieff*, the swami was "a mixture of Rasputin, Svengali and Gogol's Chichikov." I have tried in vain to get Solita and others of his disciples to explain the man's philosophy; the only response is the contented smile of a Mona Lisa and a brief remark that I "wouldn't understand." Gurdjieff influenced many serious writers; among them was Katherine Mansfield. But in the words of Fritz Peters, the author of the aforementioned book, who spent years as a pupil at the Fontainebleau Institute, he was "a real, genuine phony."

Before leaving Europe, John decided to visit the battlefields of the First World War and then take a short swing through Germany. So, leaving the Talmadges in Paris, we started on tour, and this time John allowed Ash and me to ride in our car.

CHAPTER 15

In order to examine the battlefields of World War I we had to put up in dirty taverns that were sloppily run, overcrowded by busloads of tourists, and serving food that blasted the old theory that one can eat well in any French byway. But it was rather snide to complain about lack of creature comforts in such grim surroundings. I remember how tremendously impressed we were when a guide showed us through the underground fortress of Verdun, which had sheltered the French armies in dismal comfort, with hot and cold running water, baths, steamrooms for delousing, kitchens, laundries, and libraries. We were appalled by the relics of that awful stalemate when millions of lives were exchanged for a few inches of no man's land; particularly arresting was a long line of rusty bayonets projecting a few inches above ground; their guns were still in the hands of dead men who had been engulfed as they stood in a trench. Our distress, however, was mingled with relief, for we had been informed that a certain military genius, André Maginot, was secretly planning a new defense for France, an impregnable line of fortresses which would follow the eastern border so that the Germans would realize they couldn't invade France just by looking at a map. The Maginot Line was to cost half a billion dollars, which was cheap, considering it would forever prevent a second world war. Feeling very reassured about future world security, we shook off the dust of the battlefields and went on to Munich.

My first impression of the city was that it had an intense and abiding love for art. The German word for it, *Kunst,* appeared endlessly on street signs, kiosks, posters, shop windows, and in newspaper headlines. On the surface, Munich itself appeared to be a vast art collection of monuments, museums, and galleries. Visiting the latter, I discovered the paintings of Cranach, that fifteenth-century Ziegfeld who glamorized the German girl of his day. As a rule portraits in galleries give the impression that there were no pretty girls in ancient times, but only beauties. However, the girls of Cranach are irresistible in a strictly modern sense, like Mary Pickford. Unfortunately they seemed to be the only thin girls in Munich. One night we went to an art theater where they were playing a Teutonic version of Oscar Wilde's *Salome.* I watched the dance of the seven veils with suspense, for the German Salome was so heavy she might at any moment have broken through the floor. During the *entr'acte* Ash Creelman and I were mulling about, watching those Münchner art-lovers enjoy a snack of bratwurst, leberwurst, blutwurst, sauerkraut, dill pickles, Limburger cheese, apfelstrudel, and beer, when we suddenly found ourselves in the center of a group that had gathered to stare at my windblown bob. In contrast to Madame Lanvin, they found me ridiculous and didn't bother to hide their guffaws; I had to restrain Ash from taking a poke at one of these male Münchners. But I later avenged myself on Munich by disclosing in *Gentlemen Prefer Blondes* that the thing those art-lovers mostly care about is delicatessen.

From Munich we proceeded to Vienna, which, after World War I, was supposed to have lost its *Gemütlichkeit.* It still had plenty for me. The Viennese were the most hospitable people I had ever met. We had no connections in the city, as it was far removed from the café society we had frequented in Paris, but John was recognized by theater people as having directed some of the best American movies. He was sought out, and we were entertained in restaurants, at clubs, and even in homes.

The greatest charm of Vienna lay in its undefeated gaiety; although the people were shabby and down-at-heel, they refused to recognize the dire poverty brought about by losing the war. We found that there was little language barrier to surmount; the Viennese had always been Anglophiles; it was chic to speak English. Slang was appreciated in any tongue, and I was told that before the war the Emperor Franz Josef himself affected the argot of the Viennese underworld in the same manner that the Princess di Frasso loved to talk like Bugsy Siegel. The Emperor's argot was authentic, for he too had learned it first hand, from his common young mistress, Kathi Schratt. I was informed that Kathi, then in her seventies, lived in a suburb where she was as highly respected as when, during her days at court, everyone, including the Empress, was grateful to Kathi for sharing the intellectual vacuum in which the Emperor lived. That Kathi had not been ruined by the war was due to the fact that, even at the height of her imperial glory, she had never had any money to lose. Her poverty had been the fault of a language barrier between the Emperor and herself; the German word for "money" is *silber,* and when Kathi would bolster her courage to hint to her lover that she had need of *silber,* His Highness would give orders for her to be deluged with tableware and toilet articles. These she would sell, of course, but she was a notoriously bad businesswoman. Kathi lived to be nearly a hundred, and in New York during the thirties I met an Austrian gentleman who was trying to help the old lady by selling the last of her imperial knickknacks. There is no career as frustrating as being an emperor's moll.

Our days in Vienna were to be further enlivened by the presence of Janet Flanner, who came on from Paris to join us. She shared our enthusiasm for the Viennese; we all agreed that to be in Vienna was like living in a musical comedy. The very beggars in the street had style, a sense of humor, and impeccable manners. Salespeople in shops were interested in their customers; the first time I made a purchase at Zweibach's large department store, the package was delivered with a handwritten note thanking the *gnädige* American for her patronage, and pinned to the envelope was a rose. Janet and I met an English lady who had been marooned in Vienna through-

out the war and she told us that during all that time not a single
Viennese had mentioned the war in her presence; it would have
been bad manners to remind her that she was an enemy alien.

We spent our evenings in the theaters or at protracted dinner
parties, the gayest of them in an intimate dining room of the old
Sacher Hotel. The hotel was redolent of Edwardian luxury, as it is
even today, and it then sparkled under the superb housekeeping of
old Frau Sacher herself. Her iron-gray hair formidably coiffed in
the manner of imperial Austrian ladies, the *gnädige Frau* was impressively corseted and dressed in rigid elegance, an autocrat who
took it upon herself to order people out of her dining room for no
other reason than that she didn't like their looks. Luck was with us;
she fell for John and was tolerant of Janet Flanner and me.

At the beginning of Frau Sacher's reign over the hotel, she had
been a confidante of the young Crown Prince Rudolf. He kept an
apartment at the Sacher, which he used for purposes of carousal,
during which he was likely to emerge into the halls and public
rooms without any clothes on. During these crises it required
young Frau Sacher herself to argue Rudolf back into his private
quarters.

Frau Sacher had been the principal go-between in the Crown
Prince's love affair with the semi-aristocratic but overly ambitious
Marie Vetsera, which had its tragic culmination in what was called
a double suicide at the royal hunting lodge at Mayerling. Dozens of
motivations for the crime have been put forward, but the version I
heard from Frau Sacher bears earmarks of truth that make it seem
worth repeating. It appeared that after Rudolf's affair with Vetsera
had run a hectic course, her too ardent and hysterical nature began
to bore him; he had decided to break with her and face up to his
imperial duties.

Among his intimates Rudolf made a joke of the fact that, in announcing their break to his sweetheart, he placed all responsibility
on the Emperor and assured Vetsera that he still loved her madly.
Rudolf also made a joke of the fact that Vetsera had wheedled him
into taking her to his hunting lodge at Mayerling for one last night
of love. But subsequent events indicated that Vetsera was quite

aware that her lover had cooled off and had decided on a terrible revenge.

On the morning that followed their night of drunken debauch, the lovers' bodies were found by Rudolf's confidential valet; both had been killed by shots from a pistol. The valet immediately got word to the palace, and emissaries were rushed out to Mayerling. In a search for evidence they found the pistol with which the two had been shot, but they also found a hunting knife with which the Crown Prince had been mutilated in a way that would have forever ended the imperial succession. Guilt for the crime was later established when it was found out that, the day before their departure for Mayerling, Vetsera had purchased the hunting knife. (One afternoon Janet and I were shown a shop in the Graben where she bought it.)

As observers reconstructed the murders, it appeared that Rudolf must have drunk himself into a stupor, which made it possible for Vetsera to commit her unspeakable act of vengeance, one which ruined her lover both as a monarch and as a man. In an aftermath of agony and rage Rudolf apparently killed his mistress and then, unable to face up to his shame, chose to commit suicide. The Austro-Hungarian court, well versed in burying evidences of Rudolf's scandals, decided to make the incident look like a romantic suicide pact of two star-crossed lovers, which was a lot more palatable than the sordid truth.

Wherever our evenings in Vienna were spent, we were generally taken to the Theatrical Club for a late session. The unusually pretty girls we met there, whether actresses or nonprofessionals, greatly admired my Paris dresses; I, on the other hand, began to appreciate Viennese style. Those girls, who had so little money to spend on clothes, dressed with a romantic and subtle femininity that is overlooked by the Parisiennes in their striving for spectacular effects. At the Theatrical Club we met the famous young Hungarian playwright and wit Ferenc Molnar, who happened to be in town from Budapest; his inexhaustible line of anecdotes made Molnar's talk better than any play. Janet and I also had the thrill of meeting the matinee idol of all Central Europe, Richard Tauber, who was then singing in the Lehar operetta *Das Land des Lachelns*. It was there that he established his theme song, "Du Bist Mein Einzig Herz"; translated into English as "Yours Is My Heart Alone," it has become a standard love song, not only in our country but all over the world. Byronically handsome and desirable, Tauber was protected by a tiny, unattractive brunette who looked vicious enough to claw any female who got too near her property. She had plenty of provocation, for Tauber's attitude toward all women—young, old, pretty or not—was one of a perpetual caress.

The Opera House had just reopened in Vienna. Although tickets were ruinously expensive for the Austrians, there was always a long line of shabby opera-lovers at the box office. One day when Ash was waiting to buy us tickets for a performance of *Rosenkavalier*, a ragged Viennese was next in line, his feet wrapped in gunny sacks as a substitute for shoes. That performance of *Rosenkavalier* was a gala event, with Richard Strauss conducting and Maria Jeritza singing the Marschallin. At the end of the first act John felt impelled to make a phone call to New York. The only available phone was in the basement of the Opera House, and before John could get his connection a bell announced the end of the intermission. As John started to cancel his call, Richard Strauss happened to pass by and heard him. To the maestro John was merely an American tourist, but Strauss interrupted him to say, "Please don't cancel your call, sir. It's quite simple for me to put off the second act until you complete it."

There was an occasion when we were motoring back to Vienna from Semmering and, hopelessly lost, stopped at a farmhouse in the dead of night to ask our way. In answer to John's apologetic knock at the door, a boy of about fifteen appeared at a window in his nightshirt. John begged pardon for disturbing his sleep and asked for directions. The boy replied in English (which so many Austrian peasants had learned during the war) and asked us to wait until he could come down and guide us to the right road. "But we don't want to disturb you," John protested; to which the boy answered, quoting Goethe, "Great souls are never disturbed!" It may have been the brilliant moonlight, or the perfume of pines in the mountain air, or the fact that in Austria the waltzes of Strauss constantly seem to ring in one's ears, but for whatever cause, had that boy been just a little older I would have fallen in love with him. At any rate, I think I began subconsciously to look for an Austrian in the right age bracket, bypassing both Mencken and Ash Creelman, but on my first trip to Vienna I didn't find him.

While in Vienna, John got in touch with Arthur Schnitzler, in the hope of buying one of his plays which might be produced in New York. One day he invited the Herr Doktor for lunch, which we took in the garden of a restaurant on a high terrace that overlooked the city; as always, an orchestra played the melodies of Strauss. Although Doktor Schnitzler's brown hair and small beard were going gray, he had the slim figure and buoyancy of youth. His attitude and comments were attractively cynical; in mentioning his only play that hadn't been sold abroad, Schnitzler claimed that it wasn't worth buying. (It is called *The Legacy*; I still own a manuscript of it and can only agree with the author's opinion.) However, John insisted on reading the play and, dazzled by Schnitzler's reputation, considered it excellent. He telephoned Schnitzler an offer of $1500 for an option and made an appointment to bring the money to his apartment the next afternoon.

Vienna was then in the throes of inflation, and when I accompanied John to the bank for those $1500 in Austrian schillings, the package, wrapped in an old newspaper, was as large as two shoeboxes. John loaded it into a fiacre and we proceeded to the Herr Doktor's apartment. But on arriving there we learned from a maid that Schnitzler had forgotten our appointment and was off at a coffee house. It was typical of a Viennese to attach more importance to a cup of coffee with friends than to the $1500, which would have bought more than a lifetime's supply of coffee. Greatly as we were charmed by the Doktor's lack of interest in money, we found that package to be an incubus. It was too big to go into the safe at the Bristol Hotel; we finally locked it in a wardrobe of the royal suite we occupied (for which we paid all of $3.00 a day).

Important as that money must have been to the Herr Doktor, it took us nearly a week to catch up with him and turn it over.

One day we were witnesses to poverty that lacked the comic aspect of the Schnitzler incident. It was at a university luncheon which the American Quakers provided for the professors in an effort to save the best brains of the city from malnutrition. I sat next to a science teacher who, at the end of lunch, brushed the crumbs into an envelope to take home to his family.

We found that Vienna was always crackling with gossip; one item concerned Doktor Schnitzler, who was then trying to withdraw from the public a series of his one-act plays called *Reigen*. The plays had a single theme based on the tragedy of venereal disease. Being a physician, Schnitzler knew the subject all too well, but after writing the plays he felt they were lewd and that the subject ought not to be discussed outside the privacy of a doctor's office. I wonder what the ghost of Schnitzler feels if it ever slithers into an evening of Monsieur Genet, Mr. Beckett, or Mr. Albee.

I learned in Vienna that Professor Freud was *persona non grata* to the Viennese, who accused him of trying to dirty people's minds and destroy romantic love. He was then rumored to be carrying on an affair with his sister-in-law, one to which the Viennese would have been most sympathetic had the professor considered it in a sentimental light, but they objected to his attitude of guilt and an alibi that the romance was motivated by his degrading theories. The fact that John was interested in meeting Freud caused our Viennese friends to chide him; they argued that we Americans were paying the professor much more attention than he got elsewhere. But it was attention for which the professor had no gratitude. He claimed that America had misinterpreted his theories in a crudely childish manner and that we were largely responsible for the neglect he suffered in Europe. In fact the professor was so extremely anti-American that a request from John to meet him would have met with a flat refusal.

The Viennese denied that Freud had made any contribution to the understanding of human psychology, and they claimed this lack might be proved by the classics of any literature. Had Shake-

known Chris then, for he would have shown me an impoverished Berlin that was much more attractive than the one I saw.

One day we were invited to visit the UFA movie studio, where we watched the young director Ernst Lubitsch shoot a scene with the youthful Pola Negri. Ernst was then negotiating a deal which would remove him to Hollywood for keeps and, torn with anxiety, he quizzed John about what his reception in the United States would be as an enemy alien. That Americans find it impossible to hold a grudge seemed to Ernst too good to be true.

In Berlin I had my first thrilling experience of being considered stupid. While John and Ash were meeting with members of the Berlin Actors Association on matters of social import to the profession, I was taken on sightseeing tours by an aristocratic Berliner whose attentions were typical of the sexy arrogance of the Prussians. He didn't know English, and our conversation was limited by our equally bad French. On one of our lunch dates he pretended I was too frail to cut up my apfelstrudel, and when he proceeded to do it for me I experienced the unwonted ecstasy of being cherished as a helpless female. (I met the same gentleman on my second visit to Berlin but spoiled everything by knowing enough German to make a few wisecracks, from which time the jig was up and I went right back to being a neglected brunette.)

One morning I experienced at first hand a demonstration of the strangely double Prussian nature. I was in our suite at the Adlon when a phone call from the lobby announced that a Kapitän von Something-or-Other wished to see me. Being curious, I invited him up. The Kapitän proved to be robust and impressive, a typical Junker in uniform, with a monocle and any number of medals. He introduced himself pompously, saluted, and then suddenly fell to his knees, burst into tears, and began a plea for financial aid so emotional that he might have been a hysterical woman. I was terribly embarrassed by his outpouring of self-pity, from which I finally escaped by calling John, who came in, heard the Kapitän's plea, and offered him a hundred marks. The Herr Kapitän grabbed them with alacrity and beat a fast retreat.

The contrast between the Prussian viewpoint and the Austrian is illustrated by this vignette: in the Berlin museums we sometimes found ancient clocks on display that had been kept in perfect running order for centuries and still told the correct time, but in the railroad station of Vienna, where the correct time was really important, an enormous clock that had lost both its hands had never been repaired. Between German efficiency and Austrian *laissez-aller*, I will forever choose the latter.

Following our month's tour, we returned to Paris, where I was thrilled to learn that I had indirectly taken part in a fashion trend which, frivolous as it was, would be worldwide in scope. It appeared that every day while we were gone one of the manikins at Lanvin's had been exhibiting a windblown bob, and we now saw examples of it all over town, at galas at the Pré Catalan, in the Ritz Bar, and at the theater. I noticed any number of such haircuts the night we went to the Russian Ballet and saw Nijinsky dance *The Afternoon of a Faun*.

But just as I was deciding that Paris was the place where a girl like I belonged, a cable arrived calling John home to take part in the actors' strike. I was not only disappointed but a little resentful because while we were in Vienna I had gotten a first inkling that John's championship of the underdog was phony. One day we had visited several housing projects which the socialist government was building for the poor. John breathed deep satisfaction over the onward march of that cause to which he had given his devotion; that is, until one morning when a Viennese official tapped on the door of our suite and stated he had come to collect a luxury tax on our touring car. I had to smother my giggles over John's explosion of outrage at having to pay for his manifestation of swank, a car so enormous that it was ultimately sold to an institution to be used as a bus.

When we arrived in New York, John was greeted by a delegation from Actors Equity with horns, cheers, and confetti. Almost hidden by the mob was Swatty, who looked on in silent amusement. But as we drove home later he kidded John for using his socialism as a gimmick for publicity. Caught off guard, John admitted as much. Having always adored flimflam, I was delighted; John's duplicity seemed suddenly to open up a new *entente* with him. But when I tried to assume he meant his confession, John refused to go along with it and went right back to being a clean-shaven Abe Lincoln bent on emancipating Broadway chorus girls. Subconsciously aware that to me our marriage was a bore and to Emerson a tragedy, I tried to fool both myself and him by assuming an attitude of devotion while in public. Perhaps I thought that by feigning domestic bliss I could bring it into being. It never works; and I finally came to realize that when a married couple holds hands out in the open it's a sign that the marriage is pretty far from robust.

CHAPTER 16

~§In the actors' struggle for better working conditions, their first move was to unionize the Actors Equity Association, which up to that time had had only the mild status of a guild. Once established as a union, Equity faced the producers with its demands, which were promptly turned down. Equity, now backed by the unions of stagehands, musicians, carpenters, and electricians, threatened to strike. The producers retaliated by setting up a company union which they called The Actors Fidelity Association, promising actors untold benefits if they would join and keep the theaters open. After which the producers felt sure they had scotched the rebellion, never dreaming that actors would support any regime that prevented them from acting. But it soon evolved that the strike would give them a more imposing stage than they had ever occupied before. And when strike activities began to give actors more publicity than they could earn onstage, the call to strike was sounded. The Equity membership rallied to the cause and with gestures of high defiance closed down every theater in New York. Never had actors, *en masse*, attained so many headlines or had more fun, for the strike turned every producer into a villain, and every striking supernumerary became a star. The Actors Fidelity Association, now derisively nicknamed "the Fidos," found itself with a full-scale battle on its hands.

Leaders of both sides took to soapboxes in meetings which were electric with ardor and wit. The president of Actors Equity was

Frank Gillmore, a scholarly and gentle man who greatly dignified the cause; his pretty blue-eyed, blond daughter, Margalo, then an ingénue, was among those who supplied Equity ranks with sex appeal. (Margalo Gillmore has become one of the first ladies of the American theater, which is generally hard put for actresses of intelligence, wit, and distinction.) The Fidos had counted on the support of Broadway's royal family, the Barrymores, never dreaming they would join the ranks of bit players, extras, and chorus girls. Ethel, in particular, belonged to the upper echelons of real-life society, into which she had married. However, Ethel Barrymore took sides with her humble fellows, entered vigorously into the campaign, stirred the strikers on in her famous husky voice, and became the glorious queen of the rebellion. But one of its greatest assets was the rational and carefully prepared oratory of John Emerson.

The actors' strike of 1919 was one of the first ever to be organized by white-collar workers and it was more de luxe than any labor activity had ever been. Its cast of characters sparkled with stars; one of the foremost was the aging actor Frank Bacon. He had spent a lifetime in obscurity, playing small character roles, and at long last had attained overnight stardom in a play called *Lightnin'*. It concerned a lovable, slow-moving ne'er-do-well, sarcastically nicknamed Lightnin'. Bacon required no make-up for the part, for he was a spare Yankee type with a ruddy complexion, a shock of unruly white hair, and a prominent Adam's apple. *Lightnin'* was the biggest hit of that season. Frank Bacon could have joined the Fidos, kept the play open, and earned lifetime security, when to close it might well have ended his career. It is a well-known fact in show business that to break a successful run is a great hazard against the play's ever being revived. The producers of *Lightnin'* offered Frank Bacon a healthy percentage of the show if he would continue its run, and Equity might well have understood had Bacon accepted, for he was a poor man with a family to support. But he never wavered, and the day Frank Bacon led his company down Broadway carrying a banner, "Lightnin' Has Struck," the whole street went wild with joy.

The strike was to split up families and old friendships and to break business associations, which in the theater are so deeply sentimental. It resulted in George M. Cohan's toppling off the pedestal from which he had dominated the Broadway scene for years. His desertion to the Fidos was all the more shameful because his partner in the producing of plays, Sam H. Harris, took sides with Equity. Now, George was himself an actor, while Sam was not. Their firm was the most prominent in New York, with an impressive catalogue of hits, most of which had starred Cohan. Both men were loved for their charm, wit and good fellowship; they enjoyed numerous family associations, for they had married sisters. But from the time George M. Cohan joined the Fidos, he and Sam Harris never spoke again or even met, except by chance. Sam's producing career faded out with the loss of his partner, and Cohan sacrificed his place in the affection of actors; he never again set foot in that holy of holies, the Lambs Club, and remained a pariah to the end of his days. There is a statue of George M. Cohan on Broadway; I doubt if many passers-by stop to look at it; perhaps it has no galvanism, because George M. Cohan deserted his kind in time of stress.

During the weeks when John was absorbed so happily in the strike I was free to spend nearly every evening with Mencken's cronies and with Menck himself when he happened to be in New York. The group met most frequently at a small walk-up apartment in a converted brownstone of the East Fifties. It belonged to a young bachelor, Herman Oelrichs, who used it for the sole purpose of entertaining in a more relaxed manner than was possible at his elegant Fifth Avenue home. Herman belonged to the rich and socially prominent Oelrichs family but he had both talent and sophistication; had he been poor, he might have become an artist of some sort, but vast wealth had turned him into a sybarite. He drank a great deal, as did the entire group, but there was no drunkenness, and alcohol never dulled anyone's wits. Herman was in his mid-thirties and rather good-looking, but he showed the effects of his non-active indoor life; he was a little too heavy, a lot too pale, and somewhat balding. He spent much time and effort on as ingenious a parlor trick as there ever was. He was an ardent disciple of that old friend of my Pop's, the escape artist Houdini, who had now become the marvel of audiences and the despair of jailkeepers all over the globe. (Harold Ross, the brilliant editor of *The New Yorker* magazine, used to claim that only two names are familiar to everybody in the civilized world: Sherlock Holmes and Houdini.) Herman had a collection of handcuffs which included every type in existence. I must say we weren't as interested in the subtlety of their variations as he was, but we used to attend politely while Herman escaped from them in full view of his audience, with his hands covered by a handkerchief.

At those gatherings of Herman's I got a hint of how much more fun men must have when there are no women present. Very few girls were honored by invitations, but I was given the supreme compliment of not being regarded as a female or, at any rate, I could be assimilated, for I was there to listen and, except for casual brief comments, I kept my mouth shut. The one married man in the group was Ernest Boyd, so his wife had frequently to be included, but she wasn't very welcome; Madeleine Boyd was talky.

In that social life I was leading apart from John there was a colorful character named Tommy Smith. I had been meeting him from time to time during the past few years, but we were now meeting very often at Herman Oelrich's. Tommy was short, cherubic, and foppish, with a pink complexion, silvery hair, and pince-nez glasses attached to a ribbon that was rather too wide. He was a rowdier version of Mr. Pickwick; Tommy had also been written up by a better author, who called him Falstaff. He drank enormously, became a little glassy-eyed, but was never incoherent, and he never indulged in that drunkard's curse of repeating himself. The reason Tommy was able to carry on his drinking career was supposed to be that, no matter where he spent his nights, he ended them at a certain dairy lunch counter where he drank a quart of milk. I don't know the scientific basis for this prescription, but it kept Tom going, more or less steadily, throughout his middle years. He prowled the city on the late shift, the last New Yorker ever to get to bed; spent every night making the rounds of speak-

easies, *maisons de joie,* and literary gatherings; knew every call girl
in town and was a confidant of them all. Tommy would often go
all the way down to the House of Detention in order to bail out
some unfortunate beauty caught in a raid. Manhattan's most prominent night-club hostess, Belle Livingston, depended on Tommy for
aid, comfort, and sucker lists.

Tom earned his living as an editor at the Liveright publishing
house. In the practice of his profession he scouted for new authors,
read manuscripts, and appraised them. Any business that put up
with so unorthodox an employee had to be eccentric, and the firm
of Liveright was downright bizarre, a monument to that epoch of
innocent heyday, of sex without guilt, the childish sin of the twenties. Horace Liveright was a ladies' man of such wide accomplishment that he became a legend. His private office was lined with
bookcases in which the books were a hollow sham, for when Horace pushed a button the wall opened and a boudoir appeared, complete with a seductive bed. It was like *Alice through the Looking
Glass,* with the added attraction of sex appeal. With Horace the
first business of the day was to insure the evening's fun, not only
for himself but for his string of authors and his friends. Sometimes
Mayor Walker phoned, asking Horace to provide girls for visiting
VIPs. But in the midst of all this hanky-panky Horace Liveright
and Tommy Smith discovered some of the most important writers
in America, among them William Faulkner, Theodore Dreiser,
Ernest Hemingway, Eugene O'Neill, Sherwood Anderson, and
two distinguished Californians, the novelist Gertrude Atherton and
the poet Robinson Jeffers. (At a time when Sherwood Anderson
was outraged by what he considered Hemingway's unwarranted
success, he refused to be published by any house that patronized his
rival and Horace had to choose between the two; unwisely he
chose Anderson.)

In contrast with his employer's, Tommy Smith's interest in
women had little to do with sex; he was gallant in the most courtly
sense of that word and quite innocently fond of female company.
He was also lonely. In his early youth Tom had gone through an
unhappy marriage with a Catholic who refused him a divorce. Al-

though they had a daughter, the child remained with her mother and Tom never saw her. His relationship to me became that of a perverse chaperon; he introduced me into very heady company, but then protected me as if he were Lewis Carroll and I were Alice in Wonderland. Long before Tommy ever thought of me as an authoress he took me on a tour of the Liveright premises, showed me the bookshelves in Horace's private quarters, and warned me never to let Horace trap me in his office.

At the same time Tommy loved to dramatize me as being wicked. When, on leaving for Europe, I had said good-by to him, Tommy had asked me to send him a photograph, which I did, from Vienna. His thank-you note:

Dearest Anita:

I cannot tell you how happy for a moment, but also how very sad upon further contemplation, your photograph made me. Here was a lovely creature with the manner, conversation and gait of one of the wickedest tomboys I have ever known. But the hair—what can I say about that? God help us when our best bad girls are changing! Still if you *must* be this way, I am happy to have a picture of the wind-blown hair.

                              Love always,
                                  Tommy

Sometimes Tommy took me into the upper-class bohemia that had its center in the home of Willie Chanler, eccentric member of the elite, wealthy, and colorful Chanler family. Willie, a hulky, thundering giant of a man, was a sculptor of sorts with a studio in the attic of his brownstone house on East 19th Street. But his most solid claim to fame had been a marriage to the great Italian beauty of that era, the diva Lina Cavalieri, who had deserted Willie the day after the wedding. The marriage had prompted one of Willie's brothers, who was locked up in an asylum, to send the bridegroom a telegram that became a catch phrase of the twenties and read: "Who's loony now?"

Life for Willie Chanler was one continuous romp, compared to which even the flaming youth of the twenties was kid stuff. His house was a rendezvous for an artistic sect whose diversions were male and female in the extreme. The classical dancer Isadora Duncan hung out there when she was visiting New York from her home in Paris. Isadora had started a revolution in the art of the dance by going back to the ancient Greeks for inspiration. On stage and off, she wore robes of heavy material that were hand-woven by her avant-garde brother, Raymond, who also affected a Greek type of dress. (Raymond, who is now crowding ninety, recently lectured at Carnegie Hall and bitterly attacked Hart, Schaffner and Marx and all their ilk for disfiguring the male form divine.)

Isadora was an exponent of free love, and her affair with the multimillionaire Paris Singer, of the Singer Sewing Machine hierarchy, was carried on in the same blaze of publicity that illuminated her career. As a gold-digger, Isadora far outdistanced Peggy Hopkins Joyce and Jean Nash, who were famous for that exploit, but she cared nothing at all for diamonds and spent the huge sums given her by Paris Singer in educating girls to carry on her tradition of the dance.

When I encountered Isadora Duncan at Willie's, my flip little mind put her down as arty and a figure of fun. Several years later I went, in that same spirit, to see a recital she gave at the Théâtre des Champs Elysées in Paris. By that time Isadora had developed a figure of monumental proportions; she danced in bare feet, with movements copied from pictures on Grecian urns, but her astonishing grace made the heavy woolen garments seem as fluid as chiffon. When Isadora danced she became a goddess; she was one of the few authentic geniuses I ever met. I left her performance in a spirit of humble apology. (On the way out of the theater that night I had a less elevating experience. In the lobby I was introduced to a sleazy-looking old Englishman with a flabby face and motheaten beard. My brain reeled when I heard his name, for in his youth that creature's beauty and poetic gifts had placed him, too, among the gods. He was Lord Alfred Douglas, for love of whom Oscar Wilde had gone to prison in disgrace.)

It is most likely that I met Isadora's rich lover at Willie Chanler's, but I can't remember him, so Paris Singer must have been rather nondescript. But Isadora had a friend of her own age whom I shall never forget. She went by the name of Desti and was in the cosmetics business; a dark, sultry type, she looked like a woman of destiny. Desti catered to the vampire trade, and her beauty products featured heavy Oriental perfumes, kohl for the eyes, face powder white as chalk, and purple lipsticks. In private life Desti's name was Mrs. Sturges, and I presumed that the invisible Mr. Sturges had a tendency toward the normal, for their son Preston, then away at college, was engaged in writing an extremely down-to-earth comedy, *Strictly Dishonorable*, that became a huge success. (Preston Sturges later repaired to Hollywood, where he wrote sophisticated comedies which he directed with brilliance.) Another frequent guest at Chanler's was Jack Coleton, who had dramatized *Rain* from the Maugham short story. Jack, who was addicted to cocaine, often showed up with Jeanne Eagels, who starred in his play.

It was at Willie Chanler's that I had a first brush with the eminent English portrait painter Augustus John. On the night we were introduced he used the crude tactics of a traveling salesman and enticed me up to the attic to "look at Willie's sculptures." With the naïveté of a farmer's daughter, I walked into the standard old situation. I screamed for help to no avail, for the whole house was vibrating with the revels going on downstairs. John was a colossus of a man with a Michelangelo beard in which I was about to be smothered, when good old Tommy Smith discovered that the two of us had disappeared and, knowing John, dashed upstairs and rescued me just as Augustus was pressing the lighted end of a cigarette into the palm of my hand, not in revenge over my resistance but with the assurance that the pain was going to be delightful. Tommy told Augustus to find himself a more willing victim, at which he was quite ready to look further, and I had one more rude experience to laugh off.

An incident of that type was so run-of-the-mill that to have mentioned it to my husband would have been dealing in clichés. He had other things to think about, things that provided me with a taste of what it means to be a celebrity's wife. I saw very little of him, for he left the apartment in the early morning, and it was late at night before he got home. ("Home" at that time happened to be on East 79th Street. We moved every year, tried out all the city's luxury neighborhoods. I, being easily pleased, could have settled for any one of them, but John always became restless after a few months and could hardly wait for our lease to expire. I finally came to suspect he was trying to run away from something. He never succeeded, because the "something" was poor John himself.)

Sometimes when he returned from late committee meetings John would be either too exhausted or too keyed up to sleep, so I spent hours ministering to him, treating his ailments, both real and imaginary, listening to his outlines for the next day's campaign, or reading aloud the countless fan letters he had been too busy even to open. But my duties were enlivened by John's astonishing caprices. I remember one night when he claimed he couldn't sleep because of the imagined odor of laundry soap on the bed sheets; he decided the only way to get rid of it would be to sprinkle them with violet cologne. There was cologne of other scents in the apartment, but the job required violet. It was three a.m., when all the shops were closed, but I called a phone operator and learned there was an all-night drugstore in the Grand Central Station. It was a long way to 42nd Street, but it intrigued me no end to cover my dishabille with a trench coat, pull a slouch hat over my eyes, and start out into the night, a lone female on a strange mission. At that hour there was no doorman in our hallway; it was an adventure even to find a taxi, and when I did the driver treated me with thrilling curiosity. I finally reached the drugstore and made the purchase. There were plenty of taxis at the station when I started back, but even so, the whole venture took almost an hour. I hurried into John's bedroom with his prescription for insomnia, only to find him sound asleep. He slept until morning and never mentioned violet cologne again.

On another occasion I was sitting on the floor, reading John's mail to him while he reclined in bed. A majority of the letters were mash notes from actresses; John saw nothing incongruous in having his wife read these love letters aloud. I remember one which told of an abiding passion for him and said in effect, "It's a tragic that a great man like you, who ought to have the understanding and comfort of a real woman, is tied to an inconsequential little doll." I might have been annoyed over that letter, for John's "inconsequential little doll" was his nurse, secretary, masseuse, collaborator, and friend beyond all other friends, and had earned the better part of the family fortune. But I chose to look on its funny side; and in defense of John let me here observe that men who are unfailingly considerate tend to be dull companions. Also I find gratitude the dreariest form of hypocrisy.

John's comment about the many women who were mashed on him was only "How little those women understand my Bug!" But his gratitude was merely oral; it never changed his tactics. Once, when I found a bill for dresses John had sent some girl, I was afraid he might have run out of alibis. He hadn't. "You're so generous, Buggie, that I have to be with some gold-digger from time to time in order to appreciate you." Moreover, there was a very good alibi for John's self-centered behavior; after so many years as an invalid he couldn't assume the habits of a healthy man now that he was well. At any rate, his antics were invariably entertaining and, just as a character is sometimes loved all the more for being naughty, almost everybody loved him. But it is also to John's credit that self-love never took the form of arrogance; actually he was quite humble; it was just that he quite frankly cared more for himself than for anyone else, and his main thought at all times was to see that he was comfortable and happy. He was never a hypocrite. He used to make the most disarming requests, such as, "Try to find yourself a cab, Buggie. I'll use the car on account of this blizzard."

As the actors' strike continued and the producers stubbornly held out, Equity, in desperate need of money, organized a variety show as a benefit for the strike fund. Performances were given at the old Manhattan Opera House on Lexington Avenue and, seeing that they supplied the only theatrical entertainment in town, they did a sell-out business. Every Equity star took part in the show; its master of ceremonies was Ed Wynn, already a prominent comedian in spite of his youth. The Shuberts, who had Wynn under contract, got out an injunction that prevented him from appearing on any stage. So when performances began Ed would walk down the center aisle, stop just short of the orchestra pit, and address the audience. "Ladies and gentlemen, the Shuberts, to whom I am under contract, have put an injunction against my working on any stage. But, if I could only have gotten up on that stage, I was going to tell you a story about . . ."—at which Ed would legally go into his entire comedy routine, to squeals of delight from the audience and the utter rout of the Shubert lawyers.

As a climax to the campaign, the Fidos challenged Equity to a debate. The protagonist for the Fido cause was an Irish-American actor of enormous wit and aplomb, a brilliant extemporaneous speaker named Wilton Lackaye. John Emerson, as Equity's most effective orator, was chosen to meet him. On the afternoon of the debate the Manhattan Opera House was a seething mass of actors dedicated to both sides. The Equity group far outnumbered the Fidos, but the latter were all the more vociferous. John Emerson and Wilton Lackaye were evenly matched; both were extremely handsome and had superb stage presence, John with his calm, ministerial bearing, Wilton, a robust bon vivant with a touch of the Irish country squire. John had all the assurance of careful preparation, but his antagonist's native wit gave him enough of an edge that John was hard put to it to keep up with him; Lackaye drew laughs that were louder, longer, and more sardonic. But in his rebuttal Lackaye closed his argument with a declaration that was extremely unfortunate for the Fido cause. "As an artist," he said, "I have no desire to share the union label of a carpenter." Not realizing to what extent he had left himself open to attack, Lackaye resumed his seat. John rose to make a quiet response: "There was

once a very great Man who was a carpenter." I shall never forget
the look of consternation on Wilton Lackaye's face. A gasp of triumph went up from the Equity ranks, followed by thunderous applause. That instant clinched the decision; Equity won the debate
hands down; John hit the heights and for one dazzling moment
was the man he always dreamed he might be.

With the actors' victory everything turned out for the best in
the best of all possible worlds. Frank Bacon resumed his run in
Lightnin', and the publicity he had earned by striking served to
increase business at the box office. (His family affairs were also to
prosper; his son Lloyd went to Hollywood and became an outstanding movie director.) Producers were now forced to buy
chorus girls' stockings, to pay actors half salary after the second
week of rehearsal, and to post bonds so that when traveling troupes
were stranded they wouldn't have to walk back to Broadway. Actors were now entering into the twentieth century's melodramatic
switch of power; no longer underdogs, they now had their turn to
trample on the boss, and this is only fair, considering the many
centuries that the converse had been true. I had seen an early demonstration of the triumph of the underdog in Berlin, where Soviet
commissars, "in town on business," were spending government
funds on German baby dolls with all the abandon of capitalistic
sugar daddies. Along Broadway the theatrical unions can now op-
press management to their hearts' content. They can curtail rehearsals to a point where there isn't a chance for smooth performances;
plays can flop victoriously, actors, stage hands and electricians can
all be triumphantly out of jobs. Unions can achieve the same results by running up production costs. In a play of mine called
Happy Birthday there was a jukebox used onstage, which gave the
musicians' union an opportunity to consider the production a musical. Therefore the management was forced to hire eight union
members who, not being needed, sat in the cellar of the theater
playing pinochle. For all their large investment in *Happy Birthday*,
the producers cleared only $8000 on its lengthy run of a year and

eight months. The only reason why producers don't quit must be that they are dangerously stagestruck.

While the stardust of triumph was settling over Broadway, John, in a last blaze of glory, was elected President of the Actors Equity Association. But now that there was nothing left to fight for, it soon turned out to be a dull assignment and I only hope the actors were more content with peace and quiet than John was. At any rate, his three years as head of Equity didn't interest John sufficiently, so when Joe Schenck made us an offer to write one more picture for Constance Talmadge, John accepted the assignment. This meant I would be forced to spend several months in Hollywood, far removed from my pals, from Mencken, Tommy Smith, Herman Oelrichs, and George Jean Nathan. But a disturbing new element was added to my grief over the parting for, during a recent session at Herman's, George Jean had broken the general rule and introduced one of his transient sweethearts into the gathering. Her name was Mae Davis. She was a natural blonde of the type I characterize as an old man's darling. I knew any number of them who were favorites of my husband. I find that such girls are stamped rather early with the marks of a sort of juiceless middle age; their skins are fragile and tend to wrinkle easily; their hair, a little too fine, is inclined to be scraggly. Gentlemen may be wise in preferring girls who are not likely in a few years to look embarrassingly youthful. That particular specimen of George Jean Nathan's had a naïve, stupid viewpoint on everything, which happened to intrigue Menck; he took to egging her on to make idiotic remarks, and George Jean was so pleased that his choice in girls was approved by his better that he failed to be jealous. I, on the other hand, *was* jealous, even though the little blonde supplied me with cues for wisecracks that amused Menck.

When it came time to go to Hollywood I was torn at the thought of leaving Miss Davis behind with Menck while I was three thousand miles away. But as John and I were crossing the Grand Central Station to take our train, who did we run into but Miss Davis. Accompanied by a mountain of luggage, that silly

A GIRL LIKE I (265

blonde was also en route to Hollywood. It transpired that she had made a screen test which came to the attention of Charlie Chaplin, and he wanted further to test her for the ingénue lead in his next picture.

Miss Davis was entranced to latch onto John and me, apparently being her own worst company. Relieved as I was that she was no longer a threat to Mencken, I didn't relish the thought of spending the next five days with Mae. I realized there would be small chance of escaping her, for she was just the sort of company any husband would adore.

En route to Chicago on the Twentieth Century for the first lap of our trip, that blonde, although she was considerable less fragile than I, was waited on, catered to, and cajoled by every male we encountered. In the club car, if she happened to drop the magazine she was reading, several men jumped to retrieve it, whereas I was allowed to lug heavy suitcases from their racks while men, most particularly my husband, failed to note my efforts. We had to change trains in Chicago and take the Santa Fe, on which I faced three more days of being bored by that golden-haired birdbrain. As our train raced across the plains of the Midwest, I watched her disorganize the behavior of every male passenger on board. I tried to puzzle out the reasons why. Obviously there was some radical difference between that girl and me, but what was it? We were both in the pristine years of youth. She was not outstanding as a beauty; we were, in fact, of about the same degree of comeliness; as to our mental acumen, there was nothing to discuss: I was smarter. Then why did that girl so far outdistance me in allure? Why had she attracted one of the keenest minds of our era? Mencken liked me very much indeed, but in the matter of sex he preferred a wit-less blonde. The situation was palpably unjust but, as I thought it over, a light began to break through from my subconscious; possibly the girl's strength was rooted (like that of Samson) in her hair. At length I reached for one of the large yellow pads on which I jot down ideas and started a character sketch which was the nucleus of a small volume to be titled *Gentlemen Prefer Blondes*. That book was destined to earn millions of dollars, but to me money was of second importance, for it was to gain me the objective of which I had first started to dream at the tender age of four.

Any such female accomplishment could have been motivated only by sex. Bernard Berenson, that wise and witty critic of art and the humanities, put his finger on the matter in one of his diaries called *Sunset and Twilight*. "A woman finds it very difficult," he wrote, "to separate sex from a career, in literature especially. Her own dreams, aspirations, romances, stick out ever so much more than in a man's work. Yet when she in any career manages to get rid of sex entirely, she becomes a monster of implacable activity for her unsexual ends." Had I been unsexual I might have written viciously, but I was in love with Henry Mencken and had taken up my pencil in order to laugh into nothingness a blonde he cared more for. As I scribbled on that yellow pad, my little sketch became a mixture of fact and fiction. The name of my heroine, Lorelei Lee, was invented, although her birthplace was not, and Mencken himself had a hand in that. For I wanted Lorelei to be a symbol of our nation's lowest possible mentality and remembered Menck's essay on American culture in which he branded the state of Arkansas as "the Sahara of the Bozarts." I therefore chose Little Rock for Lorelei's early years; Little Rock, which even today lives up to Mencken's choice as a nadir in shortsighted human stupidity.

As our train was nearing Pasadena, I finished the few pages of my sketch; it was time to pack up and go back to the chores of a movie studio. I stuck the manuscript into the pocket of a suitcase and forgot about it as completely as I forgot Mae Davis. There was little reason to remember her, because she didn't land that job with Charlie Chaplin; he gave it to a discovery of his own, named Paulette Goddard. With my mind and heart back in New York, I had little interest in my movie script; so little, in fact, that today I can't remember what the picture was. Our stay in Hollywood was enlivened principally by Dutch Talmadge's current romances, which were, as usual, onesided. This was the time she was courted unsuccessfully by Irving Thalberg, the thin, pale young man who, still in his teens, had just been promoted from office boy to head of production at Universal Pictures; his boss, Carl Laemmle, having as great a genius for recognizing genius as Irving's own.

As soon as John and I finished our movie stint we returned to New York, as usual to search for another new home, which turned out to be an apartment on East 54th Street next to the Hotel Elysée. The building was brand new, the apartments small, only two on each floor. Ours was in the front. Our neighbor at the back was a tremendously pretty girl, the sister of Barbara Bennett whom I knew from Paris; her name, Constance.

It was with feelings of keen anticipation that I unpacked the chic Vuitton luggage I had acquired in Paris. I was home again and ready to begin the life I loved; we had now retired for keeps. I might never have thought of my little critique on that blonde who had interested Menck, had I not run across its rumpled pages in my suitcase, and, in order to give Menck a laugh at his own expense, I mailed my sketch to him in Baltimore. Menck read it and was amused; on his next visit to New York he suggested that my sketch be published. Were he still editing *Smart Set*, he said, he would gladly use it, but he didn't think it was right for *The American Mercury*, the more serious publication he now edited. He frankly told me he felt my heroine would be an affront to most readers. "Do you realize, young woman," said Menck, "that you've made fun of sex, which has never before been done in this grand and glorious nation of ours?" But Menck suggested that I send my sketch to *Harper's Bazaar*, where it would be read by a frivolous public and, lost among the ads, wouldn't offend anybody.

It was at this point that another catalyst entered my life in the person of young Henry Sell, then editor of *Harper's Bazaar*. It happened that he had recently engaged the cartoonist Ralph Barton to do a series of drawings for his magazine, and as yet the two hadn't been able to fix on a theme. Henry Sell had begun to worry about having put Barton under contract without previously working out an assignment for him; it smacked of faulty editorship. When my manuscript reached his desk, it seemed like a good subject on which Barton could extemporize. Henry Sell sent him my short sketch, and Barton agreed. Sell breathed a sigh of relief; his editorial judgment had been vindicated.

When Henry Sell sent for me to come to his office, he was surprised that his new author appeared to be so young. But he was young himself, although he looks much the same today, except that his hair has whitened. He is small, slender, wiry, with sharp features and eyes that reflect perpetual amusement. When Sell told me he would like to publish my story in the *Bazaar* he failed to inform me that it would be only an excuse for Ralph Barton's drawings; not that I'd have minded if he had. I admired Barton's cartoons; to collaborate with him seemed a vast compliment. Still with an eye on Barton's requirements, Sell then stated that if we considered my manuscript complete, it would be long enough for only one issue and suggested that, having started my heroine on a trip, why stop her? "Take your blonde to Europe and let her have some more adventures," said editor Sell.

As always, luck was with me, for it so happened that John, having again entered a restless phase, had recently decided on another tour of Europe. When I told Sell about it, he was delighted; it would give me a chance to gather fresh material for the entire series. It was agreed that I would mail a chapter of Lorelei's adventures each month, in ample time for Barton to do the drawings.

Sell then made an appointment for me to meet Ralph Barton at the *Bazaar* office. Like George Jean Nathan, Barton had a wide reputation as a Lothario, but whereas one always felt George was boasting, Ralph had no need to boast. Several of the most extraordinary women of that time were successively in love with him; he married two of them. When I met Barton, his marriage to the dark and sleekly beautiful actress Carlotta Monterey was about to break up, although they were still living under the same roof. Following her divorce from Ralph, Carlotta was to marry America's foremost playwright, Eugene O'Neill, and, after his death, assume a guiding hand in the production of O'Neill's plays throughout the world. Ralph was next to marry a pretty young French woman, Germaine

Tailleferre, the composer and member of *Les Six*, a sextette of avant-garde musicians, one of whom, Georges Auric, was to become world-famous.

Little did I realize when John and I sailed for Europe that we would return to a life that would never again be the same for either of us. I wrote the second chapter of Lorelei's diary on board the *Paris*, using the ship as a background. Our first stop was London, which I had never before visited. I looked the city over and immediately started the third chapter. The characters involved with Lorelei were all based on people I knew, either friends I had previously met away from London or new acquaintances. It was fun to write about them, and I could hardly wait to see Ralph's drawings; in some cases their resemblance to the originals was startling. I think it was in Paris that I had the thrill of seeing the first printed chapter in a copy of the *Bazaar* I found at an international bookstore there.

After we had pushed on to Vienna, an amusing contretemps happened in connection with Chapter Four. A little late in finishing it, I worried about its reaching Barton in time for him to do the illustrations. I was on my way to the post office to mail the manuscript when I ran into a good friend, Jules Glaenzer, the cosmopolite who managed (and still does) the New York branch of the Cartier firm of jewelers. He was leaving the next day for New York, and it seemed a good opportunity for me to send my script to Sell. Jules was more than happy to oblige. The only trouble was that en route Jules forgot all about it. But the day after his arrival in New York he happened to run into a very harassed Henry Sell on the street. Stopping to chat, Jules casually mentioned that he had just seen me in Vienna, at which Henry gave a start. "Did Anita say whether she'd finished her chapter of that series she's writing for me?" It now dawned on Jules that the manuscript was in his own possession. If he hadn't run into Henry Sell that day by chance, the next issue of *Harper's Bazaar* would have lacked my Chapter Four. But luck was with me as usual, and, in Lorelei Lee's own words, "fate kept on happening."

The very first day after our return from Europe, I began to realize to what an extent fate *had* kept on happening while I had been
away. On Fifth Avenue I was stopped by several acquaintances to
tell me how much they enjoyed my pieces in *Harper's Bazaar*. And
on my going to pay my respects to Henry Sell, he said, chortling
with amusement, that the newsstand sales of the magazine had trip-
led; all on account of Lorelei Lee. Not only that, but gentlemen
themselves had taken to reading *Harper's Bazaar;* ads for men's ap-
parel, cars, and sporting goods were pouring into the office.

I was so delighted and amused that I failed to notice a vague
uneasiness in my husband's behavior. But another fly in the ointment was more apparent; darling Frank Crowninshield was
shocked by my story. In a confidence to John, he said, "I wish little
Anita had never written that story"—which goes to show how
much stronger the stomachs of the reading public are today and
how far they have advanced in shock resistance. Dirty words, which
are now printed in bold type, would never have entered Lorelei
Lee's mind. So refined was she that she completely overlooked the
basic fact of procreation and, like the true Christian Scientist she
was, Lorelei pretended it didn't exist. There isn't a single line in her
story that couldn't be read aloud in a kindergarten. But back in
1926 she was considered by my mentor, Crownie, as such hot stuff
that she would smirch my reputation. John heartily agreed with
Crownie, but I'm afraid his secret reason was professional jealousy.
At any rate both men were relieved when, at chapter six, Lorelei's
adventures ended in *Harper's Bazaar,* and they felt she had disappeared forever. They hadn't counted on my good friend Tommy
Smith.

As usual, Tommy and I started our peregrinations around New
York. It was late summer, and the speakeasies were all in bloom.
One night Tommy and I were sitting in one of the liveliest. It was
called Reine Davies' Country Club and was run by an older sister
of Marion Davies. In spite of Reine's being a judge's daughter, she
had a few brushes with the law over conducting a speakeasy. On
one occasion Reine was picked up by Prohibition officers just as she

and an escort were leaving the club. They were taken to the police station, where the matron in charge discovered that Reine's clothing consisted of nothing more than a mink coat and a pair of sandals. The episode had reached the gossip columns, and Tommy began commiserating with Reine on the unfair publicity, at which I piped up to remark that no garment could cover a girl more respectably than a full-length mink coat. Tommy agreed and said that Reine's unfortunate adventure might easily have happened to Lorelei Lee. His remark led to a suggestion: how would I like him to print a few copies of my story so that I could give them to friends for Christmas? And let me here state that Tommy's offer was no compliment to me as an author. Tommy was a beau who merely wanted to make a nice gesture.

But when John Emerson and Frank Crowninshield heard of Tommy's project they took a firm stand against it, their common argument being based on my reputation as a nice girl. Tommy proved an equally firm antagonist. He insisted that the edition would consist of only twelve hundred copies, a large percentage of which would be Christmas presents to friends who were already familiar with the work; the few remaining copies could make a very small dent in my very unimportant reputation. At any rate, Tommy talked Crownie and John down and the edition went into work.

The galleys were finally sent to me to be proofread, and when I was about to send them back there occurred one of the most amazing psychological phenomena I had yet encountered in my experiences with John. He ominously stated that he had something to talk to me about, the type of announcement that always made me quake with apprehension. It generally meant that I had done or said something that disgraced him. However, this time he was exceptionally gentle; placing his arm around me, John said, "Buggie dear, do you mind using this as a dedication in your book?" He handed me a paper on which he had written in block letters the following: "To John Emerson, except for whose encouragement and guidance this book would never have been written." Considering all his attempts to squelch *Gentlemen Prefer Blondes*, I was stunned, and then, as usual, the reason for it struck me as amusing. After he had unsuccessfully tried to stop publication of my book, there remained only one way through which John could save face: by pretending that he himself had been responsible for it. I agreed to use the dedication, but Tommy, although he, too, was amused, refused to print it *in toto*. It would be much more effective, he assured John, if it merely read: "To John Emerson." And that is how John Emerson's name appears on the dedication page, rather than that of the man who really inspired and was responsible for the destiny of Lorelei Lee.

The first small edition of *Gentlemen Prefer Blondes* came out in late November 1926; of its twelve hundred copies, Tommy sent me twenty-five, which went off to friends in lieu of Christmas cards. Horace, Tommy, and Ralph Barton used a few books for the same purpose, and the remaining volumes were distributed among New York shops. By noon of the day it appeared, the entire edition was sold out. Horace and Tommy were as delighted as they were surprised. Tommy phoned in amazement to tell me the news; he said that, as he spoke, the Liveright switchboard was jammed with calls for more and more books, that orders by the hundreds were forced to wait for another printing. A second edition that would number sixty-five thousand copies was put right to press. And there were forty-five more editions yet to come.

My heroine's adventures led to unexpected dividends which were pretty undeserved. The satisfaction of getting even with Mae Davis for seducing the man I loved more than paid for the pains of bringing Lorelei into the world. The money my heroine made and still continues to make never seemed any more legitimate than the loot she herself collected inside the covers of my book. What with hardcover and paperback royalties, serializations, translations, a play, a musical, two films, and all the other rights to which a bestseller falls heir, Lorelei's diary turned into an annuity. In the entertainment world my heroine was portrayed by its two most eminent blondes: Marilyn Monroe of the movies, and Carol Channing of the stage. The musical version of the play goes right on running in summer stock and winter stock.

The horoscope that Ella Woods cast for me when I was so young all came true. A certain comment of Lorelei's which would ring round the world like the welkin was inspired by an adventure she had in Paris. Lorelei wrote: "An American girl has to watch herself or she might have such a good time in Paris that she wouldn't get anywhere. I mean, kissing your hand can make a girl feel very good, but a diamond bracelet lasts forever."

Any disparagement of Lorelei as being just one more witless blond is ill deserved. Her girl friend Dorothy appreciated this. "Her brain reminds me of a radio," said Dorothy, in effect. "I listen to it for days and get discouraged, but just when I'm ready to smash it something comes out that's a masterpiece." Besides being a sound thinker, Lorelei is so normal that when, in Vienna, she undergoes analysis at the hands of Freud, the learned Professor can only advise her to try to cultivate a few inhibitions.

In 1950 Lorelei came to be included in the new edition of *The Oxford Dictionary of English Quotations*, making me, as her instigator, one of the extremely few living writers to attain those august pages. But by that time Lorelei's philosophy had infiltrated every cultured language. In China her adventures were serialized in the Shanghai newspaper edited by Lin Yutang, who informed me that the dialogue went quite naturally into the argot of the sing-song girls. When the book reached Russia, I was told by our then Ambassador, William Bullitt, that the Soviet authorities embraced it as evidence of the exploitation of helpless female blondes by predatory magnates of the capitalistic system. As such, the book had a wide sale, but Russia never sent me any royalties, which seems rather like the exploitation of a helpless brunette author by a predatory Soviet regime.

Apart from all the money my book earned, most of which filtered into the dress salons of Mainbocher and Balenciaga, it became a passport to all sorts of unusual places and a letter of introduction to diverting people in every walk of life. I have been able to meet princes and panhandlers, diplomats and dips, geniuses and clowns; people as disparate as Aldous Huxley and Hoppy Hopkins, the movie gagwriter at MGM; Wilson Mizner, the dazzling international gambler, and Los Angeles' favorite evangelist, Aimee Semple McPherson; the astronomer Edwin Hubble; and Officer Dan, an expert blackmailer who, while operating around Southern California, actually disguised himself in the uniform of the Los Angeles Police Force; Lord d'Abernon, the British diplomat who dedicated his memoirs to me; and the great Colette, who recorded sex life at the turn of the century, and whose novel, *Gigi*, I was privileged to introduce to the American stage.

Other connections I've made are as similar as the two philosophers George Santayana and Edith Hamilton. When Santayana was asked to name the best philosophical work by an American, he said with a grin, "*Gentlemen Prefer Blondes.*" Edith Hamilton wrote in her last work, *The Ever Present Past*, published in 1964: "In that book of balance and proportion, *Gentlemen Prefer Blondes*, Miss Anita Loos does not bring an indictment against the universe in the person of Lorelei. She knows how to laugh, and that knowledge is the very best preservative there is against losing the true perspective. Let the young men beware!" (meaning the *angry* young men). "Without a sense of humor one must keep hands off the universe unless one is prepared to be, oneself, an unconscious addition to the sum of the ridiculous."

The determination I had first uttered as a child, that I would never be bored, turned out to be a prophecy. As Hoppy, the gagwriter, once said of the weekly salon over which I presided in Santa Monica for eighteen years, "Pal, you ought to charge admission to this joint of yours. I'm damned if it ain't better than a side show."

From all those varied sources I learned much wisdom. Officer Dan, the blackmailer, advised me, with deep emotion, always to respect the feelings of a mother; Lord d'Abernon once told me, with Machiavellian candor, that "one can be too kind to widows and orphans." In recent years, when the operations of wheeler-dealers down Washington way keep breaking into unfortunate headlines, I think of Wilson Mizner's sage advice: "Never try to get rich quick in the daylight."

But much as I owe to Lorelei Lee, I mustn't forget to add my thanks to the brunette Dorothy. In the book, Ralph Barton's pictures of Dorothy resemble Arlene Pringle of *Three Weeks* fame, because Ralph happened to be involved in a flirtation with Arlene and used her as his model. But my brunette's true inner self was inspired by girls I could laugh *with* and not *at* (as I did in the case of Mae Davis); by girls like my beloved Peg Talmadge (although by the time we met Peg's hair had long been gray); by a pert and stylish friend of several decades who shall be nameless unless she wishes to tell on herself, as I am about to do. For in affairs of the heart I was Dorothy's most accurate prototype. My ability from early childhood to earn money had always attracted the type of gentleman toward whom a girl like I aspired. I believe that my character was best summed up in a comment from Gladys, my devoted companion of over thirty years. It was prompted by a phone call from one of the Argentine gigolos I had met in the days of my first gay, windblown appearance in Paris. Using gallant terms that were a sort of verbal "kiss on the hand," my beau stated he wished to talk to me about something and invited me to the zoo in Central Park, there to partake of a cheap lunch at the cafeteria. Although I sensed that his "talk" might hinge on the subject of a little loan, I nevertheless accepted the invitation with delight. But as I hung up the receiver Gladys brought me back from the clouds to stern reality. "Miss Loos," she said, "you sure are flypaper for pimps!"